WHEN
WE
WERE
SILENT

WHEN WE WERE SILENT

Fiona McPhillips

FLATIRON
BOOKS
NEW YORK

WHEN WE WERE SILENT. Copyright © 2024 by Fiona McPhillips. All rights reserved. Printed in the United States of America. For information, address Flatiron Books, 120 Broadway, New York, NY 10271.

www.flatironbooks.com

Library of Congress Cataloging-in-Publication Data

Names: McPhillips, Fiona, author.
Title: When we were silent / Fiona McPhillips.
Description: First edition. | New York : Flatiron Books, 2024.
Identifiers: LCCN 2023046390 | ISBN 9781250908230 (hardcover) |
    ISBN 9781250908247 (ebook)
Subjects: LCGFT: Thrillers (Fiction) | Novels.
Classification: LCC PR6113.C5866 W47 2024 | DDC 823/.92—dc23/eng/20231222
LC record available at https://lccn.loc.gov/2023046390

Our books may be purchased in bulk for promotional, educational, or business use. Please contact your local bookseller or the Macmillan Corporate and Premium Sales Department at 1-800-221-7945, extension 5442, or by email at MacmillanSpecialMarkets@macmillan.com.

First Edition: 2024

10 9 8 7 6 5 4 3 2 1

For James, Anna, and Harry

when we are silent
we are still afraid

　　—Audre Lorde, "A Litany for Survival"

PART ONE

Now

1

For years, I tried not to think about Highfield Manor. The pompous rise of its granite walls, the secrets hidden in its stone-cold shadows. The dark veil of cedars shrouding the school from the outside world. But still the memories fester in me, real as a disease.

Even now, as I watch the new students gather on the cobblestones of Trinity's front square, I can't help but think of the intimacy of teenage girls, their social hierarchies and my naive certainty I could conquer them.

It doesn't take much for Highfield to trespass on my life. Just a whisper of chlorine at the gym or the groan of leather on bare skin and my heart picks up pace. The body remembers everything the mind wants to forget.

In my office, slatted sun brushes parallel shafts of light and shade onto the books that fan out across my desk. Beads of sweat gather on the bridge of my nose as I prepare the words I'll deliver at my afternoon lecture, a revival of Irish female writers of the last century. It's a crime, I think as I write, that these voices were suppressed for so long, always deemed too quiet to matter.

As I lose myself in my work, my phone vibrates on my desk and I glance over. It's a number I don't recognize. I hesitate and then grab it.

"Ronan Power," he says, and it only takes a second for the terror and guilt to find me.

And I know whatever happens next, one thing is certain: my story is about to be resurrected, more than thirty years after I tried to bury it.

RONAN'S AT AN OUTSIDE TABLE WHEN I arrive, sunlit and tie-less, nursing an americano. He's better looking than I remember, the graying beard only adding gravitas to the sculpted lines of his face. As he leans in to greet me, I catch sight of the ice-blue Power eyes through the tint of his Ray-Bans, and the soft edges of nostalgia ease my trepidation.

He was only fifteen back then, three years our junior. Shauna's cocky younger brother, nothing more. I've kept an eye on him over the years, his litigation successes and society engagements. But Shauna, she has managed to live a life offline, without a trace left behind for the casual observer. The sole reason I'm convinced she's still alive is that a Power surely could not die without mention. It's only now, in the fluster of this formal summons, that I'm numb with the possibility.

"I wanted to tell you in person," says Ronan.

And so it's here, surrounded by fumes and footsteps and the blinding gaze of the midday sun, that it's all finally going to come to an end. I'm almost as eager for the news as I am fearful of it. Shauna's death would put our story back in the headlines, but it would mean the end of the dread I've lived with all these years, the reason I can't sleep at night.

"It's happening again," he says. "At Highfield."

"What?"

"I'm taking a case on behalf of a swimmer."

This is not what I was expecting. A return to Highfield instead of an escape from it.

"Only fourteen years of age."

"Oh god." I put my hand to my head to shade it from the force of his words as much as the flare of the sun.

"I need your help," he says, and the strength seeps out of me. "I want you to testify."

Something shatters deep inside, but I am nerve-numb to it, my rigid exterior unbroken.

"I don't see what any of this has to do with me."

"Come on, Lou. Surely I don't have to spell it out for you?"

I shake my head, both in disbelief and to stop him forming the words I know I won't be able to handle. All I can think is, I've done this before, I can't do it again.

"Look," says Ronan, "none of us wants to revisit the Highfield affair, but we can't let something like that happen ever again."

The Highfield affair. That's what they call it online, the armchair detectives and internet sleuths. But the past is not contained within those wrought-iron gates. It is part of all of us, the Highfield girls you think you know, born into privilege, the world at their feet. And me, the intruder. Our testimony does not begin and end on that one fatal night. We are the before and the after, the culmination of cruelties that made it all seem inevitable: just a consequence of the time.

A different time. The era of synth pop and mixtapes, hair gel and new wave. Of Prince and paramilitaries, Madonna and moving statues. Magdalene laundries, the Eighth Amendment, bodies as battlegrounds—pig slit and gaping. Different but the same. Absolution for the guilty but not for us.

"I'm sorry, Ronan, I can't. I have a daughter now."

He sits back in his seat and takes a deep breath.

"You can come forward as a witness," he says, "or I can summons you."

I close both hands across my face.

"And there's enough testimony from you on record already to back me up."

I've done this before, I can't do it again.

"What does Shauna think?" I say, rubbing my neck.

"She's already preparing a statement. She's ready to tell everything."

It doesn't sound like the Shauna I knew, the girl who went to unimaginable lengths to keep a secret. That was always the one thing Highfield valued more than grades, more than silverware or celebrity alumni: silence.

Even now, there are still so many questions, the answers buried deep in the sacral belly of Highfield. We all have them, our secrets and half-truths, the memories that rage in the delirium of night. Some of us will take them to our graves. Some of us already have.

"I want to talk to Shauna," I say, "before I make any decisions."

"I'm sorry," says Ronan. "She doesn't want that."

"Can I call her? Or email even?"

He shakes his head. "I'm under strict instructions."

So that's how it's going to be. Everything on Shauna's terms, like always.

"It's better this way," says Ronan. "Believe me."

I want to say I've no reason to believe anything a Power tells me, but I stay quiet.

"I'm going to need you to write down everything," he says. "As much detail as you can remember."

"Everything?"

"Yes."

I can only hope the impatient flick of his hair means he doesn't know it all. That she hasn't told him *everything*.

"Concentrate on your friendship with Shauna, how much you confided in each other. Her testimony is worth so much more with your corroboration. And, of course, we want to focus as much as possible on what happened before that night."

That night: Monday, December 8, 1986. The Feast of the Immaculate Conception. My head pounds with the thought of it and Ronan's voice fades to a distant mumble as I sink into the murky depths of memory. I tried for so long to make sense of it, as if there was a single moment that could have changed it, as if any of us had been owed a happy ending. But I'm still not sure it could have ended any other way.

2

The city air is sour with the weekend residue as I lumber through the alleyways off Grafton Street, taking the shady route back to work. It's not only Ronan's bombshell that's shaken me, or how I'll explain it to my family, to my colleagues at Trinity. It's the rage simmering in my gut, that after everything we went through, it is still not the end. Not just for us but for a whole new generation. I thought I'd left it behind, and Shauna with it, but now the memories catch my breath so intensely I can barely work out what is real and what is trauma and the sleight-of-hand tricks it plays.

She doesn't want to be contacted; Ronan made that clear. After what happened, I only ever saw her from the sidelines—glamorous photos in the society pages, magazine features on her burgeoning law career. And then after a while, there was nothing, as if she had simply stopped existing. I've tried to find her online many times of course, those dark nights when her memory is a silhouette in the shadows, a haunting of us. If I could even see a photo, the middle-aged version might help me leave the teenage Shauna where she belongs. But the hollow thud of that heart keeps beating, no matter how much I try to make it stop.

At the end of Dawson Street, my head whirls with the incessant glare of the sun and the solid throng of tourists and I fluster through the dappled shade of the side entrance to Trinity, and into the cool concrete shelter of the Arts Block. In the toilets, I run cold water over my hands and wipe them under the dark fringe that hangs low over my eyebrows. My green eyes are shot with rivulets of blood and there's a tremor in my hand that I see only in the stark glare of my reflection.

The woman in the mirror is not me, the Lou Manson I've worked so hard to build from the ashes of the girl I left in Highfield. I want to help Ronan and his client, just a child for god's sake, but even news of the case could jeopardize my career. The Highfield affair has never gone away completely; it still lingers on the fringes of the internet. A trial would bring it all back into the open and I'm not sure the department would stand by me through the scandal. And Shauna, she has the ammunition to take everything from me. I've no idea how far she's prepared to go and I'm dizzy with the possibility that she really is prepared to tell all. I've carried the weight of that secret all these years, the memory still as brutal as the deed. The taste of blood still fresh on my tongue. I don't want to face my students like this. I need to get out of here.

WHEN I GET HOME, OUR GOLF is not in the drive, and I breathe a sigh of relief. I'm not ready to explain anything to Alex just yet. I turn the key in the front door of the 1930s semi we recently restored, the project that was as much of a commitment as our wedding three years ago. It fills me with joy every day to return to this house, this family I've worked so hard for. I won't let the Powers steal them from me.

I throw my keys onto the hall table and I'm about to push open the double doors to the extension when I hear laughter upstairs, the sort of uninhibited outburst I haven't heard from my teenager in years. I'd be delighted if it wasn't still early afternoon, almost two hours before she's supposed to finish school.

"Katie," I shout, but there is no reply.

I trudge upstairs, primed for battle, when I hear her phone vibrate on the drawers beside her room. Behind her bedroom door, she's chatting lightly on her laptop, a tone I barely recognize, and I know she hasn't heard me. I hold my breath as I pick up the phone, which is clearly, unmistakably, unlocked.

I never meant to be a suspicious parent, but years of second-guessing Katie's anxiety issues have left me exhausted and paranoid. She wasn't shy when she was younger, but she started to retreat into herself in the last few years of primary school. It got so bad when she started secondary that we ended up home-schooling her between us for most of the last term. Now she's in a private all-girls school, two things I swore off after my Highfield days. She seems happier, but she tells us nothing of her life there and I'd give anything for a brief glimpse.

I wrestle with my conscience for precisely two seconds before my thumb hovers over Katie's social media icons. I don't want to disturb her alerts, leave a trace. Instead, I click on her photo gallery, a collection of selfies and gifs and other people's video clips. I scroll down, and it's more of the same until I come to a series of photos that can't be her, not my baby, only fourteen years of age.

It's Katie's long, brown hair, pulled back behind bare shoulders, Katie's full lips puckered at the camera, Katie's hazel eyes both eager and docile. And her naked breasts in one photo after another, then intimate, close-up shots, and I have to look away as the phone drops from my shaking hands onto the carpet.

I try to rationalize what I've seen, that she is exploring her sexuality, that boys had already put their fingers inside my own fourteen-year-old body, but I can't get my head around how exposed she looks. Not to just one other boy her age but to every single person who might gain access to those photos.

I pick up the phone and click it to sleep, and I've just put it back when her bedroom door opens and I'm caught in a guilty side-step away from the drawers. She looks at me, her face a confusion of outrage and horror.

"How long have you been there?"

"I just got here," I say as I regain my composure. "And hold on a minute—I'm the one who should be asking the questions. Why aren't you at school?"

She half shrugs, as if it's none of my business, and I feel the onset of an impotent rage at this young woman who towers over me already.

"I didn't get any message from the school," I say, as calmly as I can.

"Study class," she says, barely moving her lips.

"And they let you go home? For the whole afternoon?"

She says nothing, just stands there with her long, dark hair draped across her royal-blue crested jumper, her hazel eyes giving nothing away.

"Katie, honey, I'm going to have to check with the school if you won't talk to me."

I put my hand in my pocket to get my own phone.

"No," she says, baring braces across both rows of teeth.

"Well, please explain to me then."

"It was only PE after," she says quietly, "and nobody cares if I go to that."

"I care. And that school is responsible for you until 4 p.m. so they should care too."

I have to admit Northwood Park's laid-back attendance policies suit

Katie, but sometimes I wish for the heavy-handed discipline of the High-field nuns.

"You can't leave school just because you feel like it," I say, but I don't know what else to do. I can't ground her; she never goes out anyway. And I could confiscate her phone or her laptop, but they're her only social outlets and I don't want to isolate her any further from her peers.

"Sorry."

She smiles sheepishly and it wrenches my heart. I never know whether to chastise or hug her and even though I want to reach out I can't bring myself to validate her behavior. I'm about to walk away when her phone buzzes again and she startles. She sees it on the drawers and grabs at it.

"Were you looking at my phone?" she says.

"No. Of course not."

She clicks on the alert with half an eye still on me.

"Dad's coming to pick me up at a quarter to five," she says. "To bring me to the orthodontist."

I nod. And I realize with a sickening dread that I'll have to tell Katie's father about the lawsuit, the re-emergence of Highfield into our lives. I can't begin to explain it to Katie without his support, but even he doesn't know the full extent of what happened that night. If he knew what I was capable of, what I've kept from him all these years, I'm not sure he'd ever forgive me.

I CAN'T TELL YOU EVERYTHING about that night. I do know, as twilight lifted over the chapel tower, as a brittle frost crept across the playing fields and woodlands, that Claudia Doyle walked the graveled path from the front gates of Highfield to the swimming pool at the rear of the school. I know nothing there was any different to usual, not the flickering of fluorescence in the changing rooms, or the air thick with chlorine, or the lukewarm ripple of the water's edge against her skin.

But after that, I can't say. I don't know if Claudia screamed underwater at the end of her first length, when she saw the hunched and lifeless shape on the floor of the pool. I'm not sure how she gathered the strength to drag her shaking body out of the water and across the hockey pitches to alert the nuns in the convent. And I've no idea if she still dreams about it, like I do.

3

To learn the truth of a narrative, you have to examine the narrator carefully. That's what I tell my students when I introduce them to Molly Keane's *Good Behaviour*. Iris Aroon St. Charles is a protagonist so ridden with repression and denial that we perceive as much from her silence as from her words.

You'd think such a skill would be second nature to teenagers, with their whispered intents and coded language, but it still surprises me how much they take at face value. Reading between the lines is also a strategy for life, but it's all the more important when words are tight and motives are hidden behind them.

I love teaching, the focus it requires. For an hour or two, I am lost in a literary world with my students while we investigate the stories and minds of my favorite writers. When I was an undergraduate, I studied Joyce, Beckett, Yeats, men celebrated by surname alone. It took me several years to ask *where are all the women?* and several more to put them on the curriculum.

Now, as female voices soar into our collective consciousness, I struggle even more with my own. I've published widely in the academic field, but I've never dared share any of my own creative writing. I have dabbled periodically but I've never been able to let go enough to make it real. Maybe I just don't have what it takes, but it doesn't stop me wanting it, wondering what would happen if I could break the seal on what I know.

"Can you name me any other unreliable narrators in literature?" I ask the new first-years in the tiered seating before me.

A tentative hand goes up in the front row, a girl with a pink fringe and pierced eyebrows.

"Amy Dunne in *Gone Girl*."

"Yes, she's a classic," I say.

"*Atonement*," shouts a girl several rows up.

"That's a good one," I say. "Briony Tallis changes the truth to try and atone for what she's done. Anyone else?"

"Humbert Humbert."

It's a quiet voice to my right, a boy with pockmarks and earnest eyes.

"Have you read *Lolita*?" I ask.

"Em, no," he says. "I mean, I always thought it was . . . problematic?"

"Well, if you read it as a love story between a middle-aged man and a twelve-year-old girl, then, yes, it certainly is. But you already know that. So you'll come to it with a cold eye, ready to discern the truth by dissecting Humbert's account. Because Lolita doesn't have a voice, only the lie given to her by him."

My phone vibrates on the desk in front of me and my eyes shoot to the alert. It's an email from a Liam Kelly, the subject line below his name:

I know what you did.

"Did you read *Lolita* when you were younger?" asks the girl with the pink fringe while my pulse surges to double time.

I stare at her as I try to engage the trademark Lou Manson cool. It's a survival skill that's never left me and I show no emotion as I struggle to separate her words from the ones I've just read.

"I, eh . . . sorry, what's your name?"

"Maisie Taylor."

"And what was your question, Maisie?"

My tongue sticks in my mouth and I put my hands on the desk to steady myself.

"Did you read *Lolita* when you were our age?"

Maisie is eighteen, nineteen. Old enough to get it, young enough to think she'd never fall for it.

"Yes, I did."

I glance at my phone to see if it's time to wind up the lecture, but there are still ten minutes to go. I see the words again and my stomach clenches. I don't know a Liam Kelly; it might be spam, but I won't be able to breathe until I find out.

"Did people understand it back then?" asks Maisie. "I mean, did they know how bad it was?"

They didn't want to know. I close my eyes, but it does nothing to dull the ringing in my ears nor the glare of the overhead lights.

"Everyone knows child abuse is bad," I say.

"But it wasn't as taboo, was it, in the seventies and eighties? Like, pop stars went out with fourteen-year-old girls and nobody said anything."

"Well, I don't really remember the seventies, thank you very much, Maisie," I say with a smile as I pick up my phone with a shaking hand.

I hear the start of a "but" as I snap my laptop closed and I speak over her with the first words that come to mind.

"I want you all to read *Good Behaviour* with an eye on what Iris does that conflicts with what she says, and we'll discuss next week."

And then I take the stairs two at a time and keep putting one foot in front of the other until I'm safely behind my office door. I don't even make it to my desk before my phone is out and I skim the email, looking for the right words, seeing only the wrong ones. I throw the phone on my desk and fall into the chair, trying to catch my breath as my chest tightens and my shoulders heave. I open the laptop, as if the words might make more sense on a bigger screen. My heart hammers in my ears as I read.

If you testify, I'll tell them everything.

I look away, the unreliable narrator caught in the lie of omission. I suck the breath into me as I try to think about what this means. If it's really out there, the secret that has haunted me all these years. There were times I almost let it out, to Alex, to Katie's dad, but I was never brave enough to take that risk. Only Shauna ever knew the truth about that night, and I have no way of knowing what she might have done with it.

4

There's no way I can run out on work again, so I carry Liam Kelly's email with me for the rest of the afternoon while my head pounds with the weight of it. When I leave Trinity, I can't face the bus home so I make my way on foot across the Liffey, through the north inner city to the open calm of the seafront promenade. It's only here I feel a distance from Highfield's shadow, as if the water separates not just Southside from Northside but also before from after. It's far from the working-class estates of Ballybrack, this beautiful seaside suburb that I call home, and I breathe in the salty freedom of it.

The evening has lost its luster and a thin shadow of cloud rolls in over the gray-green sea. In the distance, the red and white stripes of the Poolbeg chimneys rise through a dusty haze and I focus on them, an anchor in this changing landscape. I remember a drunken summer's evening on the other side of them, sharing a naggin of vodka in Blackrock Park with my best friend, Tina. The perfect flick of her eyeliner, the giddy rush of her laugh and the two of us with hardly a notion of what was out there, beyond our comprehension.

I remember when Tina told me she was joining the Highfield swimming club, I was so proud of her. There weren't many kids round our way whose talent took them out of Ballybrack, and she inspired me to want that too. I dreamed of being a writer and Tina made me feel like it was possible. Afterward, she was remembered as a tragedy, that poor girl. She would have hated that.

ALEX IS HOME ALREADY, PREPARING dinner at the kitchen island in our minimal, open-plan extension. I'd been hoping for a bit of down time, but she hands me a bowl of pistachios and I dutifully shell them as the melancholic groove of Bicep's "Glue" fills the space between us. She shaves Pecorino into a pasta dish and I'm afraid to ask why she's making such an effort on a Tuesday evening.

I still haven't managed to broach the subject of Highfield, as if it's going to be any easier, the longer I wait. I thought if I slept on it, I'd wake up with a palatable way of introducing it into our lives, but Liam Kelly has killed any chance of that. Now, I'm so on edge I'm starting to wonder if someone has got to Alex already, if all this is just the calm before the storm. The music finishes and she seizes the silence.

"I've got some news," she says.

It's the coy half-smile that eases my fears, and I stop thinking about myself for a minute.

"Wait," I say. "Did you get it? The license?"

"Yes!"

The joy that spreads across her face banishes all thoughts of Highfield and I skip around the island to wrap my arms around my brilliant wife. Alex is an independent festival and concert promoter, a tough gig in a market dominated for decades by the same two companies. But Alex saw a niche, an opportunity to curate events in existing urban spaces, and now she's secured a license for a series of concerts in Trinity during the summer. She already has Sinéad O'Connor and Villagers lined up so I know it's going to be a very big deal indeed.

"You fucking genius," I say, and kiss her hard on the lips. "I knew you'd do it."

"Well, I'm glad you were so sure because I have been shitting my pants for days."

I realize with remorse that I hadn't noticed. I can only hope she's been distracted from my own shifty behavior.

"Never a doubt," I say as I take a bottle of champagne from the wine rack and put it in the freezer.

"It will mean longer hours and more travel," says Alex, twisting her auburn curls into a bun.

"I know that."

"And I won't be around for Katie so much anymore."

Alex has been a second mother to Katie for the eight years we've lived together. She's the voice of reason, the measured calm to my overprotective paranoia. She's always had the distance to see clearly and, ten years my junior, she also has Katie's ear. It was Alex who talked me down last night when I told her about the photos on Katie's phone, when I couldn't trust my own trauma not to force my hand. She convinced me that a confrontation would cut off all lines of communication, that we'd be better off keeping a close eye on her than risking the loss of her trust. And now it looks like I'm going to have to be the one to police that.

"Actually, I wanted to talk to you about her," says Alex. "She came to me this morning."

"And?"

"She wants to start swimming."

"But she already does that."

Katie's new school has a pool, so swimming is part of the PE curriculum. It's no different to hockey or netball, just a forty-five-minute class once a week.

"No, I mean she wants to join the swimming club."

I freeze as the stench of chlorine floods the kitchen.

"She's really good, Lou. She's faster than girls who've been swimming for years."

Of course she is. I always feared this day would come.

"You know," continues Alex, "it's a really big deal for her, putting herself out there. It's the first thing she's even asked about since she started in that school."

If it was any other activity, I'd be thrilled, but this one comes with too much baggage. And Katie knows exactly why I won't want her anywhere near a swimming club. We've never kept the basic facts from her, but there's so much more out there online—truth, lies, opinion. I know what Alex will say—that we have to equip her to live in the world—but Alex's childhood was on a different planet to mine. Not just the privilege of it, but the expectation of fairness and balance that is alien to me.

"Oh god," I say as I put my hands to my face. "It's all up to me, is it? That's not fair, Alex."

"I know. None of it is fair. But I'm not going to give her the go-ahead without your blessing."

"Ah, Jesus. You know it's . . . complicated."

"Not for Katie," says Alex. She smiles sweetly to show she's not on the attack. Alex doesn't make demands, just gently eases you in her preferred direction. It's the reason she's such a good promoter. She makes her clients feel they're in control at all times while she carefully guides them down the path she's already chosen for them. It's a comfort, usually, to be with someone who knows exactly where they're going.

"I'm sorry," I say, "I'm scared . . ."

. . . of so many things I can't explain. I'm scared Katie will bear the brunt of my mistakes, that she'll be an easy target for bullies. I'm scared she'll find out too much. And I'm scared that if this new case goes to trial I could lose them both.

"I know," says Alex, reaching for my hand, "but please, just think about it."

And I do. I think about the secrets I've told her and the ones I haven't and I just can't do it, not tonight. I force a smile instead and take two champagne flutes from the cupboard.

I'M STILL TIPSY WHEN RONAN calls, the sharp edges of the past softened by champagne and celebration. I jump up a little too quickly and mouth an apology at Alex as I skip out to the front room. The amber glow of a streetlight pulses outside as Ronan petitions me, detailing the bravery of his young client, Josh Blair, until I have no choice but to surrender.

"You know, he's the one who sought me out after the DPP decided not to prosecute?" says Ronan. "Only fourteen years of age and he's got more courage than the state."

Ronan speaks with conviction, yet I still can't work out if this is just another game to him, or if he really is after justice this time around.

"How is he?" I ask.

"I think he's doing OK. He's very upset not to be swimming, especially with the nationals coming up, but he's got a lot of support from his family and he's not afraid to talk about what happened. He told a friend fairly soon after it started so it could have been a lot worse."

"How . . . bad was it?"

"I can't really disclose that, but it wasn't like back then."

I breathe a sigh of relief for Josh, for the friends and family who were willing to listen, and I can only hope it's because my generation has provided the support system we never had.

"But we don't know how many other kids might be affected," says Ronan. "Highfield had to suspend him—Damien Corrigan, that's the bastard's name—but they reinstated him when the case was dropped. Unfortunately, the DPP has sent out the message that there's no point in speaking out, but if things go well for us, then hopefully any others will feel like they can come forward."

"Why are you so sure you can win when the DPP thinks there's a lack of evidence?"

"Because the burdens of proof are different," says Ronan. "A criminal case has to be proven beyond reasonable doubt, but a civil case needs to succeed only on the balance of probabilities. In other words, which party is more likely to be telling the truth."

"Oh, I see," I say, and I wonder if a civil action could have saved any of us back then. Not that Tina or I had the money or the clout for anything like that.

"So that's where you come in," he says. "Because we're suing High-field's board of management for negligence, anything that confirms a pattern of behavior will help our case. If we can show a systemic cover-up of abuse in the school and the swimming club over decades, it should tip the balance. Especially as they won't want any of this getting out. Josh may not be a student at Highfield, but the school still runs the swimming club, so this is very much their responsibility."

"Hold on a minute," I say. "What do you mean, Highfield won't want it getting out? Surely the media will be all over it?"

"Yeah, if it goes to trial. But none of us wants that. The plan is to make sure Corrigan never coaches again and to get a generous settlement for Josh."

"So I won't ever have to take the stand?"

My relief is audible, a physical release of the anguish of the last few days. Maybe I can do this, help that poor boy and keep my career and my family intact.

"Ah Lou, I can't promise anything, but I've got Shauna and at least four other victims prepared to testify. You might remember Julie Gillespie and Paula Fletcher."

I remember their bravery, how much they were prepared to risk to save me. Maybe it's the champagne or Ronan's easy sales patter but I don't feel like I can let them down again.

"OK," I say before I can change my mind. "I'll write a statement."

"Thank you, Lou," says Ronan with the air of someone who's just sealed the deal. "I really appreciate it. I know this can't be easy for you, but it is the right thing to do."

I want to ask about Shauna, how forthcoming she's been with her own testimony. What she's written about me. But I don't want to alert Ronan to the can of worms he might not even know exists.

"I'll set up a time for you to come in," he continues, "and we'll go through the statement and make sure it's as tight as it can be. I'm confident it will help us get a swift and fair settlement."

It's only when I've hung up and caught my breath that I realize what I've done: Liam Kelly has every reason to come for me now.

THE VOICES OF NIGHT PULL me out of a thin sleep. The clack of pipes, the whisper of wind, the creak of these mortgaged walls. The rise and fall of Alex's breath is a ticking clock, one that keeps pace with my nocturnal illusions.

In the blue light of my phone, I read the email over and over, probing and parsing it, trying to fit it into the cracks of my life like Tetris, as if there is some order to this chaos. I google Liam Kelly and Shauna, Ronan, Highfield, but there is nothing. It's a common Irish name chosen for exactly that reason, a mask for someone who doesn't want to be seen. He could be any one of the players so invested in Highfield's reputation. I need to know why he's so sure of himself, what proof might be out there apart from the memories Shauna and I have held close all these years.

I think of the photo, the one we hoped would lift the veil of secrecy that shrouded Highfield. But that was lost along with everything else that night.

I try to trace the email, find the sender's IP address, but even with the help of several tech websites, the only IP I find points to a Google server in the States, one through which the email has been routed. It takes a further round of investigation before I finally accept the answer that no, it is not possible to trace a message sent from Gmail.

I can't confront an enemy who is undeclared and elusive so I'll have to do what he wants instead. I've got to make sure this case never goes to trial, for everyone's sake. I need to go after Damien Corrigan myself.

PART TWO

Then

5

It's a damp Monday in September 1986 when I first enter the 6A form room. You could fly a kite in here, the height of it, and the sash windows almost as tall. The clack of heels and the clatter of chairs bounce off the timber floors and the bare walls as the girls saunter into the room in their purple uniforms, satchels slung across shoulders, curly bobs tucked behind one ear. They stare and whisper as they settle at their desks, while I stand at the front of the class, arms folded, trying not to look like a complete eejit. I've got the uniform, even if it is second hand, but my spiky hair and patent brogues are clearly not the in-thing at Highfield.

Soon, I'll be expected to speak and the words that stumble out of my mouth will brand me as pure outsider. I have a normal accent, the same as everyone else I know. It's them, the Highfield girls, that are different. They don't know that, but why would they? There's no need for them to step off their pedestals; they'll be expecting me to step up.

Sister Mullen, the English teacher, sits upright at the podium, white hair tucked into a dark gray veil. The way she looks out over the girls, beaked nose in the air, it's not that she's better than them, I think she wants me to know she's one of them. Isn't that the whole point of this place, that everyone knows it? Sure, why else would you spend so much money? Luckily, I am on a scholarship, so I don't have to pretend to be on their level. I'm on the floor, blowing smoke up their skirts.

You'd swear they were saints, with their "moral values" and "inclusive ethos." But beyond the braids of rain that trickle down the sash windows, past the tennis and netball courts, I see the cedars that shroud the grotto, a sacred shrine and the scene of Highfield's summer scandal. Róisín Tunney, a third-year swimming champion, just fifteen years of age as she gave birth under the statue of the Blessed Virgin. They'd have kept it all quiet, only she was found by a visiting tennis player from rival Fairfield Grove and rumor has it you can't trust those sneaky cows as far as you can throw them. Needless to say, Róisín hasn't been welcomed back for fourth year.

I'm trying to suss out the lay of the land when Sister Mullen raises her hand for silence and the last few stragglers find their seats. She nods at me to begin and, in the hush, I'm half paralyzed by the glare of expectation and the smell of 4711 cologne. I focus on a lonely crucifix splayed across the back wall, a naked metal Jesus hanging from a wooden cross.

"I'm Louise Manson and I'm going to be here for sixth year."

Sister Mullen rotates her hand impatiently and I shrug like I don't understand.

"Tell us a bit more about yourself, Louise."

"Like what?"

There are a few sniggers, and the aggro gives me something to work with. I throw side-eye across the room as if I'm the boss up here.

"Like where you come from and how many brothers and sisters you have."

"I'm from Ballybrack and I have zero brothers and zero sisters."

Whispers ripple across the back row and a hand goes up.

"Yes, Carol?" says Sister Mullen.

Carol has the look of someone who uses her cheekbones as currency. She's smiling sweetly but I've known enough Carols not to believe it.

"Where's Ballybrack?"

I look at Sister Mullen, but she's waiting for me to answer.

"It's beside Loughlinstown . . . Carol," I say.

The hand is up again.

"Carol?"

"Where's Loughlinstown?"

There's a flitter of laughter around the room and it takes me a few seconds to realize it's a badge of pride that they don't know the working-class areas of their own city. I want to tell Carol where to go but Mam has warned me to keep my head down. She knows these people, grew up with them, she says. Before I came along and dragged her down to my bastard level.

"It's near Killiney, isn't it?"

At the end of the front row is a face I know from the school brochure: pale blue eyes and sun-kissed skin, white-blonde hair tied back in a high ponytail. Shauna Power, Highfield's star swimmer and Olympic hopeful. She's wearing the dark purple sash and implicit confidence of a prefect and she's throwing me a bone.

"Thank you, Shauna," says Sister Mullen.

I give Shauna a grateful smile and I'm edging away from the front of the class when another hand goes up, a girl next to Carol with thick wire braces and a fit of the giggles.

"Stephanie?" says Sister Mullen.

"Is it Lou-eez or Lou-wee-uz?"

I wonder if she has a hearing problem, or if the acoustics of the room have distorted my voice in transit. But the smirk unfolding on her lips leaves no room for doubt. I turn to Sister Mullen to protest, and I swear I see a conspiratorial glance flash between them.

"Give it a rest, Stephanie." It's the girl beside Shauna, all dimples and ringlets like a Billie Barry kid, and I wonder what her deal is.

"Melissa," says Sister Mullen, "can you please watch your tone?"

"What?" says Melissa. "Me and not her?"

The three of them eye each other in a Mexican stand-off and you could hear a pin drop.

"It's actually Lou," I say. "I hope that's simple enough for you."

As I walk past Melissa to the spare desk behind her, she says, "Ignore Carol, she's a bitch."

When I think about everything that happened, when I wonder what I could have done differently, I always come back to this moment, the crumb Melissa threw that I devoured.

HIGHFIELD SITS ON A HILL of the same name, looking down on the rest of Dublin. It's the sort of school that expects everyone to know it by reputation and, to be fair, I did. After all the trouble at my old school, Mam was ecstatic when I suggested repeating sixth year at Highfield. In a rare burst of optimism, she filled out forms and went to meetings. I did the tests and we both went to the interview and pretended to be devout Catholics, and they must have believed us, or else my results were too good to turn down. Whatever it was, I got a scholarship and Mam got a break.

I'm not sure what I expected. That it would be like my old school only grander? That I'd be left alone to observe from a distance? It's not just the dim corridors with their dark wood paneling and checkered floor tiles, or the clocktower turret that rises into the clouds. Everything at Highfield is shade and shadow, forged by hidden hierarchies and unspoken rules as much as granite pillars and cedar boughs. Even the prefects, their privilege worn across their chests, are evidence of an inner circle within the elite. One that would never be open to me. But I haven't come for any of that. I don't want to stand up or stand out. I'm at Highfield to watch and listen and bide my time, until I'm ready to pounce.

I'm not here for prestige. I'm here for revenge.

6

We're in the locker room getting changed for PE and Melissa's making a show of chatting to me, and I'm happy enough to be a pawn in her power struggle with Carol and Stephanie and their bitch friends.

"So, where did you go to school before?" she asks.

Rich kids always wanted to know where you went to school. *Tell me your school so I can know who you are.* She couldn't begin to imagine.

"Santa Maria."

"Oh, which one?" says a girl with large welts of acne across her chin and forehead. "My cousin goes to Donnybrook."

"I'm guessing it's not Donnybrook," says Melissa, "seeing as you live in Ballybrack." She hoists her blouse over her head to reveal the sort of lace bra you'd see on a model.

"Where's Ballybrack?" asks the girl.

"God, Aisling, it's near Killiney," says Melissa, rolling her eyes at me. "Don't you know anything about Dublin?"

"Sor-ry," says Aisling, rubbing a flake of dried skin from her chin.

"It's the Sallynoggin one," I say, yanking my unbranded polo shirt down over a gray-white bra.

At the end of the lockers, Shauna changes discreetly, face to the wall. As she bends over to tie her laces, I stare a moment too long at a narrow scar on her inner thigh, turning away as she catches my eye.

"There was a girl from your school in the swimming club here," says Aisling. "Tina Forrester, did you know her?"

"Is that the girl who . . . ?" Melissa stops as Aisling glares at her.

"I . . . I didn't know her well," I say, as dismissively as I can.

"So sad," says Aisling. "She had a real chance at the nationals."

"She had everything to live for," I say. I just can't help myself.

IT'S STILL RAINING WHEN WE get outside, angry droplets that spit against bare arms and legs. A sullen mist hangs low over the hockey pitches and I'm shivering when I see him. Mr. McQueen, with his feathered fringe and that thick bristle of a mustache, scooting across the pitch as he lays out the marker cones for class. You'd expect him to be taller, larger than life, the legend he's built for himself. But he's just a man, like one of the dads from the estate, with his electric-blue Adidas tracksuit and casual swagger. Maybe you'd find him attractive if you were the sort of person who fancied Magnum P.I., but that's a no from me.

You can't spend five minutes here without knowing who Maurice McQueen is. He teaches PE at the school and also runs the prestigious Highfield swimming club, and his photo is center stage in the vast echo chamber of the school's entrance hall. He sent two Highfield swimmers to the LA Olympics two years ago and there's already an expectation for Seoul in '88. If you believed the hype, you might think he pissed rivers of gold.

Mr. McQueen's ordered two laps of the pitches and you'd almost be winded by the batting of eyelids and pleas for clemency. Only Shauna is not amused, starting her run while the laggards are still trying to charm their way out of it. I follow behind, keeping pace with her when Mr. McQueen catches up with me.

"You must be Louise Manson," he says. "Welcome to Highfield."

"Thanks."

"How's your hockey?"

"I dunno. I've never played it."

"Really? Well, we'll soon find out," he says, and he's off, sprinting ahead to catch Shauna.

Mr. McQueen puts me on the wing, and I spend most of the match minding my own business on the sideline. It's coming up to the end of class and I'm unmarked when the ball comes shooting toward me. I stop it dead and take off with no particular plan in mind, hurtling down the pitch toward the circle. Melissa's in goal, looking like she'd rather be anywhere else, so I hammer the ball at her, and she kindly makes no effort to stop it. As the ball glides past her into the net, an unexpected rush of joy lifts my hand above my head and when I turn around I see a chorus of fists in the air behind me.

Afterward, we're walking back to the sports center, sodden and muck-splattered, when Mr. McQueen calls me back. Shauna gives me the up-down as she passes.

"Is this really your first time playing hockey?" he asks.

"Yeah," I say. "I mean, I played camogie when I was younger so . . ."

"It's a shame we didn't get our hands on you earlier," he says, packing the bibs and balls into a large sports bag. "Do you swim?"

I've been asked this question at every step of the enrollment process. The answer is no, I don't even float.

"Well, if you make half the progress you've made in one hockey lesson, we'll have you on a team in no time."

"I can't swim," I say. "I have a perforated eardrum, I'm not allowed in the water."

He fixes his brown eyes on mine, and I can't look away.

"Let's see if we can get that looked at for you."

WHEN I GET HOME, I can hear the *Countdown* clock galloping to a climax from the hall.

"Lou?" says Mam from the living room.

She's lying on the sofa, lights off, curtains closed, the glow from the telly just enough to catch the flush in her cheeks. With her bleached hair and lace top, she looks more like a brittle Debbie Harry than a thirty-six-year-old council-estate single mother.

"Well?" she says, pushing herself upright.

"Well what?" I'm too tired to play along.

"Ah come on, Lou. How was it?"

"Barter," I say, looking at the letters on the screen.

"What?"

"No, Rebater. Yes, seven!"

"Very good," says Mam.

The quiz obsession is her way of holding on to her past self. Even with a few drinks, she can blitz the mental-agility round on *The Krypton Factor*.

"But tell me, how was school?"

She pats the cushion beside her, but I stay where I am.

"It was fine, I suppose."

"Is that it?" she says. Her shoulders slump and the guilt slices through me.

"OK, it was great," I say, sitting beside her. Her breath has a sharp, chemical tang and I know to tread gently. "I played hockey, made some friends and the work was a piece of piss. And I finally met the famous Mr. McQueen."

"Oh yeah, he called," she says.

"What do you mean?"

"Mr. McQueen, he phoned."

"Why?"

"He wanted to talk about your ear, to see if you'd be able to start swimming. A very nice man. You seem to have made some sort of impression on him."

"I told him I didn't want to join his stupid club."

Even if it was just the ear and not the crippling fear of water that came with it, I'd still be surprised at the audacity of him.

"For god's sake, Lou. After everything you've been through . . ."

"Here we go."

"You've got a fresh start now and opportunities most people don't even dream of. Mr. McQueen is a very influential man. If anyone can help you get back in the water, it's him. Will you not think about it?"

I say nothing and Mam pushes on, mistaking my angry silence for consideration.

"You know, Tina would be so proud of you."

But she's wrong. Even if she wasn't dead, pride is the very last thing Tina would feel for me.

7

The rain continues into my second week at Highfield, a leaden beat that fills every corner of the city with its perpetual monotony. I arrive at school each morning in various dank states after a thirty-five-minute cycle across South Dublin from Ballybrack to Sandyford. Mam doesn't drive and the city's radial bus service means there's no other way of traveling the seven miles without going into town and back out again.

I love it, the freedom of the bike. That in-between time that's not concerned with the past or the future, only an infinite present that stretches ahead like those days of summer that merge into night. When the tape in my Walkman decides my persona and I'm taken so far away from myself I don't care if it's grief or joy that surges my heart. Today it's The Cure's *The Head on the Door*, and I'm an eagle, soaring along the Leopardstown Road to the piano riff of "Six Different Ways," reveling in the burn of "Push" as I make the final ascent to Highfield, sweat pooling in the small of my back. It's the challenge of pain with a purpose that drives me, even with the earth damp and the tarmac wet and the sticky-sweet hair gel melting onto my forehead.

Most days I head straight to the locker room to change from my tracksuit to my uniform before assembly, but I'm late today and make it to the hall just in time for roll call. The whole school meets here every morning, all six years with four classes in each, almost five hundred day students in total. The last of the boarders graduated two years ago so they remain only in legend, stories that have already been elevated to mythological status. Melissa's told me all the gory details, the sixth-year who had two boys climbing the drainpipe to her dorm on alternating nights. The daughter of a government minister who gave the Christmas address in the chapel while high on her da's cocaine. The fourth-year who seduced a teacher and was promptly expelled. These myths are not about academic or sporting achievement—Highfield has plenty of that already. They're a dangerous dip into the thrills of the outside world, the one that isn't supposed to exist within these protective stone walls.

I slip into the back of the 6A line as Sister Shannon's footsteps creak up the wooden steps at the side of the stage. Rain blurs the windows, all the blues turned gray, dulling even the heavy maroon curtains behind her, the ornate plasterwork overhead. Silence falls across the hall as she leads us in prayer, our reverence as mechanical as our refrain. It's an illusion of control, the power the Church has over our lives. No matter how much they try to threaten and shame us, you can't stop teenagers being themselves. Sometimes the more you have to rebel against, the harder you push.

As Sister Shannon starts her announcements—sick teachers, classroom changes—I take off my soaking school gabardine, hang it over my arm and lean forward to ruffle the rain out of my hair. The air is still warm and heavy, despite the damp, and I get a whiff of the sweat festering in my armpits.

Eva O'Brien, a prefect with windswept hair and red cheeks, makes her way along the line with a clipboard, marking off those present. When she gets to Carol Sheridan, a few places ahead of me, Carol leans into her, sniffing the air.

"What's that smell?" she says.

I catch a sideways glance from Eva as I flick my head upright, and at least she has the remorse to look away, but Carol's face is scrunched with intent as she looks down the line.

"Oh my god," she says to Eva, "whatever about personal hygiene, it's just good manners to shower in the mornings."

A couple of girls turn around and back again when they see the state of me. Melissa is in front of them, either oblivious or indifferent. I'm about to explain to Carol, of course I washed, I just haven't had time to change, but I know it's not about that.

"I think somebody needs to have a quiet word with B. O. Baracus there," says Carol to Eva, and I see the acne on the back of her neck shake with suppressed laughter.

You could pass it off as a few bitches but there are three fifth-years sniggering in the line beside us and nobody is telling Carol to shut up. Maybe it's not even Carol at all, maybe she's just a catalyst for the exclusion that is inevitable for people like me. I want to tell them all to fuck themselves and storm out, back to my natural habitat, where drugs and sex are not considered some high achievement. But nobody listens to the girl from Ballybrack, that much is clear. I have to take their crap, play their game and blend in as much as possible. It's only from the inside that I have any hope of exposing the truth about Tina.

AFTER ASSEMBLY, I SLINK OFF to the locker room to banish my offending clothes and douse my bare skin in deodorant. My brain rattles with the need to show Carol I'm not the vermin she thinks I am while also trying to think of a killer comeback that will show her up as the ignorant snob she definitely is. I'm mouthing my way through an imaginary encounter with Carol when Shauna arrives at the door, blonde hair dark and wet around her shoulders. She doesn't see me and she's muttering too, as if practicing a speech.

"Hi," I say.

"Oh." She stops, startled, and pulls a smile together as she walks past me to her locker. "Hi, Lou."

"Sorry about the smell," I say, flapping my hand through the air. "I think I overdid it on the deodorant."

"That's OK," she says. "All I can smell is chlorine anyway."

"Have you been swimming?"

Of course she's been swimming.

"Yeah, I just finished training. I hear Miss Carter is sick."

"Oh yeah, I heard that at assembly," I say, buttoning my blouse. "I don't do German. I have French now."

"With *Madame*?"

She puts on a husky voice and a French accent that makes me laugh. Mme Martel is a bona fide Parisienne, a sultry femme fatale who should be an icon to any teenage girl but instead is mimicked and mocked for her accent, for her status as a mere teacher. All behind her back of course—they wouldn't dare do it in class. At Santa Maria, I never had a French teacher who sounded remotely like anyone from a Jean-Luc Godard film, and I can't get enough of her. Unlike my classmates with their holiday homes and student exchanges, it's film that has taught me French. *À Bout de Souffle* and *Le Retour de Martin Guerre* taped off the telly and watched with my finger on the pause button. It was the plan, before Tina died, to study French and English at Trinity, but I ended up dropping out of school before the final Leaving Cert exams had even begun.

"Yeah," I say. "I better make a move."

I hang my damp clothes on the hooks inside my locker and shove the door closed.

"See ya," I say as I sling my bag on my shoulder and head for the door.

"You knew Tina Forrester, didn't you?" says Shauna, and I stop.

"I was in school with her, but . . ."

"How was she before, you know?"

Before she killed herself? She was depressed, angry. I barely recognized her.

"She was quiet, I suppose. Looking back, like, it's obvious there was something going on."

"Like what?" She feigns indifference but those blue eyes are begging for an answer and I want to know why.

"I dunno. Maybe boyfriend trouble or something like that."

"Oh." She looks away, reaches into her locker.

"Do you know anything about it?" I ask.

She hesitates and I wonder if I've pushed too hard.

"No, god. All we ever talked about was swimming."

She underlines her comment with a smile that makes me certain she's hiding something.

I DON'T HAVE ANY MORNING classes with Shauna, so I keep an eye out for her in the dining hall. Lunch at Highfield is a reverberation of chatter and clatter as girls queue for hot drinks and scramble for seats on the long oak tables and benches that line the hall. Light floods the walls that bear photos of girls past, prefects and teams gone but not forgotten. I wonder if they'll ever let me up there, if I'll do enough to achieve Highfield notoriety.

I spot Shauna at the end of a table with Melissa and Aisling, and I push past a large group of irritated fourth-years to reach them. I squash in beside Melissa while the others pick at their food opposite. It comes in colored containers with compartments that house batons of carrot and stuffed olives and brown bread topped with smoked salmon. I have my ham sandwiches wrapped in tinfoil, a slightly bruised apple and a United bar that seems to have survived the schoolbag.

"You made a real show of Carol in French this morning," says Melissa to me, smirking. "She did not like that one little bit."

"She was raging," says Aisling.

"What happened?" asks Shauna, peeling a satsuma.

"Carol was talking about her summer in the south of France," says Melissa. "They have a villa in . . ." She turns to me. "Where is it?"

"Beaulieu-sur-Mer," I say.

"Yeah, it's on the Riviera, near Monaco. So of course Carol thinks she's the world expert on France. She was going on and on about the houses and cars and the shops and how she got a real Hermès scarf, except she pronounced it *Air-may* instead of *Air-mez* and Lou was straight in there correcting her. God, the look she gave you when Mme Martel said you were right."

The glee on Melissa's face tells me this is how to keep her sweet. The hierarchy in the school is based on money first, sports second and looks third, so even though Melissa's pretty and thin and lives in Donnybrook, the power balance must always be wrested from Carol's hands.

"I think you've definitely evened the score there," says Melissa.

"For what?" I say, and she looks at her lunch as her cheeks flush. So she did hear her at assembly.

"Oh, you know, she's just been having a bit of a go at you since you got here," she says. "Hey, are you coming to the Rockdale social next month?"

Rockdale is a private boys' school, Catholic of course, that is closely aligned to Highfield in ethos.

"Will it be any good?" I ask.

"Oh no, it'll be terrible," says Shauna.

"A school disco with no alcohol, supervised by priests," says Melissa with a grin. "It's every girl's dream night out."

"But you'll still go," says Shauna to Melissa.

"Of course. I don't expect David Sharkey to ravish me right there on the hall floor, but there are ways and means."

Shauna ignores her and looks at me.

"What do you do for fun, Lou?"

"I've been known to shuffle my feet to a bit of popular music."

"What are you into?" asks Melissa.

"The Smiths, The Cure, The Jesus and Mary Chain."

"You're not a goth, are you?" asks Melissa, sharing a look of mock horror with the others.

"Nah. A Curehead maybe. But definitely not a goth."

"I'm sure there's a big difference, but maybe glam it up a bit if you come
to Rockdale."

"Sorry, Melissa, but this is Rockdale we're talking about," says Shauna.
"It's not exactly the Pink Elephant."

"Oh my god, Shauna," says Melissa. "Not all of us want to hang around
with men old enough to be our dads. I'll take a Senior Cup player over
Bono or Joe Elliott any day."

Shauna slumps back in her seat. "In your dreams," she says meekly.

"Do you want me to tell you about my dreams?"

"Melissa, we really don't . . ." says Aisling.

"In my dreams, David Sharkey knocks on my bedroom door and I open
it, stark naked, and . . ."

"OK, we get it," says Shauna.

Melissa leans across the table and lowers her voice.

"You don't want to hear about the bit where he fucks me till I scream?"

"Fuck off," says Shauna quietly.

"What?" says Melissa, looking to me for support. "What have I done
wrong?"

"You know he's only after one thing," says Aisling.

"Would that be the same thing I'm after?" says Melissa.

Aisling shakes her head, but Melissa's looking at Shauna, waiting for a
reaction. Shauna puts the satsuma peel into her lunchbox, piece by piece,
as if she hasn't heard a word.

I've seen it before, the slow build of resentment that can tear a friendship apart. I should know to steer clear, but I can't look away. Maybe those
of us with secrets are destined to find each other. Maybe there was never
any choice.

8

I'm at Highfield less than three weeks when I'm first accused of a crime. I'm the last to find out as the transgression happens during double swimming on a Wednesday morning, that glorious hour and a half I get to spend alone. The library is my refuge, a long, dignified room that smells of old newspapers and floor polish. Light filters through the cedars outside onto the long wooden desks that carry their own secret histories, the messages gouged into the dull, faded oak. I trace my finger along etchings of hearts and flowers, boys and bands, and wonder if Matt really was the one, if The Sisters of Mercy are the goths or the nuns. You never can be sure in this place.

On the bookshelf behind me, under dusty dictionaries and ragged reference books, is a pile of *Paris Match* magazines. This is my go-to library read and I spend a happy hour learning about Princess Stephanie's burgeoning pop career and her sister Caroline's new baby. I read about Luc Besson's much-hyped film *Subway* and vow to see it when it comes to Ireland.

If I'd come to Highfield under different circumstances, I'd probably love it. The overspill of lilac at the front gate, the vast corridors of science and language labs, music and art rooms. The expectation of excellence and the small classes and rigid discipline that ensure it. At Santa Maria, it was always the loudest voices that set the agenda and I'd have to decipher my notes with the help of textbooks later. They made such a big deal about all the As I got in my Inter Cert, but the truth is I learned more in the quiet calm of Shankill library than I ever did at school.

When I get to our form room, I can tell something is up. There's no sign of Sister Keating, our religion teacher, and the girls are huddled around desks and in the window alcoves, whispering and chattering. Carol Sheridan sits head-in-hands near the door while Eva O'Brien crouches beside her, a thick arm around Carol's narrow back. Conversation withers to a hum as I enter and Carol is on her feet, wiping kohl-blackened tears from under her eyes.

"Where have you been?"

She folds her arms and fires disdain from the slits of her eyes.

"In the library. I don't do swimming."

"Were you in the locker room?"

The low autumn sun catches the side of her face and, even in this ambush, I marvel at the jut of her cheekbone, the deep blue of her eye.

"No. I told you where I was. Why d'ye want to know?"

"Somebody stole my grandmother's earrings from my locker while we were in the pool."

I know them: gold flower studs with diamonds for petals. They're beautiful, too precious to take for granted.

"I'm sorry to hear that."

I scout the room for a free desk, for any means of escape.

"You know, the locker room is being searched as we speak."

I think of the packet of Silk Cut cigarettes in my coat pocket, the trouble I'll be in if it's found, and maybe I show a spark of discomfort. Triumph sweeps across Carol's face and I try to walk away, but she grabs my wrist from behind.

"Where are they?" she says as I turn, stunned into silence.

I pull my hand free and look to the room for support, to Melissa perched on a desk beside me, but they're all waiting for my answer. It's a lesson, how easily Carol can put on this display, how eager everyone else is to go along with it.

"Keep your hands off me," I say, my voice unsteady now. "It's got nothing to do with me."

"Are you sure?" says Carol. "We never had a problem with security before you arrived."

It's true, nobody locks their lockers here. Books and belongings are left on open shelves in classrooms, hockey sticks and tennis rackets line up along changing room walls.

"Ah come on, Carol." It's Shauna who finally breaks the deadlock. "She said it wasn't her."

She smiles sympathetically and I scuttle to the empty desk next to her.

"You think you're so clever," says Carol, "but you'll never fit in here." And even though I ignore her, the words ring in my ears for the rest of the class.

I SLIP OUT AFTER CLASS to check the contraband in my coat pocket. Smoking is a suspendable offense, even outside of school grounds, and it's not like Mam can throw money at the problem if I'm caught. It's the scholarship I'm worried about, and I need to know. I tell the others I'll see them later and I skip down the stone staircase to the locker room.

Highfield gave me that scholarship with such ease I'm afraid they could take it away just as quickly. I never had any worries about the entrance exams but I was always surprised the award had been granted without a cross-examination of my obvious failings—my Ballybrack address, my absent father, my abandoned Leaving Cert. And the headmistress, Sister Shannon, must have known I'd gone to the same school as Tina, although she never mentioned it. I'm not their ideal candidate, despite my results, and I'm sure there will be no special dispensation for any lapses of judgment.

My coat is where I left it, on one of the hooks inside my locker, my tracksuit opposite. I squeeze the right pocket, shove my hand inside it. It is empty. Adrenaline courses through me as I pull at the left pocket and dig deep down into it, but there is only a tissue and a few coppers. No purple cigarettes, no yellow lighter. I grab the jersey fabric of the tracksuit with shaking hands, pull everything out of the locker, run my fingers along the top of it. There is nothing. Somebody has taken them and it's just a matter of time before my punishment is served.

I'M ON MY WAY TO the bike shed after school, head full of the day's dilemmas, when Shauna scoots up behind me.

"I'm sorry about Carol earlier," she says. "She's really not that bad when you get to know her."

I want to tell her there's no danger of that ever happening.

"Thanks," I say. "You know, for standing up for me."

A smile breaks across her face and I can't take my eyes off the apples of her cheeks, the perfect curve of her lips.

"Ah, it was nothing," she says. "Like, I know she was upset, but there was no need to take it out on you."

"Well, it was a nice thing to do." I'm grinning, the cigarettes forgotten for now, and I don't want her to leave. "Are you walking out this way?"

"Yeah, my mum's picking me up outside."

"Here, let me just get my bike and I'll come with you."

As we walk and talk, I take it all in, the way her blue eyes smile intensely when I speak, how she catches a wisp of hair with her fingers and slides it behind her ear. There are no wasted words, each one considered and thoughtful as we bond over music and books, and I start to see beyond the purple sash and the perfect teeth.

"I've never met anyone else who's read *Oranges Are Not the Only Fruit*," I say, and when she smiles, I want to believe it means something.

I keep the conversation going, even when we get out past the front gate, and I try not to look disappointed when a silver-blue Mercedes pulls up beside us.

"I'll see you tomorrow," she says, and I swear I see an expectant pause before she opens the car door. I don't know what it is, the scale or scope of the connection between us; all I know is I don't want it to end.

WHEN I GET HOME, MAM'S in the hall, running a neon-red lipstick over her smoke-thinned lips. She leans forward, scrunches her hands through her peroxide bob and flicks her head upright.

"How do I look?"

"Only gorgeous," I say, and she smirks at me.

"I don't know if I should believe a word that comes out of your mouth," she says, but she's still pleased with herself.

She always scrubs up well for work, her customers at the Black Swan the only company she keeps these days. Now and again, I catch a glimpse of one of them, a balding rocker or a cocksure young fella, skulking out the door before sunrise, but I don't pass any judgment. She hasn't had anyone on the scene since Keith left four years ago and after that car crash, I'm happy with any setup that keeps the peace in the house.

I've one eye on *EastEnders* when the doorbell rings, and I curse it. I've half a mind to ignore it, but Mam's warned me Bridie Brady from next door might call round with the out-of-date fruit and veg she gets working at Quinnsworth. Mam has no problem taking handouts from the neighbors. When you've known poverty, she says, you choose the principles that keep it furthest from your door.

It's not Bridie that's looming over me in the fading light, and it takes me a second to focus on the once-familiar face, the sandy mullet and hazel eyes of Joe Forrester, Tina's older brother.

"Howiye, Lou."

"Alright."

I don't know what else to say. I haven't seen Joe since the funeral almost six months ago and the memory of it still haunts me. My ill-timed allegations upset him and his ma so much, I was asked to leave. Now, I can't even guess what he wants and I'm not sure I'm able for it anyway.

"So it's true?" he says.

"What?"

"You've gone over to the dark side," he says, pointing at my uniform.

I look down at the purple jumper and think how quickly I've got used to it.

"Oh yeah, yeah, I'm one of them now."

Joe sucks his teeth and I wish I could explain.

"You never made it to Trinity then?" he asks.

Joe is a journalism student at Rathmines College, and he always thought I had notions with my talk of university.

"Not yet," I say, with more conviction than I feel.

"Can I come in?"

There's a pleading in his eyes, and I relax, relieved to let my guard down.

"D'ye want tea?" I ask as he follows me to the kitchen.

"Yeah, go on."

I put the kettle on and start spooning tea into the teapot, my back to Joe.

"You were right," he says.

I stop and the air stills around me.

"Tina was pregnant."

It's as if I've been holding my breath for five months and I've just been given permission to exhale. I turn to Joe, and his awkward smile fills my stony heart with such gratitude there are tears racing down my cheeks before I can stop them.

"I'm sorry," he says. "We didn't find out until the inquest, and Ma, well, she ended up in John of God's hospital again and I just . . . I dunno, there was so much to deal with, you know?"

I did know. I saw her around the estate, eyes glazed and empty as she wandered the streets.

"I want to apologize," says Joe.

I rub my fingers roughly under my eyes, across my cheeks.

"And I want you to tell me everything."

9

September clings to summer, sun-dappled days that chill into night, the pear trees by the tennis courts still heavy with their wares. There is still light, ephemeral and transient, and it's easy to linger in its dying glow before October comes and cloaks everything in its drab reality. The Leaving Cert exam pressure, the scramble for college points, the everyday business of living, will take over soon and these in-between days will fade into memory.

I watch the last gasp of it from the 6A form room, the girls lying on the grass beside the tennis courts, barefoot, skirts and blouses hiked up for optimal tanning. Even from this distance, I can spot the glossy white of Shauna's hair, the discarded purple sash on the grass beside her. I imagine the caress of the sun on her skin, the calming warmth of it. Aisling's lying next to her and I'm gutted I've missed the chance to spend lunch with them, their senses softened and their guards down.

"Louise, are you paying attention?"

Sister Mullen clasps her hands together and rests them on the gray pinafore that covers her knees. She sits upright next to me, her feet crossed at the ankles and tucked under her chair. It's a performance of calm, this controlled pose she adopts, even when she's reprimanding insolence from the podium in front of the whole class.

"Sorry," I say, trying to focus on the text in front of me.

"Lady Macbeth," she says, jabbing her finger on my copy. "What do you think she means when she says, 'Come, you spirits that tend on mortal thoughts, unsex me here, and fill me from the crown to the toe top-full of direst cruelty'?"

I'm getting English grinds from Sister Mullen at lunch every Tuesday and Thursday. In most subjects, I'm ahead of the pack as I've already done most of sixth year at Santa Maria, but the English syllabus changes each year so I've a new Shakespeare play and two novels to learn before June.

"She wants to be more like a man," I say. "More violent so she'll have the strength to kill Duncan and take the crown off him."

"Take the crown from him, Louise, not off him. She's not literally going to pick the crown off his head now, is she?"

She can do what she likes, I think, he'll be dead. I shrug and she sighs like a disappointed parent.

"Did you study grammar at Santa Maria?"

"Em, not specifically."

She nods her head as if she'd hardly expect any more from such a dump of a school.

"I think we need to do a class on grammar and deportment," she says, "although I fear you may already be lost to solecism."

She looks at me with such weary malaise I can't work out why she'd give up her time to help me only to slag me off. The conceit of it stings, the assumption that my upbringing has failed me—I got an A in my Inter Cert English and she knows it. Maybe it's simply her vocation, that inherent drive to help those less fortunate than herself.

"If you want people to take you seriously—and I presume that is why you came to Highfield—you need to be able to speak with authority," she explains. "That means no mumbling, no slang and no lazy grammar. We have high standards here and we expect you to meet them when you're representing the school."

I fight the instinct to push back against her measure of worth because there's a part of me that knows she is speaking the truth, that the only way I can get them to listen to me is if I sound like them.

"Actually, I would like that."

THERE ARE TEN MINUTES OF lunch left after we've finished with Lady Macbeth and I run down the stone staircase to catch the girls on the lawn. I'm walking over to them, Shauna sun-splayed on her back, Aisling propped up on one elbow beside her, when I see Mr. McQueen waving from the entrance to the sports center. I look over my shoulder, but no, it's me he wants. As I get closer, I see he's holding something up between his thumb and forefinger. Something yellow, cylindrical. It's a Bic lighter. My stomach clenches and I feel the fluster rising through my chest.

"I believe this belongs to you, Lou," he says with a smile. "Come on in and we can chat about it."

He leads me into the sports center and along a narrow corridor as I pull nervously at the sleeves of my jumper. His office is a small, windowless space, the walls lined with filing cabinets and framed photos. Mr. McQueen with the president, with the archbishop, with the Irish Olympic team. He closes the door, motions to a plastic seat on one side of an uncluttered desk while he takes the leather chair opposite. He opens a drawer, takes out the ten-pack of Silk Cut and puts it on the desk in front of him with the lighter.

"You don't need me to tell you this is a serious offense."

I open my mouth to say something, feign ignorance or make an excuse, but I get the feeling that's not where this is going.

"However . . . I don't think you deserve to be suspended, not in your first few weeks of school."

I exhale heavily and he leans forward, arms folded on the desk.

"What you do with your body is your own business." He pauses, his dark eyes locked on mine. "But I would like to see you put it to good use. Have you thought about trying out for one of the hockey teams? The seniors could do with some fresh blood."

I wouldn't mind having a go, but the matches are all over Dublin and beyond and, with no car at home, I don't know how I'd manage it.

"It's a bit tricky," I say, shifting in my chair.

"It's OK," he says. "I understand you have . . . challenges."

"What do you mean?"

"I spoke to your mum on the phone. Don't worry"—he holds his hands up—"it's all in complete confidence."

I feel exposed and my cheeks flush with it.

"I know Rose doesn't have a car so if you want to play—and I really hope you do—I can talk to the parents of your teammates and organize lifts. How does that sound?"

It's her name that throws me, the familiarity with which he uses it, as if he knows us already.

"Yeah, OK," I say. "Thanks."

He stands up, hands me the cigarettes and the lighter, and I take them with the unsettling sense that this is our little secret. As he leads me out of his office, he lays his hand on the small of my back in a way that's so fleeting I barely notice he's done it.

MAM HAS ALREADY LEFT FOR work when I get home so I put all thoughts of homework aside and lie on the mottled brown carpet of the living room floor with the stereo up to eleven. It's The Smiths, *The Queen Is Dead,* a record that came after Tina, one that doesn't crack under the weight of unbearable sadness.

All music is divided into before and after. There are records that are so full of her I can no longer navigate them in this uncharted territory of grief. The synth pop songs of our first discos, full of hormones unleashed and intoxicated. Echo & the Bunnymen's *Songs to Learn & Sing* and the gig in the SFX only last Christmas. It could have been a decade ago.

It was music that drew us together that first year at Santa Maria. Duran Duran's *Rio* and a mutual appreciation for John Taylor. Later, we'd pool our babysitting money, buy Siouxsie and the Banshees and Cure albums and tape them for each other. This was the music that predicted how we'd move through the world, the one that was within our perception. We weren't under any illusions; we'd both lost fathers—Tina to prostate cancer when she was only ten and me to the fact that Mam couldn't go through with the abortion. We thought we understood the light and shade of it, that we could hold hands in the dark.

After, I submerged myself in Depeche Mode's *Black Celebration,* the album we'd listened to on her last night. It was supposed to be a peace of-fering, my attempt to cross the unimaginable void her secret had opened between us. I'd brought it round and put it on the tape deck in her room and we sat on the floor smoking, her orange shag-pile rug melting under the ash that fell unheeded from her cigarette. I remember every song, the soundtrack to our final bloodshot moments together. "A Question of Lust" as she started to open up, her freckled beauty raw with her tears. "A Question of Time" while she told me of her pregnancy and begged me to help. "Stripped" when I walked out and left her, exposed and alone.

I want to rewind the tape, remember what it's like to breathe without thinking. Before every song was filled with her absence. I can't bring her back, I know that. All I can do is retrace her steps, find out what happened and make sure it never happens to anyone else again. If I can save a life, maybe I'll have a chance to reclaim my own.

10

The hockey trials are a mess of endeavor and adrenaline as I do my best to keep pace with Stephanie Burke, her long, easy stride and smug metal grin. Stephanie's an A player but I make the Senior D, not bad for a beginner in a school that has teams all the way down to H. The details are posted on the notice board in the sports center and I'm running my finger down the list of Saturday morning's matches when Melissa sidles up to me.

"Please tell me the school vacuum hasn't sucked you in."

"What do you mean?"

"It comes for everyone. First it's swimming, then hockey, choir, debating. And if you're no good at any of that, there's always"—she sticks two fingers in her mouth—"charity work."

"Well, at least I've dodged that," I say, and she squints at the lists, looking for my name.

"Um . . . congratulations?" she says before turning to me, eyebrows raised. "Lou, are you seriously going to be playing hockey on Saturday morning?"

"Yeah, looks like it."

It's in Clonskeagh and I've no news yet on how I'm going to get there.

"You know Rockdale is on Friday night?"

Of course I do. There's been talk of little else all week, but it's not really my scene, slow sets and rugby players. Shauna is still undecided and I'm not sure I want the hassle of it if she isn't going to be there.

"Oh, yeah. Are you going?"

"Of course. It's on at half eight so that means the party starts in my house at seven."

I'm trying to think of an excuse when Shauna and Aisling come through the door speaking in whispers, their short purple skirts and polo shirts touching with their closeness. I smile instinctively at Shauna and I could swear her face lights up too.

"Drinkies at mine before Rockdale tomorrow," says Melissa. "See you around seven?"

"Sorry," says Shauna. "We have an early start on Saturday. The Leinsters are next month and training's going to be insane until then."

"You're not coming at all?"

Melissa does her best to harden her eyes, but I see the disappointment hidden in them. I know that feeling well, the resentment and guilt of losing your best friend to success.

"We might come to Rockdale for a couple of hours, but no way will we be getting pissed."

She looks at Aisling, who nods in agreement.

"OK," says Melissa. "Suit yourself."

She grabs hold of my arm and directs me into the hall.

"We'll just have to drink twice as much to make up for your uselessness, yeah, Lou?"

I must roll my eyes or grit my teeth because Shauna grins and I smile back as Melissa drags me away.

PE IS VOLLEYBALL WITH MISS Aherne, a short, sinewy woman with cropped hair and boundless enthusiasm—her first mistake. Her second is being barely older than us, a sure sign she must be clueless. She's well able for the backchat from the usual suspects but the sexual innuendo is harder to tackle.

The class is set up on two adjacent courts and I'm at the net with Stephanie looming over me from the other side. Miss Aherne is behind me, her arms around Mary Connolly as she helps her with her serve.

"Lezzer," coughs Stephanie into her hand, and a couple of the girls around her snigger their support.

Behind them, Shauna shakes her head and I stare at Stephanie, hands on hips.

"Have you got something to say?" says Stephanie to me.

"Yeah, grow up."

Stephanie takes a step closer to the net and peers down at me.

"Maybe you're OK with being felt up by a perv, but it's not my scene," she whispers.

"If you're so concerned, why don't you make a complaint? I'm sure

Sister Shannon would be horrified to learn one of her teachers is sexually abusing the students."

Stephanie returns only a withering look.

"OK, OK, girls," shouts Miss Aherne as she claps her hands and jogs in between the two courts. "We're going to play up to ten points and then we'll swap teams. Are you ready?"

I sure am, ready to spike the arrogant grin on the other side of the net. I look back at Mary as she serves and I stay low as the ball soars over my head. It's bumped mid-court and then set by Shauna and I keep my eye on it as it falls to Stephanie.

I wish I could say I see it coming but I don't stand a chance. It's so beautifully choreographed, such strength and agility in the twist and turn of Stephanie's body as her legs propel her into the air and her arm rounds the ball with all the power of her muscular shoulders. I'm still marveling at the follow-through when the ball smashes into the side of my face and I give in to it, limbs folding, the ground coming at me, cold against my skin.

"Lou, Lou, can you hear me?"

Miss Aherne's voice is distant and I'm in no hurry to move toward it.

"Shit, Carol, go and get Matron. Run."

"But I have a note for running, my doctor says . . ."

"Jesus, fuck'n . . . Shauna, please, as fast as you can."

Miss Aherne smells of fresh grass and ginger, her hands soft against my face. She rolls my head gently until light starts to filter through the gray fuzz and she's closer, her voice thin and raspy.

"Lou, can you hear me?"

I flick open my eyes and she's so close I see the pores on her nose and the flare of her nostrils as she sighs with relief.

"Oh, thank god. Are you all right, Lou? Are you feeling dizzy?"

"No."

I'm feeling calm, serene almost, but there are too many faces above me. One of them is Stephanie's and, even though she looks concerned, I don't want any more attention from her. I try to get up but it's only in motion that I feel the rolling pain in the side of my head, and I put my hand to it.

"Does it hurt, your head?" asks Miss Aherne.

"A bit."

"You got a fair whack of the ball. Are you sure you're not feeling faint or confused?"

"No, I'm fine."

"Good. Matron's on her way and I'm going to send you to the infirmary, just to be safe."

Shauna arrives back with Matron, a cheery woman from Manchester with pale skin and red lipstick. Her blue uniform is tight across her chest, as if it can barely contain her compassion.

"Shauna, can you stay with Lou and make sure she's OK?" says Miss Aherne.

Matron leads me to the bench that runs along the wall and Shauna sits beside me, the bare skin of her thigh smooth and warm against mine. I feel the rhythm of her breath on my cheek as Matron crouches in front of me, checks my eyes and moves a stubby finger in an arc in front of my face.

"I think you'll live, Lou," she says, "but I want to keep an eye on you in the infirmary until lunchtime, OK?"

"OK."

I stand up a little too quickly and I stumble sideways. Shauna puts her arm around my waist and I let her hold me for several seconds.

"Are you all right?" she says, her hand still firm against my hip.

"Yeah, thanks," I say, and she links her arm through mine.

As we walk away, someone wolf whistles, and it's probably Stephanie but I don't care.

MY HEAD IS FINE BY hockey practice on Friday afternoon but I still haven't heard from Mr. McQueen about a lift to my match. Afterward, I seek him out at the swimming pool, a place I've managed to avoid so far. Even the thought of it triggers that engine in me, the low hum of anxiety and inertia. It's not just the memory of water that fills me with dread, it's the whole stifling environment—the air thick with chlorine, the ghostly echo of shifting sounds.

My heart pounds as I tread carefully through the stands, and he's there, the squeak of rubber soles piercing the air as he sets up for evening training. He gives no indication he's seen me, his back turned as he pulls the lane ropes into place. I hold fast to the wall between us and breathe, trying not to remember.

I was just nine when it happened. A natural-born water baby, Mam says, never out of the pool. It was our first time at Mosney holiday camp and I'd only ever swum in the sea before that, the paralyzing chill of Sandycove or Killiney beach. So I'm sure I loved it, long afternoons in the indoor pool, playing with a constant supply of kids as Mam sat at the window of the bar next to it, making friends of her own.

None of them were there when she needed them. When the night and the drink had taken her away from herself. I'd been watching her in the bar long after she'd sent me to bed, waiting for the droop of an eyelid or a slump of the head, a sign it was time to help her back to the chalet. I thought she was at the toilet when I saw her, barely conscious, teetering around the darkened pool enclosure in her shiny jumpsuit and knee-high boots. She didn't hear when I banged on the glass, when I screamed her name as she lurched forward and flopped into the water.

What I remember most is the unreality of it, when she didn't resurface, when the people around me just stood and stared through the window as if they were watching a film. But they were half-cut themselves and I knew not to reason with booze. I ran out by the toilets, down the stairs and along the corridor, rattling one door after another until I found her point of entry and threw myself into the pool after her.

Under water, time slid to a sluggish pulse, flickered in shapes and shadows in the murky silence. Each second screamed its departure, sucking oxygen with it as it disappeared out of reach. The chlorine burned my eyes and tore at my eardrum as I prowled the pool floor for movement, grasping at the darkness. My diaphragm stuttered, its rhythm broken, and all I could think was, I must breathe for her until she can do it on her own.

I think I expected to see a struggle, some sign she was fighting for life. But all I found was the leaden shape of her, water billowing through the legs of her jumpsuit, boots weighted to the ground. Her torso was twisted away from me and I tugged at her arm, my shouts bubbling upward as her head lolled toward me, her soundless mouth open and her eyes glazed and vacant.

That's the image that never leaves me, the one that ripples through my head as Mr. McQueen fixes the lane rope to the wall. Not the later scenes, how I somehow hooked my arms under hers and dragged her to the surface, the teenage hostess who pulled her out of the water and pumped her chest, the moment she spluttered back to life. What lingers is the feeling of coming face-to-face with a life so loosely tethered to a body and knowing that you hold the final thread.

"Lou, what can I do for you?"

As Mr. McQueen walks toward me, I wonder if he's forgotten, if I'm going to have to beg for help.

"I have a hockey match in the morning."

"Oh, you made a team. Well done you."

He looks back to the pool, as if I'm a distraction.

"It's just, you said you'd ask some of the other parents for a lift for me."

"OK," he says, as if I might be making it up. "You're stuck for a lift?"

I wish I'd never mentioned it now and I need to get out of this putrid air that's sticking in my throat.

"It's OK, it doesn't matter."

"Let me think," he says. "Yes, you're right, I did say something. I'm sorry, I've just been so busy this week with the fundraising campaign. I'm sure you've heard about it."

I couldn't avoid it. He's been in all the papers, trying to raise money for Ireland's first fifty-meter Olympic-standard pool, to be built at Highfield.

"Where is your match?" he asks.

"St. Catherine's in Clonskeagh."

"I'll pick you up at twenty past ten," he says.

I suppress a shiver as I hold his gaze. I never mentioned the match was at eleven.

11

Behind the modest red-brick facade, Melissa's house is a Tardis of corridors and high ceilings. She has the room at the top, sloped walls, purple chenille and a window that looks out over the evening hum of Donnybrook village.

Melissa is head-deep in a wardrobe, a leather pencil skirt tight across her bum as she rummages behind a large shoe collection. I take two cans of Coke from my satchel and scan the room for a glass. A collage of photos frames a floor-length mirror and I look at tiny Melissa in a pink tutu, Melissa and Shauna on Santa's knee, Melissa and Shauna in bikinis on a pedal boat. They can't be more than fifteen there and I don't see any more recent pictures of the two of them.

"Ta da!" Melissa emerges triumphant, a bottle of vodka raised like a trophy. I wonder why the big secrecy; we're both practically eighteen already. Or maybe it's just my house where alcohol hangs around casually like a perpetual guest.

"Did you buy it?" I ask.

I still find it hard to get served. I'm small and skinny with short hair and an aversion to heels that does me no favors in the maturity stakes, no matter what my fake ID card says. It's the girls with curly bobs and clothes from Next that get past the bouncers, but nobody round our way wants to look like that.

"Rob did."

Melissa's older brother, a second-year at Trinity, is an absolute ride, according to Aisling.

"Is that him?" I ask, pointing to a photo of a Matt Dillon look-alike, all moody with dark hair and upturned lips.

"Yep. He has his uses."

I've assured Aisling I'll keep my hands off Rob, but honestly, I'm not sure I could muster the energy if Matt Dillon himself was in the house.

Sex has been disappointing, certainly not the explosion of fireworks I'd been led to expect. All that anticipation for a quick fuck in the park that lasted barely five minutes, and no better after that. For a long time I thought that being wanted was what mattered. Boys were attracted to me and I loved the power of that. But it was never enough, Tina helped me to see that.

There are no glasses in the room and Melissa's parents are in the kitchen so we drink half our Cokes and top up the cans with vodka. I'm all on for a bit of drunken camaraderie but I'll need to take it easy; I can't afford a nasty hangover for my match in the morning. And I'm not one to lose control of the situation anyway, a consequence of watching Mam drink herself to sleep for so many years.

We sit on the edge of the pastel-pink duvet on her double bed and clink cans and Melissa takes several large gulps before she surfaces, face full of divilment. Her hair is pulled back with a large bow, two ringlets falling onto her cheek, and her brown eyes pop with shades of pink and brown. I've taken it easy on the eyeliner and fishnet but I'm still head to toe in black, fitted skirt and mesh top. This is a moment I want to capture so I reach for my bag and take out my camera, an Agfamatic so small I can fit it in my coat pocket. I slide it open and Melissa blows me a kiss as the flash lights up her face.

"C'mere," she says, "let me have a go."

I hand it over and she runs her finger over the buttons, trying to work them out.

"It's the black switch to open and the red button to take the photo."

I raise my can to her as she clicks.

"I want one of me and David together later," she says as she hands me back the camera.

Melissa refills her drink, but when she tips the vodka in my direction I put my hand over the can.

"Can't we bring it with us?" I ask.

She puts the bottle on the bedside table, swings her legs onto the bed and leans back onto a pile of pillows.

"Yeah, OK. I'll stash it in the bushes before we go in," she says. "We can sneak out when they play 'The Birdie Song.'"

"They won't."

"They will."

"Will they inflict the slow set on us too?"

"Don't knock it," says Melissa. "That's the highlight of the night. Dancing at arm's length with the boy who expects to finger you on the rugby pitch after."

"Oh," I say with a grimace.

"Oh god, you're not allergic to sex too, are you?"

"No, don't worry," I say. "I'm a fully paid-up slut. But yeah, what's the story with Shauna and Aisling?"

"Swimming, swimming and swimming."

"What does swimming have to do with sex?"

Melissa swigs her drink and considers her answer.

"Well, Shauna wasn't always like this. She used to be wild when we were younger."

"Oh yeah?"

"She had loads of attention—you know, blonde hair, big tits. She was always going out with someone. And breaking it off and going out with someone else. And then at the start of last year, she stopped going anywhere except swimming. No more drinking, no more boys. I mean, she'd always had training before but she'd still want to go out whenever she could. That all stopped practically overnight and every time I tried to talk to her about it she got all defensive, like I just wouldn't understand."

"All because of swimming?"

"I dunno. Yeah, maybe."

"Do you think there's something else going on there?"

Melissa keeps her eyes on me as I try to drink casually from my can.

"Hold on a minute," she says, "did your friend from your old school say something?"

"No," I say quickly. "I barely knew her. Ah, I'm just being a nosy cow. Forget about it."

"OK," she says, with a look that means she definitely won't.

STREETLIGHTS GLISTEN AGAINST A BLUE-BLACK sky and chill air shimmies between us as we dance through the village on our way to Rockdale.

Melissa pirouettes at the pedestrian crossing, twirling sideways into the street, and an Austin Maestro swerves and hammers on the horn. I reach out to catch her and we laugh and hug, immune to the earthly hazards around us. The night is ours to lose now.

Rockdale is every bit as grand as Highfield, only bigger, stronger, faster. It has more Senior Cups than any other school and that doesn't come without top facilities, serious commitment and plenty of money. I get a sense of it in the long, imposing driveway to the school, pitches lined up on each side as far as I can see. It's as if us girls are only playing at hockey while the boys get to tackle the serious business of rugby.

"Vodka storage," says Melissa as we round the corner to the stately castle of the main school building. The driveway curves around an area thick with trees and shrubs and we take a final swill before stashing the bottle under a cascade of flowering fuchsia.

We're bursting with bravado as we enter the hall, arm in arm, strutting through the double doors to the steady shuffle of UB40. The lights are dim but still alert to the teen temptations that could huddle in darkened corners. Bunting of blue and yellow, Rockdale colors, drapes across the stage, and priests and lay teachers stand behind parallel rows of Formica tables laid out on either side of the room, a design that keeps us in the center where they can see us. Jugs of orange juice and plates of custard and bourbon creams are undisturbed by the groups already here—boys in cargo pants and boat shoes, polo shirts with upturned collars, and girls in fishtail and puffball skirts, posturing in stilettos, feigning disinterest in the whole setup.

Carol and her jet set are at the back of the hall, Stephanie and Eva and a couple of other clones in designer blouses and skirts, and pearls that must surely belong to their mothers. I don't get it, their inherent desire to conform, unless it's us they're rebelling against by aligning themselves to the wealth and status of their parents.

They're sniggering at the DJ on the stage, a balding man wearing a silver blazer and a bored expression as he flicks through a box of singles. In defiance, we take to the center of the floor, moving our hips as the reggae beat fades out and gives way to the opening vocal of Bon Jovi's "You Give Love a Bad Name." In a moment of synchronous rock irony, Melissa and I punch the air with our fists and leap as the guitar riff kicks in. That gets the party started and a few of the lads join us on the makeshift dance floor, their air guitars betraying their own inebriation.

By the time we're dancing, arms raised Madonna-style to "Into the Groove," it's the jet set that are the odd ones out, peering miserably from the sidelines. Melissa gyrates up to me, puts her arms around my neck, and it's only when I feel the weight of her slump against me that I realize she's drunker than she looks.

"Vodka time," she says as she plants a kiss on my lips before grabbing my hand and leading me outside.

"So he's not here yet?" I say as we retrace our steps in the sobering chill of the night air.

"No he fucking well isn't," she says. "I can't believe it. Especially after last time."

"Wait, there was a last time?"

"Um, yeah. He was all over me at Bective last month. I had to drag him out of my pants."

"So he, like, owes you or something?"

"Let's just say he better be coming or I'm going to have to hop on one of his teammates."

She stumbles sideways and I grab her arm.

"The blond one," she says. "No, the one in the stripy top."

"The one with the gammy nose?"

"Which one has a gammy nose?"

"I dunno. All of them? They're rugby players, aren't they?"

We explode with laughter, and we're still doubled over with it when three lads strut around the corner, chests out, collars up.

"Hi, Melissa," says the cutest one, chestnut hair gelled up at the front.

I'm impressed at how quickly she affects a polished smile and I know this can only be the man himself.

"Hi, David."

"I'll see you inside," he says.

"Oh. My. God," says Melissa as soon as they're out of earshot. "Oh my god, oh my god, oh my god. Did he see me?"

"It's fine," I say. "You were just having a laugh with a friend. He said he'd see you inside, right?"

"He did, didn't he?" she slurs. "OK, I need another drink."

WE ARRIVE BACK TO THE Communards, "Don't Leave Me This Way," and I move through the room carving out shapes with my hands. The flashing lights on the stage fill the fringes of my vision with a gauzy haze so I don't see Melissa fall, only the scatter of bodies as they clear the dance floor. When I look down, she's sprawled on her back, skirt riding up her thighs and a nervous grin on her face. I bend down, take her hands and hoist her to her feet, and she's shouting *fuck, fuck, fuck* in my ear as David Sharkey makes no attempt to hide his laughter and another boy slaps him on the back.

"Let's go and sit down," I say.

As I guide her to the seats at the end of the room I see Shauna and Aisling standing at one of the tables, plastic cups in their hands, and the room lights up. Shauna's wearing a gold lamé skirt, cinched at the waist, and all I want is to bask in her radiance. I'm about to go over when I clock the disapproval on their faces and the wary look of the priest behind them. We make a beeline for the chairs instead, and I'm wondering how I'm going to deal with Melissa when the opening sax of "Careless Whisper" signals the start of a slow set and she is alert with expectation.

"Where is he? Is he looking at me?"

David Sharkey walks toward us with intent. He takes her hand and leads her to the dance floor, and I put on my best sober face and join Shauna and Aisling.

"What have you had?" asks Shauna.

I inhale the floral scent of her and gaze at the glow of her skin, blond hair soft against it.

"Just a teeny-tiny bit of vodka. We've got some hidden outside if you want some."

"No, thanks," she says. "But keep an eye on Melissa. She's in a right state."

The boy in the stripy shirt asks Shauna to dance, and I'm right, he does have a gammy nose. I sit out the rest of the slow set in the toilet and when I get back Melissa has disappeared.

"Have you seen Melissa?" I ask Aisling, still on her own at the side of the room.

"Yeah, she left."

"What do you mean? She never said anything."

"I think she was preoccupied," she says with an awkward grin, and I realize Melissa's got what she came for. I hop onto the dance floor and force the moves out of me, but the rush of it all has departed and my limbs are heavy and tired. I'm just going through the motions when Shauna comes up and leans into my ear.

"Can you show me where that vodka is?"

The thought of getting drunk with Shauna catapults me straight out of my slump.

"Yeah, definitely. What changed your mind?"

"Oh, no, I don't . . . I just want to find Melissa."

"Oh."

I'm so crushed by the letdown, I don't even think about where Melissa might be.

"I don't trust David Sharkey," says Shauna as we leave through the double doors.

Outside, a chill and bitter air pricks my skin and low-hanging clouds have captured the sky.

"I think Melissa can look after herself," I say.

Shauna's eyes cut through me and I want to take it straight back.

"Are you sure about that?" she says. "When you've only known her for a month?"

I want to tell her she's wrong, that we have become close, but I say nothing.

"It's a defense mechanism," she says, "all that bravado."

"Defense against what?"

"She has a tough time. At home."

"Her home looks all right to me."

"Yeah well, things aren't always as they seem," she says.

"What do you mean?"

She sighs, caught between clarification and loyalty.

"I'm not just being nosy," I say, even though I am. "I really like Melissa, I want to help."

"It's her parents," she says. "They have a really fucked-up relationship."

"But they're still together?"

"Yeah, they're together. In an open relationship that suits her dad just fine and who cares about anyone else."

"Jesus, that's . . . heavy."

"Look," says Shauna. "Don't tell her I said anything, I'm sure she'll tell you yourself. She treats it like it's no big deal."

"OK."

"But it is a big deal. That's why she's so needy."

I'm about to say I haven't noticed Melissa is needy at all when Shauna puts a finger to her lips. We're almost at the turn in the driveway and she points into the undergrowth, beyond the hanging fuchsia. I can't see anything and I'm starting to wonder what right we have to stalk Melissa like this, if Shauna's concern is more about control. I hear it then, a whisper of leaves, a low shush and then nothing but the distant rumble of bass. We don't move, just wait and listen.

It starts as a rustle, shoes or hands dragging across the dirt, slowly at first, then rough and repeated, and a feeble moan of protest. Melissa. Shauna turns to me, eyes wide and searching, and I don't know what else to do but shrug and throw the decision back at her. Another scrape and a groan, louder this time, and Shauna can't wait any longer. She pushes past me into the bushes.

"What are you doing?" she shouts, and from behind her I see a pair of boat shoes, soles up, scrambling to one side.

David rolls off Melissa, her skirt hitched up at her waist, tights around her knees and the empty vodka bottle at her feet. I'm still not sure if we've just caught them in the act until Melissa's head rolls to one side, eyes closed, and I see her face is black with dirt.

David makes a half-arsed attempt to pull up her tights, but Shauna waves him away.

"I think you've done enough already," she says.

"Suit yourself," he says, standing up and brushing the soil from his chinos.

As he walks out of sight, he says, "I'd have had more fun fingering a corpse."

"Bastard," says Shauna, but her attention is on Melissa. She kneels beside her and lifts her head gently into her lap.

"Melissa, can you hear me?"

Melissa opens her eyes and smiles weakly.

"Where's David?" she says.

"Forget about him," says Shauna, and she takes a tissue from her gold clutch bag and gently wipes Melissa's face.

There's no anger or disappointment in her, only love and concern as she pushes the curls out of Melissa's eyes and runs her fingers along her cheeks, and right now all I want is for her to touch me like that too.

12

It takes a moment to remember when the shrill blast of the doorbell shatters my ragged sleep. Melissa face down in the Rockdale dirt, Shauna's disapproval at everything I said. The digital alarm clock blurs and pulses with the throbbing pain behind my eyes and I jolt upright to see it properly. It's 9:55, still twenty-five minutes before Mr. McQueen is due. I fall back onto the pillow, mouth bone dry, and glare back at Robert Smith's dour, crumpled face on the wall beside me. The bell rings again and I hear Mam swear and then pound down the stairs.

I know it's him by the sound of her, that posh voice she uses on the phone. There's no way out now; I'm going to have to get up. I drag myself into the bathroom, cup my hands under the tap and gulp at the water as it slips through my fingers. I meet my own bloodshot gaze in the mirror and try to analyze the damage, how much of a fool I made of myself, what my drunkenness weighed against Shauna's sobriety. She'll have been swimming already this morning. I wonder if she thought of me at all as she crawled her lane at Highfield, what she'd say if she knew Mr. McQueen was in my house, laughing with my mam like they were old friends.

When I get to the kitchen, he's lounging in a chair, legs spread wide. Mam is cross-legged beside him, swathed in a silk paisley dressing gown.

"You never told me your mum was so young," he says. "I thought she was your sister."

Mam giggles like a child and I roll my eyes at the pair of them. He must have known it was just the two of us, he'd have seen it on my file when he checked for the address I never gave him. I knock back a glass of water and then pour myself a cup of tea.

"Are you not going to eat anything, love?" asks Mam.

I know I should force some toast into me but my stomach is knotted with nausea and the tea is all I can manage.

"Listen to your mother, Lou," says Mr. McQueen. "You can't win a match on an empty stomach."

I take a mandarin, a Mars bar and a scowl with me to the car, a black Saab Turbo that reeks of aftershave and disinfectant, and I sit in surly silence, answering Mr. McQueen's questions as briefly as I can.

ST. CATHERINE'S IS A SCHOOL in limbo, a run-down old house that stands tall in a sea of prefabs. It stirs an arrogance in me, a hope that I can shine here in this needy environment, and it strikes me how easy the transition has been. There are times when I forget, when I slide so easily into the rhythm of Highfield life that it's like waking from a dream when I remember. It makes me all the more determined to grab everything that's on offer while I still can.

My hangover surrenders to the cool air and a bracing warm-up, and by push-off, I'm not feeling too bad. I'm playing at right half, a position that lets me use my speed to follow the action, and I spend most of the first half in the thick of it. I don't score but I shoot a cross to Laura Gallagher and she flicks it past the goalie and into the net. It's 2–0 at half time and I'm feeling pretty good about my play until I see our captain, Karina Kenny, a fifth-year with a permanent frown.

"You need to stay in your position," she says.

"Oh," I say. "What do you mean?"

The two girls beside her, arms folded in solidarity, seem to know exactly what she means.

"Who do you think you are, coming in here and trying to take over?" says Karina.

The chill in her voice goes right through me and the throbbing in my forehead is back. Maybe I was naive to think the social hierarchy wouldn't extend to the hockey pitch, but I didn't think that stuff would matter if I played well.

"I didn't . . ." I look from Karina to Laura, who shakes her head like she doesn't want to get involved. "I thought we were trying to win the match."

"Do you think just cos you're teacher's pet you can do whatever you like?"

"What?"

Mr. McQueen dropped me at the gate and he hasn't hung around, and it's only now I can see how suspicious that might look.

"We don't have a car," I say, but Karina's already turning away.

"Stay at right half and leave the wing to me."

THE BLUSTER'S GONE OUT OF me and I do what I'm told, vowing to end
my hockey career with this match. As soon as it's over, I sneak off, leaving
the rest of them to refreshments in the school hall. Mr. McQueen's waiting
in his car at the gate.

"How did you get on?" he asks as I buckle my seat belt.

"We won 3–1."

"Did you score?"

"No."

"You will next time," he says as he pulls off.

"I dunno."

He takes his eyes off the road and looks at me with concern.

"What do you mean, you don't know?"

"I don't think I'm cut out for hockey."

Maybe there's another team, another way of getting close to him. We
stop at a red light and he turns to me.

"Lou, I knew the first time I saw you just how capable you are. To be
able to come into a school like Highfield and perform like you did, that's
not just raw talent. That's determination and grit, and you've got plenty of
it. You're not a quitter, I know that."

He's right of course, and I start to wonder just how much I can leverage
our relationship.

"It's just one of the girls," I say while he looks at me intensely. "Oh, it's
nothing, I've probably got it wrong."

"No," he says, "go on."

I look at my hands, as if I'm ashamed.

"She saw me with you and made fun of me when I said we didn't have
a car."

He rolls his eyes and lets out a sigh.

"Lou, the entitlement of some of these girls . . . I don't understand it.
But if you tell me who it was, I'll make sure it doesn't happen again."

It's not that I want to throw her at his mercy, but there are more layers of power at Highfield than Karina knows and I need to grab whatever
scraps I can to survive.

"It was Karina Kenny," I say. "But please don't say anything about me."

The light turns green and he puts the car into gear. Then, with his eyes straight ahead, he rests his hand on my bare thigh. "I won't say a word."

FROM THE HALL, I HEAR Mam in the kitchen listening to the red-hot sound of Sunshine 101, so I run upstairs and lock the bathroom door behind me. I fill the olive-green bath with scalding water, the thrash of it drowning out the ringing in my ears. I let it come, higher, deeper, until the bath is full and water spills over the side as I lower myself into it. It burns and pricks my skin but it's still not hot enough to drive the shiver out of me.

It's real now. The physical handprint searing my thigh no matter how much I scrub at it. The sickening smell of disinfectant and aftershave, and those dark eyes, black with intent. Even though it's what I planned, why I came to Highfield, I'd almost hoped at one point that a lift was really all that was on the cards. My face flushes in the steaming air and when I close my eyes I see his hand on Tina's leg as she sat on that same leather seat of his Saab.

Tina had everything to lose, but I have nothing. I've already been branded a liar by the Guards, when I tried to file a police report about McQueen's abuse of Tina after her death. And by Mrs. Forrester and anyone else who overheard me shouting about it at Tina's funeral. I had no evidence, just the words of a dead girl who wasn't there to defend herself. As if she was the one to blame.

It can't happen again, the accusations of jealousy and narcissism that cut as deep as a blade. Before I'd ever met him, he'd plunged me into a dark and reckless despair. Long weeks in my room, the tables turned as Mam nursed me through hopeless days and drunken nights, and still the whispers that I was the one to blame. This time, I will document everything—times, dates, places. And when he thinks he's got me right where he wants me, that's when I'll make sure we get caught. Then they'll have to believe me.

A loud rap on the door wakes me from my reverie.

"Lou, are you OK in there?"

I don't want to talk, about hockey or him or anything else. I sink down until my eyes and ears are submerged and the water smothers the noise above. My heart pounds but I know I am in control, that I can stop this any time I want. I stay under until my chest aches and my legs kick out in protest. When I splutter to the surface, Mam is banging on the door.

"Open up, Lou, please," she shouts. "I just want to see that you're OK."

I push out of the water, wrap a towel around myself and unlock the door.

"See, I'm fine," I say.

Mam exhales heavily.

"I'm sorry, it's just . . ." She frowns. "Your skin, what's wrong with it?"

She reaches out to touch my arm and I recoil. She's right, it's raw red, though I barely felt the sting of it until now.

"It's nothing, I just had a hot bath."

"Ah Lou, honey, you gotta be careful, mind yourself."

"Yeah."

"Come on down," she says. "I'll make us a fry and we can have a catch-up, OK?"

I smile and nod, but Mam is not the person I want to talk to. Not yet, anyway.

13

Joe Forrester is already in Byrnes, a suburban pub in neighboring Shankill that doesn't refuse legal tender on the basis of age. I order a pint of Fürstenberg and the barman doesn't bat an eyelid, although he's seen me wave over at Joe and he's nineteen and six feet tall. It's a tatty old pub, faded landscapes on beer-stained walls, and we blend into the background, Joe in a biker jacket and Docs and me in a black skirt and tux jacket.

"Hair of the dog," I say as I take a seat opposite Joe. I down several mouthfuls before I put the glass on the table. Joe takes out his fags, offers me one and then lights both of them with a single match. He lets me take a couple of drags before he says anything.

"So, he made a move on you?"

I nod.

"Are you absolutely sure? Like, you didn't misread the signs or anything?"

"He put his hand on my leg and he left it there for five minutes."

I'd stared out the window, conjugating French verbs.

"Yeah, but did he say anything or . . . ?"

"No, but it was no accident. He even changed gears and put it back."

"But that was it?"

It sounds like nothing, an over-exuberant uncle or the touchy-feely parish priest, but it didn't feel like nothing.

"Yeah, that was it. For now. I'm sorry he didn't expose himself to me on our first date. Is that what you were expecting?"

"Ah Jaysis, Lou," he says. He pulls hard on his cigarette and exhales slowly. "I'm just playing devil's advocate here. Imagine what the Guards would say if you told them he touched your leg."

"Yeah, well, why don't you imagine how you'd feel if he did that to your girlfriend?"

Joe winces and I wonder if I've hit a nerve. I've no idea if he has a girlfriend; I haven't seen him with anyone since he brought me to his debs ball almost a year ago. I'd gone because we'd always got on great and I was flattered to be asked while I was still at school. Of course, we'd ended up getting hammered and having a snog and I'm not sure we'd got past the awkwardness of that before everything fell apart.

"OK, point taken. But even if he had"—he wrinkles his nose—"exposed himself to you, how would you convince anyone that you hadn't been, you know, leading him on?"

"Oh for fuck's sake," I say, and I'd walk out right now if he wasn't my only ally. "You still don't believe he forced Tina, do you?"

"I don't know what to believe, Lou. And I don't know what I'm capable of believing. Do you know how hard it is to think my sister killed herself because of something I didn't even know was happening? It was bad enough when we thought she had some mental imbalance or something, but you've brought this man into our lives and it's fucking torturing me, thinking about him."

He stubs out his cigarette and sinks back into his seat.

"So yeah, I want you to be wrong. There, I've said it."

I suck on the cigarette, buying time to think. I need to work with Joe's grief, not against it.

"I know how you feel," I say, "because I feel it too. I was supposed to be her best friend and I didn't even know until she was already pregnant."

But that's not true. I knew he was taking over her life and all I felt was jealousy and resentment that he was stealing her from me. I couldn't bring myself to think he was touching her, what that might mean for her, for me.

"Did you know she was cutting herself?" asks Joe.

"No."

Not until that last night when she showed me the scars. The raised welts at the top of her inner thighs that *he* must have seen every time. Thoughts of Shauna flicker to mind and I try not to think of the thin line on her thigh, only the soft wave of her hair, the upturned curve of her smile. Just knowing I'll see her on Monday morning is enough of an antidote to the fear that I'll have to face him too.

"I don't understand why Tina couldn't have told someone," he says.

"He told her she'd never swim again. She was totally under his control."

He closes his eyes and I feel his anger, deep and raw and open to suggestion.

"Don't you see what he did? He put her in a position where she had no choice. He had the power to take away the one thing that meant everything to her."

"So she just let him . . ."

"No," I say as I stub my cigarette hard in the ashtray. "He forced her."

Joe puts his elbows on the table, his head in his hands.

"I want to fucking kill him," he says.

I leave him with his thoughts until they've had enough time to fester.

"Joe, it's still happening. If he's trying it on with me already, there must be others."

He shifts uncomfortably in his chair.

"So what do you want me to do?"

"I dunno, you're the journalist."

He laughs. "I'm a second-year student, Lou, not Kate Adie."

"Couldn't you do a piece on Highfield? You could write about their Olympic chances and that would give you a reason to talk to the swimmers? Maybe him too?"

"I dunno," he says, but as he taps the bottom of his cigarette packet I can see he's thinking about this new angle, the one where he's a hero instead of an aggrieved relative.

"You told me ages ago you wanted to write about sport," I say.

"Yeah, football and rugby, not the personal lives of swimming coaches."

He takes two cigarettes out of the packet, but I wave mine away.

"That's the problem, isn't it?" I say. "Everyone acting like it's none of their business."

"I don't know, Lou. I don't know what's going on."

"So it's OK to turn a blind eye?"

There's a darkness in his eyes then, a resignation more than a realization.

"Yeah, Lou, I get it. I'll think about it. But don't get your hopes up, OK?"

"Thanks."

"If I do anything—and it's a big if—it'll be for Tina. Swimming was her life."

It's the finality of that last sentence that gets me, that her story has already been written. And I wonder then whose justice I'm after—hers, or mine.

ON MONDAY, I'M HARDLY IN the door from school when Mam's on my case, the bag in the hall, the dishes in the sink. She's clearly in one of her moods, banging around the kitchen, and I can't work it out. She hasn't been drinking—I can always tell, even when she denies it—and it's too early in the day for a hangover. I tread carefully up the stairs to my room, taking my bag with me.

There are two things that start the slow spiral into despair in this house: men and money. There are no boyfriends lurking in the shadows and I thought we were ticking along financially. Mam's even been giving me pocket money since she encouraged me to leave my job as lounge girl at the Black Swan. In fact, it's the first time in years we've had a break from the endless cycle of counting and pinching.

When the girls at school moan about being poor, all they mean is their allowance isn't due for a few days or they haven't enough to buy the Patrick Cox shoes they want. They're not watching the electricity meter, measuring out the days until the next dole payment or wage packet. Mam always has an eye and a hand out for a bargain, even when she's pouring the savings down her throat. It's the reason we've never had anything as unpredictable as a car or a pet, why it's so important to her that I do well at Highfield and go to college.

It's the path that was laid out for her, until she could no longer hide her pregnancy. In her first term at university, she was sent to England with a cover story about a sick aunt. She was expected to return with empty arms but, once she held me, she couldn't give me away. She walked away from a family that didn't want to know me, from the money and stability she'd always taken for granted.

What Mam sacrificed for herself, she holds tight for me, that hunger to improve. I've always felt it, the certainty that there's more than this estate and signing on and cash-in-hand, week-to-week work. Sister Mullen has been feeding that notion, chipping away at the rhythm of my accent and language, and I try it all out on Mam to see what I can get away with. Yesterday, I complimented her spaghetti Bolognese as "utterly glorious" and, after she made sure I wasn't slagging her, she replied that it was her "absolute pleasure." We laughed, a solidarity in our softly shifting voices.

I'm lying on my bed, counting the rings of damp on the ceiling, when Mam pushes the door open.

"Can I come in?"

"OK."

She stoops to pick up the discarded clothes on the floor and I groan.

"Mam, would you leave it?"

"Well, somebody has to do it."

"I'll do it, OK, just stop."

She hangs the clothes on the back of a chair and sits on the edge of my single bed.

"I want to talk to you about something," she says. "I've taken on some more shifts at the Swan."

I roll onto my side to face her, the draft from the window cold against my neck.

"And I was thinking maybe it's time for you to get your old job back."

I'm up on my elbow now, alarm bells in my ears.

"But you said I needed to concentrate on my studies. What's changed?"

"Things are . . ." She looks out the window with tired eyes. "Money's just a lot tighter than I thought."

My heart sinks at the thought of working evenings on a school night, giving up hockey on a Saturday.

"I'm sorry, love," she says. "I'm going to have to look at other ways to raise money too."

"Like what?"

"We could take in a lodger."

"We've only got two bedrooms."

"You could move into my room."

"I will in my hole," I say as the full horror of it dawns on me. She's never made this threat before, no matter how bad things have been. I try to stifle my anger but it's already hurtling out of me.

"What have you done?"

Mam puts her head in her hands, and she's shaking, maybe even crying, but I'm not letting her get away with this.

"Tell me," I shout, sitting up now, inches away from her.

"Ah Jesus, Lou," she says, her breath catching between sobs. "I've borrowed some money, that's all."

There's a tightness in my chest and I almost don't want to ask the next question, let her deal with it herself, but it's never that simple.

"You didn't borrow it from Kenny O'Kane, did you?"

She doesn't need to answer; I can hear it in her silence, see it between the fingers still clinging to her face.

"Fuck," I roar. "How could you be so stupid?"

I think of the easy pocket money, how eager I was to go along with it, how I should have known better.

"How much?" I ask, and her hands slide down her wet cheeks, the fight gone out of her.

"Only a couple of hundred. It was all fine until he started increasing the payments."

"But you know that's what he does. How many people round here have you seen fall into his trap? Mam, how could you do this to us?"

The tears are rolling down her face and I know she wants me to reach out and tell her it'll be OK, like I always do. But I can barely breathe with it all—Tina, Highfield, McQueen and now Kenny O'fucking Kane too. I lie back onto the pillow and stare at the dirty brown rings on the ceiling until she lets herself out and closes the door behind her.

14

At Highfield, there are words that are missing from language, as if they have ceased to exist. The unspeakable shielded by silence. Deeds and symptoms cleansed from memory until we are all complicit in our collective amnesia. It's just how things work here, and there is a kindness to some of it. How we never speak of David Sharkey to spare Melissa the shame and stigma. How the swimmers rarely mention Tina, lest they unleash her anguish. It goes against my instinct, this controlled restraint, and I struggle to read the space between the words and their absence.

I hear nothing more about Carol's earrings and she starts to thaw out. Mme Martel has paired us in French and we've grudgingly bonded over a genuine love of the language and culture. My rapid move to the Senior B hockey team hasn't harmed my image either and I almost feel sorry for Karina Kenny, slumming it down on the E team. I could love it here, if I didn't already know too much. If I'd been bred to hold my silence like a true Highfield girl. I envy them, the certainty of their position, the rewards offered by the privilege of their birth, and at times it kills me to think what could be mine if I chose to play by their rules.

I take what I can when I can. Those quiet hours in the library, diving below the surface of the truths we're taught in class, the alternative views of history and literature that open up the heart of them. The pure buzz of the hockey pitch and the camaraderie that goes with it. And the stolen moments with Shauna, each of us making time to chat about books and films and anything at all. I'd be lost without that intimacy, the simple joy of being around her, and I'm sure she feels the same way too.

The earrings return to class without fanfare. I notice them when Carol sits beside me in French, although she says nothing.

"Where did you find them?" I ask.

"What?"

"Eh, the earrings you accused me of stealing?"

She sighs heavily, as if I'm making a big deal out of nothing.

"I suppose I owe you an apology," she says.

I keep looking at her for an explanation and she rolls her eyes.

"They somehow got from my locker into my bag, OK?"

"And you never thought to tell me?"

"For all I know, it was you who put them there," she says, and even though I laugh, I know it's a narrative she could get away with, given her standing at Highfield. It's always the inner circle who'll be believed, no matter how unlikely their story.

MCQUEEN PAYS ME NO SPECIAL attention for a couple of weeks until my next away match. He picks me up on a Saturday morning and delivers me without incident to Fairfield Grove in Enniskerry, just over the county border in Wicklow. It's a school that has a long sporting rivalry with Highfield and we're all aware of the weight of expectation. My precarious position at home and at school makes me all the more determined to justify my place on the team and I chase that ball relentlessly in pursuit of my first competitive goal. It comes with just five minutes to go, a solo run down the wing and a flick into the corner of the goal, giving Highfield a 2–1 lead. By the final whistle, we're all bonded by adrenaline and I'm flushed with a rare joy as I follow my teammates back to the gym for refreshments and celebrations.

Mam will have to fight me if she thinks I'll give this up for the Black Swan. It's the challenge, the thrill, the simple fairness of it. Today, there's been no aggro on the pitch, no impenetrable hierarchy, just the skill and collaboration of a team that's worked hard and played hard. If only all of life was this rewarding.

It's at least half an hour before I get back to the car, hidden down a side street, and he won't even look at me when I slide into the passenger seat. We drive off in tense silence and I clench my fists for several minutes before he acknowledges me.

"I'm going to stop off at a café," he says. "We can get some lunch."

The very last thing I want to do is spend any more time than I have to with Maurice McQueen. The plan was to get close to him, lure him into a false sense of security and then have Joe and an unconnected third party discover him assaulting me. For that, I was prepared for small talk, suggestive

glances, a hand on my knee. But this departure from the routine fills me
with a sickening dread. I don't speak until we get to the main road and he
takes the turn for Greystones, the opposite direction to Ballybrack.

"Where are you going?"

"I told you, a café. It's not far."

I stare out the window at the stone walls and hedgerows, digging fingernails into palms until he pulls into Greystones village and the safety of
others. The Copper Kettle smells of bacon and coffee but I'm riddled with
unease so I settle for a chocolate éclair and a cup of tea, and take a table in
the corner by the window. McQueen talks about music, seeing U2 play at
the Dandelion Market, being invited to their gig at Croke Park. I pretend
I'm not impressed but he carries on, stories of backstage and Adam Clayton's twenty-year-old whiskey.

"You know the feeling when whiskey hits the back of your throat? I
know you know what I'm talking about, Lou."

I say nothing and he laughs.

"Well, imagine it doesn't feel like you're being cut by a knife. Imagine
it's the sweetest, smoothest feeling that grips your whole body like an or-
gasm."

I wish I had the balls to look him in the eye but the blood rushes to my
cheeks as I study my tea. He lets his words hang for an indecent amount of
time while I breathe slowly and remind myself that I'm one step ahead of
him. I know what's coming and I'm prepared for it. That's what makes me
different to all the other girls.

"But you know what it can't beat?" McQueen tucks into his bacon and
fried eggs, swallowing a mouthful before answering his own question.

"Winning." He points his knife at me. "You got a taste of that today, and
don't tell me you didn't get the biggest rush from your goal."

He's not wrong, and I smile despite myself. It felt fucking fantastic.

"And believe me, there's no greater feeling than representing your country. You're talented, Lou, you could excel at any number of sports. Look
how far you've come at hockey in just a few weeks."

He mops up the egg with a slice of toast and pushes it into his mouth.
The runny yolk smears on the bristles at the side of his mouth.

"I can see you wearing a green jersey one day," he says.

"I dunno about that."

"Stick with it and you'll do us all proud, I'm sure of it."

He wipes his mouth with a napkin but there's still a glob of yellow in his mustache.

"I know a lot of people in a lot of sports, not just swimming—hockey, netball, tennis, athletics."

I know he probably says that to all the girls, but still I wonder how much I can get out of him before I turn him in.

"It's an honor most people only dream of," he continues. "When I hear about athletes boycotting the Olympics and rugby players refusing to tour South Africa, I want to throttle the lot of them. If any of my swimmers tried any of that, they'd be out on their ear."

"But by going to South Africa, you're saying you don't care about black South Africans. You're supporting apartheid."

"Oh, no, no, no," he says, wagging his finger at me. "Playing a sport that you love, representing your country, that's a personal privilege, and whatever you believe politically shouldn't come into it."

"Haven't you heard? The personal is political."

It's Mam who taught me that if you don't stand up and talk about the things that are important to you, the people in power are never going to know about them. But these days, I'm not sure what matters to her anymore.

"You're not a women's libber, are you?" He rolls his eyes. "Jesus, Lou, I never had you down as a militant lesbian, you're way too pretty for that."

There must be a sure-fire comeback for what he's trying to do to me, pitting my looks against my brain, but I can't think of anything that doesn't sound as pathetic as I feel.

"I believe in basic human rights," I say, my voice thin and strained.

"That's nice," he says, tapping his finger on the table. "But that's not how the real world works, Lou. In the real world, these poor black South Africans you love so much are murdering whites and burning down their homes, did you know that?" He snorts and throws his arm over the back of his chair. "It's very easy to be an idealist when you never have to make any of the big decisions."

I want to lift my teacup, do something to dilute the tension, but my hands are shaking and I can't let him see. Words are backing up inside me and I'm afraid if I release them, tears will follow.

"I want to make big decisions," I say carefully. "That's why I want to go to university."

He laughs and shakes his head.

"I won't say I told you so, but you'll find out soon enough how the world works."

There is nothing I can say to counter his bravado and by the time we get back to the car I don't know if I can do it anymore. I've made sure to wear my tracksuit so I won't have to feel his clammy hand on my bare skin, but it's half an hour back to Ballybrack and if he tries something, I won't be able to ignore it for that long.

We're only a few minutes on the road when his hand lands on my thigh and he massages it through the jersey fabric of my tracksuit bottoms. I say nothing, although I'm screaming inside my head. He changes gears and his hand is back, higher now, his little finger pushed up against my crotch.

"What are you doing?" I say, my words catching in my throat.

"Do you mind?" He looks straight ahead as if nothing unusual is happening.

I hate it, I hate it, I hate it.

"Lou?"

All my words are frozen inside me and I can't scream or move or think. He puts his hand back on the steering wheel and we carry on in silence. I pray that's the end of it, but the indicator's on and we're turning into a country lane, twisting past woodlands and hedgerows. I bite down on the inside of my lip and the blood, sharp on my tongue, keeps me lucid until he pulls into a clearing and parks under a cloak of dark and heavy foliage.

"I can't stop thinking about you, Lou."

The metallic taste drips down the back of my throat and I swallow heavily.

"But I don't want to do anything you don't want to. I'm taking my lead from you."

The air is taut with silence. His eyes burn a path through it.

"But . . . we're not allowed," I hear myself say.

I look away, at the trees behind him, sycamores or horse chestnuts.

"How old are you, Lou?"

"Seventeen."

"You're old enough to make up your own mind."

He takes my hand between both of his. Horse chestnuts, I think, the leaves turning golden already.

"Lou, I couldn't live with myself if I wasn't honest with you. I think you're extraordinary. You're so different to all the other girls at Highfield. You're mature and perceptive and you have life experience they can only dream of. I never meant to have feelings for you. How could I? I'm your teacher."

I see his rueful smile in the corner of my eye while his devious fingers caress my wrist.

"But I won't always be."

I don't know what I'm supposed to say or do so I don't speak, don't move. He puts my hand to his lips and my nail catches the egg yolk crusted in the hairs of his mustache and all I can think about is the filth festering in my finger. He unbuckles his seat belt and leans over and kisses me, stale coffee breath and wire hair rough against my lips and my nose, and his tongue is in my mouth and I take it, rigid and removed, until I can't breathe anymore and I pull away, gasping.

All the way back to Ballybrack, I think about how I never said no. Whether everything I've done has invited this outcome from the moment I entered his office. I thought I'd be able to control him, manipulate him into a compromising position, but he is stronger than me. In the distance, the Wicklow Mountains float into the clouds, detached from the blurred and foggy earth below, and I wonder how far he'll go next time.

15

It's that time of night at the Black Swan when voices drift into laughter, rising like spirals of smoke into suspended reality. As if there are no consequences outside the privacy of this public house, no Monday morning waiting on the other side of sleep. We work the lounge, a long, carpeted attempt at comfort with upholstered booths opposite the bar and smaller tables dotted in between. Mam's regulars, the thinkers and the talkers, slouch on the tall stools at the bar, their solitary lives lined up along the ring-stained mahogany stage.

I tackle the floor, the courting couples, the gangs of lads squeezing the last bit of fun out of the weekend. They're buoyed by booze at this stage of the evening and it's part of my job to ignore the suggestive comments, the brush of a hand against my arm or leg. I'm taking an order from a group of regulars, a quartet of red-faced men in their thirties, when I feel a pinch on my bum so hard I cry out.

"What's the matter, sweetheart?"

The culprit grins up at me, sweat beading across the bridge of his crooked nose.

"Is it all too much for you, the level of talent at the table?"

He bursts into laughter, elbowing the mullet in the Liverpool shirt beside him. But his mate across the table has seen what's happened and he points his cigarette at the crooked-faced offender.

"Jesus, Mikey. Would you ever behave yourself?"

Mikey clearly has no regrets. If anything, he's emboldened by the attention.

"Come on, Dermo, would ye blame me? When you see an arse as sweet as that, it'd be rude not to."

He turns to me as I dig my thumbnail into my finger, an attempt to stop the tears.

"Gimme a Jameson with that Harp, will you?"

I take a breather behind a pillar by the bar, but Martina, the other lounge girl, is on me before I've had time to pull myself together.

"What's up with you?"

"It's that prick, Mikey. With the beer-belly gang."

Martina is bigger and brasher than me and the likes of Mikey and his mates would know better than to get physical with her.

"What did he do?"

"He pinched my arse so hard. It really hurt."

Now that it's out, the tears follow, and that makes me feel even worse, that I'm losing it over a bunch of gobshites who've probably forgotten me already.

"Ah here, don't cry," says Martina. "Look, you take a break and go to the toilet or something and I'll hold the fort here, OK?"

"Thanks, Martina, you're a star."

"No sweat. I'll spit in his pint for you."

I have to walk around the bar to get to the toilet, and I don't want Mam to see me but her guilty eyes are watching and she catches me before I can make it round the corner.

"What's wrong, love?"

"Nothing."

I haven't had a chance to wipe all the tears away yet.

"It doesn't look like nothing. Is someone hassling you?"

"No."

"Please tell me, Lou."

She looks so dejected that I tell her just so she can be the hero.

"Mikey, with the curly hair . . ."

"That fucking goon, what did he do?"

Her face flushes with such fury I know he's going to pay for what he did, and I want the price to be high.

"He grabbed my bum and pinched it. Hard. Really hard."

She wipes her hands on a towel, flips up the bar hatch and walks over to Mikey's table.

"You . . ." She points at Mikey and then flings her finger at the door: ". . . out."

"What?" His eyes travel from her white stilettos to her bleached hair, but she doesn't flinch. He tries to laugh, as if it's a game. "You can't do that."

"Get. Out."

"Jesus, Rose," says Mikey. "Can you calm down and tell me what's going on here?"

"You assaulted a member of staff and we don't put up with that sort of shit in here."

"Assaulted? For fuck's sake, Rose. I gave the girl a compliment, that's all."

Mikey looks to the lads for support, but they're way too interested in the contents of their pint glasses.

"Get out. Now," says Mam.

Mikey takes his cigarettes and lighter from the table and stands up slowly, keeping his eyes on Mam.

"If your kid can't handle a bit of banter," he says when he gets to the door, "what the fuck is she doing in here?"

"You're barred," shouts Mam. "And if any of the rest of you have a problem with that, you can leave, too."

I'M HAVING A COKE AND a packet of crisps in a booth by the door when Joe arrives, stone-washed denim jacket buttoned all the way up, cheeks pink from the cold. He chats to Mam while his pint settles and I know he'll be on the way over. He's been calling all weekend for an update on my outing with McQueen, but I haven't had the stomach to deal with any of it.

"Howiye, Lou," he says, sliding in opposite me.

"Howiye."

"You're a hard woman to reach," he says. "I'd almost think you were avoiding me."

I say nothing, hoping he'll take the hint.

"How'd it go?" he says. "Your hockey match and . . . everything."

He offers me a cigarette but I shake my head. I never smoke around Mam so we can both keep up the pretense that I don't smoke at all. She gave up two years ago and she clings to that virtue as if it absolves her of all other vices.

"Yeah. It went."

"What d'ye mean? Did he try anything?"

I know I have to tell him. Maybe it will help me work through it.

"Yeah." I drop my head and lean closer to Joe, but I can't look at him. "He put his hand right up between my legs and he pushed his tongue into my mouth."

"Shit," says Joe. He takes a long drag on his cigarette and blows a lung-ful of smoke at the ceiling. "But this is good. We've got him where we want him."

His elation at the news I've been molested sinks my heart, even though I get it. It's what I thought I wanted, to lead McQueen on enough to entrap him. But I know now for certain that nobody would ever do this unless they had no choice.

"I don't know if I can do it," I say. "I thought I could, but . . ."

"What can't you do?"

"I don't want him to touch me again."

Joe sighs.

"Lou, we're so close. We could set something up for next week. You tell me where you're going to be and I'll get one of my classmates to come with me and we'll walk in on you."

"Why don't you fuck him and I'll walk in?"

Our eyes lock and the pain and the memories shift between us until I look away, determined not to cry twice in one shift. Joe swings round the table, pushes in beside me and puts his arms around me, and I let him hug me. When I've calmed down I pull away, but he leaves his arm around my shoulder.

"I'm sorry," he says. "I'm just so wound up thinking about him. I wouldn't get a chance to fuck him cos I'd batter him first."

I smile in solidarity, and he smiles back, a look that lingers a little too long.

"Look, Lou, I'll step up. I'll do whatever I can. Research, interviews. I have an assignment coming up in college I can use for cover."

He's still smiling, his arm heavy on my back, and I shift awkwardly. He moves toward me and I think he's going to whisper in my ear until his lips are on mine and I stiffen with the shock. I push him away with the scrap of strength I have left.

"I thought . . ." he says.

"You thought what? That I was the school bike?"

"No!" He recoils, and I'm finally free of his arm. "Jesus, Lou. I just . . . you know I always liked you. I didn't just stop having feelings for you."

"But you didn't think about what I wanted?"

I stand up and he's forced to do the same to let me out. I squeeze past him and grab my empty glass and crisp packet.

"This is the last fucking thing I need right now," I say before I leave.

I WANT TO WALK HOME in silence, leave all thoughts of the night behind, but Mam's tongue has been loosened by vodka and she won't let me forget.

"A bit of banter," she says, her voice thick with outrage. "The cheek of him."

The wind follows us along the main road to our estate and my tuxedo jacket is not enough to stop it shivering through to my bones. I pull my lapels tight across my chest.

"I can dish it out and I can take it, but there's a line and that eejit crossed it tonight. I'm sorry it happened to you, love, but I'll make sure he never bothers you again."

I'm grateful, but I know better than to get into a heated discussion when she's on this trajectory.

"Yeah, thanks, Mam."

She turns into the laneway that leads to our estate and I follow close behind.

"If he tries to set foot in the Swan again, he'll have me to answer to."

Mam gets to the end of the lane and stops, and I see taillights outside Bridie Brady's house.

"What's going on?"

She shushes me and I look over her shoulder at the red Ford Capri. It's Kenny O'Kane.

"Let's take the long way round," I say, pulling at her sleeve, but it's too late.

The stooped shape of Kenny is coming down the drive, hands tucked into the pockets of his leather jacket.

"Evenin', Rosie," he says.

"Howiye, Kenny," says Mam cautiously.

He's a short, skinny man with a wedge of red hair, intimidating only by reputation.

"You up in the Swan tonight?"

"Yeah, working," says Mam.

"Glad to hear it," says Kenny.

He nods at me and I fold my arms across my chest.

"I hope you're looking after your ma," he says.

"Yeah, I am," I say, although I don't know why Kenny would care about that.

"What with her working all hours now," he says, opening the car door. "I hope you appreciate her."

The Capri shoots off with a guttural rumble that's audible long after it's turned out of sight.

"What did he mean by that?" I ask.

"Just ignore him," says Mam. "He's trying to wind us up, that's all."

She picks up speed and I trot after her.

"Mam, what's happening with all of that stuff?"

I've been afraid to ask.

"I'm on top of it," she says. "Don't worry. With my new shifts and the extra you're giving me too, it'll be all paid off by Christmas, I promise."

When we get in, Mam goes straight for the vodka and Coke and settles in the sitting room in front of some late-night tennis. I'm left alone in the kitchen, staring at the bottles on the counter until they morph from threat to comfort. I take a large glass of the sickly sweet concoction to my room and let it burn a path down my throat as the distorted reverb of *Psychocandy* by The Jesus and Mary Chain takes control. I lie on my bed with my eyes shut and the fuzz and feedback swirl around me until the noise in my head fades to a whisper.

16

In the morning, I let The Beatles banish thoughts of McQueen, *The White Album* in my head as I drive my bike up the final hill, pushing through the pain barrier to the endorphin release at the top. I've almost forgotten when I see his Saab outside the pool and the cold nausea of his hot breath comes rushing back to me. I hurry past to the bike shed and I'm about to leave when I see him sauntering across the lawn.

"Morning, Lou," he says. "Have you got a minute?"

He gestures to the sports center and I realize he probably means behind the closed door of his office.

"If I'm late again this month, I'll get detention," I say.

"I'll make sure you don't get detention."

In the split second I have to make a decision, I can't think of an excuse, and I don't want to make a fuss in front of the girls who are still milling around the bike shed. So I do what I've done in so many awkward situations where a man has maneuvered me into an uncomfortable position: I go along with it and pray it will be OK.

Afterward, I will think, I chose to go there, I went of my own free will. But it doesn't feel like that. It feels like my only choice is between doing what I'm told and being labeled difficult. And there's always the voice that wonders, what if I'm being paranoid? What if he just wants to talk, maybe even apologize, and I make a scene and have to live with the embarrassment of being stupid as well as difficult? No, easier to walk the path of least resistance and hope for the best.

I follow him into the sports center, down the narrow corridor and into his office. Voices pass outside the door and I think, he won't try anything here.

I turn around and he slides his hand inside my coat, onto my hip, coffee breath on my cheek. I try not to retch as I feel his mustache wet against my neck, his hand sliding onto my bum. There's a clatter in the corridor and I pray this is all that will happen. But his fingers are on my thigh, inside my skirt, and he pulls me close, his erection hard against my stomach.

"You are so fucking gorgeous," he whispers in my ear, and he presses into me once more before I pull away.

His dark eyes flick with irritation and his hand reaches for me again.

"Not here," I say, as firmly as I can. The only way I can possibly endure this is with a solid plan, and I need to work out exactly what that's going to be if I can't rely on Joe anymore. Because the one thing I've learned from McQueen is that I can't beat him on my own.

He stares at me for several seconds, not the hint of a smile on his lips.

"You're the boss."

He pushes aside a strand of hair that has fallen onto my forehead and runs his fingers across my cheekbone.

"Don't worry about detention. I'll sort it out."

He turns to the door and, now that it is over, I want to get my money's worth.

"What about my other late marks? You know, it's hard getting here from Ballybrack on the bike."

"Consider your record wiped clean."

He reaches for the door handle, but I'm not finished yet.

"Just one more thing. D'ye think I'll ever make the Senior As?"

He laughs.

"Yeah, I'm sure you will."

As I walk back across the lawn to the school I can't shake the feeling of him hard against me and I wonder with a shiver if someone else is going to have to suffer for it.

I'VE HAD ENOUGH OF MCQUEEN for one day, so I develop period pain just in time for his hockey class after lunch. Matron is kind and obliging and it's in the muted lamplight of her infirmary that I finally have a chance to try and let go of the ache he's put inside me. It's been hidden deep in my gut all day, a solid knot I've managed to ignore while the rest of life continues regardless. For the first time, I'm starting to understand how Tina carried on while the rest of us were oblivious.

When I leave the infirmary, the corridors are still calm with the silence that settles between classes. I take in the grandeur of the wood-paneled walls, the stained-glass panels in the arched windows and the ornate coving above them. It could be perfect here, if it was allowed to be.

In the distance, I see Shauna and my heart fills with the pure joy of her. I wave as I skip down the corridor but she turns into the toilets before she sees me. I follow her in but she's already in a cubicle and I wash my hands while I wait. It's only when I turn off the tap that I hear her sobs.

"Shauna," I say. "Are you OK?"

She's silent and still.

"It's Lou."

The door opens and she goes straight to the sink and runs her hands under the tap. She wipes under her eyes and then looks in the mirror, a stare so vacant I'm not sure what she sees.

"Is everything OK?" I ask.

"Not really," she says.

"D'ye wanna talk about anything?"

"No," she says softly, without conviction.

"Well, if you ever do want to talk, I'm a good listener."

I touch her arm and, for a moment, her reflection looks at me with such longing I don't want to let go. I smile awkwardly and turn to leave, but she grabs my hand.

"I'd like that," she says, and I swing back to her.

We stand at the mirror, fingers touching, for several seconds. I don't want to break the spell and neither does she. My heartbeat slows to a crawl as I try and stop time, until the door behind us swings open. We break apart as a fifth-year passes by into a cubicle.

"Do you want to come round on Saturday night?" she says.

"Yeah, that'd be deadly," I say with a giddy smile. "I mean, yes, I'd love to."

FRIDAY IS THE SORT OF day that lulls you with the brightness of a blue sky, while a brisk and bitter air lies silently in wait. It slinks into the locker room as we prepare to leave for October mid-term and we pull our gabardines around us as we head out into the unblinking light. It's a half-day and Shauna doesn't have training till later so I saunter out the back door with her, confident McQueen won't approach me in her company. Now, even the glint of sunlight on the rear of his car can't spoil the prospect of ten glorious days off without him.

The sun shimmers in Shauna's blue eyes as she recounts a Halloween six or seven years ago, trick-or-treating with her younger brother, Ronan.

A beloved wizard's hat that blew off his head and tumbled down onto the rocks on Dalkey seafront, the daring rescue where she climbed out to the water's edge. She smiles and gestures as her frosty breath billows, her movement loose and unguarded, and I fantasize it's because she's as excited as I am about Saturday night. A whole evening of unbounded potential without Aisling's protection and Melissa's rivalry.

We're walking the gravel path when we hear voices from across the lawn. McQueen is at the entrance to the pool, hands raised in defense as an older, stockier man paces in front of him. The other man doesn't look like he has any business at Highfield, his ill-fitting jeans and flecked jumper as tired and worn as the look on his face. McQueen speaks in hushed tones and reaches out to the man, but he pushes his hand away.

"You know exactly who I am," he shouts. "I'm Elaine Dowling's father."

I can tell by Mr. Dowling's voice, the harshness of his consonants, that Elaine is not a student at Highfield. I turn to ask if she's a swimmer and Shauna's rigid, caught in the glare of sun and shock. Her piercing eyes are aimed at McQueen, waiting for his next move. He holds his hands out, palms down, and speaks softly and calmly as Elaine's father shakes his head.

"I don't know what to believe anymore."

Mr. Dowling's voice quivers and cracks and he puts his head in his hands. As he falters, McQueen pounces, a gentle hand on Mr. Dowling's shoulder, and this time he doesn't resist. McQueen leads him into his lair, the safety of his pool and his patter.

He might think he's got away with it, but he hasn't seen the revulsion on Shauna's face. I touch her hand in sympathy and she curls her fingers around mine. And in that moment of intimacy, I feel a sickening certainty that she knows as much as I do.

Shauna lives in a detached Victorian house near Dalkey village, barely three miles from our estate. I've been along this road before but I've never seen beyond the gates and tall trees that guard every entrance. You could build ten of our houses along her gravel driveway and still have space for the three cars that line up at the end of it. Granite steps lead to a scarlet door and, beyond it, the sparkle of a low-hanging chandelier. In a distant room, Cilla Black introduces tonight's *Blind Date* and I relax at the thought that behind every front door, we all watch the same shit telly.

Either Shauna has spent hours tidying or she lives a life as ordered as her facade suggests. There is no clutter in her room, no evidence of teenage chaos within the sparse and elegant walls. Across the plush beige carpet, on the other side of a large bay window, is a wall of fitted wardrobes and shelves, the artifacts of her life confined behind sliding glass doors. Painted dolls, love-worn teddies and soft toys line up along the top shelf, with medals and trophies on display underneath. Even the books on the bottom shelf are from childhood—*The Secret Garden*, *Anne of Green Gables*, *The Famous Five*. It's only the desk inside the door, the piles of books and tapes and the music center beside it that give any outward display of an inner life.

"What do you want to listen to?" she asks.

"Whatcha got?"

She chews her lip as she looks through the cassettes on her desk and scrunches her nose as she picks one up.

"I have the Housemartins' album."

Her hesitance puts me at ease, and I take off my coat and lean back onto her double bed.

"I love The Housemartins."

She smiles as she puts the tape in the deck and kicks off the night with "Happy Hour."

"Your house is amazing," I say. "I can't believe you have all this space for four people."

Shauna sits cross-legged at the end of the perfectly made bed, leggings tucked into soft, woolly socks and a baggy sweatshirt hanging off one shoulder.

"Yeah, I suppose."

I take off my Docs and mirror her pose, my neon-orange mini riding up over my own black leggings.

"I did have a younger sister," she says.

"Oh. I didn't know that."

"She died when she was ten days old."

"God, I'm sorry," I say. "That's awful."

I don't know what else to say and I reach to touch her hand, but she folds her arms.

"Yeah. I don't remember it. I was only one. Mum had a nervous breakdown after and Dad . . . I dunno. Mum says he was a different person before, but we've never been close."

"I've never met my dad."

"Really? Do you know who he is?"

Now it's my turn to fold my arms.

"Well, he was my mam's boyfriend for two years so yeah, she did get his name."

Her cheeks flush with heat but she still tries to cover her tracks. It's the Highfield way.

"All I meant was, like, have you . . ."

"Don't worry about it," I say. "I made a lot of assumptions about you too."

"Like what?"

"Like you'd have a pole up your arse. And you'd have really crap taste in music."

She gasps, grabs a pillow and laughs as she hits me on the arm. I pretend to be hurt as I reach behind me and then lash the other pillow at her.

"Stereotypes work both ways, you know," I say as I take my pillow back. "And there are a lot more of us than there are of you."

She lands a blow to the side of my head and then stops, as if she's considering my perspective for the first time. I seize the advantage and knock her sideways onto the bed.

"You're the freak, not me," I say, laughing as I collapse breathless beside her.

"Fuck off," she says, but she's smiling too, her face just inches away from mine.

Her breath is shallow and quick, and I draw it in, taste the floral sweetness of her perfume. It fills my lungs like nicotine, the chemical rush of it rocketing through my veins. Inside, I'm buzzing, but on the surface I'm frozen, unable to disturb the universe no matter how much I want to reach out and run my fingers through her hair.

Shauna makes the first move, breaking the trance as she pushes herself up onto her elbow. Her hair is loose, hanging across her face as she looks down at me.

"Tell me something else I don't know about you," she says.

I don't know where to begin, how to broach the many conversations I want to have with her, so I blurt out the first thing that comes to mind.

"Um, it's my birthday tomorrow."

"No way. How come you never said?"

"I dunno." I grimace apologetically. "I don't like any fuss."

"But it's your eighteenth, right?" she says, sitting upright. "You have to celebrate."

I don't have to do anything, but I love that she is excited for me and, right now, I'll follow wherever she leads.

"Wait there," she says, and she's gone, skipping down the stairs.

I walk to the window and pull a gap in the heavy velvet curtains. Beyond the wrought-iron front gates, past the slate rooftops with their ornate gable ends, I see the purple-gray shades of the horizon lit only by the slivers of moonlight that sneak through the clouds.

Shauna returns with a bottle of champagne and two glasses.

"Where did you get that?" I say.

"In the wine cellar. There are loads of them. They won't notice if one is missing."

"You have a wine cellar?"

"It's just an old coal bunker in the basement."

"You have a basement."

I want to get out of this place where she is queen and drink champagne on neutral ground. Somewhere we can be equal partners in the conversation that's ahead.

"Let's go there."

"Where?"

I point through the curtains to the mottled light over the sea. "The seafront. Down to the rocks you were telling me about."

"You want to get drunk and climb out onto the rocks?"

"We can climb first, drink after. Then we only need to worry about getting back."

Shauna laughs.

"You're crazy," she says.

"I'm probably the sanest person you know."

Maybe if I say it enough, she'll believe it's true.

THE SEA IS STILL AND silent, its sedative spell broken only by the gentle lap of it against the rocks. The streaks of moonlight that glimmer on its surface highlight the blackness of what lies beneath and I pull my heavy overcoat tight against the reflective chill. Just a few hundred yards across the water is the silhouette of Dalkey Island, its Martello tower rising out of the somber shadows.

"Did you ever swim out to it?" I ask Shauna.

"Yeah, once. It was for a fundraiser though, so we had boats watching us in case anyone got into trouble. You can get pretty strong currents out here."

I shiver at the thought of it, the silent grip of the sea, and I wonder if Shauna would come after me if I slipped and fell. We're elbow to elbow on a rugged rock formation that slopes down to the water with only the warm buzz of champagne for protection.

"Were you really not going to celebrate your birthday?" she asks.

"Mam probably has something planned, but I kinda got out of the habit of celebrating."

"Why?"

Her eyes are daring me to tell, and I will. I want her to know.

"I was really fucked up after Tina . . . after she killed herself. I still am, really. I'd only be pretending to have fun."

"Are you pretending now?"

"No."

My heart skitters and I can taste the tension between us.

"It's different with you," I say. "You get it."

"I think about Tina all the time," says Shauna.

"You do?" I want to tell her everything. But not yet; I'm not ready to let him come between us.

"I wish I could have saved her," she says. "I mean, I could have, but . . ."

I take her hand and we hold on tight, breath coming in short, urgent bursts.

"You just didn't know how," I say.

Our eyes lock, and we know. That we're telling the truth and lying to ourselves at the same time. That the weight of the guilt is going nowhere and there's nothing we can do but share it.

I don't remember who moves first, if she tilts her shoulder toward mine or I slide my thigh next to hers. We lean into each other, breath hot against icy skin, soft lips drawn together like magnets, hands on faces, fingers laced through hair and the crash of glass as a champagne flute kicks off the foot of the rock and splinters into the sea.

18

Shards of light filter through a cracked concrete sky on our return to Highfield after mid-term. A winter smog hovers over the last of the fallen leaves, crisp with frost, as the wind whistles in the bare branches overhead. There's no hiding from it now; we're all just waiting for the cover of darkness to descend on the year.

I shuffle through the back door of the school, hoping for a glimpse of long, wet hair on a purple sash, but I don't see her, not in the locker room nor the assembly hall. I think of the possibilities, that she will ignore me, belittle me or act like nothing has happened. That's what boys do. But kissing Shauna was nothing like kissing a boy.

I don't get to see her properly until lunchtime, and when we meet in the dining hall with Melissa and Aisling, it's not Shauna who's making snarky comments about me.

"I bet mid-term in Ballybrack was a hoot," says Melissa. "I hear it's all happening at the . . . what's the name of it again, the Dead Swan?"

"No."

"Well, you missed a classic night at Stradbrook. And another at Wesley last weekend."

"You went to Wesley?" says Aisling.

"Not babies' night on Friday," says Melissa. "You know, the proper adults' disco on Saturday."

Shauna catches my eye for the first time, and I know it's a reflex action, her concern for Melissa, but my stomach still flips as I hold her gaze, willing it to mean something more. She looks away and takes my hope with her, the hollow void of it tight in my chest.

I wish I could stop the clocks. At that moment on the rocks, the perfect stillness of us. It's all that feels right; everything else is just time stretching in the wrong direction, pulling us apart. I've hardly thought about anything else since, not the fading memory of Tina nor the looming threat of McQueen. I've ignored the calls from Joe and the questions from Mam as if I could grind it all to a halt, but my heart keeps pumping regardless. I need to talk to Shauna, alone.

"Any scandal?" asks Aisling.

"That's for me to know and you to find out," says Melissa, tapping her nose. "All I'm saying is I'm sworn off schoolboys for good. Now that I've had a go of an actual man."

"A go of?" says Shauna.

Melissa smirks, triumphant now she's got Shauna's attention.

"Jesus Christ," says Shauna. "Will you ever learn?"

The legs of Melissa's chair scrape across the floor as she stands up and slaps her palms on the table.

"You're one to talk," she snaps. She picks up her lunchbox and walks away.

"What's wrong with her?" asks Aisling, and both Shauna and I shrug and shake our heads.

AN ICY WIND CLAWS AT us as we make our way to PE after lunch, the spectral shapes of our breath whipping to nothing in the air before us. I chat casually to Aisling as we pull the sleeves of our jumpers over fingers stiff with cold, but my mouth is dry, all my senses raw at the thought of seeing McQueen again. He shouts from the pitch, an impatience in him as he hurries us along and separates us into groups for hockey practice. Shauna reminds him we're supposed to be training for the cross-country trials next week and he answers her with a curl of his lip.

"Are you the teacher today, Shauna?"

"No, I was just saying—"

"You were just saying." He holds his hands up to the rest of the class. "Go on then, educate us all with your expert knowledge."

Her lip quivers as she opens her mouth and the usual suspects can barely hide their glee.

"It's nothing."

"Well, maybe keep your mouth shut in future if you've got nothing to say."

As the other girls run off sniggering, I catch a glance from Shauna to McQueen, a pleading for mercy. He gives it to her, a leering nod of his head before he turns away, and that's when I know with absolute certainty that he is abusing her, too.

I've seen that look before. When I watched from the stands as he criti-cized Tina's third place in a hard-fought race at a swimming gala, her dev-astated tears and the scrap of absolution he threw her with a single nod. At the time, I didn't understand. But I do now.

As he walks away, I mouth "Prick" to Shauna, but she's lost inside her head.

There's no mention of cross-country training for the rest of the class and we're making our way back to the school when I hear my name.

"Lou."

McQueen waves me over, a smile on him now and a flick of his feath-ered fringe as he shakes off the formality of class.

"Your turn," he says, and I freeze. "To help tidy up?"

I grab Aisling's arm. "Come with me."

She stumbles as I pull her along, but she never asks why. McQueen says nothing to either of us until the holdalls are full and it's time to head to the sports center.

"You go, Aisling. We can manage."

She looks from him to me and my wide, urgent eyes.

"It's fine," she says. "I don't mind helping."

"Aisling, there are only two bags. There's nothing for you to carry. Go on, get outta here."

She throws me a sheepish look before she leaves, and I return a grimace.

As we walk to the sports center, McQueen chats about my match on Saturday and I realize with a mounting dread that he assumes he's bringing me. He hasn't even bothered to ask this time.

"Your stick work has improved so much. If you keep practicing those drills we did today, you'll be unstoppable."

"You didn't . . ."

"What?"

"You didn't blow off cross-country so I could practice my hockey?"

"Aren't you the cocky one today?" He laughs. "And what if I did? You're not going to tell on me, are you?"

I force a smile and hold it in place as we walk to the sports center and put the hockey gear away. As if compliance will save me. We still have to pass his office on the way out, that long, narrow corridor where I'll have to hold my nerve and plead for a stay of execution. I try to think of an excuse, any reason to leave, but my brain has stalled, frozen as my face.

"I need to talk to you in my office," he says when we reach the door. He opens it and steps aside so I have no choice but to enter first. The chink of light from the corridor throws shadows across the room, dark and swollen as a bruise.

"No," I say, pointing to the exit, "I have to go."

"It will only take a minute."

He puts his hand on my hip to usher me inside and I squirm and elbow him away. He grabs my wrist and holds it so tight I can't speak.

"What's going on, Lou?" His voice is a menacing growl. "I thought we both felt the same way about this."

My throat tightens and the words won't come.

"After everything I've done for you," he says.

It's the threat of darkness, the close confinement of his office, that loosens my tongue, and I say the first thing that comes to mind.

"Who is Elaine Dowling?"

His grip slackens as it dawns on him that I was there, the last day before mid-term. He bites his lip, nods and then snorts, as if his allure could ever have been in doubt.

"Are you jealous?"

"Maybe."

"She's nobody. Absolutely nobody."

I slip my wrist from his grasp and he flinches before placing his hand gently on my shoulder.

"Let me prove it to you," he says. "Let me take you to lunch. After your match on Saturday."

"OK," I say as I engage those facial muscles again and pray this means he'll leave me alone until then.

FRENCH GOES BY IN A haze of anger and futility, and I can't focus on the irregular verbs on the blackboard. Carol beside me notices there's something up.

"You're even more intense than usual."

"Oh."

"Is that all you have to say? God, it's like getting blood out of a stone sometimes."

At least she has the gumption to ask. There hasn't been a word out of anyone else and by the end of the day I can't take it anymore. I know I came here to play the long game, but that was before I understood what it meant to live under his threat every day, to pretend nothing is wrong when everything is wrong. There's me, Shauna, Elaine and how many others? I can't understand why we're not talking and trying to help each other find a way out of it. In this moment of clarity, I'm so convinced of what I need to do I don't stop to think about anyone else.

"Where's German on?" I ask Carol as she packs up.

"G11, I think. You know, behind the music room."

I'm gone before she can ask why, running to try and catch Shauna before she leaves for swimming. I find her in the corridor, chatting to another prefect.

"We need to talk."

She winces without dropping her smile.

"Not about that," I say, although I'm gutted at the coolness of her response. "It's something else."

She shrugs and follows me down the stairs and out to the refuge of the cedars at the back of the school. She hugs her arms around herself in protest as the wind rattles the thinning branches overhead.

"It's about Mr. McQueen," I say.

A car engine rumbles in the distance but Shauna doesn't make a sound.

"You know he was molesting Tina. I mean, he was forcing her to have sex with him."

Still, her face betrays nothing.

"She was pregnant. That's why she killed herself."

It's only now she reacts, a tiny gasp she swallows quickly.

"And now he's trying it on with me. And Elaine Dowling and god knows who else. What about that swimmer who gave birth in the grotto?"

The wind whips Shauna's hair into her eyes but it can't disguise the horror on her face.

"What did you say?" she says. "About you?"

"He tried to force me. In his office."

"Here? In the school?"

"Yes. Today. Last week. In his car as well."

She recoils with the impact of each word, her eyes growing wider with the sting. "You never said anything."

"Neither did you."

She looks away then. Her hair blows clean behind her as she stares out across the lawn, past the sports center to the hockey pitches beyond. I give her time and space to think, to come round. But when she turns back, it's pure anger that fuels her.

"Why did you come to Highfield?"

"I wanted to see for myself."

"So you came here because you heard a rumor. And then? You decided to try and make it come true?" She shakes her head, as if I'm the worst of us all, and I clench my fists in frustration.

"No, of course not."

"You don't get it, do you?" she says. "Mr. McQueen is a hands-on sort of person. He tries to make everyone feel special. That's what makes him such a great coach."

"Oh, I'm not saying he's not a great coach. He gets results, I know that."

"That's not what I mean," she says. "He doesn't just teach, he connects with people. He finds out what drives you so he can get the most out of you."

"Don't you think that's what makes him so dangerous?"

There's a hardness in her eyes, a single-minded determination that unsettles me.

"I wouldn't be where I am without him. I could make the Olympics in two years. Do you have any idea what that means?"

I do now. It means she has so much more to lose. It means she'll sacrifice me before him.

"But what about Tina? You said you wished you could have saved her?"

"I wish she wasn't dead, but it's not my fault."

"I didn't say that."

I put my hand on her elbow, a last desperate attempt to reach her. She unwraps her arms and my heart leaps with hope until she shrugs me off and turns away.

"I have to go," she says, and I let go of the rage that's been gurgling inside all afternoon.

"So that's it? You keep fucking your way into the Irish team and who cares about the rest of us?"

She doesn't look back as she walks away and leaves me in the wind-blown space beneath the cedars, anger swelling and collapsing in my chest and a smothered gasp of despair that sounds like surrender.

19

A visit from Bridie next door is like opening the house to the whole estate. She brings all of life with her, the inane gossip, the comings and goings of the neighbors we try to ignore most of the time. We never exactly invite her in, but I think we're both glad of the lift it gives us. It's like exercise or study: you're happy you've done it, even if you haven't exactly enjoyed it at the time.

She knocks on the door more often now her three older kids have moved on and she only has Derek to worry about. He's a fully-grown man, twenty-five or -six, who lies around the house all day and stays out all night, and he has poor Bridie's heart broken. He's a smart lad, she says, maybe the smartest of them all; even in this recession, there must surely be some work out there for him. I think about the glassy blue of Derek's eyes, the lazy slur of his speech and his fondness for Kenny O'Kane and his cronies. That's what I'd be most concerned about, if I was his mother.

I prefer to hear about Sheila O'Rourke's varicose veins and Maureen Feehily sneaking a Walnut Whip into the shopping and her supposed to be on a diet. I'm brewing another pot of tea and getting out the good biscuits when the doorbell rings.

"It's like Grand Central Station in here," says Mam.

"It's Grand Central Terminal," I say as I get up, "not Station."

"How do you know?" asks Mam.

"Because I read," I say.

I've been zipping around the world with *Time* magazine in the library. From the Sandinistas in Nicaragua to Cory Aquino in the Philippines to the fight against AIDS in New York. And I've been learning the truth about feminism and power and the lie that women already have it all. I wonder which of the nuns put in the order for *Time* and if they'd intended to radicalize those of us who dig a little deeper below the surface. I hope the answer is yes, that there is one of them beating us a path that goes beyond UCD and a nice boyfriend from Law or Commerce.

"Would you listen to her," says Mam to Bridie. "Only a couple of months in that school and she knows it all already."

I don't mind her slagging; I know she's proud of me. And Bridie will be sure to tell the whole estate.

"Ah Jaysis," says Bridie as I leave the kitchen, "she's a little treasure but."

Bridie has me so distracted with the normal rhythm of life I don't even think to brace myself before I open the door. It's Joe Forrester, backlit by the orange sheen of a streetlight, a big, angry head on him.

"Oh, hi," I say.

"Your phone broken, is it? For outgoing calls only, like?"

I still haven't returned any of his messages, but I say nothing. I'm not going to be drawn into an argument.

"Look, I'm sorry, OK?" says Joe. "I'm sorry I tried to kiss you and I'll never do it again. Are we cool now? Because I have a lot of things I need to talk about and I'm pretty sure you'll be interested to hear them."

It's the sheer force of his bluster that wins me over.

"OK. Come in."

I show him into the sitting room and return to the kitchen to make tea and face the inquisition.

"Is that Joe Forrester?" asks Mam.

"Yep."

"He's been following her round like a lapdog," she says to Bridie. "Of course, she won't tell me what's going on."

"He's a lucky lad," says Bridie. "Lou, make sure and give me plenty of notice if I need to buy a new hat?"

"Ah, would you stop, Bridie," says Mam, but Bridie's off, cackles of laughter escaping through the crooked gaps in her teeth.

As I slip out with the two teas, I pull the door handle with my elbow and Bridie lowers her voice.

"Poor fella," she says.

"Ah yeah," says Mam.

I take the teas to the living room and hand one mug to Joe.

"Milk and two sugars."

"Lovely."

"So go on," I say, taking the armchair next to him. "Put me out of my misery."

"Guess who's got an interview with the man himself next Thursday?"

"With McQueen?"

"Yep. A profile for the college magazine."

"That's so cool. A real writing credit too."

"Ah, it's not a real magazine, it's just some shitty pamphlet the journalism students put together. But that's not the point. I have half an hour with him and I'm going to go round during training, you know, see his genius in action and all that, so I'm hoping to get to talk to some of the swimmers too."

"Shauna Power," I say.

"Who's that?"

"She's the star of the show. And he's fucking her."

It's a picture I can't get out of my head and a pain that sits heavy in my heart. No matter how many reasons she has for choosing him over me, it doesn't hurt any less.

"What?" says Joe. "How do you know?"

"I got talking to her about Tina and she didn't tell me outright, but she knew what was going on."

"Then why the fuck didn't she say anything?"

"Because it was happening to her too."

Joe shakes his head.

"Jesus fucking Christ. He's a monster."

"Yeah."

"Has he . . ." He sucks air through his teeth. "Has he done anything more to you?"

"No, not really."

"Well, that's something."

"Yeah."

As Joe drinks his tea, I think about the interview, what we can do to catch him off guard.

"Hang on a minute," I say. "Does he know who you are?"

"Me? I'm Joe Doyle from Ballyfermot, sure how the hell would he know me from Adam?"

"Joe Doyle?" I laugh. "Could ye not've come up with something a bit more imaginative?"

"And what do you think I should be called?"

"I dunno, like . . . Joe Fontaine. Or Joey Spinosa."

He shakes with laughter, and he has to put his mug on the coffee table.

"You want him to think I'm an American gangster?"

"Why not? You could really put the shits up him."

"I know what your game is, McQueen," says Joe in a terrible New York mafia drawl. "And that game is up."

I let the laughs come, waves of them rolling out of me as if they've been trapped in my belly for weeks.

"Jesus," I say, "if only it was that easy."

"Yeah, but lookit, we're getting somewhere," says Joe. "It's gonna take a while but he's not getting away with this."

"Are you sure?"

"Yeah, I am. We're gonna nail that prick if it's the last thing we do."

I DON'T EVEN TRY TO get up on Saturday morning. I've told Mam I've got terrible period cramps and she's brought me painkillers, but I'm still writhing around the bed half an hour later.

"You need to call Mr. McQueen," she says. She's wearing a tight skirt, a face full of makeup, and she's blow-dried her hair. I hate him even more for making her so desperate.

"I don't know his number."

When the doorbell rings I hear the murmur of Mam's apologies and his faux concern. The front door closes and relief floods my body until I hear his voice in the hall, moving into the kitchen. And then the laughter, forced and falsetto, each of them chasing something they can't have.

He's in there for twenty minutes when I hear the kitchen door open and close and his heavy footsteps in the hall. I wait for the sound of the front door latch but instead, the stairs creak under his weight as he moves closer. He must be going to the toilet, the room next to me, and I hold my breath in case he hears it thundering through my head.

At first I'm sure I'm imagining it, a symptom of my distress, the click of the handle on my bedroom door. But then it turns, slowly, inch by inch, and he's there, his mustache peering through a crack in the door. I lie very still, hoping the threads of light that filter through the curtains won't betray me, but he slides into the room and closes the door softly behind him. I say nothing as he looks around, the discarded knickers on the floor, the dirty plates on my desk, yesterday's bra and tights hanging over the back of the chair.

"Your mum tells me you're not feeling well," he whispers.

It's only two steps to the bed and he's standing over me and, with him, that cloying smell of aftershave. I lie on my side under the duvet, knees tucked into my tummy.

"I've got stomach cramps."

"Let me help you," he says, sitting on the edge of the bed. "I can massage it for you."

"No."

I shake my head and push back against the wall.

"It's OK, Lou," he says, all smiles. "I'm trained. I know what I'm doing."

He rests his elbow on my leg and squeezes my knee through the geometric pattern on the covers.

"No," I say again, pulling my knees tighter into my chest. "It's not muscular. It's . . . it's . . . women's problems."

He nods in sympathy.

"That's the muscles of the womb contracting. I can make it all go away."

He slides his hand under the duvet, onto my knee, and I push it away.

"No, don't."

He's straight back, his fingers moving the length of my thigh, insistent now, ignoring the thrust of my hand against his wrist.

"Stop," I say, but he doesn't, his breath hot and hard and a low moan out of him as he finds the edge of my underpants and pushes inside. It's like he can't see or hear me anymore, I'm just flesh at his disposal.

"No." I don't mean to scream so loud or kick so hard, not with Mam downstairs and the threat of him looming over me. But once I start, I can't stop.

"Get off me!"

He jumps off the bed, his hands raised in defense.

"Jesus," he says, "it's just a massage."

It's the first time I've seen him lose his cool, creeping backward like a cornered rat.

"Get out, get out of here," I shout.

In between the thump of my heart and the grating sound of my voice, I hear the pound of Mam's feet on the stairs and the crack of the handle as she flings the door open.

"I'm sorry, Lou," says McQueen, "I was only trying to help."

Mam looks at me, cowering on the bed with the covers clutched tight around me, and then at him, the picture of sympathy and compassion.

"What's going on?" she says.

"It's a really bad cramp, Rose," says McQueen. "I tried some physio but it's deep in the muscle. I think bedrest and painkillers are Lou's best options for today."

To be fair to Mam, it's not like she buys it straight away. She throws me a quizzical look, but I can't think straight with the screaming in my head and all I can manage in return is a strained smile.

"Is that what's wrong, Lou?"

"I'm sorry," I say, my voice timid and thin, "it just hurt more than I expected."

"Don't worry about the match, Lou," says McQueen. "We'll miss you, of course, but your health is far more important."

I meet his searing gaze, but I cannot return his sickly smile.

"OK, thanks," I say.

Mam looks from me to him, his mournful resignation at my plight, takes a deep breath and opts for damage limitation.

"She's been through a lot recently," says Mam. "She's obviously not herself today and, well, I'm sure she'll apologize to you properly when she's feeling better."

"Don't worry about it, Rose," says McQueen as Mam leads him back out onto the landing. "I'm at this job far too long to take anything personally. The only thing I care about is that Lou gets better."

Mam closes the door and his words fade to a rhythmic hum, a pacifying lull of poisoned syllables that will lie in wait for me on Monday morning. I know I've crossed a line today, and I realize with a shiver that I will need to prepare for a very different sort of battle. Everything is going to change now.

20

I see him as soon as I turn the corner, his nylon tracksuit swishing down the stone corridor toward me. Time slows as I shift the weight of my school bag across my back, hold my English folder to my chest and concentrate on putting one foot in front of the other. I sneak a glance as he approaches and his eyes whip me with a gloating, a flash of swagger to match his stride. I feel the heat of him in my periphery, the electric-blue arrogance, the sterile, mealy smell of him, and I hug my folder tight as if it's body armor. And then he is there, close enough to reach out and grab me or slam me to the floor with a single strike.

"You're not as smart a cunt as you think you are," he whispers.

I turn to catch a glimpse of the sneer curled across his lip as he passes, his arm almost brushing my shoulder. I keep walking, eyes fixed on the Sacred Heart of Jesus that hangs over the door to the staff room ahead of me. The words pound in my head, *cunt, cunt, cunt, what a thick fucking cunt you really are*, and the smell of him lingers long after his footsteps have faded out of earshot.

I AVOID HIM FOR THE rest of the morning but we've hockey with him after lunch and I'm not even going to try and attempt that. I'm straight up to the infirmary with a grimace and a familiar sad tale of period cramps. Matron nods sympathetically. She understands she is the guardian of girls who need a break and opens her infirmary to anyone who asks. She sits on one of the two beds and pats the space beside her.

"Tell me, Lou," she says as I sit down, "is everything OK with you? Apart from the period pain, of course."

Matron smells of strawberries and Savlon and I want nothing more than to trust her with my secret, but I'm not ready to take that risk.

"Em, yeah. I suppose."

"It's just, I hope you don't mind me saying this, but you seem upset when you come here on Mondays."

I was hoping she wouldn't remember. I've had period pain twice in the last month.

"Is there anything in particular you want to talk about? In complete confidence."

I don't know if it's the Mancunian accent or the bold red lipstick but there's something about her outsider status that I trust and I need unbiased advice more than anything.

"There's this man, em, at work. He's been hassling me."

I stop, unsure if it's OK to be explicit. As if naming the act is worse than doing it.

"In what way is he hassling you, Lou?"

"He touches me and kisses me and I'm scared nobody would believe me if I told them."

Matron isn't shocked. In fact, her expression barely changes and I'm afraid she's thinking, is that it?

"Is this man someone in a position of power over you?" she says.

"Yes."

She turns to me and takes my hands in hers.

"Thank you for telling me this, Lou. I believe you."

I'm so relieved to hear those words I could hug her.

"I want you to listen to me," she says. "This is assault. It's not your fault and it's not OK. You've taken the first step by telling me, but now you need to tell your parents or your manager or somebody else at work. Men like this, they rely on your silence and shame to get away with it and, as long as you don't tell, they will keep doing it."

"I don't know if I can," I say. "I might lose my . . . job."

"Can you keep doing your job if he's going to be there upsetting you all the time? Just think about it. And come and talk to me any time. I mean that."

"OK, I will. Thanks."

Matron believes me. She'll back me up. I leave the infirmary with a lightness I haven't felt in a long time and the certainty that all I have to do is tell my story. No entrapment, no games, just the truth.

IT'S A LONG WALK TO Sister Shannon's office down a corridor of checker-board tiles, and the click of my brogues reverberates in the vast, open space, announcing my arrival from a distance. I haven't made an appoint-ment; I don't want her to be forewarned of what I have to say. I spent all of last night organizing my notes, the list I've kept of times, dates, places and actions. Every inappropriate thing he's said and done, documented in detail. Joe's given me the go-ahead to tell Tina's story too. There's so much evidence here she'll have to listen.

Sister Shannon answers promptly after my first knock, a voice deep with authority and poise.

"Enter."

I haven't been in here since my interview and I'm only vaguely aware of the orderly clutter around me, the floor-to-ceiling bookshelves, the paint-ings and certificates that line up against the dark, embossed wallpaper. Sis-ter Shannon is upright in a leather chair, hands clasped on a large mahogany desk. She wears no veil, just a veneer of kindly compassion that does little to bridge the space between us. She gestures to a low chair opposite her, and I sit obediently, holding tight to my precious papers.

"How are you getting on at Highfield, Louise?"

I clear my throat and make eye contact.

"There's something I need to tell you," I say, my voice thin and reedy.

"Go on."

"It's Mr. McQueen."

There's no change to her benevolent pose, no indication she knows what's coming.

"He molested me. On four separate occasions."

She still doesn't move, not a shift in her seat nor a tilt of her head. I look down at my notes and start to read.

"On Saturday the 4th of October, he gave me a lift to my hockey match . . ."

"Yes," she interrupts, "he's very good like that."

I look at Sister Shannon in her elevated position across the desk and wonder which of us has misheard. I need to be absolutely clear.

"Mr. McQueen assaulted me in his car on the 4th of October on the way home from a match at St. Catherine's. Then on the 25th of October, he—"

"Louise," she says in a sharp voice. "Before you go any further with these . . . outlandish accusations, I want you to know Mr. McQueen has told me all about this already."

It starts slowly, the dread rising from the pit of my stomach.

"And all I can say is, you're very lucky to have a teacher that cares so much about you."

"What?"

My breath fractures, the unease stuttering in my chest.

"Mr. McQueen is not going to make a formal complaint, nor will he be pressing any charges. His only concern is your welfare."

"Charges? What did he say?"

She sighs, as if she really didn't want to involve herself in the minutiae, but if I insist.

"He told me about your crush on him—"

"That's not true."

"And he told me about your attempts to be intimate with him."

"It was him that kissed me."

"That's enough," she shouts as she holds her hand up.

In the simmering silence that passes between us I finally understand I will never win at their game.

"Mr. McQueen also told me about your outburst at home," she says with renewed composure. "I understand your mother witnessed that too."

I'm on my feet now, my pages scrunched tight in my fist.

"Do you know what he was doing in my bedroom on Saturday, while I was in bed sick? He put his hand under the covers, inside my underwear, even though I told him to stop. And he raped Tina Forrester, in the storeroom behind the pool. Did you know she was pregnant when she killed herself?"

I could swear there's a flicker in her eyes, right before she stands up and lays her palms flat on the desk.

"I've heard quite enough, Louise. Now, I don't know what your game is, but I will not have you making such vile accusations against a member of staff. This ends here."

She punctuates each of the last three words with a slap of her index finger on the table.

"If you persist in this . . . this slander, there will be serious repercussions. Do you understand?"

"I understand it's not slander if it's true."

Sister Shannon lowers her eyes to the desk, exhales and then looks straight at me.

"We took you in here in good faith, Louise, despite your incomplete record at Santa Maria. If you continue to cause trouble for Mr. McQueen, it will be the end of your Highfield career."

I want to tell her to shove it up her hole, but I can't think straight and I need to get out of here.

"Just one more thing," she says as I turn to leave. "Please tell your mother the most recent installment of your fees is now overdue."

"I don't pay fees," I say. "I'm on a scholarship."

She looks at me with bemusement, as if I've just told a joke.

"You were never awarded a scholarship, Louise."

My heart clenches tight and I can't tell if this is simply another attempt to undermine me.

"I wouldn't be here without it, believe me."

"I think you need to go home and have a conversation with your mother. She's paid part of the fees for this term but there is still a sum outstanding."

It comes to me in a smack of despair, Kenny O'Kane, his interest in me, his faux concern for Mam, and I stumble out of the room, trying to piece it all together. I don't know who to believe anymore. All I know is I've been acting as if I had a free ride at Highfield when there is always a price. And mine is bound to be higher than most.

I COULD BE SUSPENDED FOR mitching off school, but I need to know. I freewheel down the hill and let the road come at me, as if letting go is a function of free will. I'm so tired of curating every move; I just want life to happen to me. Powered by Violent Femmes' *Hallowed Ground*, I sail through red lights, weave in and out of traffic along the dual carriageway until the sharp sting of deceit has subsided to a dull ache. When I get home, I slam the door so hard the puckered glass rattles in the frame. Mam appears from the kitchen, a towel wrapped around her head and her eyes bleary with morning.

"What are you doing home so early?"

I let my bike fall against the radiator and she jumps with the clatter of it.

"Jesus Christ, Lou, what did you do that for?"

She picks up the bike and leans it against the side of the stairs.

"Why did you tell me I got a scholarship?"

Mam pulls her paisley dressing gown around her, as if the flimsy fabric will protect her.

"What do you mean?"

"What do I mean? Hmm, let me think, what could I possibly mean? I mean I did not earn a scholarship to Highfield and yet I am attending Highfield. That's what I mean. So why don't you tell me what's going on?"

Mam puts her hand to her mouth and lowers herself onto the stairs.

"Who told you?"

"That bitch, Sister Shannon, got great satisfaction out of telling me my fees were overdue."

She puts her head in her hands and the towel flops forward onto her feet.

"So it's true?" I say.

"Yes."

"So let me guess. I wasn't good enough so you hit Kenny O'Kane up for a loan without ever thinking of how you'd pay it all back."

"No," she says, and when she looks up she's as angry as I am. "You were good enough, I know you were."

"So why didn't I get a scholarship?"

"Sister Shannon told me it would be a formality with your exam results. She gave me all this shite about the inclusiveness of the school and how much they value students like you. It looks good in their brochure, you know, helping the underprivileged."

She rolls her eyes.

"And then I got a letter to say you hadn't achieved the required results."

"So what happened?"

"I don't know. You'd already been offered a place, so I went into the school and told Sister Shannon herself that you'd be taking it anyway."

She shakes her head.

"Lou, I know I've messed up, but it wasn't just about my hopes for you, it was the unfairness of it. I wasn't going to let them toss you aside because you didn't fit their idea of a deserving pauper."

"I know why. It's because I'm connected to Tina, isn't it?"

She doesn't argue, and I know she didn't have the heart to say it herself.

I don't tell her it's not the stigma of Tina's suicide that's the problem, it's what lurks behind it. I can't. Mam doesn't cope well with an emotional crisis, and I don't have the energy to look after both of us. And if she didn't believe me, if she even questioned one bit of it, it'd end me.

"What were you going to do?" I say. "About the fees?"

"You don't have to worry about that."

"Don't pay them. I don't want to go back there anyway."

It's only after I've said it that I realize it's true. After everything that's happened, this is a relief more than anything. But Mam grimaces and I think it must be because of my university chances.

"I'm going to college no matter where I go to school. I don't need Highfield for that."

She rubs her hand across her forehead.

"You'll be staying at Highfield. Until Christmas anyway."

"What d'ye mean? Sister Shannon said you hadn't paid?"

"I put the money in their bank account yesterday."

It takes a second for the full implications to hit me.

"Ah no, Mam. Please, please tell me you didn't."

She can't look me in the eye and I know. It's not just McQueen I'm going to have to face for the foreseeable, it's Kenny O'Kane as well.

21

Thursdays at the Black Swan are a unique beast. It's almost but not quite the weekend so punters come for one or two, the best of intentions all round, and then stay until they're thrown out after midnight. It's already busy when I get here, but at least it means I've little time to think about school. I flit from the floor to the bar in a choreographed whirl with Martina, leaving her to deal with the rowdies at the far end of the room. I'm up near the door with half an eye on it. Joe's said he'll call in with news of his showdown with McQueen, though I'm so tired of it all I'm not sure what difference any of it will make.

Joe arrives as momentum builds at the bar and he has to hang at the end of it, chatting to one of the old-timers. It's only after final, final pints have been pulled that I get a chance to join him. Mam slips me a glass of Fürstenberg with Joe's last pint and we find a corner to chat.

"It's heaving in here tonight," says Joe. "Hope you're making some money out of it."

"Are you joking? I'm lucky if I scrape together a pound from the measly tips I get here."

"You serious? I've friends working in The Bad Ass Café who make almost as much in tips as they get paid."

"That's the food. And the Americans. They know how to tip, but they've fuck all reason to come to Ballybrack."

"That's true."

Joe sinks the top of his fresh pint and then wipes a Guinness foam mustache from his top lip.

"So how did you get on?" I ask.

"Yeah, right. Well, I didn't get any confessions out of him, but it was . . . weird."

"Whatcha mean? Weird, how?"

"He was obsessed with what I was writing down. He kept joking about it, but it wasn't funny after the fifth time."

"Like, in a control-freak kinda way?"

"Yeah, sorta. I think he's so used to journalists fawning over him, and he probably thought I'd be even worse, like I'd be in awe of him with me only being a student. He was obviously expecting a puff piece where he'd give me a few lines and I'd be eternally grateful for them, d'ye know what I mean?"

I laugh at the idea of Joe making the great Maurice McQueen squirm.

"He started off on a charm offensive, saying he'd look out for me and give me exclusives when I'm out in the real world. I can see how all that shite works on people who don't know him. And I got all the big-man stuff, you know, all his achievements and awards. Sure I knew all that already."

He pulls out a cigarette and offers it to me. I shake my head and he fires it up and blows the first lungful out the side of his mouth.

"But I noticed something when I was talking to him, only with the girls, never the boys. The way they'd wait at the side of the pool for him to tell them what to do. Like they had no minds of their own. It was just some of the girls but enough to make me wonder what sort of mind games he's playing with them."

"Did you get to talk to any of them?" I ask.

"That was the other thing," he says. "He had a go at me when I asked to talk to the swimmers, said he'd never agreed to it. But I gave him all this guff about human interest and students inspiring students, blah, blah, blah, and he called Shauna over—I didn't even have to ask for her."

My heart picks up speed at the mention of her.

"She's certainly, eh . . ." he says.

"A ride?"

He laughs, but there's a flush in his cheeks.

"That's one way of putting it all right."

He tilts his head as he takes a drag of his fag.

"Yeah, so anyway, she talked about her hopes and her plans, you know, classic one-liners about inspiration and commitment. But then, when I started asking about her relationship with McQueen, you know, working so closely and spending so much time together, she froze. She kept looking over at him, and then he must have got spooked too cos he came over and told her to get back in the pool. He couldn't get me out of there fast enough after that."

"Jesus," I say. "So, what are you going to write about?"

"Honestly, I dunno. I've got no evidence of anything, just a hunch he was hiding something. I'd get thrown out of a real newsroom trying to make something out of that."

"Use me," I say before I get a chance to engage my brain. "Interview me. You can write about everything he did to me."

Maybe this will be enough. I have suffered too, and I've no reason to keep quiet anymore. I can shout about what I know and nobody can stop me.

"Ah Lou," says Joe, frowning, "I can't do that. You'd be expelled from that school for starters."

"I'm leaving at Christmas anyway."

"What?"

I do trust Joe, but he doesn't need to know about my family finances.

"I've had enough of him," I say. "I want to get as far away from him as possible. But first, I want to crucify him."

When he's sure I'm sure, I see the start of a smile curl on his lips, and I feel the heaviness rise from my chest. My testimony is a start but it's not worth as much without proof. And I know exactly where to look for that.

"MR. MCQUEEN IS A RAPIST."

Melissa splutters out a laugh and looks at me wide-eyed and incredulous, waiting for the punchline. I let my words hang in the air as a sullen drizzle starts to spit and we take shelter under a cedar that seems to stretch into the clouds.

"What are you talking about?" says Melissa, her smile fading slowly to a mystified pout.

"You know my friend, Tina? The one who killed herself?"

"The swimmer? Yeah."

"He raped her and got her pregnant."

"What? No way." She's all ears now. "How do you know?"

"She was my friend. She told me."

Melissa bites her lip as she takes it all in.

"But why would Mr. McQueen need to rape anyone? He's got half the swimming club swooning over him."

That's what everyone will say. I've asked myself the same question so many times: why would he bother? Wouldn't a good-looking, successful man be able to get sex without having to force himself on teenagers?

"It's about power," I say. "He thinks he can get whatever he wants from anyone."

"How would you know?"

"Because he tried it with me too."

I'm sure Melissa doesn't mean to laugh, but it's all she can do with this onslaught.

"Sorry, I need to get this straight. Mr. McQueen tried to rape you? Where? When?"

"It started in his car on the way home from a hockey match."

"Yeah," she says. "I heard the rumors about the two of you."

This time, I can't hold back the fury.

"Jesus Christ, Melissa, I'm trying to tell you about something horrible that happened to me. Please listen to me, I'm begging you."

She holds her hands up in apology.

"OK, OK, I'm sorry. I'm listening."

I steady myself as I tell her about the car, his office, my bedroom. She raises her eyebrows at that, as if the other locations were somehow more understandable. I bet she thought I'd given off the wrong signals, getting into his car, going to his office.

"But . . ." she starts, "do you think anybody is going to believe you?"

"No."

"So . . . ?"

"It's not about me, that's over. It's about who he's still doing it to."

I give her a moment to let my allegation sink in. The rain taps a rhythm on the canopy above us, only solitary drops falling through onto the soft, needled ground.

"No." She shakes her head. "Shauna?"

"She hasn't told me outright, but I tried to talk to her about him and, well, she didn't deny it."

"But . . . she would have told me," says Melissa.

"I didn't know about Tina, and she was my best friend too. I was so angry with her for deserting me when all the time he was threatening to drop her from the team if she didn't have sex with him."

I know what Melissa is feeling, the gut-punch that she was right all

along, that Shauna has been involved with McQueen. And then the guilt
that she is still jealous of their relationship.

"Do you know the worst thing?" I say. "I still resented her for being with
him, I couldn't help it. If I could do it all again . . ."

"What?"

"I'd destroy him."

"How?"

"I'd catch him in the act, take a photo."

There's a glimmer of mischief in her now as I start to reel her in.

"And do what with it?" she asks.

"First, I'd make sure he knew I had it. That'd keep him away from her.
And then I'd start talking to other people at the club, girls who might have
seen or heard something, and let them know I had proof. It might help
them remember things they'd conveniently forgotten."

"And would you go to the Guards then?"

"Yeah, but only when I'd got enough people to back me up."

Melissa smiles.

"You've got it all worked out."

"All I need is an accomplice."

She looks out into the threads of rain that fall like a veil across the lawn
and laughs, shaking her head at the same time.

"Fuck it," she says. "I'm in."

PART THREE

Now

22

I t's never her face that catches my eye, just the slow dance of her hair in the swirling water. I reach out, but she drifts away in the shudder of a wave, and I know that I will lose her again. The dream has no sound, no rhythm of its own, not even the rumble of an underwater scream. Nothing I can do to save her. I want to share my breath with her, rising and falling, faster and faster until the water fills my lungs and floods into every part of me.

"Lou."

I gulp at the air, try to suck the life back into me.

"Lou, baby, it's OK."

I feel the warmth of her breath on my face before I dare open my eyes.

"It's just another nightmare," says Alex as my breathing slows and her fingers brush the sweat from my face. "It's over now."

I grab hold of her hand as if it's the only thing that tethers me to this solid earth. In the fever of this half-sleep, it feels like all I have left.

DAMIEN CORRIGAN DOESN'T LOOK LIKE an abuser. He's a man at ease with himself, sleeves rolled up, arms folded across a branded sweatshirt and a smile that declares, you can trust me. His Instagram is set to private but from what I can see of his profile photo, he's mid to late thirties, older than McQueen was back then. The idea that he could have been at this for a very long time hits me with an unexpected force. And as much as I want Ronan to nail Highfield for decades of institutional negligence, I still don't want to think about what that means on an individual level.

It's not the same as it was then, coaches with unrestricted access to children and reputations that couldn't be challenged. Garda vetting and safeguarding training are legal requirements now, and I know from the research I did into Katie's swimming club that coaches are never supposed to be left alone with students. But there is still so much physical contact, so many opportunities for behavior that might fly under the radar.

The looming threat of Liam Kelly's email, the promise that he will "tell them everything" has been hard to ignore, but still it's taken me all day to work up the courage to search for Corrigan. It's only now, with Alex out at a gig and Katie upstairs, that I feel both isolated and protected enough to let him in. I sit back on the sofa, feet up and a glass of wine to hand, but still my mouth is dry, my chest tight. With every click, the memories surge and grief comes at me in waves of rage and regret, a mourning for the girl I used to be. The sheer bravery and persistence I can hardly remember. I owe it to her, to all of us who were left behind there.

Corrigan has a blog, very Web 1.0, which hasn't been updated since 2015. It's fairly dull: swimming techniques and upcoming competitions from years past. As I scroll through it, I learn he's a Rockdale boy and has also coached at the primary school there. I wonder what they know about him, if they've been complicit in the cover-up at Highfield, or if they've had to have any of their own.

There are no photos, of him or any of the kids he taught. No names I could note, no email address or phone number I could google. But I know how to go deeper, where to find evidence of a younger, more reckless existence. It's knowledge gained from my own paranoia, a consequence of having to cover my tracks all these years.

I copy the URL of Corrigan's website and paste it into the Wayback Machine, an online archive that has been saving internet data for decades. Any previous iterations of the website should be there, even if the information has been deleted from the live site. There are indeed copies of his blog from as far back as 2009 and, with a single click of the mouse, I dive into the depths of Damien Corrigan's past.

The internet in 2009 was a much more innocent and trusting place. A time of social networks instead of social media, when people wanted to connect rather than broadcast. Privacy wasn't so much of a concern back then, nor permanence, the idea that the internet was forever. And it's there, in the side panel of an early blog, that I find Damien Corrigan's email address and mobile number. I copy the email and throw it into Google, the results yielding nothing but a list of old swimming websites and Facebook pages. There are no incriminating details in any of them, yet I still shiver at every photo, hoping each child I see is safe and well.

I'm not expecting much more from his phone number, but still I google and scroll through a similar assortment of results until I come to one that is very different from the rest. It's only when I see the name of the site that I realize how much I wanted to be wrong. But even before I've clicked on the link I can see that this is no innocent mistake. The words "underage boys" jump off the screen and I brace myself for the worst.

Irish-Punters.com is a message board where people discuss and rate sex workers. In this post from April 2008, a user called funboy23 asks where to find underage boys on a weekend away in Cork, and he's added his mobile number so that any suitable candidates can get in touch. It's the same number that's on Corrigan's 2009 website.

I slap the laptop closed and listen to the sound of my rapid, shallow breath. There will be more, I'm sure of it. And whatever I do with this information, I need to be certain it will make a difference. There can be no margin for error, no chance for anyone to dismiss or excuse it.

I finish my wine before I open the laptop again, and I'm glad of it because each post from funboy23 is more grim than the last. His final contribution comes in 2011, a message that fills me with adrenaline and nausea, the dual charge of power and responsibility.

Wanted: Underage boys for playrape. Anywhere in Ireland.

This might not prove anything, but I bet there are private messages that will. And I know just the person to help me find them.

23

R onan's offices are on the top floor of a contemporary, glass-fronted
building overlooking Grand Canal Dock. It's only when I've exited
the lift into the understated retro cool of the vast, modernist foyer
that I appreciate the full extent of his material success. Power & Co. is a
firm started by his father, Charles, but it's Ronan who runs the show now.
As I wait for the man himself, I watch the day fade over the docklands below, dusk capturing the old city mills as their modern counterparts cast a
kaleidoscope of light onto the water.

I see the boy first, the dull gray uniform unadorned by colors and crests.
A woman with brassy hair and slouched shoulders follows behind, deep
in conversation with Ronan, and I finally understand the lack of interest
in the case. Josh Blair is not the private-school boy I'd pictured, the one
who would set two bastions of South Dublin society against each other.
He's just an ordinary kid with no media-friendly angle, one of a multitude
without leverage who fly under the radar. I wouldn't have paid him any
attention if I'd passed him in the street, with his cropped brown hair and
pale, freckled skin.

Ronan walks them to the lift before crossing the polished concrete floor
to greet me.

"Was that . . . ?" I ask.

He grimaces, a deference to his duty of confidentiality, but he doesn't
need to answer. I could feel the defiance in Josh, the head held high despite
it all. Some memories are written on the body. That's what I focus on now,
the struggle for justice, the desperate hope of it. Because if I think about
why Josh is here in the first place, I might fall apart.

Ronan leads me past reception, into a bright and spacious office full
of vintage leather and teak. I sit on one side of a large desk and he takes
position opposite.

"Thanks for doing this, Lou," he says, turning his computer monitor
toward me. Laid bare on the screen in my carefully chosen words is the

stark reality of my Highfield history. "This is fantastic work. It's all so vivid, and intimate at the same time. You're a great writer."

"Thank you."

I don't want to tell Ronan about Damien Corrigan's online exploits, at least not yet. I know from before just how easily evidence can be dismissed by savvy lawyers and legal loopholes and I need to find out exactly how to leverage my discovery first. Joe is an investigative journalist with the *Irish Times*; he'll help me get what I need. And he'll know what I can threaten to publish and how best to do it. I want to come at Highfield with the full force of this and without warning. There's too much at stake now, for me, for Josh and for every other kid who swims at that club.

"There are just a few points I want to clarify," says Ronan.

"Before we get into that, I really do need to know what Shauna's going to say. Will I get to see her testimony?"

"No, not if it doesn't go to trial."

The frustration gusts out of me, and the illusion of control with it.

"She won't talk to me, she won't communicate with me in any way. What you're both asking of me is a big deal, and I could do with a bit of support, or at least some clarification."

"It's not personal," says Ronan. "She just wants to leave the past in the past."

"OK," I say as I struggle to control my anger. "That sounds like a plan . . . let's all leave those *inconvenient* memories behind."

"It's a lot more complicated than that."

"You know what, Ronan? I'm not sure I can really remember any of it anymore. I mean, it was all such a long time ago."

"Come on, Lou."

"No, I think it's a great idea. Let's just forget any of it ever happened."

Ronan folds his hands on his desk, a performance of control that reminds me of the nuns before they went in for the kill.

"I didn't want to do it this way," he says quietly, "but if you do have trouble remembering, there are plenty of things that could help."

"Like what?"

"There's the interview you gave to a certain student newspaper. I still have a copy of that, if you want a refresher."

Joe's article. If Ronan's held on to that, he could have any number of obscure documents from back then. I push back the chair and I'm on my feet before I realize I'm shaking.

"Look," says Ronan, standing up to face me. "Can we start again? Let's have a drink."

He pours two whiskeys and I sit down and drink until the ice clinks against my teeth. Outside, the docks are backlit by a pink and orange sky that does nothing at all to soothe me.

"I know how difficult this must be for Shauna," I say. "Of course I do. I'm just trying to understand why she won't even talk to me."

"She's a very private person these days," he says.

"So private she's prepared to confess everything to the world?"

Ronan winces and I wonder if I've hit a nerve.

"I've told you, it probably won't come to that. Shauna's prepared to sacrifice her privacy to help Josh and, let's face it, all the other kids at risk, but that's the only boundary she's willing to push."

I concede a sigh of weary resignation and Ronan's shoulders relax.

"Look," he says, "it's been hard. For all of us, not just Shauna. I hold my hands up, it took me years to come to terms with it, maybe even to believe it."

"You were very quick to believe the worst of me."

Ronan's eyes don't leave his desk as he takes a deep breath. It's only on the exhale that he looks up.

"I'm very sorry about that, truly."

All I can do is nod.

"I wish I'd had the tools to understand," he says, "but that took a while. It wasn't until a few years after that Shauna told us what he'd done to her and . . . I dunno, I didn't want to believe it. I even blamed her, for being the way she was. But she couldn't move on so the rest of us couldn't pretend it had never happened. It started to eat away at me, you know? Especially after I had kids of my own."

"How old are they?"

"Tommy's fifteen, Milo is ten and Oscar is eight."

"And how's Carol?"

He smiles at the mention of her name, my old classmate, my Highfield nemesis.

"Carol is good, yeah. Actually, she's the one who pushed me to take this case."

"Really? Why?"

He laughs knowingly and I break a smile.

"Carol was Miss Highfield," I say. "Born and bred."

"It's caused a few ructions in her family all right. But Carol's been close to Shauna since we got married."

It shouldn't hurt as much as it does, that Carol has spent all this time with Shauna. But it feels like Carol got it all when she already had more than her fair share.

"I'd like to see Carol," I say. If she has Shauna's ear, maybe she can help me understand.

"OK." Ronan nods slowly. "I'll have to check with her first, but I can't imagine she'd have a problem with that."

"Thanks."

He eyes me as he sits back, drumming his fingers on the arm of his leather chair.

"Lou," he says hesitantly. "You came out of it all OK, didn't you?"

He registers the bewilderment on my face and holds his hands up in apology.

"I mean, after . . . everything. You survived, you made a life for yourself."

"I guess so."

"Well, your testimony will help Josh to do the same."

I'm not sure Ronan knows what that means, if anyone else really understands. Yeah, I survived. If you don't count the insomnia, the night terrors, the unbearable weight of sadness, you could almost say I made it. But I never escaped Highfield. It's still the yardstick by which my life is measured, the distance traveled from it. If I'm a survivor, it's only in relation to those who didn't make it.

"Like I said," says Ronan, "we need to go through some of the details of your statement, but, all going well, I'm going to file proceedings to the High Court on Tuesday, so you'll need to be prepared."

"For what exactly?"

"There's always media interest in my big cases, and once reporters see Highfield on the paperwork . . ."

"They'll be able to see everything?"

"Just the names of the parties and an outline of the claim. But as far as you're concerned, it won't take them long to connect the dots. It could get nasty."

My whole body tenses, the fear rising through my chest. I already know how brutal online strangers can be, those dark nights spent trawling the true-crime message boards and blogs. My past words and actions dissected and distorted and not a thing I could do to answer back.

"What exactly do you mean by 'nasty'?"

He sighs slowly through pursed lips.

"It can be intense. It's just the way social media works these days—it's an outrage machine. Try not to take it personally and switch it off if it gets too much. Honestly, my life has been so much easier since I deleted my Twitter account."

I've never really experienced Twitter as much more than a one-way conversation, sporadic literary criticism tweeted to an audience of a few hundred. The prospect of a public hate campaign fills me with such dread, I'm more determined than ever to put an end to this before it even gets a chance to begin.

"What's the timeline for everything?" I ask.

"Once I issue proceedings, they have eight days to respond and, fingers crossed, that will be with an appropriate offer."

"Do you really think they'll settle?"

"Josh's testimony is pretty damning, and another swimmer can back up some of it. And then there's Shauna, you and six others from over the years."

It could all be wrapped up in a couple of weeks, before Liam Kelly or Shauna or anyone else has a chance to speak out. I'll have to tell Alex and Joe, of course, but there's no point alerting work to something that might never happen. I have eight days from Tuesday to confront Highfield, and that might be the last I ever have to think of that place.

KATIE AND ALEX ARE IN the kitchen chopping vegetables when I get home, thick as thieves with their smiles and glances, and I know I'll be sitting down to dinner with an agenda. I'm happy to give in to almost anything to avoid an argument but I'm not prepared for the news that's delivered with the aubergine parmigiana.

"I've been picked for a swimming gala," says Katie with a nervous smile.

"That's wonderful," I say, and I reach across the table for her hand. "Baby, I'm so proud of you."

"It's next week, on Saturday," she says, and takes a slow breath. "At Highfield, the McQueen Centre."

I hold on to my smile and to Katie's hand, while I try to control my emotions and think of the least bad thing to say.

"It's great news, isn't it?" says Alex. "And we'll both be there, won't we?"

The McQueen Centre, Ireland's first fifty-meter pool. But it's still the same place to me and I haven't set foot in there in over thirty years. I don't know how Alex thinks I'm going to be able to do it, but then again, she doesn't know the full story.

"I . . . eh . . ."

Flashes of cold, limp flesh, rough hands on damp skin and the rolling echo of the one word that screams inside my head: *No*.

"Yes," I say, "of course."

And then I let go of Katie's hand, mumble an excuse and walk slowly out of the extension to the understairs loo and vomit as quietly as I can.

24

As September comes to a close, we're granted one day of glorious back-to-school weather and the lecture halls are abandoned in favor of a sun-soaked patch of grass. Below my office window, Fellows' Square is littered with flesh, skirts and sleeves hitched up, shirts and blouses unbuttoned as the students make the most of this last flush of heat. The pageantry of yearning is on display, bare arms brushing off each other, laughter rippling across shoulders that are angled just a little closer together than usual. Two teenage girls stretch out on the grass, one propped up on an elbow leaning over the other, an arm draped across her partner's waist. And barely an eyelid batted across the lawn. It's what we dreamed of, and I'm happy for them, that love and longing are allowed to be, but I can't help a pang of grievance for those who came before, the ones who never stood a chance.

I slip out after my last class and I'm on the bus before the afternoon traffic has started to congeal. I get off a stop early and make my way to Joe's, a pretty terraced house overlooking a large green. Joe makes tea while I exchange pleasantries with his wife, Naomi, and their young son, Danny, and then he ushers me into the TV room at the front of the house.

"Is everything OK?" he asks before I've even had a chance to sit down. He knows; he always does. "It's not Katie, is it?"

"No, it's nothing like that," I say as I sit beside him on the sofa. "It's Highfield."

"What have they done now?"

I sip my tea to steady my nerves.

"Ronan Power's suing them on behalf of a fourteen-year-old boy who's been abused by one of the swimming coaches."

"Jesus Christ. Not again." Joe takes a deep breath and runs his hand through his graying hair.

"And he wants me to testify," I say.

"Shit," says Joe. "Are you OK with that?"

"Yes and no," I say. "I don't really have a choice, so I'm just getting on with it. You know me."

"Yeah, I do," he says, reaching out a hand to touch mine. "That's why I worry about you."

I link my fingers through his and it's a relief to let the mask slip, to feel my eyes fill with tears of trepidation.

"There's more, Joe. I haven't told Ronan, but I found some stuff online from years ago. You know the internet archive?"

"Yeah."

"I found the coach, Damien Corrigan, on a message board—Irish -Punters.com."

"Oh fuck, this doesn't sound good."

"No, it's not. He was looking for underage boys to," I air quote, "'playrape.'"

Joe lets out a long exhale.

"That's horrendous, but . . . isn't this good news for the case?"

"Well, it's not proof of anything. But I was thinking, there must be private messages as well." I look at Joe, and he's already shaking his head in protest. "Would you be able to access them?"

"Oh god, Lou." He sighs heavily. "Even if I could, what would you do with them?"

"I want to go directly to Highfield," I say. "I want to look the principal in the eye and ask her if she can live with this. And then I'm going to give her a very short window of time to choose between defending him and offering a settlement."

Joe picks up his mug with a look of such concentration I know he's already figuring it out and, once again, I'm grateful to have him on my side.

"It couldn't be linked to me in any way. Or you."

"I know, but . . ."

"I'll see what I can do. There's a good chance, given the . . . the nature of the site, that the owners won't want the Guards sniffing around. So they might give up those messages rather than risk a Garda investigation. But I couldn't do it myself, I'd have to call in a favor, so I'm not promising anything, OK?"

"Yeah, of course."

We take respite in our tea, but I can tell that Joe's still planning and plotting like I am.

"Would you be prepared to leak it?" he asks. "I mean, if you could find someone to do it?"

"If I did, could it prejudice the trial?"

"No," says Joe with a smile. "Those restrictions are only in place to prevent a jury being prejudiced. If this does go to court, it'll be tried by judge alone. They're supposed to be above being swayed by what they read in the press, but you'd be hard pressed to ignore something like this."

I can see it in Joe's eyes, that he wants this as much as I do. A chance to claim the retribution that was always denied us.

"You know," he says, "even if Highfield didn't back down, I'd say bringing this up with them in advance of a trial could work in your favor."

"So you're saying we've finally got them?"

"Oh Jesus." He laughs and holds up his hands. "Never write off those slippery fuckers. But yeah, from what you've told me, I'd be hopeful. What does Alex think?"

Alex. I'd planned on telling her this evening.

"Uh . . . she had to go to London for the weekend. Work stuff."

"You haven't told her?" says Joe. "Lou, you have to tell her. When is Ronan issuing proceedings?"

"Not until Tuesday. I'll talk to her as soon as she gets back on Monday."

Joe sighs. "I understand how hard this must be for you, I really do. But you're both going to have to talk to Katie before it becomes public knowledge, you know that?"

"I know, I know." I put my head in my hands. "There just seems to be so much going on at the moment."

"The gala?"

"You heard about that?"

"Yeah. Are you concerned about her going to Highfield?"

I want to scream at the thought, but the truth is, I'm more worried about me. And Katie will be gutted if I don't let her go.

"Yeah, of course I am. I won't be able to take my eyes off her the whole time she's there. But she's excited about it, so what can I do?"

I grimace and Joe holds out his arms.

"C'mere," he says, and I lean into the gentle warmth of him. I can only hope he's right, that Highfield really could capitulate this time. Because I'm not sure how much more of this I can take.

I NEVER PLANNED TO SET foot in Northwood Park's swimming complex, but here I am, sneaking in the side door, standing behind a pillar as I try to spot my daughter in the pool. I've braced myself for the caustic assault of chlorine, the dizzying recoil of voices. And still the sounds and smells grab me by the throat. I shouldn't be here, I know that. But I couldn't stay away.

In front of me, a balding man booms orders to the older swimmers who slice their way through the water at his feet. I spot Katie's yellow cap across the pool and, above her, a female coach shouting support, and the tension seeps out of me.

I wait out the rest of the session in the car and return to the pool as the swimmers are leaving. I wave to Katie, but she turns away and carries on to the changing rooms. It's the coach I want to talk to anyway. Una Clayton, she says as she introduces herself, and tells me how excited she is about Katie's progress. My daughter has all the attributes that will take her far, the height and strength she gets from her dad's side of the family, and a dogged tenacity I can't say has ever done me too many favors. Still, it's the reassurance I needed, and I leave the pool happy that Katie is in good hands.

I wait in the car, but when Katie comes out she walks straight past me. I roll down the window and shout her name and it's only when she doesn't turn around that I realize she's ignoring me. I get out of the car and run after her.

"Look, Katie, I'm sorry," I say. "I just had to be sure."

Her wet hair flies through the air as she swings round and confronts me with desperate eyes.

"Did you tell her?" she asks.

"What?"

"Coach Clayton, did you tell her?"

"No," I say. "I didn't say anything. I just asked how you were getting on."

Her nostrils flare with the force of her breath.

"I swear, Katie."

"I don't want anyone to know."

"Well, that makes two of us."

Katie searches my face for any evidence to the contrary.

"I'm sorry, OK?" I say. "I won't interfere again."

She stands her ground for a moment before her shoulders fall and she sighs quietly.

"OK," she says, with such a look of Tina at that age I can't bear it.

"Come on, let's go home," I say as I put my hand on her arm and, for once, she doesn't flinch.

As I drive, I wonder just how long we can really keep my past out of Katie's present. She has her dad's surname and I use Alex's for anything school-related, but all it will take is one parent or teacher with a long memory to connect the dots, especially if she keeps swimming. Katie's mental health is so fragile as it is, I don't know how she'd cope with any backlash. I want to give her the independence to live her own life, make her own mistakes, and I know she wants that too. It's why I held my tongue about the photos on her phone when all I wanted was to scream the dangers at her. But I know Alex is right, that I'd lose her trust completely, and we've always taught her to keep safe online. No, it's not Katie that's the problem, it's me. And once news of the case breaks, I might not be able to protect her at all.

25

I ignore the first two rings of the doorbell and it's only the third that gets me out of bed, fumbling into a bathrobe as I hobble down the stairs. Beyond the glare of the early-morning light stands a man who looks too young for his graying temples, his face fixed with the sort of bullish grin that tells me he is not expecting to be welcome here.

"Louise Manson?"

"And you are?"

He holds out his hand. "Mick Craddock, I'm a journalist with the *Evening Express*."

It's a tabloid rag and I wouldn't wipe my arse with it. I pull my bathrobe tight around me as I struggle to work out what's going on.

"Look, Louise," he says, withdrawing his hand, "I'll get straight to it. I'm interested in talking to you about Ronan Power's action against Highfield Manor. We'd love to get some insight from you into the story. For what it's worth, I think you were let down badly before and it would be great to help, you know, make amends for that."

Adrenaline whips through me as I look around the hall for Katie, before stepping onto the porch and pulling the door behind me. I knew this might happen, but I wasn't expecting it yet and I can't think of any response that won't implicate me, one way or another.

"I'm not interested," I say.

"I won't take up much of your time," he says. "I'm just looking for a few quotes. I mean, you must have some opinion on this horrendous situation."

"I said no. Now you need to leave."

He takes a step back and then stops.

"I'm not going to lie to you, Louise, the press will not go easy on you if you don't get out there and have your say first. Highfield, Shauna Power and all the others, they'll be telling their stories and if you don't, someone else will tell it for you."

"What's Shauna said?"

It's out before I can stop it, before I've had a chance to wake up my brain. Craddock's crooked smile is back and I know I've already said too much.

"I understand you and Shauna are both supporting this action," he says. "It must have taken a lot of courage for you to get back in the room with her."

"No, that's not . . ." I say, but I have to stop before I dig an even deeper hole. "I have nothing more to say."

I stumble back into the hall and close the door, and then rest my head against it until I can breathe. It's happening again, but this time, I have too much to lose. I can't let the press or the Powers or anyone else speak for me. I need to take back control of my story.

AFTER MY ENCOUNTER WITH MICK Craddock, I stop answering calls from unknown numbers. It's Monday before anyone leaves a message, a Peter Fanning, the head coach at Northwood Park swimming club. He wants me to drop in for a chat after Katie's training this afternoon. My mind races through the possibilities but I have to believe he just wants to talk about my brilliant daughter's progress.

I arrive at Northwood ten minutes before the end of training and watch the swimmers from behind a pillar in the stands. I see Katie straight away, her body powering through the water as if she's been doing it all her life. I marvel at the rhythm of her stroke, the flex of her legs, and it gives me such hope that she will finally find her way in the world.

I let Katie leave with her teammates before I re-enter the pool complex and find Coach Fanning in the office, and I'm unnerved to realize he's better-looking than he seemed from a distance.

"Thanks for coming in, Louise," he says, pointing to a chair on the other side of his desk.

"Oh, it's no problem," I say as I sit down. "We're thrilled at how well Katie's doing and I can't believe it's taken us this long to find out what a great swimmer she is. We should have known, really. Her aunt was a swimmer too, and she has the height and the broad shoulders and all of that."

I don't know why I'm so nervous. Maybe it's the solemn calm in Coach Fanning's face, as if he is simply biding his time.

"She's certainly doing very well," he says, "but there's something else I want to talk to you about. It's a fairly delicate matter, actually."

"Look, Coach Fanning . . ."

"It's Peter."

"Peter . . . Katie has suffered a lot from anxiety, and I'm not going to lie, it's been really tough for her. But this gala at Highfield is the first thing she's been excited about in ages and it's really helped her, so whatever the problem is, please let me try and find a solution."

Peter's face remains impassive as he waits for me to finish.

"The problem isn't Katie," he says. "It's you."

"What?"

"Your Highfield connection," he says, and I feel the life drain out of me.

"How do you know about that?" My voice is barely audible.

"There was a piece in the *Evening Express* today about some new legal action. It wasn't hard to work it out."

I stare at the cables that snake across the desk. I didn't expect this so soon, at least not before Ronan made it all public.

"That's got nothing to do with me," I say.

"It's just, we run a clean club here," he says, "and we can't take the risk of contamination."

"Contamination," I repeat.

"What I mean is, we've worked very hard to put safeguards in place here. We want parents to trust that this is a protected environment for their kids. I'm sure you can appreciate that."

He waits for me to respond, but there is only the rasp of my breath.

"If Katie swims at Highfield on Saturday," he continues, "and the press get wind of it—and they will—we are only inviting scandal here. I'll have to answer to journalists, and they'll come after you and Katie too. Do you understand what I'm saying?"

I laugh, despite myself. The very protections I thought I could force on to Highfield have been turned against me and I'm not sure I have anything left to lose.

"So let me get this straight, you're punishing my daughter because I was a victim of abuse."

"Come on, Louise," he says, "you know it's not that simple. I want to protect Katie, but I also need to protect everyone else at the club. Let's put this one gala aside and I promise Katie will swim at the next one."

"This gala, the next gala, what's the difference?"

He sighs, as if he had anticipated my "difficult" persona.

"Look, I'm sure there's some gutter journalist out there who can make a story out of Katie being at some random competition, but Louise Manson's daughter swimming at the McQueen Centre when you've just been linked to a case against it? That's an invitation to drag up the past and smear you and Katie and Northwood with it."

I know he's right, and it's the easy option for me. But I'm still the one who's going to have to explain it to Katie.

"I'll talk to her," I say.

What I really mean is Alex will talk while I smile apologetically and try to reassure Katie of Coach Fanning's discretion. And when she cries and refuses to look at me, a small part of me will blame her for wanting to swim in the first place.

What Alex won't understand is the lawsuit I never mentioned. Right now, she's on a plane home from London and I need to get to her as soon as she lands. If she hears it from someone else, I'm not sure how I'll salvage the situation.

26

There's an eerie chill in the shifting shadows as I leave Northwood Park and I wonder if I'll ever get to exit a swimming pool unscathed. Katie has already left with the other swimmers so I send her a quick text to let her know my plans, and then head off for the airport and pray I'll make it in time. I'm not even halfway there when my phone vibrates, and I pick it up at a red light to see what Katie has said. It's not Katie, it's Alex. She took an earlier flight and she's home already. She wants to talk.

The dread builds all the way back, and not even the raw intimacy of Hak Baker's "Like It or Lump It" on the car stereo can help carry the weight of it. When I get into the house, it's the silence I hear first. There's no music, no TV sounds or noise of any sort as I close the front door behind me. There's a light on in the extension and I push through the double doors to find Alex sitting at the kitchen island smoking a cigarette, something I haven't seen her do in the eight years we've lived together.

"Why did you let me find out like this?" she asks without looking at me.

"I'm sorry." I put my keys on the island and sit next to her. "I didn't know . . ."

"Do you know what?" she says as she swings around to face me. "I don't believe you."

Black streaks of mascara underline the velvet-blue darkness in her eyes.

"I mean, I knew about the lawsuit," I say. "I just didn't know the article was coming out today."

Her eyes harden as the words leave my mouth.

"So all this time, you were with *her*?"

"No," I say. "What do you mean?"

Alex picks up her phone and starts to read. "'Shauna Power and Louise Manson are back together. The girls at the center of the Highfield affair are all grown up now and secretly plotting to take down Highfield Manor once and for all.' What the fuck, Lou?"

"It's not like that at all," I say. "I haven't even seen Shauna. The only person I've spoken to is Ronan."

"Then what is all this shit about?"

"I don't know, it's the *Evening Express*."

"Jesus, Lou, you're going to have to do a lot better than that."

As I scramble for the right words, I'm distracted by the flaccid roll of burning ash that hangs precariously from Alex's cigarette. I slide a cup across the quartz worktop to catch it.

"Oh my god," shrieks Alex. "You care more about the fucking house than you do about me."

I think of Katie upstairs and point at the ceiling. "Can you keep your voice down?"

Alex shuts her eyes tight as tears escape them.

"Did you really just say that?"

"I'm not going to apologize for caring about my daughter."

"Oh, she's *your* daughter now?" Alex laughs through her tears. "So how come you don't even know she's not here?"

"What? Where is she?"

"She's gone to the cinema with friends."

"Why didn't she tell me?"

"Because you'd make such a big deal of it, and she hates that. So she told me—you know, her other mother?"

I should be delighted that Katie has finally made friends, ventured out into the world, and for a moment all I want is to celebrate with my wife. Maybe if I made the first move, we could put this argument to bed and have an honest conversation about the future. Maybe I could finally tell her everything. But it's the way she narrows her eyes that stops me, the accusation in the tilt of her head, and I just can't help myself.

"She only told you because she knew you'd give her an easy ride. I mean, do you even know who these friends are?"

It's worth it for just a split second, that moment of victory as I watch the betrayal darken her face, until I want to rescue her from the cruelty of it.

"Fuck you," she says.

And then she gathers her dignity, pushes past me and out the double doors, and I'm left with an overwhelming sense of guilt I can't share with anyone.

ALONE IN THE KITCHEN, I finally have the chance to see the full damage of the *Evening Express* piece. It really is the worst of the Irish tabloids, page after page of hack opinion dressed up as news, all designed to rile and feed the hate-reader within. The single mothers *living it up* on our taxes, the criminals *demanding* legal aid.

I'm still not prepared for what I find when I click into the website. Spread across the home page is a large, grainy photo of me on the doorstep in my bathrobe, my Trinity staff picture inset in a corner and the headline *Highfield Affair: Revelation or Revenge?*

I hold my breath as I skim the story, the lack of evidence for a criminal prosecution, the insinuation that we all have an axe to grind. And then a detailed summary of what happened back then, finishing with the line, "Louise Manson has some nerve jumping on the bandwagon after all these years. Let's hope she has some proof this time."

The visceral anger, for me, for Josh, quickly turns to fear, and I open Twitter to measure the fallout. It takes a second to grasp the level of activity along the bottom of the app, scores of notifications, dozens of direct messages. No matter how much I've dreamed of an academic paper going viral, there's no chance that's what's going on here. I expected comment but not conversation, and I can barely bring myself to look at it.

I feel nauseous as I click through the tweets, most of them asking variations of the question: *what has she done now?* As if this new case might be able to prove what they'd always suspected, that I was the real villain all along.

I see the words "hero," "bravery," "whistleblower," but they won't be enough to save me or my sanity. It's happening again and there's no way to close the door on it. This case is going to follow me everywhere I go.

IN THE MORNING, THERE'S NOTHING but a stinging silence in the house, and I slink out the door to work before Katie is even out of bed. As soon as I pass through Trinity's front arch, I feel naked, as if everyone knows what I've done. Until yesterday, I'd been shrouded by the passage of time, by the fact that most students and staff here are too young to remember. But now the *Evening Express* has unleashed the story on a new generation hungry for true crime, and they might as well have inked it across my face. As I walk the cobblestones to the Arts Block, I imagine all eyes are on me, watching me swipe alerts from Facebook and Instagram, even the LinkedIn account I haven't looked at in years. When a call flashes across the screen, I almost shut it down on autopilot, until I see that it's Joe.

"Bingo," he says.

"You got into Corrigan's account?"

"Oh yes," he says. "Indeed."

Hundreds of private messages, some with times, dates and transactions, others simply threatening or lewd. Evidence of cruelty and coercion, proof of abuse.

"I'll drop it all over tonight," says Joe, "and we might go through it together. But be warned, it's pretty sickening."

It's what I wanted and didn't want, a chronicle of victims. And now I owe it to all of them to expose this fucker.

ONCE I'M IN THE OFFICE, it doesn't take long before I'm summoned by Professor Judy Wilson, head of the Department of English.

"All I want to know," she says, hands folded on her desk as I sit rigid opposite her, "is that this won't have any adverse effect on the department."

I want to come clean, but there's a warning in her dispassionate tone.

"Absolutely not," I say. "Ronan Power has assured me it will all be over by next week."

"Because with the Irish Literature Festival coming up . . ."

"Yeah, of course."

"And don't get me wrong, that boy has my utmost sympathy, but I've worked so hard to bring the festival here in the first place . . ."

"Oh, I know."

". . . and somehow I've ended up fielding calls about a court case that has nothing to do with any of it."

"Look, I'm sorry about all of that, but they'll have moved on to something else by next week."

"So one week of"—she holds up her phone—"this? And that's the end of it?"

"Yes. I promise."

"OK. I think we can live with that."

"Thanks, Judy. I really do appreciate your support."

I don't mention I've already seen her tagged, along with the School of English, in a tweet demanding my dismissal. That I've been called a liar, a fantasist, a frigid cunt, that my sexuality, my failed marriage, even my daughter, have been fair game. And I know that's what will kill Alex too, not so much the truth I did suppress, but the lies I can't.

27

The social media storm peaks on Tuesday when Ronan issues proceedings and then wanes overnight with no further information to sustain it. I bluster my way through the reprieve with polite chit-chat at work and extra care and attention at home. Still, we all have an eye on the ticking time-bomb, watching to see if it will be detonated or defused. Each hour carries itself with a level of suspense that is all too familiar, a trauma I never dreamed I'd have to relive. Every phone call, every email, every passing gaze in the street has the potential to be the one that finally exposes me. And behind it all is the fear of Shauna's next move, of the testimony that could destroy me.

CAROL'S CHOSEN A SMALL CITY-CENTER brasserie with the sort of unassuming grown-up chic that always has a price. She's there when I arrive, waving over from the low-lit seclusion of a corner booth. She looks great, dark curls soft around her shoulders, skin painted with a healthy glow. But despite the obvious maintenance, the changes in her face are evident—the creases around her eyes, the slight sag of her jaw. Time comes for us all regardless.

It's only in the faces of my teenage peers that I see the reflection of my own mortality. It's that moment before my eyes acclimatize, when I see the middle-aged woman as the world sees her. Before she morphs back into Carol, once eighteen, forever her unique self. I have few day-to-day markers of my advancing age, with my university job and my younger wife. And yet, I have so much life lived already, so many reminders packed away in the past.

"It's good to see you," says Carol.

"You too."

Her smile is so sincere I can almost believe in those cheekbones.

"And thanks," I say, "for this."

"Oh, I would have done it sooner, if I'd known you wanted to. I've thought about you a lot over the years."

"Really?"

"Yes, of course. I mean, obviously none of us could forget what happened, but it was only when I got close to Shauna . . ."

She searches for the right words and I hold my breath coiled in my chest.

"I know how much you meant to her."

The pain inside tightens until it is too much to bear and tears blur my eyes.

"I'm sorry," I say, grabbing a linen napkin.

"It's OK," she says. "This is bound to drag up old feelings."

I dab under my eyes while Carol smiles sympathetically.

"Will we order?" she asks.

I look at the menu of shaved asparagus and scallop ceviche as ambient jazz plays in the background. Carol orders wine and I slide my afternoon research over to tomorrow's schedule. By the second glass, I'm relaxed, and I've heard enough about her kids and my forgotten Highfield classmates. I want to get down to business.

"How is Shauna?"

"She's . . . OK."

"Ronan didn't say much. Is she married? Kids?"

"No kids, but she did marry." Carol looks up from her baked celeriac. "Didn't last."

"Oh," I say more enthusiastically than I intended. "I didn't know. That's awful."

"It was. He was a bit of a fucker in the end."

I'm relieved to hear the "he" part of it. For some reason, that doesn't feel as much of a betrayal.

"I don't think she ever got over you."

"What?" The walls close in as I stare at Carol and try to work out if this is a joke.

"Like I said, we've been close for the last ten years or so."

"But . . ."

The words don't come. I wouldn't know what to do with them anyway.

"You don't mind that she told me, do you?" asks Carol.

"Sorry, Carol. Shauna told you what exactly?"

"That you were in love."

Now the tears come for real and there's not a thing I can do to stop them. The denial, the betrayal, all the pent-up emotions flow out of me, down my cheeks and onto my Jerusalem artichoke. Carol hands me her napkin and waves for another bottle. I take my time to let it all out, breathe deeply and wipe my face. Then I finish my wine before I attempt any further conversation.

"Why are you telling me this?" I ask.

"Because I think you deserve to know."

Carol always did speak her mind, I'll give her that.

"Thank you." I smile my appreciation as the wine arrives and the waiter refills our glasses. "But you know I'm married, right? It's not like we can do anything about it."

"Oh god, I'm not suggesting that. I know you're married to . . ."

"Alex."

"Yeah, Alex. No, I'm not trying to break up your marriage, Jesus." She laughs. "I just thought you should know. And I don't suppose you'll hear it from her. She's a very private person now."

"Yeah, Ronan said. Is that all I'm going to get?"

"It's the truth."

"And what happened to make her so . . . private?"

"Oh Lou, what a question," says Carol. "You know most of it. It took her years to get past it. And then when things didn't work out with Nigel . . ."

Nigel, I think. *She married a Nigel?*

". . . she stopped seeing people."

"Except you?"

"And Ronan of course. Other people didn't want to hear what she had to say. There's such a culture of silence in that family, you wouldn't believe the things they've swept under the carpet."

"Alcoholism, affairs?"

"Yeah," says Carol, leaning toward me. "And that was just the start. After everything, their parents acted like it had never happened. None of them were allowed to talk about it and it was years before Ronan understood the full extent of it."

I can see now that even Carol's still dealing with the fallout.

"It must have been hard for you," I say, "to turn your back on Highfield."

"Meh," she says with the flick of a wrist. "I only have boys, I didn't have that dilemma."

"But your family . . ."

Carol puts down her fork and looks me in the eye.

"I am not my family."

I'm so shocked at the force of her reply I don't know what to say.

"I think I owe you an apology," she says, and then laughs. "Probably several. Jesus."

She takes a deep breath.

"Do you remember my grandmother's earrings? The ones I tried to blame you for stealing?"

"Yes."

"My parents wanted me to make a statement to the Guards after, you know . . . that night. They said that Sister Shannon saw you at my locker the day they went missing. That you must have stolen them and then returned them to my bag a few days later."

"Oh my god."

"Yeah. They wanted me to say under oath that I definitely left them in my locker and I was certain they'd been stolen. That was a turning point for me. I liked you, believe it or not, and when I saw that the headmistress herself was prepared to perjure herself against you, well, I started seeing things very differently."

Of all the revelations I'd anticipated today, Carol Sheridan standing up for me against Highfield was not on the list. I reach across the table and take her hand.

"Thank you," I say. "I had no idea."

She smiles and then changes the subject. We chat about old classmates, Stephanie and Aisling, and Melissa, a household name now that she presents a Saturday-night talent show on ITV. She's also well known for a string of failed celebrity relationships and the work on her face she swears she hasn't had done.

"Oh my god, did you read the story about the bee sting?" asks Carol. "On her lips!"

I laugh, not because it's especially funny but because this is the Carol I remember, purveyor of scandal and slander dressed up as camaraderie.

"And that," she air quotes, "'wardrobe malfunction' she had at the BAF-TAs? Trust me, nobody was tuning in to see a forty-six-year-old nipple."

"It was a good nipple though, I'll give her that."

Carol laughs and then stops, wide-eyed.

"Did you and her ever . . . you know?"

"Jesus, no." I grimace and shake my head. "I only had eyes for Shauna."

"So it really was true love?"

"Yeah, I think it was." My smile fades. "Until . . ."

Carol's eyes flick evasively to her dessert and I grab my chance to ask the one question that's on my mind, the reason I'm here in the first place.

"Carol, do you know what Shauna's written in her testimony?"

I freeze in anticipation as she looks at me curiously.

"You know you have absolutely nothing to worry about, right? She's doing this for you as much as for Ronan or his client."

"I don't understand."

"Everything that happened, it was because you were trying to tell the truth and nobody would listen. Shauna wants to exonerate you once and for all. She wants redemption."

Her words fill me with joy and sadness at the same time, but I still don't understand. If Shauna wants to absolve me, the last thing she can do is tell the truth.

28

Just as I'll always remember the icy mist that shrouded Highfield on that night, I won't forget the death rattle of the rain that flings itself onto my office window this morning. I take in the full force of the attack when Ronan calls to tell me it's not going to be OK.

"Are you alone?" he asks.

"Yes."

"Look," he says, "I'm sorry."

The bare arms of the beech tree outside my window swing recklessly in the wind.

"I'll go through everything, so don't panic," he says, though I can hear the strain in his voice. "Highfield are going to defend the claim . . ."

"Oh god."

". . . so it looks like we're going to have to go to court."

The rain slams against the window and my heart tightens into a hard knot.

"But you said they had eight days. It's only been three."

I'd been planning a trip to Highfield first thing on Monday. I wanted to spend the weekend perfecting my pitch.

"I said they had to respond *within* eight days. They've clearly anticipated this and must have already planned to respond as aggressively as possible."

"No," I say. "I can't do it."

"Lou, I know this is a shock, but I want you to take some time to think about it. Your testimony will make all the difference for Josh, especially when it is corroborated by Shauna."

I realize with a jolt that this means I will get to see her and it fills me with equal parts thrill and terror.

"Will I get to discuss that beforehand? With Shauna?"

"No, sorry. But I will be able to advise you."

I'm enclosed on so many sides I can't see a way forward.

"I don't know, Ronan. There's so much at stake."

"You know that's what they're relying on? That Josh or any of our witnesses will crumble at the thought of taking the stand."

I see *him* now, a smirk curled across that arrogant mustache, so confident that none of us had that sort of courage.

"How can they do this?" I say. "I mean, I could understand if it was still the nuns in charge, but surely there are parents on the board of management now?"

"It's a political move, a calculated one by their legal team, I'm sure. Unfortunately, we have no material proof of any of the abuse."

There was proof once, the photo that could have saved us all. But I never found out what happened to that.

"All we have is sworn testimony and psychological reports," continues Ronan. "I really did think that would be enough to make them go quietly, but they've come out all guns blazing. They know our case could open the door for a long line of victims and they're sending out the message that they will fight anyone who takes them on. And sadly, that means most victims won't even try."

I want to be able to save Josh and all the other kids who still need to be saved, no matter what's at stake. But I need to find the courage that was stolen from me all those years ago. And if I don't do it now, I'll spend the rest of my life living in the shadow of Maurice McQueen.

THE LEADEN BEAT OF THE RAIN FILLS MY office, drowning out thoughts of the deluge that awaits, at home, in my phone. There will be no escape from any of it. My name, my involvement, my testimony, all fair game now. Ronan's warned me to expect the worst, that Highfield's defense team will tell the press anything they think might smear our story. That theirs is a media campaign as much as a legal one.

Before I talk to Alex or Katie or anyone here, there is someone I need to confront. I open the email from Liam Kelly and read the line that could end me: *If you testify, I'll tell them everything.*

He'll know soon enough that I've given a statement, that I'll be called as a witness now. My mind races through the list of possible culprits and I wonder if Damien Corrigan himself would risk it. And I think of McQueen and his supporters, that dark cloud that followed me for so many years after. I need to solicit more information, anything that could bring me closer to Liam and his motive.

Dear Liam,

You've probably heard that Highfield are going to defend the case and I will be compelled to testify. Please explain what you want from me.
Lou

I press send and close my laptop. And then I sit with the furious rhythm of the rain until I've summoned the nerve to step outside my office.

JUDY IS FIRST ON THE scene, powering down the corridor as I leave my second-year tutorial.

"Do you have a minute, Lou?"

We walk in strained silence to her office, neither of us pretending this is anything other than the obvious.

"I've just had a journalist call me on my personal mobile," she says as we take position on opposing sides of her desk. "A Mick Craddock. Do you know him?"

"Ah, yes. Sorry about that." I've ignored his calls all morning.

"And I've only looked at a fraction of the comments on Twitter, but Jesus Christ, Lou, you could have said something."

Attention whores, lying cunts, dried-up old dykes. Is that what she wanted me to say?

"Look, I'm sorry, Judy. I just found out myself."

It's only been a couple of hours but already I've seen death and rape threats, the deconstruction of my looks, my writing and my sanity. I should know better than to read them and you'd think I'd be mature enough not to let the words fester, but they hold a power greater than their intentions. It's not the most vicious that cut the deepest, it's phrases like "talentless hack" and "fame-hungry failure" alongside quotes from my publications and, worst of all, the insinuation that I was the real predator all along: *She failed to destroy one man's reputation so now she's going after another? Did he turn her down too?*

It's the internet sleuths who never bought my story first time around, the true-crime junkies with their alternative facts dressed up as critical thinking. And a new generation who still think a powerful man's career is worth more than his victim's life.

"Lou, I don't think you are fully aware of the seriousness of this situation."

"What do you mean?"

"I mean . . ." She sighs. "You're going to have to think about taking time off while all of this is ongoing."

I'm sure this isn't a disciplinary matter, but I know what a tough opponent Judy is and I just don't have the energy.

"So you're suspending me?"

"Of course not. But I am worried about you and, I'm not going to lie, I'm worried about the effect on the department too. I'll recommend you for some extra annual leave, just until this blows over."

I don't bother to reply. I just get up and leave her office, heavy with the weight of yet another situation I'll have to explain to Alex. This trial is already infecting my home, my work and my sanity. I still have the ammunition to put a stop to it, but I can no longer leave anything to chance. I'm going to need some help.

THIS CONVERSATION IS VERY DIFFERENT to the last. Mick Craddock's voice gushes down the phone, his excitement palpable.

"So you're telling me your source can confirm that Damien Corrigan has had sex with underage boys?"

"I have evidence that he has solicited and paid for it, yes."

The rain clips the side of my face as I shelter in the archway of the campanile in Trinity's front square.

"Can you share this evidence with me?"

"You publish the allegation on Monday and I will share everything I have with you if Highfield don't settle by close of business on Tuesday."

Craddock's laughter rumbles through the phone like a gust of wind.

"I like your style," he says. "But how do I know you're telling the truth if you won't show me what you've got?"

"If you don't want it, there are plenty of tabloids who do."

While I'm sure this is true, I don't know how many of them would take it on without more substantial proof. But Craddock, I already know he has a casual relationship with the truth.

"Now, I didn't say that," he says. "But you're asking me to publish a serious allegation and I have no way of knowing if it's true or not."

"You didn't seem too worried about facts when you wrote about me last week. I haven't seen Shauna Power in thirty years yet you had us in a room together conspiring against Highfield."

There's a pause and I know I'm in with a chance. It's all about margins of probability to him and I just need to tip the balance in my favor.

"Look," I say, "the allegations are already out there in sworn testimony so you're not saying anything new. And Corrigan hasn't been proven innocent. He's not going to open up that can of worms."

"It's not Corrigan I'm worried about."

"I doubt Highfield care too much for him either. I wouldn't be surprised if he's quietly let go once our case is over. It's not him they're defending, it's their own reputation, going back decades. They're doing this to prevent any more court cases, so they're not going to go looking for one. Especially one they know they can't win."

Students sprint across the cobblestones, laughing as they try to outrun the rain.

"You're a persuasive woman, Louise," he says. "You've got yourself a deal. On one condition."

"What's that?"

"If they do settle, then you and I will have a chat about how you came across this information. You know, just point me in the right direction and I'll do my own investigating. That way, it won't link directly back to you."

I was hoping he'd say that.

Alex is home before me, eyes red and swollen as she sits at the kitchen table with her hands wrapped around a coffee cup. I called her earlier, took her through the worst of it, and I wasn't expecting to find her in this sort of distress.

"What's wrong?"

I sit down and put my hand on her arm, but she clings to the cup.

"It's everything, Lou. It's too much. If it was just you and me . . . but Katie . . ."

"What's happened to Katie?" I ask as panic rips through me.

Since the Highfield gala fiasco, Katie has lived in her room, leaving only to go to school. She's quit swimming, won't talk about it and the whole house seems to simmer with silent resentment.

"The same as what's happened to all of us. Some prick found her Instagram and was sending her abuse until she got up the nerve to show me."

The guilt weighs on me, heavy and cold as wet clothes.

"Oh fuck," I say, putting both hands to my face. "Was it bad?"

"It was mostly about you. You know . . . 'liar,' 'devil's spawn,' and other incoherent shite like that. I deleted it and blocked him straight away."

"Why didn't Katie do that?"

"Because she was scared. She's fourteen, Lou. She shouldn't be dealing with any of this in the first place."

"I know, I know, I'm sorry. I'll set her account to private."

"Yeah, I've already done that. Mine too. I've locked down every account I can think of and I've updated her parental-control app."

I let out a sigh of relief, that at least no one will get to them that way.

"But I noticed something else," says Alex. "Some boy commenting on all her photos. Did you see that?"

"No," I say anxiously. "I'm not allowed to follow her. I mean, I look now and again, but I don't remember anything in particular. What was he saying?"

"Nothing more than the rest of them, you know, how beautiful and hot she looked. It's just that he was on every post I looked at and she'd liked all his comments. I probably wouldn't think anything of it except for . . ."

"The photos? Oh Jesus." I put my elbows on the table, head in my hands. "I'll have a word with her."

"Are you sure that's wise?" asks Alex.

"I won't mention them directly, but I need her to know I'm here for her. Not just because of that, but with everything else going on . . ."

My voice cracks and the tears flow until Alex can't help but wrap her arms around me and I bury my face in the familiar warmth of her.

"We'll get through it," she says. "She'll be OK."

It's only when I start up the stairs to Katie that I remember I never mentioned work, the annual leave that has already begun. I can't put Alex through any more today; I'll do it tomorrow.

TAYLOR SWIFT SETS THE TONE upstairs, the dark, sultry vocal of "Don't Blame Me," and I'm hoping it will have Katie in a receptive mood. I knock on her bedroom door and when there's no reply I push it open and she sits bolt upright on the bed.

"Can I come in?"

She shrugs and stops the music and, in the stark silence, I see my little girl so vulnerable and exposed. I say nothing about the dirty plates on her desk, the row of cups and glasses on the windowsill. I sit on the edge of the bed and smile, but she makes no effort to return it.

"Alex told me about the messages," I say. "I'm so sorry, Katie. I didn't want any of this to happen, especially not to you."

Katie's eyes flick back and forth to her phone, still clasped between both hands.

"You know none of it is true?" I say. "It's just people on the internet looking for a fight. Although why they want to pick one with a teenager, god only knows."

Katie opens her mouth, a quiver in her lip when the words don't come.

"Go on," I say. "What were you going to say?"

"The court case," she says quietly. "I believe him. He wouldn't say that if it wasn't true."

"Ah Katie," I say as I blink back tears, "you're more generous and perceptive than people several times your age. That means a lot to me, it really does."

"But the other case . . ."

She stops and I daren't take a breath.

". . . why are people still going on about it?"

My chest tightens and I suck hard at the air around me.

"Are you getting messages about that?"

"I dunno."

"Oh my god," I say. "Was that on your Instagram?"

"Yeah."

She glances at her phone and I resist the urge to grab it from her.

"And it's locked now?"

"Yeah."

"OK," I say, and I know I need to choose my next words carefully. "Do you want to share any of it?"

"He said . . ." She can't look at me. "He said you should still be locked up."

"Oh for fuck's sake."

Katie recoils at the force of my words and I wish I could snatch them back.

"I'm sorry, I'm sorry," I say, rubbing my temples. "It's not fair that you have to deal with this. If there was anything more I could do to stop it, I would. But I want you to know that I'm here for you, OK? If anyone upsets you or bothers you, I need you to know that you can come to me any time."

She just stares at me in that way that gives nothing away.

"And there's something else I wanted to say to you. It's not just abuse you need to watch out for. You have to be just as vigilant about strangers being nice to you. If you don't know someone in real life, don't interact with them online, and never give out any personal information, OK?"

Katie takes a breath, as if she's about to speak, and then hesitates.

"What is it?" I ask.

"Nothing, just, eh . . . can I go to the cinema with Alice and Bella on Saturday?"

"Of course you can, love."

I smile and squeeze her hand and pray this is the start of better times for Katie. God knows, she deserves it.

AFTER DINNER, I GO STRAIGHT to bed, and I'm plugging my phone into the wall socket when an email alert pops up. It's Liam Kelly. I click through with shaking hands and his message fills the screen.

> This lawsuit will destroy Shauna's life. If you don't withdraw your testimony, I will have no choice but to send proof of what really happened that night to your family and to Highfield's defense team. I trust you will find it in your heart to do the right thing for Shauna and for yourself.

I fall back onto the bed, fists and chest tight with the shock. This was never about protecting Corrigan or McQueen. It's all about her. A woman who has been able to live a privileged life while I have struggled to contain a brutal truth. It's not that I want Shauna to suffer too, but it's Josh's life at stake now, as well as my own. I need to track her down, even if I have to tail Ronan for a week. I grab my phone and try every search engine, every term I can think of, in the faint hope that the drama of the past week has forged some new leads. But there is nothing, only tears of frustration that blur my vision.

I turn to Carol, the Facebook page that gives up little in recent years, just some photos of last year's thirty-year school reunion. It's only now that I remember the email invitation, the one that just might have Shauna's email address attached. At the time, I didn't even look at it, assuming it was a cruel joke that someone had added me to the list. I find it in my inbox and click it open.

> The Highfield Manor Alumni Association invites the Class of '87 to a drinks reception at the school followed by dinner at Patrick Guilbaud's on Saturday the 23rd of September.

I jump straight to the address field, but there is only a list, not individual email addresses. I'm numb with the let-down as I scroll through the replies, trying to fit names to the faces that are hidden in memory. When I get to a message from Melissa, I stop and hover over her name. We never stayed in touch and I have to admit I always resented her success, the ease with which she put everything behind her. In fact, I can't help thinking she enjoyed the notoriety of it all, that it drove her to chase a career in the spotlight. I push through my jealousy and open her email.

Dear lovely Highfield ladies,

You know there's nothing I'd love more than a good old natter with my favorite convent girls. I'm afraid I'll be recording Ultimate Idol in London that evening so I will have to miss the big bash. I trust you will find it in your hearts to forgive me and I hope to see you next time.
    Hugs and kisses,

Melissa

My pulse quickens and I read it again.
I trust you will find it in your hearts . . .
I click back into Liam Kelly's message and stare at that line until it all starts to make sense. Then I open a new email and copy across the address from Melissa's reply.
Subject: We need to talk.

PART FOUR

Then

30

Days flail by in a shimmy of unease and paranoia, my only anchor, Melissa and The Plan. Even at home, I can't escape the ripples, the late-night visits from Kenny O'Kane's lackeys, the glassy stares from Derek Brady next door. My story is now in the hands of Joe and the Rathmines College magazine, and it surely won't be long before the whole estate is giving me side-eye. At school, I lurch from one classroom to another, keeping my head down and looking over my shoulder.

The split in our group is complete now. Melissa and I huddle in corners and alcoves, plotting quietly against McQueen, while Aisling and Shauna keep to themselves, only polite conversation drifting between us. Now and again, I feel the glint of an eye on us, and I catch the flick of Shauna's ponytail as she looks away, sallow skin clinging to the hollows of her cheeks. It's been almost two weeks since we argued, that day under the cedars when battle lines were drawn. And even though I never stood a chance against the power of McQueen, I can't stop worrying about her and everything she has to endure. She is fading, slipping away, shedding confidence as well as pounds in the long shadow of the Leinster championships, and there's nothing I can do to help her.

It's not until PE with Miss Aherne, on the frost-tinted tarmac of the netball courts, that I witness Shauna in all her frailty. In the enforced closeness of her goal defense to my goal attack, she is both breathless and lethargic, and I ask her if she's OK. She dismisses me with a bitter look, and I take that as permission to put the ball in the net several times. It's only at the end of class, when we're heading back for one last center pass, that I see her put her hand to her face and stagger sideways into the goal circle. I'm on her in two swift steps and I grab her around the waist as she collapses onto my shoulder.

I'm grateful for the warmth of her sour breath against the ice-numb skin of my cheek, for the soft fold of her limbs against mine. That I get to run my fingers across the small of her back while her hands wrap around the nape of my neck. As if any of it was born of desire instead of necessity.

"Shauna, Lou, is everything OK?" shouts Miss Aherne from the center circle.

"No, please," Shauna moans in my ear.

"Yeah," I shout. "She just tripped, she's fine."

"OK, we'll wrap it up there then," says Miss Aherne as she gives the class a round of applause. "Go on, go and get yourselves a hot drink. You've earned it."

Shauna unfurls herself from me, her weight shifting away like the sun fading behind a cloud. Miss Aherne jogs up to us and puts her hand on Shauna's shoulder.

"Are you sure you're all right? You're very pale."

"Yeah, I tripped over my own foot." Shauna tries to laugh but it sounds more like a stifled sob.

"Shauna," says Miss Aherne, leading her toward the chicken-wire fence.

This is probably my cue to leave, but I hang back, enough to listen to her concerns.

"Are you eating enough?"

"I didn't have time this morning," says Shauna. "That's probably all it is."

"You should be eating double, the amount of hours you put in at that pool, you know that?"

"Yeah, I know. It's fine, I just forgot today."

"OK," says Miss Aherne, "but you need to look after yourself, all right?"

Shauna's eyes are heavy and downcast when she catches up with me.

"Thanks," she says.

"No sweat."

As we walk back to the school, I try to focus on a way to sustain this fragile connection. Now that I've got her, I'm not ready to lose her to the fractious milieu of the dining hall.

"D'ye want to go down to the park for lunch?" I say.

"Yeah, why not?"

WE SAY LITTLE ON OUR walk down the hill. In the park, a delicate mist gathers on the grass, the green floor obscured by shades of silver and gray. It's too cold to sit so we eat our lunch as we stroll under the skeletons of sycamores and horse chestnuts, meandering through the ghostly outlines as if we had all the time in the world.

"I love the smell of winter," says Shauna. "You know that sharp, smoky air? It makes me think of roaring fires, even when I'm frozen with the cold."

I think of the electric fire in our living room, three bars of glowing air, and our surrender to the elements at this time of year. I want to dream Shauna's dreams. International success, financial security, picture-perfect winter scenes.

I hop on to a fallen tree trunk lustrous with moss, and walk across it with my toes pointed and arms outstretched, as if it's a balance beam. As I come to the end, I slither sideways and Shauna grabs my wrist to steady me. I slide my fingers into hers and I don't let go, even when I've jumped back to the safety of the leaf-softened ground.

As we move slowly through our wooded sanctuary, my pulse races with possibility. Each time my fingers brush against her coat, I want to slide my hand around her waist and pull her into me. If she was a boy, one I'd already kissed, I'd be pressed up against a tree by now, our hands finding bare skin under our uniforms. But I don't know the rules with Shauna; she never gives anything away.

When we get close to the edge of the woods, the path ahead outlined in the diffuse light, Shauna throws me a glance and I catch it as quickly as I can. She takes control, stepping into me, twisting my hand behind my back. I let her kiss me, her lips soft and undemanding, and I fall into it, reaching for her face, her hair. I'm not thinking about what I'm doing, what I should be doing, what she expects me to do next. There is only this moment, just the two of us.

The faint sound of footsteps breaks the reverie, and we pull apart. On the path beyond, a white-haired woman hurries away, as eager to disappear as we are in our Highfield purple. Shauna darts behind a tree and I follow.

"Did she see us?" asks Shauna, her hands to her face.

"I don't know."

"Shit, what if she saw us? We're in our uniforms. Fuck."

I should be as worried as her, but I'm just pissed off our moment was stolen.

"She didn't see," I say. "And even if she did, who's she going to tell? She's only an old woman. She doesn't know who we are."

I take the lapels of her coat in my hands and lean in and kiss her gently.

"I don't want to stop doing that just because of some voyeur," I say. "She's probably getting off on it as much as I am."

Shauna laughs and then kisses me back, deep and long.

"Did you get off on that?" she says.

"Oh yeah," I whisper.

She slides her hands inside my coat, onto my hips, and kisses me again.

"We haven't got much time left," she says.

"We can do this again, you know?"

She smiles then, as genuinely joyful a look as I've seen in her.

"Do you want to come on Saturday?" she says.

"To the Leinsters?"

"Yeah."

"Definitely."

"We can go out and celebrate after," she says, and I can't think of anything I'd rather do.

31

It's the resonant hum of the crowd that keeps me calm under the concrete dome of the Guinness pool at St. James's Gate, the venue for this year's Leinster Swimming Championships. The muggy air swells with waves of perfume and hairspray that dilute the nauseating waft of chlorine from the water below. Condensation clouds the windows behind me, blocking out the sharp focus of a city that's bathed in sunlight, even as the icy glint of winter makes its move. There are hints of Christmas out there already, the smaller shops getting a head start before the official countdown begins on the eighth of December, and I'm grateful to be able to feel the hope and excitement of it all.

I've a bird's-eye view from the back of one of the raised stands that overlook each side of the pool. There are a few other girls from our year near the front, but I've steered clear of them. And I want to stay well out of McQueen's line of sight. He is poolside, lapping up the attention and giving his swimmers pep talks as they make their way to the starting blocks. I've already cheered on Aisling to fifth place in the 50-meter breaststroke and I'm almost sick with anticipation waiting for Shauna to appear. I need her to win. Not just so she will go out with me later but because I want her to succeed despite him and I want to be part of it. An ally in her victory, not a footnote in her defeat.

One race melds into another with Highfield leading the way, until I hear the announcement for the ladies' 100-meter freestyle final. A rush of nervous excitement kicks in as the swimmers walk out to the end of the pool, flexing and stretching their lean, toned bodies. I see the power ripple through Shauna, even as she fixes her goggles over her purple cap, not a hint of the weakness that was in her only a few days ago. She doesn't look to the stands; all her focus is on the water. I've never seen her like this before, so confident and fearless. It takes my breath away and I realize I'll never be able to go through with the plans I've laid with Melissa. It's not just the betrayal of a secret that's not mine to tell, I understand now what this means to her, how hard she must have worked to get here.

Shauna steps onto the starting block, the third lane of six, and I'm on the edge of my seat. On the whistle, she knifes into the water and shimmies to the surface in third place. The water slides by her body, her arms bending and shifting it as she pushes forward, closing the gap. She takes the first turn with ease and slices back down the pool, her movements rhythmic and controlled. When she flips back for a third length, she is second and I'm breathless with possibility.

The slosh of the water, the cheers of the crowd, all fade to a muted hum as I focus on Shauna, the power of the body that overcomes the perils of the mind. I can see it now. She's not fighting anyone else out there, she is at one with the water, turning and directing it as if she is part of it. I no longer feel the suffocation of it, that deep, dangerous trough that almost dragged the life out of me. This is different, this looks like freedom.

As she turns into the fourth and final length, Shauna closes down the leader in the next lane. They are head to head, matching each other stroke for stroke when Shauna takes off, driving forward as if she's found a new gear. The water makes way as she pulls ahead, faster and stronger with every move until there is nobody else, and I am with her all the way, on my feet, punching the air as her hand hits the wall.

The first thing Shauna does when she comes up for air, before she's acknowledged the other swimmers or sought out her coach, is look to the stands. Instinctively, I wave, and she seems to be smiling straight at me as she waves back. Maybe her parents and her brother or some other friends are nearby, but it's enough that she's seen my joy and support for her.

She's not the only one. As I cast my eye around the pool, I see McQueen staring up at me, noticing me for the first time and, by the look of him, you'd swear I'd sucked all the good out of Shauna's victory. I don't smirk on purpose, but I can't help it, the feeling that she will never smile like that for him.

AFTERWARD, I WAIT OUTSIDE THE building as swimmers and spectators make their way down the steps and out into the blue-black glow of an evening that has descended without us. I've R.E.M.'s *Reckoning* in my ears, an album Joe has foisted upon me, and despite my general distrust of American rock bands, I like this, the jangly guitars and fey indie vocals giving it a raw, melodic sound. I can't quite remember how I marked time before the invention of the Walkman, all those hours spent waiting for friends on Grafton Street, trying to look preoccupied as the punks and the legendary Diceman passed by.

The crowd thins and my excitement withers as the last of the stragglers make their way into the dusky chill. I'm on the final track when I see McQueen, and my heart sinks. He's alone, ambling down the steps toward me, and I take off my headphones and fumble in my pocket for the stop button.

"You can fuck off now," he says, wagging his thumb in the direction of the gate.

"No, thanks. I'm waiting for Shauna."

"You'll be waiting all night. She's not going anywhere with you."

"Well, she can tell me herself."

He snorts then, a hollow laugh that steals the last dregs of hope from me. I'm not going to see her tonight; she's going to be with him instead. How stupid of me to think it could be any other way.

"Do you know what your problem is?" says McQueen.

I can't be bothered playing his power games anymore. I pull my headphones back onto my ears.

"You never know when you're not wanted," he says.

I put my hands in my pockets and start to walk to the gate.

"What would someone like Shauna want with the likes of you anyway?"

I stop and I want to turn around and tell him, she wants the same thing he did. But it wouldn't be true. Shauna doesn't want to manipulate me or blackmail me into fucking her. And I realize, he probably doesn't understand that, the thrill of being wanted. His version of sex is the physical without the emotional, sensation without sentiment. And maybe that's all I've known before, but I have a real connection with Shauna now and he can't take that away from us. With that thought, his power drains away and I say nothing as I walk out the gate away from him.

32

At home, all I want to do is eat crisps in front of the telly and wait for Shauna to call, but Mam is running around, stressing about a ladder in her tights, and I have to go and search my room for an unblemished pair. She won't tell me what the big occasion is and it's only after I taunt her with jibes about a hot date that she admits there is one. That's all she'll say and eventually I relent and return to the sofa.

I don't think Mam has had a real date in the four years since Keith left. Not that Keith was big on romance, but they did go out a lot, the pub mostly. I remember dark nights in my room, the anticipation and dread of his return, the temper the drink put on him. And then turning up my tinny tape recorder while they fought or fucked, trying to drown out reality with Blondie or The Jam. Now, we're supposed to pretend none of it ever happened, as if the scars don't exist. He never did hit me, but I wish he had. It might have forced Mam to kick him out long before he left her for someone else.

I do want her to be happy, but I can't help the relief I feel every time I see one of her lovers sneak out the front door. Keith's departure was just the start, the unmooring of her life as the sober parts of it drifted out into a sea of vodka. There was an arrest for breach of the peace, a conviction for shoplifting booze. It was months before I got her to stop drinking during the day, several more before she could hold on to a job. Endless cycles of furious denial and bitter regret, all raging around me while I was trying to study for my Inter Cert. It's probably the reason I'm so good at focusing on one thing to the complete exclusion of everything else.

Mam's stable now, her drinking confined mostly to evenings, and I'm wary of anything that could upset that delicate balance. It's why I never kicked up a fuss about going back to work. I'd rather put in a few shifts a week at the Swan than risk a return to that full-time job at home. So while I'm glad she has a reason to get dressed up, I can't help dreading the consequences.

It's a toss-up between the *Royal Variety Show* and *Airplane 2* so I settle in with a packet of Monster Munch and prepare for a rehash of the one-liners that made the first film such a hit. I've already lost interest by the ad break and I'm watching the clock, willing the phone to ring when the doorbell goes instead and my heart leaps with expectation.

I stuff the crisp packet down the side of the sofa, run my fingers through my hair and under my eyes. I know it's probably Bridie or someone else from the estate, but Shauna did make a promise and maybe she's gone out of her way to keep it. I'm so hopeful when I turn the latch on the door it takes several seconds for the full horror of my mistake to sink in.

He says nothing at first, just stands there with his hands in the pockets of his leather jacket and a smile so broad his mustache curls onto the apples of his cheeks. Behind him, a taxi idles at the gate.

"What are you doing here?" I say, pulling the door tight so Mam won't see him.

"I'm not here for you," he says. "I've come to see the lovely Rose."

"She's busy. She's on her way out."

"I know," he says. "Can you tell her I'm here?"

"What?"

I hear Mam's footsteps on the stairs, and I turn around to see her looking more beautiful than I ever remember. She's like Marilyn Monroe, bleached hair curled around her neck and her tiny waist cinched by a wide patent belt. I need her to tell me this is all a ridiculous mix-up, that her real date is waiting for her in a fancy restaurant miles from here.

"Who is it?" she asks.

"It's Mr. McQueen," I whisper, pushing the door closed.

"Oh, shit," she says as she stops and grabs hold of the banister.

"What's going on?"

Mam takes a deep breath, exhales slowly and then carries on down the stairs past me and opens the door. I stand behind it, praying that whatever this is, she will fix it.

"Maurice," she says, "I thought we said we'd meet at the Wishbone."

"Rose," he says, "my god, you look stunning."

"Eh, thank you," says Mam, "but I—"

"I thought I'd surprise you and pick you up," he says. "I have a taxi waiting."

"That's very, em, thoughtful of you," she says. "Let me get my coat."

I glower at Mam before I stomp into the living room, slamming the door behind me. She comes in after me and holds her hands up in defense.

"I was going to tell you," she says, "just not tonight. I wanted to see how we got on first."

I get up and turn up the telly and then fall back onto the sofa.

"Come on, Lou. I am allowed to be happy too."

On the screen, Una Stubbs shares a cup of Nescafé with that actor from *The New Avengers*.

"I'll talk to you tomorrow," says Mam. "But you're going to have to accept that I have a life too."

She leaves the room as a double bass rolls out the opening notes of Bach's "Air on a G String" and the voice-over promises that all life's problems can be fixed with the puff of a Hamlet cigar. I give it twenty, thirty seconds after I hear the front door close and then I scream until my throat burns.

I PUT THE TWO BOTTLES on the kitchen table while Mark E. Smith shouts support from the tape deck, The Fall's *This Nation's Saving Grace*. Then, I prize two ice cubes into a glass and sit down. The ice cracks and fizzes as I drown it in vodka and Coke, and I knock the lot back in five stomach-churning gulps. I do this four times until the ice has melted and the Coke is gone and I slosh the rest of the vodka into the empty glass.

It's only minutes before the alcohol buzz starts to kick in, fifteen at most before I'm leaping around the kitchen to "Spoilt Victorian Child" and, for a brief interlude, Mark has me convinced this is all that matters. And I get it now, it's not drinking to forget but to remember. The connections and small moments embedded in the music, the life still in me.

As I twist and twirl, vodka spills onto my hand, slides down my throat easy now, and it's only when the glass is empty that I feel the weight of it inside me, limbs deadened and face flushed, and I lurch forward to the living room, slump onto the sofa, and it's that guy from *Star Trek*, the telly too bright and discordant with the pounding of The Fall, so I close my eyes and let it all come at me, shifting and spinning until I'm trapped in its vortex and I daren't move, not even when I hear the phone ringing in the distance, far beyond the roar of the suffocating din.

33

Sister Shannon takes her time, looking across the sea of faces before her. The whole of sixth-year is gathered on the tiered wooden stands in the music room, waiting for her to speak. Sister Mullen stands behind her on one side, Sister Keating on the other; this is going to be serious. Shauna glances over at me anxiously and I give her a reassuring smile. I haven't had a chance to talk to her yet, not with Melissa clamped on to me, and I vow to catch her at break.

"I shouldn't need to remind any of you," starts Sister Shannon, "about the importance of upholding the school's reputation at all times, especially when you're in school uniform."

I feel a rush of blood to my cheeks, and I can only hope somebody's been caught smoking or shoplifting.

"I have been reliably informed of a gross breach of conduct and morality by students of this school and I am here today to tell you that I will not stand for this."

There's a mass inhalation across the stands, the sheer thrill of this revelation dressed up as outrage. There are probably several of us holding our breath, but I bet only Shauna's as alarmed as I am. It wouldn't take a detective to work us out from our descriptions—I can't think of any other short, skinny girls with spiky black hair that hang around with tall, blonde-haired beauties. I've no doubt Sister Shannon would love nothing more than to parade my perverted arse around in front of the year, but I can only hope she wouldn't want to do the same to her precious poster girl.

"When we let temptation lead us into shameful, unnatural acts, we make a mockery of everything Highfield stands for, all the values we strive to instill in you as young women and upstanding, principled members of our community."

Her voice rises in pitch and volume, trembling with righteousness as she raises a finger to emphasize her fervor.

"I will not have the good name of our school tarnished by *deviants*, and

I will expose anyone who tries to bring Highfield into disrepute. You will have me to answer to, as well as the good Lord himself."

She leads us in a decade of the rosary to cleanse our souls and we're into our fifth "Hail Mary" before I realize we've probably got away with it for now. Still, I'm shaking when she leaves and we climb down from the stand and file out into the corridor.

"What the fuck was that all about?" says Melissa.

I shrug as my eyes follow Shauna hurrying down the stairs, putting as much distance between us as she can.

THE STREETLIGHTS SPILL SHAFTS OF amber and yellow onto the footpath while the moon tries to penetrate the thin film of cloud above. There's a surreal silence in the gauzy black of night as I walk from the tiny terraces at our end of the estate to the park-side semis at the other.

Out here, the smell of burned rubber pricks the air and I take the long way round to the Forresters', avoiding the open green in the center of the estate, a place where cars and loiterers come to no good. As I get closer to the park at the end of the estate, the gardens widen and an outburst of privet guards against the casual voyeur. There are proper driveways too—you could park a car in them, if you had a car. On the corner, I take a moment to steady myself before I turn into full view of the house I treated as a second home for so many years, a gray pebbledash semi with neither hedge nor car.

I know every crack and creak of this house as well as my own, the split in the concrete at the end of the drive, the rattle of the front door behind the porch add-on. Through the dimpled yellow glass, I see the shape of Joe and I breathe out the relief of my temporary reprieve. I haven't spoken to Mrs. Forrester since the funeral, and I'm not sure I'm ever going to be ready for a reunion.

"Howiye," says Joe.

"Hi," I say and take a deep breath as I cross the threshold.

I follow Joe through the hall to the kitchen at the back of the house. There's no radio or telly to distract me and I'm hit with the full force of music and laughter past. On the pine dresser inside the kitchen door is a photo of Tina on her confirmation day, the gray of her school uniform pale and drab against the flash of her smile and the neon-pink headband tied across her long, brown hair.

"Are you OK?" asks Joe as he puts the kettle on.

"I dunno," I say quietly.

I'm not here to reminisce or look for absolution. Joe's article is out tomorrow, and I need to know what I've let myself in for.

"It must be weird for you, you know, coming back here."

"Yeah. It is a bit."

It's no time at all, the eight months since I was last in the house, the night of Tina's death. Everything is the same: the orange flowers on the wall tiles, the soupy smell of leftovers on the stove, the brown rings on the speckled white Formica table. I sit down and Joe makes two cups of tea with one tea bag and takes a bottle of milk from the fridge.

"Just a drop," I say.

"I remember," he says with a smile.

He puts the two cups on the table and nods his head at the door.

"It's in my bag in the hall," he says.

He leaves me alone with the thought that Tina is never going to walk through that door, rifle in the fridge, slap on her dad's old radio. I walk to the counter, turn it on myself and flick through the wall-to-wall pirate stations until I find Capitol, her favorite. That Petrol Emotion bang out "Can't Stop" from their new album and I think she would've liked it. At the midpoint breakdown, I hear a scratching at the back door and a shadow slinks across the lower glass panel. I rush to open it, pulling the door tight toward me as I turn the key. A black cat with white paws trots in, tail aloft, and rubs her head gratefully against my legs.

"Footsie," I say as I lock the door and scoop her up. We rub noses as tears roll from my eyes onto the soft shine of her fur.

"Ah, you've found her," says Joe, closing the kitchen door behind him. "She must've smelt ye."

I laugh and brush the tears from my cheeks as Joe hands me the magazine.

"Lou," he says, "are you sure you're all right?"

"Yeah, I've just missed her."

Footsie curls up on my lap, the contented hum of her easing my heart.

"It's on page four," says Joe.

I turn the loose-leaf pages until I come to a headline that can't be anything else.

When Absolute Power Corrupts Absolutely

"Jesus," I say. "So you went for the jugular."
He's credited as Joseph Forrester.
"And you used your real name."
"Yeah, I thought if I'm going to do this, I'm going to have to be up front about it. And I didn't want to have to explain to my classmates why I'd used a false name."

Underneath is a black-and-white photo of McQueen, arms folded at the edge of the Highfield pool. I read the opening in silence, my chest tight with nerves.

> Celebrated Irish swimming coach Maurice McQueen "is a sexual abuser," according to one of his students at Highfield Manor school. McQueen is the founder and head coach at Highfield swimming club, as well as a PE teacher at the school itself. But behind Highfield's closed doors, girls at both the school and the club have fallen victim to McQueen's abuse of power. I spoke to sixth-year scholarship student Louise Manson about the sexual assaults she says took place in his car, his office and in her own home.

"Fuck," I say quietly.
Joe nods his head in sympathy, but it's the mention of the scholarship that has me rattled. I skim through Joe's observations at the pool, the girls scared to move without McQueen's instruction, his reluctance to let any of them have their say. I hold my breath when I see Shauna's name, afraid I have said too much.

> Shauna Power is one of Highfield's swimming stars and has been tipped to make the national team next year. She is the only swimmer authorized by McQueen to talk to me and she is guarded, looking over to him for approval as we speak. She tells me about her regimented training schedule, how hard she has worked to get this far and her hopes for next year's

European Championships. She praises McQueen as a coach and mentor, and lists her achievements with him. When I inquire further about the nature of this relationship, she won't answer, and it's at that point Mc-Queen puts an end to our conversation. It appears he controls what these girls say as much as what they do in his presence.

I exhale, relieved there's nothing in it that Shauna could read as betrayal. I continue on to my own story, wincing at each clinical description of his hands on my body, this double violation he's forced upon me.

"Anger is an energy," shouts PiL's John Lydon on the radio, and I don't hear Mrs. Forrester arrive home. I jump as she pushes open the kitchen door while Joe slides his magazine under a copy of the *Evening Herald*.

"Lou," she says, stopping in the doorway, an overfull Crazy Prices bag in each hand.

"Hello, Mrs. Forrester."

She puts the bags on the counter and turns down the radio.

"How are you?" she asks, her back to me.

"I'm fine, thanks."

"I hear you're over in Highfield Manor now," she says, glancing at me as she puts the shopping away.

"Yeah."

She's still got her hat and coat on, that same belted, tweed overcoat she's worn since I've known her. It's as if she's so eager to get on with things she's forgotten the order in which to do them. She says nothing more until the fridge is full and the plastic bags are shoved under the sink.

"Did Joe say anything to you?" she asks, facing me for the first time. "About the autopsy?"

I look at Joe, and he nods, almost imperceptibly.

"Yeah," I say. "He told me."

"I'm sorry," she says.

"God, no, I'm sorry," I say. "I should never have . . ."

"Shh," she says.

A half-smile passes between us and that's all the vindication I need.

"Footsie's glad to see you," says Mrs. Forrester, taking off her wool hat.

I'm shocked at the waves of gray in her short, wiry hair and I look down at Footsie and tickle under her chin.

"I'm very glad to see her too," I say.

"Do you want to go up?" asks Mrs. Forrester, raising her eyes to the ceiling.

I say nothing. I don't know what I want.

"There might be something you want to keep," she says.

"I can go with you," says Joe.

"OK," I say, before I have a chance to think about any of it.

Joe rolls up the *Evening Herald*, his magazine inside it, and puts it under his arm.

JOE FLICKS ON THE LIGHT and Tina's room is flooded with a warm orange glow from the vintage glass lampshade overhead. It takes a moment to focus, to see the details as they are instead of how I want them to be. I could close my eyes and picture it all, the constellation of our lives. The wall beside her bed papered in posters of pop and indie bands, the collage of photos and concert tickets on the back of her door. The tiny burn marks on the flimsy white curtains, evidence of our sneaky cigarettes out the window. And our beloved John Taylor looking down on our favorite hangout spot, the orange shag-pile rug at the end of the bed.

But John Taylor isn't there anymore. She replaced him with American swimmer Matt Biondi almost a year ago, and John Taylor had moved on to The Power Station by then anyway. I couldn't understand it, why he'd ever want to leave the pop perfection of Duran Duran.

Tina's bed is made for once, its yellow-and-white-striped covers smoothed into parallel lines, and the air is thick with damp and dust. I'm sure I can still smell her, gasps of White Musk from The Body Shop lurking in her wardrobe or on the cuffs of the herringbone jacket still hanging over the back of a chair. I press eject on the tape deck on her bedside locker and it glides open, releasing my Depeche Mode tape.

"It's still here," I say, taking it out to show Joe.

"We haven't really touched anything," he says.

There is one thing that has been removed, probably destroyed. The orange rug. The place I'd left her crying that night, the same spot where she'd bled to death not long after. The speckled red-brown carpet has been scrubbed, the color bleached out of it in parts, and I have to look away. The strength goes out of me and a fitful shiver forces me onto the bed, the straight lines of it warping and twisting around me. Sweat beads across my nose and my stomach lurches once and then again, and I'm on my feet, running across the landing to the bathroom. I heave into the toilet until the legs go from under me.

For so long, I've wanted to go back to that room. As if all my questions about truth and love could be answered by returning to the exact instant when I could have made a difference. But there was no single moment, we were changing all the time, even before either of us had ever heard of Maurice McQueen.

"You OK in there?" asks Joe.

"Yeah. Just give me a minute."

When I return to Tina's room Joe's on the bed, and it's only when I sit beside him that I see the tears on his face. I put my arms around his waist and he sobs quietly onto my shoulder, and I'm glad there's something I can do to ease the crippling guilt in me. Over his shoulder, I see the shape of our embrace in the mirrored wardrobe door and it looks like the only sure thing in my life.

"C'mere," he says after several minutes. "D'ye want to have a look at the rest of the article?"

"Yeah, OK."

He unrolls the *Evening Herald* and hands me the magazine. I flick through to the last page of his piece and find the end of my interview.

When I ask Louise if she knows if this has happened to anyone else, she says yes.

"He raped a good friend of mine, a swimmer at Highfield. She told me that he used to force her to have sex in the storeroom behind the pool."

I let it fall onto my lap.

"I'm sorry, I can't . . ."

"It's OK," says Joe. "You can keep it and finish it later."

I roll it up as tight as I can.

"Who's going to see it?" I ask.

"It'll be distributed around college tomorrow. After that, I dunno. I was going to post a copy to the papers, you know, *The Times*, *The Press*, *The*

Independent. I might contact some of the smaller pirate stations, ones that wouldn't be scared off by the libel laws. If that's OK with you, of course."

"Yeah," I say, out of duty more than anything else. "But what will I say to my mam?"

"I have the same problem myself."

"Oh Jesus," I say. "She'll work it out, won't she?"

"Well, yeah. Remember, you already told her most of it."

My outburst at Tina's funeral, the upset I caused her grieving family.

"You know I'm so sorry about that?"

"I know, but you were only telling the truth. It was us that didn't want to hear it."

I stare at a photo on Tina's door, the two of us at Echo and the Bunnymen last Christmas. Our faces pressed together, grinning as if we hadn't a care in the world. As if she wasn't being forced to fuck her swimming coach, as if I was nothing more than a best friend enjoying her company. And I can't say what truth is anymore. A snapshot in time or the contradictions that span a life. But maybe this was never about truth. Maybe it was only ever about revenge.

34

On Friday, the sky is dark and heavy by lunchtime, and Melissa and I take refuge in the sixth-year common room. We sit on the cast-iron pipes under the large sash window, our pale legs pressed into the thin heat as rain clatters against the glass beside us. Outside, water rushes onto the tarmac, the ground lustrous in the dying light as black clouds move across the sports center, casting a grim and ominous shadow over the domed roof of the swimming pool.

Carol and Stephanie have put *Now: The Christmas Album* on the record player and I have a Slade singalong in one ear and Melissa hissing demands in the other.

"I don't know what we're waiting for," she says. "She's in that pool every evening. We have a chance to catch them literally every day."

I've run out of excuses. What seemed like the perfect plan in the heat of the moment now feels like the worst kind of betrayal. A photo of McQueen with Shauna will destroy her too, and I won't do that to her. My Highfield days are surely numbered, now that Joe's article is out, but maybe there is still a way for me to spare Shauna. Maybe there is someone else who needs to be saved.

"Elaine Dowling," I say.

"Who's that?" asks Melissa.

"She's another swimmer who's being abused. She doesn't go to school here but I heard him talking about her."

"So?"

"So it doesn't have to be Shauna. If we caught him with Elaine, we could still expose him and save Shauna without fucking up her life."

Melissa stares at me and says nothing and I can't help wondering if she's disappointed, if she was in this for retribution against Shauna as much as McQueen. I understand that feeling, the backlash against a sense of abandonment, but I also know how dangerous it can be.

"I'll find out from Aisling when Elaine swims and we can go over there today if you want. I have my camera in my bag."

"Yeah," she says eventually. "OK."

Carol hums the opening bars of "When a Child Is Born" and Melissa's had enough.

"Come on, Carol," she says. "It's bad enough that we have to sing this shit at Mass. Nobody wants to listen to it in their spare time."

"You know your problem?" says Carol. "You've got no heart."

Carol leads her crew into the first verse and as I watch them sing and sway I wonder if she might have a point.

THE RAIN IS RELENTLESS, SOLID panes of it crashing onto us as we run from the school to the scant shelter of the cedars. From there, we watch the pool complex as Shauna and most of the other swimmers leave. Tonight is Elaine's private lesson, according to Aisling, and I can only assume she's still inside. McQueen is anyway by the looks of it, the black Saab in its usual spot near the door. I run across the lawn, Melissa close behind, and we slink into the entrance without a word.

The lights are on in the foyer and we freeze as we listen for movement from the changing rooms and the pool beyond. We hear nothing but the rattle of rain and we look at each other, both anxious and alert to what this might mean. Melissa nods at the ladies' changing rooms and I try to ignore the stifling surge of chlorine as we enter. Our cover story, that we are looking for Shauna, will only get us this far; once we're in the pool area, we'll have no excuse. We wait in silence for a moment and then look out at the eerie still of the water.

The storeroom is at the other end of the pool and we are completely exposed as we walk the length of it. When we get to it, my heart is pounding and I feel in my pocket for my camera as Melissa reaches for the door. She whips it open and I'm ready to snap, but there is only darkness, not a sound or a flicker of movement inside.

"Elaine," I call as I step into the room and my eyes adjust to the shadows. There are shelves full of floats and armbands, ropes and goggles, but no sign of Elaine or anyone else. I'm about to leave when Melissa pushes in behind me and closes the door.

"What are you doing?" I whisper. Her breath is rapid in my ear, her hair wet against my cheek.

"There's someone coming," she says, and I hear it then, the echo of footsteps as they creep closer and closer and then stop.

We don't dare move or breathe as the silence swells around us. There is no way out. I close my eyes and wait for the door to open.

Until it doesn't. The footsteps move away and there is only the rhythm of the rain and the splutter of breath as we suck the air into us. We hold on to each other as we listen and, when we are sure, Melissa opens the door slowly into darkness. We sneak back down the pool, feeling our way along the walls and into the changing rooms. It's only when we find the entrance black with night that we know we are trapped.

"We're locked in," I say as I shake the front door. A flash of light erupts through the windows as an engine starts to growl and I don't know whether to feel relief or fear that he is leaving.

"What should we do?" asks Melissa.

"There's got to be another way out," I say as the headlights retreat. "There's an emergency exit at the pool."

As I open the changing room door, the lights and the engine cut to nothing and I realize he is coming back.

"Fuck," I say. "Get in here."

We watch through a crack as McQueen strides through the foyer and into the men's changing rooms on the other side.

"Let's make a run for it," I say, and we race to the front door and we don't stop until we are across the lawn and into the safety of the bike shed.

"Oh my fucking god," says Melissa as she tries to catch her breath.

I should be shocked or shaken or scared half to death, but all I feel is a rush of elation at the thrill of the escape. It comes out of me in waves of laughter, each more guttural than the last until I am doubled over on my bike and Melissa is cracking up too.

"Who the fuck is Elaine Dowling anyway?" says Melissa as we walk toward the front gates.

"I dunno."

"Can you imagine, if she'd been in there?"

I can't. I don't know what we would've said to her.

"You know there's only one way we can be certain of catching him," she says.

I look at her face, to be sure I understand.

"We have to do it," she says.

And I know she's right.

35

I t's over."

Joe stands in the dim light of the doorstep, the rain lashing him sideways. His sandy hair clings to his face and water runs the length of him, as if his whole life is flowing into the gutter.

"Jesus, come in," I say, and I close the door to the dark clutches of the storm behind him. "Here, you go on into the kitchen. I'll get you a towel."

When I return, Joe's just standing there, his donkey jacket dripping onto the lino and his eyes red raw with rain and tears. He takes off his sodden coat and throws it over the back of a chair. I hand him the towel and wait for him to wipe his face and his hair before I slide my hands around his waist. He clutches me, hair wet against my neck, breath heavy in my ear.

"I've been expelled," he whispers.

I pull back, hoping I've misheard.

"What?"

"I've been kicked out of college."

He spits out a bitter, hopeless laugh.

"What the fuck? Joe, what's going on?"

"They got a letter, the college. From his solicitors, threatening to sue for libel."

"Oh fuck."

"Yeah."

Joe sits down, puts his elbows on the table and his head in his hands. I slip into the chair beside him and put my hand on his knee.

"I shoulda used my real name from the start, I hold my hands up to that, but what I wrote, it's all true. I told them you'd back me up and everything."

He turns to me, a rare fury in him.

"And d'ye know what they said? They asked me to prove it. Like, what does that even mean? Am I supposed to have videos of him assaulting you or something?"

"So my word is worth . . . nothing?"

Joe snorts and shakes his head.

"Less than nothing. They said you had a track record of lying. That you weren't on a scholarship for starters, and you'd already been threatened with suspension for lying in school."

"Oh god."

I could explain, but what good would it do?

"So he can make up whatever he wants," says Joe, "and all he needs is money to back it up. But me? If I don't have proof, I have to issue a full retraction and apology saying that we both made it all up." He shakes his head. "Fuck that. That's my career over before it's even begun and the end of any chance of justice for Tina."

"So they just expelled you?"

"Yeah. Well, after I told them to shove their apology up their holes."

"Oh shit." I stifle a nervous laugh. "Fuckit Joe, I'm proud of you, whatever that's worth."

"Thanks."

He puts his hand on mine and I'm grateful.

"So whatcha gonna do?" I say.

"I'm going to murder him," he says, his teeth bared in a way I've never seen before.

"Don't do that," I say. "You're not allowed. Unfortunately."

"I fucking want to. What else can I do?"

"Get pissed. Keep talking."

"Who's gonna want to talk to me now? I'll have to set up my own pirate radio station."

"Do it."

He smiles, wraps his other hand around mine and squeezes them together.

"Sure why not? He can send me as many solicitor's letters as he likes, I've fuck all money."

"I'll go in with you."

"Where? The pub or the radio?"

"Both."

"OK, you're on," he says. "Get your coat and an umbrella and we'll leg it up to the Swan."

"Ah no, not the Swan," I say as I stand up. "Mam's working up there tonight."

"No she's not."

"What? How do you know?"

"I called in on my way over to see if you were there."

Joe's words take the wind out of me and I sink back into my chair.

"She's with him," I say quietly.

"Who? Has she got a new boyfriend?"

Joe flashes a smile but it fades quickly when I don't return it.

"What's wrong, Lou?"

"She's with McQueen."

"You're joking, right?"

I shake my head slowly.

"Fuuuck," I shout. "I should have known."

"Why is she with him?" asks Joe.

"Because he asked her out and she's desperate."

"Why'd he do that?"

"Why d'ye think?"

"To get back at you? What the fuck is he playing at?"

"Maybe it's true love," I say.

"Ah Jaysis, Lou," says Joe. "What kind of twisted fuck is he?"

There's only one thing for it so I go straight to the back of the press beside the fridge, take out the two bottles and pick up a couple of mugs from the draining board. I slosh a measure of vodka and Coke into each and hand one to Joe.

"Race you," I say, and we clink mugs and knock back our poison. "Let's go to the Rambler's Rest. We can drink there until we puke."

As we leave the house, we link arms and huddle under my umbrella. The vodka's starting to kick in and I want to believe in its warm glow, to be normal for just one night. The rest of it can wait for me and my hangover tomorrow.

MAM NEVER CAME HOME. SHE should've been here giving out to me, hounding me out of bed in the afternoon, and me pleading with her to leave me alone in the misery of my own making. But there was only silence in the house all day. She came back in the evening to wash and change for work and then she was gone again before I could catch her. She'll be treading carefully this morning so it's the best chance I'll have to talk to her.

It's after midday when she comes down to the kitchen, rubbing the night from her eyes. She pulls her dressing gown tight around her, shivering as she waits for the kettle to boil.

"Sit down, I'll make it," I say, and she does what she's told.

"What are you after?" she asks, eyeing me suspiciously.

I say nothing, chew my lip and wait until she has half a cup of tea inside her before I begin.

"Mam, there's something I need to tell you."

"Actually, I need to talk to you too."

She's cradling her tea, eyes fixed inside the mug, and I know I need to get my confession out first.

"I need to tell you about something that's been happening for a while. It's to do with Tina and why she killed herself."

She looks up at me now, eyes wide with concern.

"She was being abused, at swimming."

I pause to give my words time to sink in. Mam's eyes narrow, her guard rising already.

"It was one of her coaches. He used to force her to have sex by threatening to cut her from the team."

"Who told you this?"

"She did. Mam, she was pregnant."

Mam closes her eyes tight, and I know she's holding on to the last bit of hope she has.

"And that coach tried to do the same thing to me when I started at Highfield."

She puts her hands to her face and breathes deeply through her fingers, taking it all in.

"That time, when he was in my bedroom, that's what he was trying to do to me. That's what I was shouting about."

She slaps her hands onto the table and jerks her head upright.

"OK, Lou," she says. "So you know I was with Maurice on Friday. Well done you, nothing gets past you, does it?"

"That's not . . ."

"It's not what? The whole point of this character assassination? Well, what exactly is your point then?"

"Mam," I say, my voice cracking. "I'm trying to tell you something important. I wish I'd told you months ago."

"So you forgot to tell me all this time and now I've finally found someone I could be happy with, you've conveniently remembered? Come on, Lou."

"Mam, please," I cry. "This has nothing to do with you going out with him. I mean, yeah, I don't want you to go out with him, but it's because he's evil, you have to see that."

"Wow," she says. "I always knew you hated Keith, but I didn't think you'd stop me trying to be happy with someone else."

"I hated Keith because he hit you. And now you want to go out with a rapist?"

"A rapist?" The word rolls indignantly off her tongue. "I've heard it all now."

She pushes her chair back, starts to walk away and then stops. She swings back and points her finger at me.

"You know what, Lou? Fuck you."

She turns to leave and it's too much. The rage, the disappointment, the crushing futility of it all.

"Fuck me?" I shout. "That's exactly what he was trying to do."

It happens so fast I barely see it coming. The spin of her head and the swift flick of her arm as her hand claps against my cheek. I wish I could say that I'm shocked or stunned but I feel nothing, not even the bitter sting of it. He's taken almost everything I love. There's only one person left who can save me and that's where I need to be right now.

36

The weekend has seen Christmas wash across the city, a constellation of lights that clusters tightly in our estate. We have nothing yet, not so much as a mention of the garlands and baubles that are taken down from the attic and arranged lovingly at this time every year. Mam's so caught up in the illusion of romance she's forgotten our shared memories and rituals and I hate him even more for taking that away from us.

As I rush past one glitzy house after another, I think about this time last year, counting down to Christmas with Tina. The ceremony of picking dresses for our pre-debs ball and planning exactly how far we'd go with the poor fellas we'd invited. But that was an illusion too, because Tina was only pretending everything was normal. Or maybe I was just refusing to see that it wasn't.

When I get to the gate, the house looks like an advent calendar, half its windows glowing with the promise of warmth inside. In the living room, a spruce fir beams incandescent while, above it, her bedroom is a pool of darkness. I tread carefully down the drive and press the doorbell.

The door swings open, behind it a nonchalant boy in 501s and a white T-shirt, his skin still soft and unblemished. And those ice-blue eyes—it has to be Ronan.

"Is Shauna here?" I ask.

He regards me with leering curiosity, a power game that seems too old for his years.

"Just a minute," he says and pushes the door closed, leaving me out in the cold.

Shauna opens the door slowly with an awkward smile. She seems younger, more relaxed in a baggy sweatshirt and leggings, her hair loose around her face.

"Lou," she says, almost meekly, "come in."

Ronan stays in the hall as we pass through, arms folded in an adversarial stance, and Shauna throws him a withering look.

"What was that all about?" I ask when we get to Shauna's room.

She grimaces. "I wasn't going to say anything, but he saw us together that first night, when we kissed goodbye at the gate. He's been blackmailing me to buy booze for him ever since."

"Oh shit." I wonder if that's why she was so elusive after our first kiss, why it took us so long to find our way.

"I denied it, of course, and it's not like he'd ever say anything, I mean, he wouldn't want people to know about it anyway. But it's just easier to do what he wants than listen to him go on about it all the time."

"Little fucker."

"He is. He's a little shit with no life experience of his own who thinks he knows it all. God help any girl who ends up with him."

I laugh and then we're just standing inside the door, unsure of what to do next. She leans in to embrace me, all roses and jasmine, and we hug tentatively, her hands on the elbows of my coat and my fingers uncertain if they should be touching her hips. And then her face is buried in my neck, her breath hot in my ear, and I turn to find her lips and we're kissing as if nobody's watching. She pulls away to close the curtains and flicks on the lamp on her bedside locker while I take off my coat. I hang it over the back of her desk chair, and she slips her hands around my waist from behind. She kisses my neck, biting softly and then harder, sending electrical shivers through me, and it would be so easy to melt into her, forget about everything else.

I prize her hands apart and turn around and her eyes harden with confusion.

"I want this," I say, taking her hands in mine, "I really, really do. But I need to talk to you first."

She bites her lip and nods slowly, as if she's anticipated this conversation.

"It's about Mr. McQueen," I say.

"OK, go on," she says, and I smile with relief.

We sit on the edge of her double bed, and I tell her about McQueen and Sister Shannon and, this time, she listens with empathy, squeezing my thigh and running her fingers along my black leggings. It's only when I explain who Joe is that she withdraws her hand and her approval.

"So, you . . . set me up?"

"No, of course not. Joe didn't ask for you, McQueen offered. But you don't need to worry about Joe, he's on our side."

She frowns and I'm afraid I've used the wrong words or made the wrong assumptions.

"Have you seen the article?" she asks. "What does it say about me?"

"It says that you seemed afraid of him. Not just you, some of the other girls too."

Shauna sighs and shakes her head.

"Why can't everyone just leave us alone?"

"Because it's not right."

I put my hands on hers and I'm grateful when she doesn't flinch.

"Shauna, it kills me to think of what he's doing to you. I'd do anything to make it stop."

She stares at me intensely and I know it's true. I'd do anything for her.

"How would you stop him?" she asks.

I think about the plan I made with Melissa, how we could pull it off together.

"What if I was to walk in on the two of you? Would that scare him off?"

Shauna winces at the thought and then shakes her head.

"Honestly," she says, "I don't think he cares what you think."

"Wouldn't he be afraid I might tell someone?" I ask.

"Who'd believe you if you did?"

I know she's right; I've blown through all those options already.

"If I took a photo," I say, "d'ye think that'd be enough to keep him away from you?"

Shauna bites her lip as she considers this, as if the idea scares her as much as it gives her hope.

"He couldn't know I had anything to do with it. You'd have to make out like it was just you getting revenge on him, maybe on me too. We wouldn't even be able to be friends in school anymore."

I grimace but I know she's right.

"It would be worth it. As long as we can still do this." I wave my finger between us. "Whatever this is."

Shauna puts her hand back on my thigh and I lean in to kiss her.

"Deal," she whispers.

"There's one more thing," I say, pulling back, and she groans, my honesty just cramping her style now.

I start to tell her about Mam and McQueen and she doesn't move or say a word. She stares at me deadpan, enduring the whole story from beginning to end.

"What night did she stay with him?" she says.

"Last Friday. Why?"

She sucks on her bottom lip and I'm not sure if she's going to laugh or cry.

"Was he . . ." I say, unsure of how to finish the question, ". . . with you on Friday?"

She nods.

"He even told me he loved me before he left. Not that it means anything to me anymore."

"Did it ever?"

She looks at the ceiling and releases a long, slow breath.

"I used to think it was important for him to love me, to see me as special. I needed that, for him to think I was better than everyone else. I thought it mattered."

"Did you ever love him?"

There's such sadness in her eyes I can't bear it.

"I think I always hated him."

She turns away and takes her hand from my leg. I'm not sure if I've lost her but I've come too far to give in without a fight.

"Shauna, I'm really sorry," I say. "I hate him too. I wanted to kill him when I saw him with Mam, so I can't imagine . . ."

"What the fuck is your mum doing with him anyway?"

"He's nice to her. Most men aren't."

"Fuck men," she says.

"Not literally."

"No, not literally, just fuck them."

Her eyes are wide now, daring me to make the next move. I lean into her and she holds up a finger.

"I'm just checking you don't have anything else to get off your chest first."

"No." I laugh.

She swings her legs onto the bed and lies back. I climb onto her, straddling her waist as I pin her hands behind her head.

"Is this OK?"

"Yeah."

I bend down and kiss her, my body pushing into hers.

"And this?"

"Yeah."

"I don't want you to feel . . ."

"What?" she asks.

"I dunno . . . uncomfortable."

"Jesus, Lou," she says. "You're not him, OK? I can tell the difference."

I laugh nervously.

"I hope so."

"I want you to touch me."

I smile as I slide down her body, lift her sweatshirt and move my mouth across the flat of her stomach. She gasps and it shudders through me, as if we share the same nerve endings. I've no idea what I'm doing but it feels as natural as breathing. I'm kneeling over her, my fingers hooked into the waistband of her leggings, when I hear the rattle of the door handle and I jump backward away from her. Shauna shoots upright, pulls her sweatshirt down and tucks her feet under her.

A tall, thin woman in tight jeans and heels slinks into the room and surveys me with a smile. She's not at all what I expected Shauna's mother to look like, hair slicked back, red lipstick like one of the models in a Robert Palmer video.

"I thought I'd better introduce myself," she says, "seeing as Shauna didn't do it for me."

She raises an eyebrow at her daughter, who ignores the gesture completely.

"I'm Olivia," she says, holding out her hand. "Shauna's mum."

"Hi," I say as I shake her hand, my heart still clattering in my chest.

"And you are?" she says.

"Oh, sorry, I'm Lou. I'm in school with Shauna."

"Really?" she says. "At Highfield?"

"Lou's new," says Shauna. "Well, since September."

"Uh-huh," says Olivia. "And how are you finding Highfield?"

"I love it," I say.

"That's cos she's good at everything," says Shauna.

"I'm glad to hear it," says Olivia. "Shauna, dinner is takeaway. I've left some money on the hall table."

"Can Lou stay?"

"Of course. If that's what you want."

"It is."

"I'm going out with Lucinda," says Olivia as she leaves. "I'll be at the Guinea Pig if you need me."

WE SHARE A BAG OF chipper chips and sneak past the Guinea Pig as we head to Finnegan's at the end of the village.

"Looks fancy in there," I say.

"Oh, she won't be eating. She only consumes black tea and gin."

"Oh," I say.

"So she can't complain if we spend the rest of her money on booze."

Shauna puts her arm around me, and I reciprocate.

"Don't you love being a girl?" she says. "Nobody suspects a thing."

She leans in and kisses me on the cheek.

It's still early and we find a quiet corner in Finnegan's, a spot hidden by a wooden panel from the rest of the pub.

"What are you going to have?" I ask.

"I might have a vodka and tonic."

"Ugh," I say. "I can't drink vodka anymore. It's what Mam has at home."

"I feel the same way about gin."

"How about Pernod and black to start us off?"

"Why not?" says Shauna, and hands me a five-pound note.

When I return with the sickly purple liquid there are two older guys in leather jackets sitting opposite Shauna. They have a local swagger about them, like they know the lay of the land and they've spied the new blood in the house.

"How's it going?" says the one with the bleached hair. He'd have a look of Larry Mullen if it wasn't for his terminal acne.

"All right," I say, trying not to engage as I push in beside Shauna.

"You're not from round here, are ye?" says the other, a big thick head of hair on him.

"We're from London," says Shauna in a fierce posh accent.

"Camden Town," I say in my best mockney.

I hand Shauna her drink and we clink glasses and knock them back in one. She gags and sticks a purple tongue out at me.

"My brother's over there," says Larry. "In Kilburn."

"Sorry, we don't know him," I say, and Shauna laughs.

"Can we buy you ladies a drink?" asks the other one.

"What do you think, Louise?" asks Shauna.

"I think not, Shauna," I say. "Sorry, boys, it's not your lucky night."

The legs of their chairs scrape slowly across the floor as they stand up.

"Fuckin' dykes," says Larry as they leave.

"What gave us away?" I shout, and Shauna can't help giggling as she shushes me.

BY THE TIME WE GET back to Shauna's, we're heavy with drink, stepping slowly and deliberately through the house. Shauna goes downstairs to get a bottle of wine and I carry on up to her room. As I close the door behind me, I see Ronan across the landing, sizing me up with a critical eye. He can think what he likes; I'm not going to let him come between us. I flop onto Shauna's bed, relieved I don't have to get up in the morning. It's the eighth of December, the Feast of the Immaculate Conception, and schools are closed. There is a procession and Mass at Highfield in the evening, but I'll worry about that tomorrow.

"D'you've swimming tomorrow?" I ask Shauna when she gets back with an open bottle of white and two glasses.

"Yep."

"Morning or evening?"

"Both."

"Shit," I say. "So you're not going to the procession?"

"Nope."

I push myself up onto my elbows and take the glass of wine from her as she sits down beside me.

"Don't you know there's one thing at Highfield that trumps Holy Mary and Jesus Christ himself?" she says.

"Fucking swimming."

"Shh," she says as she puts her finger to her lips. "No blasphemy, please."

"Sorry. I'll say no more."

She rests her arm across my tummy and runs her fingers up and down my hip.

"Will you stay?" she says.

"Yeah."

We finish our wine, only the jagged rise and fall of our breaths breaking the silence. As I undress, she puts on Sade's *Diamond Life* and I sway to the opening sax riff of "Smooth Operator."

"You're so pretty," she says.

"No, I'm not."

"How can you not know that?"

"Because I don't have blonde hair and big tits and blue eyes and tanned skin."

"You say that like they're bad things."

"Oh god, they're really fucking not." I laugh. "They're all great things, believe me."

I take off my T-shirt and stand in front of her in my bra and underpants.

"Don't move," she says, and pulls out a Polaroid camera from her bedside locker. "Say cheese."

I put my hands behind my head and strike a pose as the flash lights up the room.

"Your turn," I say, taking the camera from her.

She lifts her sweatshirt over her head and she's only wearing a black lace bra underneath.

"You could've told me," I say. "All evening and I didn't know."

"I thought you noticed when you were kissing my tummy earlier."

"Well, I was preoccupied then."

I look through the viewfinder as Shauna slides her bra straps down over her shoulders and then folds her arms across her tummy. Her hair frames the photo, falling from her bare shoulders onto her breasts, and I take it all in for a breathless moment before I click. The photo glides out of the camera and I shake it dry.

"I want one of both of us," I say.

"OK, but you have to promise not to show it to anyone."

"Cross my heart," I say, running a finger each way across my breast.

She leans her head against mine as I hold the camera out in front of us and I turn to kiss her lips as I snap.

"Let's see," she says as she sits on the bed and takes off her leggings.

"It's perfect."

She's perfect, her soft, full lips on mine and that unmistakable white-blonde hair across her face. I sit beside her, our bare arms and legs brushing off each other.

"What now?" she says.

"I dunno, I've never done this before."

"Oh, good," she says.

"Why? Have you?"

"No."

"So we'll just have to feel our way around it," I say.

"Yeah, I think we should."

I run my fingers along the inside of her thigh and she moans gently.

"Like this?" I say.

"Yes, definitely."

I move my hand across her tummy and on to the cup of her bra.

"Take it off," I say.

She unclips the back and slides the straps down her arms without taking her eyes off me. I take off my own and then kneel before her and slowly pull her lace underpants down over her hips, her knees, her feet. She opens her legs and I slide my hand between them, and then we're kissing hard, biting and sucking on lips and skin, pushing into each other as if we've always known exactly what to do, and it's all so easy and so fucking good, and when she goes down on me, I have to bite the inside of my lip to silence my cries when I come harder than I ever have before.

Afterward, we can't stop kissing, as if detaching from each other would break the spell. We lie entwined until Sade stops singing, and the stop button clicks us out of our reverie.

"That's never happened to me before," says Shauna. "I mean, with someone else."

"Me neither."

"We should definitely do it again."

She runs her nails down my back, onto my bum.

"Now?"

"No." Shauna laughs. "I mean, I wish, but I have to get up in . . ." She leans across me to look at her alarm clock. "Oh god, five hours."

"Boo."

"Come round tomorrow, after Mass. I can meet you after swimming."

"Yes, please," I say and, when we kiss, I can't think of a single thing in the world that could possibly stop us.

37

It's the floral scent of her perfume that grounds me when I wake. The air is black, not a chink of light through the velvet curtains, not a whisper of morning beyond them. I slide my fingers across the sheet but she is out of reach. As I roll over, the muffled ache in my head slides behind my eyes and it takes a second to focus and another to register the crashing disappointment when I see the empty space beside me. I know she never misses swimming and I don't know what I expected. Not a kiss goodbye or a declaration of love, just some sort of nod to what's happened.

My breath stutters when I think of them together, the power he has over her, how brittle she is in his hands. The sickening thought of his fingers on her wet skin. It's personal now, urgent, and I have to believe she meant what she said, that she really does want to be saved.

The red glow of the alarm clock shows 6:55 a.m. I need to get out of here. Soon, Shauna's dad will be up for work and, without her, I'm just an intruder in this vast and hollow house. What would I say to him? "I stayed over to drink your wine and fuck your daughter." Jesus. And it'd probably be my accent that would freak him out the most. I sling my legs onto the carpet and my ankle brushes against a glass I don't remember leaving there. It's a highball filled with water, still cold. A nod.

I dress in darkness and I'm about to leave when I remember the photos. I flick on the bedside light and there they are, a near-naked Shauna smiling up at me, the two of us lost in a passionate kiss. It's real; there's proof. I put the photo of me in a drawer and slide the other two into my coat pocket.

I open the door slowly and I'm startled to see a man frozen on the stairs below me, like a burglar caught in the act. He's wearing suit trousers and a white shirt open at the neck and his cold blue eyes are more ragged than mine. We're locked in a silent stare until I remember I'm definitely not supposed to be here, whatever about him.

"I'm a friend of Shauna's," I say. "I was just leaving."

"Oh," he says, shoulders straightening now that balance has been restored. "I'm Mr. Power." And then, in case it wasn't clear, "Shauna's dad."

He climbs to the top of the stairs and, when he passes, I smell a mix of stale booze and expensive perfume, and I wonder if he gets the same from me.

AT HOME, MAM IS CRASHED out on the sofa, face tucked into her chest like a baby. The dregs of vodka sit in the belly of an overturned bottle and the air is thick with that old familiar stench of alcohol seeping through her pores. I bring a glass of water upstairs and try to sleep off the hollow void of my hangover, but there are too many conflicting thoughts rolling around my head and I can't calm the fear that I'm not in control of any of them. All I want to think about is Shauna, the curve of her hip, the quickening of her breath in my ear, but I can't unshackle her from *him* no matter how hard I try.

After a while, I hear Mam creeping up the stairs and I drag my duvet down to the sofa and try to numb my brain with the hum of daytime TV. Floella Benjamin shows us how to make our own Christmas decorations on *Play School* and there's trouble in the Ramsay household in *Neighbours*. By mid-afternoon, I'm starting to doze when the phone rings, and adrenaline has me on my feet before I know what's happening. I'm so elated at the thought of talking to Shauna that I don't even try to hide my disappointment when I hear Melissa's voice.

"What's wrong with you?" she says.

"Nothing. Actually, I'm sick."

I am sick. I haven't eaten all day and I'm shivering with the bitter cold that creeps into the hall at this time of year.

"What, like vomiting and stuff?"

"Yeah."

I sit on the stairs and huddle my elbows to my knees.

"I caught Shauna barfing in the loos on Friday," says Melissa.

"Oh. Was she OK?"

"No. But it wasn't because she had a tummy bug."

"What do you mean?" I say, even though I've felt the jut of her hip bone, the skin taut across her ribs.

"If you have to ask that question then you don't know Shauna as well as you think you do."

I want to tell her everything then, steal the smugness from her voice, but I've no doubt she'd destroy me with it.

"Oh," I say.

"Yeah. But I just called her house and she's already left for swimming so she must be OK. Listen, I've been thinking, it has to be this week. It can't be during the holidays, like, what excuse would we even have for being at the school? And there's no way we can leave it until next year. I mean, could you enjoy your Christmas dinner knowing what that fucker is doing to her?"

She pauses to let me picture it, and I do.

"She has her private half-hour lesson with him at half six tonight, Wednesday and Thursday. Take your pick."

"Not tonight." I can't begin to explain to Melissa how things have changed, and I can't take the risk that she will go ahead without me. Or worse, tell Shauna we conspired behind her back.

"So Wednesday then?" she says.

The free local newspaper flaps in the breeze that slides under the front door and the cold goes right through me.

"I dunno. Can we wait and see?"

"Look, Lou, I'm going over there this week, with or without you, so you better make your mind up quickly."

After that, everything Melissa says fades to a distant mumble and all I can think is, I'm going to have to confront them tonight, alone.

AS SOON AS I TELL Mam I'm going to Shauna's later I know I've made a mistake. She's lying on the sofa, eyes dark and hooded, the angry stage of drunk already, and *Countdown* hasn't even started yet.

"This is what I was afraid of," she growls. "They've taken you away from me."

She sits up, pulls a slouched jumper back onto her shoulder and reaches for the glass of vodka on the coffee table.

"Don't forget, I know these people." She sinks a mouthful and smacks the glass onto the table. "You can't trust any of them."

I know there's a sermon coming if I engage and I've only forty-five minutes to get to Highfield.

"I'll see you tomorrow."

I put my hand on the door.

"Was it her that put you up to it?"

My heart sinks. She's determined to do this now and I'm going to have to let it play out. I can't risk leaving her with her own destructive thoughts.

"No, Mam. Shauna's a friend."

"Well, somebody in there's got to you. Why else would you say those things about Maurice?"

"Please, can we talk about it later?"

She stares into space for a second before her eyes flare with urgency.

"I'm going to ask him myself."

She starts to get up and then falls back onto the sofa.

"I don't have his number," she says with a pout. "He never gave it to me. Do you have it?"

"No."

"Then I need to go and see him. I'm coming with you."

"No, you can't," I say. "I'm cycling."

Her lip starts to tremble and I can't tell if she's going to snarl or surrender.

"Well feck off then," she shouts.

She flicks her wrist at me with such force her arm swipes against the glass and it shoots off the end of the table and smashes against the radiator.

"Oh Christ," she says, sinking to her knees, leaning over the broken fragments.

I want to run, let her clean up her own mess, but a latent dread stops me. Mam and booze and sharp objects shouldn't be left alone. I crouch down beside her and reach for the glass, but she shoos me away.

"Just go," she says. "Leave me."

I stand up slowly and she holds my gaze, and she must have forgotten about the glass because she leans back and I shout, "Mam, no," but the palm of her hand falls flat against the upturned shards, and maybe it's the vodka or the fact that she's got my attention but she doesn't seem to notice until the blood is soaking into the cuff of her jumper.

"Oh shit," she says, holding her hand up to the light.

I run into the kitchen to grab a tea towel and, when I get back, she's on her feet, walking across the carpet, blood painting a trail to the door. I lead her to the kitchen, sit her down, and she's almost serene, barely flinching as I clean and dress her wound. My eyes flick to the clock on the cooker—thirty-five minutes to make the seven-mile cycle to Highfield. I could skip Mass completely, but then I wouldn't have a reason for being there at all, and somebody's sure to see me somewhere on the grounds.

"Will you talk to him?" she says, head lolling to one side, and I wonder if I can get her upstairs to the safety of sleep.

"Yeah. I will."

I clasp my arm around her waist and lift her off the chair.

"Let's go and lie down for a bit."

"Tell him I'll be up there later," she says. "After I've had a bit of a rest."

As I help her up the stairs, I try not to think about my fingers on the ledge of her ribs, the sharp angles of her arms, how everyone I love is fading away. When I've tucked her in, cleared the glass, half-scrubbed the blood from the carpet, I've less than half an hour to make it. I take off into the biting cold and pedal like my life depends on it.

38

There's a ghostly calm in the chapel, purple uniforms lined up in silence across the pews. Only the altar is lit, shimmering with tiers of candles that make shadows of the choir next to them. The darkness in the nave is softened by torches wrapped in colored tissue paper, blooms of soft pastel petals that glow in the hands of each of the girls. I could almost lose myself in the luster of it if my heart wasn't drumming a beat in my head.

I know I'll be noticed if I walk down the aisle and push into a bench so I take the stairs to the organ loft and squeeze in at the edge of the balcony that overlooks the rest of the chapel. Someone hands me a torch, a glimmer of pink that I hold tight as I listen to the choir sing the "Ave Maria" and scan the silhouettes downstairs. I find Melissa on the right, a glint of soft blue torchlight in her corkscrew curls. I need to keep her in my sights so I can sneak out without her later.

The priest talks of Holy Mary and the sheer purity of her immaculate conception and I wonder how many of the sixth-years are still the untarnished virgins we're supposed to be. I know Carol's allowed to stay over at her college boyfriend's house, and it's an open secret Stephanie spent the night with Ian Hardy after the Rockdale social. Everybody's at it, but nobody's confessing.

As we prepare to leave the chapel and parade our radiance around the school, Carol steps up to the pulpit to lead us in the "Salve Regina." It's a revelation, her voice so pure I want to believe it comes from deep within her and not just years of expensive vocal training.

We sing the refrain as we file out through the neo-Gothic archway of the chapel entrance into the darkened corridors of the school. As the procession rounds a corner, I flick off my torch and slide into the passageway that leads to the rear staircase. The air is cold and still and I move slowly through the blackness, feeling my way along the wall as the voices fade to a distant hum. When I get to the stairs, I grip the banister and place my feet lightly on each of the wooden steps. I'm halfway down the second flight when I swear I see a flash of light above me. I freeze but when I look up, there is nothing, only shades of black.

Unease follows me down the stairs and along the narrow corridor by the assembly hall. I stop every time a floorboard creaks and I feel the air twitch in sympathy. I turn the corner and don't look back, even when I hear the groan of timber and see the shifting shadows on the home stretch to the back door. I burst out into the raw and bitter cold and pick up pace, and I'm almost on the gravel path when I hear the door slam behind me.

"Where do you think you're going?"

She's lit only by a pale haze of stars flushed across a black sky and the muted blue of her torchlight.

"Oh, hi. I . . . I just felt claustrophobic in there," I say. "It was too dark and creepy."

"I would have thought that was right up your alley," says Melissa. "You know, weird and black."

"I'm not really the religious type."

Melissa cackles like a cartoon villain.

"Too many sins? Or is it all those skeletons in your closet?"

Her caustic tone unsettles me and I try to think what I might have done. Then it hits me, that she has spoken to someone in Shauna's house today, that she could already know I spent the night there.

"Look, I don't know what you're getting at, but I'm tired so I'm going to go now."

"Of course you are," she says. "I'm going to hang around for a while. Maybe pay a visit to the pool."

A rash of panic prickles my skin but it's anger that comes to my rescue.

"Seriously? You're going to do that to her with the whole school watching? Come on, Melissa, you're supposed to be her friend."

She hesitates and I know my words have hit the target.

"Sorry, I forgot you're the world expert on Shauna."

"I'm not," I say softly. "I know you know her way better than I do. I want to help, but not tonight. Please."

I need to make sure I get to Shauna before Melissa does, to explain everything she will tell her. But I need to be her savior first.

"Wednesday," I say. "When there's nobody else around. I'll bring my camera. You confront them and I'll take a photo. I'll give you the film and you can do what you like with it. You can be the hero. I've had enough of all of this."

She peers at me with doubtful eyes and I can only hope she has no other options.

"Ten to seven on Wednesday, at the grotto," she says. "If you're not there, I'll do it on my own."

She walks back into the school and the door bangs shut behind her. I look at my watch; it's ten past six. The grotto seems as good a place as any to hide out for the next fifty minutes. I just hope Melissa and everyone else will be long gone by then.

FROM THE DISTANT SECLUSION OF the grotto, Highfield rises above the cedars, stretching into a sky gauzed with stars. An austere darkness glowers from the school, the latticed sash windows silver mirrors in the haze, and the only sign of life comes from the checkerboard of light in the neighboring convent. The clock tower shows five to seven, almost the end of Shauna's private half-hour lesson with McQueen and the start of her ordeal. I have ten, maybe fifteen minutes before it will be over.

A thin mist hovers over the path before me, blurring the winter-green borders on either side of it. As I walk through the icy silence, I hear each piece of gravel crunch underfoot, feel every heightened thud of my heart beat against my ribs. My stomach clenches with the reality of it all, what's happening to Shauna at this moment, the confrontation that's ahead. I wrap my frozen fingers around the camera in my gabardine pocket, the Agfamatic primed and ready for action.

Beyond the cedars, I see a latent blue glint and I wait for it to fade out of sight, the last of the embellished torches to leave. A car engine fires up, and I dart behind a tree as headlights flood the bike shed and a lone cyclist pulls out onto the path around the front of the school. I wait there until they are gone, and my jagged breath is the only perceptible sound.

The pool lights are off, but his black Saab is still there, parked beside the entrance like a getaway car. I can't even look at it as I walk past and I try not to think of his clammy hand on my thigh, his grubby fingers probing my crotch. This feels like a very different mission to the one I attempted with Melissa last week. This time, everything is at stake.

I push the door slowly, listening for the usual swollen sounds from the pool, the sloshing of water, the echo of voices. There is nothing but the steady purr of the pump. The air is heavy with chlorine, and I breathe through my mouth as I feel my way through the entrance, past the noticeboard, the front desk, into the changing rooms. Shauna's satchel sits on a slatted bench, her sports bag and tasselled loafers below it, and I shudder because now I know for sure that this is real.

I move past the toilet cubicles, the row of showers opposite, and stop in front of the foot bath that leads to the pool. Beyond that, every step is crucial, each one bringing me closer to his covert hideaway. I hold on to the walls as I stretch over the water, past the point of no return. A glimmer of night passes through the domed roof, outlining the pool and the door behind it, the one that separates me from Shauna. I slink slowly along the poolside, past the stands, stopping every few steps to listen, until I hear the first sounds of muffled breath. I'm just feet away and I hear the blood pumping in my ears because I have him now, the callous power that he wields, the cocksure arrogance that he is untouchable.

As I reach for the door, I hear his strangled, hungry moans, and I waver, as if I had a choice. I'm caught in the jolting rhythm of his groans until it's all too close, too palpable, I just want it to . . .

Stop.

The door opens a crack, enough to see his hand on Shauna's wet, tangled hair, her face squashed against the wall as silent tears roll down her cheek.

"Shauna."

My voice is a whisper, frail with her pain. Then, his face on hers, that wiry mustache furled across her wet skin as he swaddles her from behind, his possession absolute even as his eyes flare with confusion first and then realization.

"What the fuck's going on?" I say meekly, trying to stick to the plan, the notion that I have simply walked in on them. But there is no remorse, no guilt, just a slow smirk spreading across his face.

"Really, Shauna?" he says, his mouth against her ear. "You'd throw everything away for that cunt?"

He places his palm flat against the wall and pushes into her.

"No," I scream. "What are you doing?"

He is punishing me, for Joe's article, for telling Sister Shannon, for daring to challenge a man like him. He's showing me he can do whatever he wants and nobody of any consequence is ever going to ask him to stop. He keeps his eyes on me as he pulls back Shauna's hair, kisses her neck and pushes into her again. She grimaces and shuts her eyes tight. I feel in my pocket for the camera, slide it open and put my finger over the shutter release button.

"It's like we're having a threesome," he says, his face warped with a joyless grin.

There's a fury that swells with time, smoldering inside, rising and falling, instinct versus conditioning. It can blaze right through you, and I feel it now, the furnace of my rage and the frenzied pleasure at the fear in his eyes as I push open the door. The camera flashes onto his bare chest pressed up against Shauna, anguish etched into every crevice of her face.

As soon as I've taken the photo I know I should run. I only need to get to the front door; he's hardly going to follow me through the school grounds in his swimsuit. He knows this too, and instead of giving chase he puts one arm around Shauna's neck and pulls her tighter onto him until she starts to splutter. He holds the other arm out to me.

"Give me the camera."

I look at the exit and then back at Shauna, grasping at his arm, struggling for breath. I can't leave her.

"Let go of her first," I say.

He loosens his grip on her neck and she sucks wildly at the air, but her body remains slack in his grip.

"Step away from her and I'll give it to you."

His lip curls in disgust at this shift in power, but he takes his arm from around her neck and slowly pulls himself away from her. She doesn't move, her crumpled shape still pressed against the wall. He is languid, standing impotent behind the door with his hands in the air as if I'm wielding a gun. He reaches out and I hold up the camera, fingers wrapped tight around it.

I slide forward and then, when the door is within my reach, I hurl my shoulder against it. It slaps against him, throwing him backward onto the storeroom floor.

For a moment, I think I can grab Shauna and run, but he is on his feet, coming at me with his hand raised high and then sharp against my cheek. I stumble and he is on me again, hands hard against my chest, and the legs go from under me. The side of my face smacks onto the tiles and blood fills my cheek as the camera skates across the floor to the edge of the pool.

"Did you really think this would work?" he says, standing over me.

"Fuck you," I scream, spluttering blood onto the floor. "You're a rapist and a murderer, and I'm gonna make sure everyone knows about it."

"A murderer? I haven't heard that one before."

"Tina would still be alive if it wasn't for you."

"Tina?" He puts his hands on his hips and laughs. "Tina couldn't handle it when I dumped her for Shauna. That's all there was to it."

"She was pregnant. Because you raped her."

Behind him, Shauna shivers in the doorway, arms wrapped around her chest like a straitjacket.

"Believe me," he says, "you don't need to rape a slut like that."

I'd always thought, if he knew, if he was confronted with the stark truth of it, he'd show some regret, a crumb of humanity. But isn't that the problem? Everyone gives him space to change but he uses it to keep doing what he's always done. I want to destroy him.

"She told me everything."

I expect him to falter, to fear or loathe me, but he just shrugs.

"Nobody's ever going to believe a little skanger like you," he says. He steps over me and walks toward the camera.

It's not just that word, it's all the put-downs and insults Highfield has layered upon me, all the times I was told it was just a bit of banter, that I couldn't take a joke. The anger flies out of me and I'm up, running at him, arms wrapped around his legs in a rugby tackle that lifts him right off his feet. He falls forward as I let go, arms flailing as his forehead smashes onto the edge of the pool with a single, violent crack that reverberates around the room until I can't tell if it's just the ringing in my head.

He lies still as blood seeps from his hair. We watch a black pool of it bloom slowly onto the tiles and drip into the water. We wait, until we are sure, until he can't touch us anymore. Shauna walks across the floor and stands over him.

"You've killed him," she says.

I fall to my knees. It's over.

39

The veil of night begins to slip, light bleeding context onto the shapes and shadows of my bedroom. The discarded satchel at the foot of a chair. The school gabardine draped across the back of it. The open textbooks on the desk, diagrams and definitions from another life. Only my dried blood on the pillowcase betrays the night's dark dance, the heavy crust of it the only material evidence in this reluctant dawn.

Under the duvet, I lie rigid, still fully dressed in purple, afraid to move in case I disturb the silence. I already hear him in every grumble of pipes, each groan in the walls, the roar of his voice and the hollow death crack of his head.

It perseveres, the light seeping into the room no matter how hard I blink it away, and I need to move with it, embrace the day like everyone else who was never there at all. I squat in the bath and ice water rolls off my back. In the kitchen, black coffee scalds the roof of my mouth. Mam's voice is a distant rattle, a tangle of words and cadences meant to chastise and hurry me along. I hear "unholy racket" and "awake half the night" and I nod and drag my bike through the house. A pedal scrapes against the architrave on the kitchen doorway and Mam's words swell and swoop until I leave the house and slam the door behind me.

The estate is a shadow, a ghostly blur of mist and morning that glides past as I autopilot through the visible world. The air is thick with smog and I think of Shauna and roaring fires, our limbs intertwined on a sheepskin rug, somewhere far away from this earthly hallucination. As if insomnia is my only problem, as if sleep will release me. But every time I close my eyes, he is there.

Traffic snakes down Highfield Hill, the road narrowed by the cars parked on both sides of it. I slide off my bike and push it slowly toward a gathering of purple uniforms, girls crying and hugging each other tight. I try to squeeze past but there's a hand on my elbow and I'm pulled right into Mary Connolly's shaking bosom. Through gulping sobs, I hear the words "swimmer" and "dead" and the sound of my bike clattering onto the footpath.

I want to tell her she's wrong, that no swimmer has died, but my sleep-broken brain can't be sure of anything anymore. All I know is that I left a living Shauna with a dead McQueen. She was going to get help, say he slipped, and I was never there at all.

I'm allowed to cry, but there is nothing. Not when Mary and Eva O'Brien wail in harmony beside me, not even when I see the fleet of Ford Granadas by the school gate, both marked and unmarked Garda cars. The Guards and girls move at such a low frame rate, I can't seem to interpret any of this waking dream. I need Shauna to tell me what's happening, what we're supposed to do next.

Guards usher girls and parents away from the main gate and toward the convent entrance farther down the hill. I follow, around the convent, through the cedar grounds to the back door of the main school building. From there, I see the Garda tape around the sports center, the ambulance at the pool. And I realize that means he's still there, almost fourteen hours after I left him.

There's no sign of Shauna or Melissa as we gravitate to our usual positions in the assembly hall and await further instruction. Parents line the walls, as eager as anyone to find out what's going on.

"Have you seen Shauna?" I ask Eva O'Brien, and she clamps her hand over her mouth.

"You don't think . . ." she says before she can stop herself.

"What?"

"Oh my god, not Shauna."

A ripple runs along the line and then spreads in all directions like a domino run. Voices rise and quiver with the syllables of her name, the tension palpable now that this tragedy has a human face. There are shrieks and more tears and I wonder if anyone has noticed Melissa is missing too.

A crowd blooms at the side door and I see Sister Mullen, hands raised, pushing past parents and daughters, all desperate for an explanation. Terror tears through me because it is coming; I can see it in her face. Gone is the collected control I'm used to, a dark resignation in its place. There's a hush as she creaks up the wooden stairs, past the unlit Christmas tree to the front of the stage. She clasps her hands as she looks out over her congregation and bows her head as she starts to speak.

"It is with great sadness that I must tell you . . ."

There's not a breath taken in the room, a collective paralysis as we hang on her every word.

". . . that Mr. McQueen has died."

It is over. My legs buckle, and I reach out to Eva, but she is gone, wrapped around Mary or Carol or any one of the girls who scream and cry and throw themselves at each other in disbelief that something so tragic, so cruel, could enter their lives. I crumple to the floor, and I'm not sure anyone even notices I'm here.

A STRANGLED SILENCE SETTLES OVER the hall as girls sprawl across the floor and the stage, waiting to give a statement in one of the nearby classrooms. Only those of us who were here last night remain; everyone else has been sent home until further notice with strict instructions not to speak to the press. There's a looming unease in the deadened air, a sense that this is something more than just a terrible accident. Or maybe that's my paranoia. Sleep hangs heavy behind my eyes and I drag them open and try to stop my head lolling back against the wall. I need to get out of here and talk to Shauna, make sure she's OK.

A third-year and her mother arrive at the door, the girl trembling, eyes wide and red. I know her, Claudia Doyle, one of the swimmers. Her mother speaks to Sister Mullen and the nun places a tender hand on Claudia's arm. As Claudia leaves the hall, her mother's arm around her shoulders, I shiver at the thought of what she has endured to deserve such an uncharacteristic display of compassion from Sister Mullen.

My turn comes quickly and a uniformed Bangharda leads me in silence along the corridor to the first-year classrooms. She opens a door to a harsh fluorescent glare, both lucid and disorientating. The shutters are closed and the overhead light paints a glaze of unreality onto the walls, the blackboard, the Guard sitting at a front-row desk. It makes me wonder if I'm really here at all.

"Hello, I'm Garda Kearns."

He's a broad-chested man with bushy eyebrows and a country accent, Galway I think. There are no formalities, no cordial smile to help put me at ease. Garda Kearns gestures to the chair opposite him and the Bangharda leaves. He takes my name and then my address, glancing up to get the measure of me before writing it down.

"Louise"—he sits back and looks me in the eye—"what time did you leave Highfield last night?"

I breathe slowly. These are straightforward questions with answers I've rehearsed all night.

"Ten past six."

"Before the end of the procession?"

"Yes. I felt sick so I left early and went home."

"Did anybody see you leave?"

"Melissa Courtney."

He looks up suddenly and, in the fluorescent haze, I panic I've made a mistake.

"I met her on the way out," I say, "and I talked to her for a few minutes. She'll remember."

"Yep," he says, "I'm sure she will."

I can't tell if his words are loaded, and I look away. On the blackboard is a mnemonic that describes the fate of Henry VIII's wives: divorced, beheaded, died, divorced, beheaded, survived.

"So you went home after that?"

"Yes. I got my bike from the bike shed and went straight home."

"Is there anyone who can confirm what time you got there?"

"Yes, my mam." She'll back me up. She won't want anyone to know she was blacked out drunk. "It was probably a bit before seven, ten to or five to."

"And did you see anything, or anyone, on your way out of the school? Anyone entering or leaving the sports center?"

"No, there was nobody else around. Just Melissa."

"OK, thank you, Louise. If we need anything else from you, we'll be in touch."

As I walk back down the corridor to the hall, my heart rattles in my chest and my face creases under the strain. I'm still wincing when the Bangharda rounds the corner with Mary Connolly and, even though I straighten up, she keeps her eyes on me as we pass.

I collect my bag and coat from the side of the hall and I'm making my way to the rear exit when Carol shouts my name.

"Lou, c'mere."

She's lounging on the stage with Stephanie and Eva, waving me over. I do what I'm told, lacking the energy for any alternative.

"What did they ask you?" she says.

"Not much, just what time I left and if I saw anything."

"What did you say?" asks Stephanie.

"Nothing. I mean, I saw nothing."

"Did they tell you anything?" asks Carol. "Like, is this a murder inquiry or what?"

The three lean forward, all ears.

"No. I mean, they didn't say. I don't think . . . murder? Surely there's no evidence of . . ."

"Look around you," says Carol. "We're all being questioned. Do you think they'd do this if Mr. McQueen just had a heart attack or something? There's something more going on and I'm starting to wonder if I should call my dad's solicitor."

"Oh, do we need to have a solicitor with us for the interview?" asks Stephanie. "I didn't think about it, but we should ask about our rights."

"I can talk to Sister Mullen," says Eva.

"What would she know?" says Carol, and Eva recoils. "I'll talk to the Bangharda as soon as she gets back."

"I'm gonna go now," I say.

I want to sleep with every fiber of my being, to cleanse my mind of fractured thoughts and memory gaps, but I have to find Shauna first. I need to find out what happened after I left last night, but more than that, I want to see that she's OK, that we're OK. I'm at the back of the hall, the exit door within my reach, when I hear my name again. A male voice this time, deep and assertive.

"Louise Manson."

I swing round to see two Guards marching toward me, their shoes clicking on the wooden floor as the hum of voices shrinks to nothing. I stand frozen at the door, my sleep-deprived brain unable to react. When they reach me, it's the tall one that breaks the silence, his thin lips delivering the final blow.

"I'm arresting you on suspicion of the murder of Maurice McQueen. You have the right to remain silent . . ."

After that, his voice slows to a dull thud and I want to disappear, but when I close my eyes, all I see is an explosion.

40

The red raw creases on my wrists, the inky residue on my fingers. All evidence of due process. The flash of a camera, a hand clapped on the back of the thin-lipped guard and the clank of the cell door as it's locked behind me. There will be no easy escape from any of this.

The room is lit only by the chink of light that slides through the bars on the door and it takes a few seconds for my eyes to adjust to the fact that I am not alone. The shape of a girl not much older than me sits on the edge of one of the two beds, her face tilted toward me. I stare at her yellow-bleached hair, her full suit of stonewashed denim, but she says nothing. I sit on the other bed, head in hands, and drift in and out of a suffocating dread.

"Whaddaya in for?"

Her voice sucks me back into the moment and the stark symmetry of these four walls.

"Shoplifting?"

It's the school uniform, the depiction of innocence and youth. I can only hope the press will see it that way, the reporters and photographers who were lying in wait when we arrived at Dundrum Garda Station. I'm just a schoolgirl and this is all a simple misunderstanding, a terrible mistake.

"No," I say. "Something I didn't do."

Her laugh echoes hollow in this hardened space.

"What about you?" I say.

"Something I did do. A while ago."

I want to ask her everything, how she was caught, her chance of conviction, questions I'm not ready to ask myself.

"How long will we be here?" I ask.

"They've got six hours to process us. So you'll be home in time for dinner."

It's all I want right now. To get out of here, sleep and work out how to make it all go away.

"Unless you've murdered someone or something."

She sniggers, and I'm not sure what sort of facial contortion betrays me, but her jaw drops and a smile spills across her face.

"What?" she says. "Not actual murder? Who d'ye kill?"

"I didn't kill anyone," I say quietly.

"Yeah, we're all innocent here," she says, and I throw her a look of such venom she holds her hands up.

"Look, I believe you. It's those bastards out there that don't care about the truth. But you and me, we're on the same side. So if you say you didn't do it, I know you didn't do it. But, you have to tell me . . . what is it that you didn't do?"

I don't know if it's my half-deluded state of mind or the fact that we're in the same boat but I feel the urge to unload some of this burden of guilt.

"They think I murdered him."

"Who?"

"My teacher."

"Your teacher? Oh Jesus fucking Christ."

She puts her hands to her face, and I look at the floor.

"Did he . . ." she says, "was he hurting ye?"

I nod.

"Like, abusing ye?"

"Yeah. Lots of us."

"Fucker," she says, and even though I know I shouldn't have said a word, that validation still gives me strength.

AS SOON AS MY CELLMATE leaves—Sonia Curley, I learn when the Guard calls her name—the bravado seeps out of me. I lay my head on the soiled mattress and fall into the black space between memories.

The sharp clatter of the door pierces the illusion of sleep and I am up, heart racing, lungs pounding. Through the crack in the door, I see my arresting officer and I know I need to pull myself together.

"Louise Manson?"

I follow him into a smothering of artificial light that glowers from the sterile surfaces of the corridor. Other Guards stop and stare, and I wonder what they know of the betrayals that have brought me here. I can't begin to imagine. I just need to stick to my story and hope the Guards don't have a better one.

The Bangharda from school is waiting in an interview room and I'm relieved to see a softer, more forgiving look on her face. Her dark hair is pinned to the back of her head and her eyebrows are plucked into an arch of permanent surprise. I find comfort in that small frailty, that tiny piece of exposed humanity. She sits at a desk in the middle of the small room, cut off from all earthly distractions apart from the gray sky that peeks through a single high window. Her colleague takes the seat beside her, thin lips pursed and ready, and I sit opposite, forcing myself to breathe in and out again.

"I'm Detective Sergeant Grace," he says with a Cork cadence, "and this is Garda Coleman."

She nods and writes on a yellow notepad.

"May I remind you that you have the right to let someone know where you are," he continues.

I shake my head. Mam would be no help to me at all. In fact, the combination of booze and what I've told her about McQueen could only make things worse for me. And I need to get my story straight with her before she talks to the Guards.

"And you can have a solicitor present if you choose."

I think about how the likes of Carol or Stephanie would swan in and insist on calling their dad's solicitor, but I don't have a dad or a solicitor. I wouldn't know who to call and, anyway, I'd be afraid it would only make me look even more guilty.

"No, thanks."

Sergeant Grace sneaks a glance at Garda Coleman. The air around me is chill and damp and my face stings with the cold sweat of a festering nausea.

"Tuesday the ninth of December at 12:35 p.m.," says the sergeant as Garda Coleman scribbles the details.

On the glossy gray-white wall behind their heads a tiny spider moves upward in short bursts of activity. I want to know how it arrived unbidden in this sterile room, how it's going to find a way out.

"Louise," says the sergeant, opening a notepad, "tell us again about last night. What time did you arrive at Highfield?"

"I was a bit late for Mass, so probably around five past, ten past five."

I clear my throat while Garda Coleman notes the time.

"Was there a reason you were late?"

"My mam cut her hand and I was helping her dress it."

"That's Rose Manson?"

"Yeah."

A jolt of panic shoots through me that they know Mam already, that they might get to her before I do. I keep my face frozen and my breathing steady.

"So you were in the chapel from ten past five until six o'clock, when you joined the procession around the school?"

"Yeah."

"And when and where did you leave the procession?"

"After about five minutes. I felt sick so I turned down the corridor to the music room and I went down the stairs and out the back door."

"Which is where you met Melissa Courtney."

"Yeah, I think she followed me. I thought I could hear someone behind me the whole time."

He looks up from his notes and squints down his long nose, intrigued at this piece of trivia that I wish I'd never mentioned at all.

"And you went straight home after that?"

"Yeah. I got my bike from the bike shed and cycled home."

"And you said you got home at ten to or five to seven."

"Yeah."

"Can your mother confirm this?"

"Yeah. I mean, I didn't talk to her, but she must have heard me come in."

He looks at me curiously.

"Why are you so sure she heard you if you didn't speak to her?"

"Because it's a tiny house, she would've heard the door."

"Right. She would have heard it from where exactly in the house?"

"She was in bed," I say reluctantly.

"OK," he says with unsettling cheer. "And what did you do then?"

"I was tired, I didn't sleep well the night before. So I went to bed."

"So you went to bed around seven and came into school this morning?"

"Yeah."

"Right," he says. He rolls his pen between his fingers as he reads back over his notes. Behind him, the spider reaches the ceiling and I will it to turn right, toward the window. At least there it will be able to see beyond the confines of this room.

"So . . ." he says, "you left the school at five past six and encountered Melissa Courtney outside the back door."

"Yeah."

"What did you talk about?"

I've thought about this, how much I should reveal. I can't be the one to tell Shauna's secret—that can only come from her—but I don't want to say something Melissa might contradict later.

"We were worried about our friend, Shauna. We were talking about checking in on her, to see if she was OK."

"That's Shauna Power, the swimmer?"

"Yeah."

"What were you worried about?"

"She hasn't been in good form, and she wasn't at Mass, so we just wanted to make sure she was OK."

"Where was she?"

"At training, in the pool."

"So you were going to go over to the swimming pool to see her?"

"Well, Melissa wanted to, but I said we should leave it. So we didn't go."

He nods and then taps his pen against his notepad. I scan the wall behind him for the spider, but it is gone.

"You said you think Melissa followed you outside. Why would she do that?"

"I dunno. Maybe she wanted to get away, too."

"But she didn't leave," he says. "She went back into the school."

It's his deliberate tone, the way he emphasizes every syllable. He wants me to know he has spoken to her already. But I don't know how that's possible when she wasn't at school this morning.

"Yeah," I say. "But I didn't see her after that."

"You didn't notice her anywhere on the grounds?"

I don't remember. Only the pale blue glow of a torch that I couldn't have seen if I was never there at all.

"No."

"Are you sure? Take a moment to think about it."

The sympathetic smile of Garda Coleman unnerves me as much as the smug satisfaction of her colleague.

"I . . . I don't remember seeing her."

"Well, she saw you."

The guilt burns across my face and he sits back in his chair, mission accomplished.

"What? How?"

Sergeant Grace flips over a page of his notepad and starts to read.

"Melissa Courtney states that, at 7 p.m., she saw you walk from the rear of the school to the swimming pool. You entered the pool complex and then exited at 7:15 p.m. You walked to the bike shed, got on your green bicycle and cycled straight past her on your way out."

I can picture her now, the long purple coat buttoned tight across her chest, the bitter loathing in a face lit only by the soft blue light of a torch.

"I think I want to speak to a solicitor," I hear myself say as I gasp for breath and sink into the darkness.

41

Russell Geary was clearly not expecting to work today. He's a slapdash mix of crumpled cotton and frayed tweed and the sweat oozing from the pores on his nose tells the story of a night spent without an eye on the clock. In the close confinement of the consultation room, a sickly stew of cheap antiperspirant and stale smoke wafts between us, keeping me alert and nauseous as I run through the events of last night. I keep my account short and concise, wavering only over the emergence of Melissa into the picture.

"Now, you have to be completely straight with me, Louise," says Russell. "Is she the only person who could have seen you?"

There is Shauna of course, but her testimony will surely vindicate me.

"Yes."

"Well then it's just her word against yours," he says, his voice a low and rasping warning. "Stick to the story you told me and don't be drawn into any questions that don't seem relevant, OK?"

"OK."

There's a rap at the door and I jump up, although my legs are shaking with the strain.

"Just try and stay calm," says Russell as he wipes the sweat from his forehead. "Keep your answers short and direct and you'll be grand."

Regardless of his yellow-stained fingers, the layers of grime around his cuffs, I need to believe in Russell Geary. Because once I leave this room, I'm on my own again.

GARDA COLEMAN AND DETECTIVE SERGEANT Grace are back in position, and I can barely focus with the pace of the panic in me.

"So, Melissa Courtney saw you enter the swimming pool complex at seven o'clock last night and then leave it at seven fifteen," says the sergeant. "What do you have to say about that?"

"She couldn't have seen me because I wasn't there," I say with a strained composure.

"You were at home? With your mother, Rose Manson?"

"Yes."

"You see," says the sergeant, "I have a problem with that. Rose Manson has no memory of you being home at 7 p.m. In fact, she seems to think it was a good bit later when you got back."

My mind races and I don't know how, why, they've got to her already. But I know I have to sacrifice her if I want any chance for myself.

"Mam was drunk," I say as tears prick the corners of my eyes. "That's why she cut her hand. She was so out of it she wouldn't know what time it was."

"How much did your mother have to drink?"

"Probably most of a bottle of vodka. I can check when I get home. She's an alcoholic," I say, lowering my eyes at the shame of the betrayal.

"Can anyone else verify her drinking habits?"

"Yeah."

I've protected her for so long, but I know it's an open secret.

"The staff at the Black Swan in Ballybrack," I say. "We both work there. And the Rambler's Rest. She lost her job there because of it."

I stifle a sob as I wipe a finger under each of my eyes.

"Well, Rose thinks she first heard you around eight or nine. She said you were playing loud music in your room. The Jesus and Mary Chain, she thinks. She turned it off, but you put it back on again. Would you agree with this part of her testimony?"

I don't know. I can't remember.

"I suppose."

"And it continued well into the early hours. Was there any reason you were up so late?"

"I couldn't sleep."

"Why not?"

As I scramble for words, I remember Russell's advice; I don't need to have all the answers. "I don't think that's relevant."

Sergeant Grace smirks as he sits back in his chair and looks me in the eye.

"Is it true Maurice McQueen was your mother's boyfriend?"

"What? No."

I can't believe Mam would be deluded enough to say that.

"I mean, they went out twice," I say. "That was it."

"Is it fair to say you weren't happy about it?"

Nothing about this is fair and I can't take the veiled threats anymore.

"When did you talk to Mam?" I ask, looking from one Guard to the other. "What have you told her?"

"We spoke to her earlier today," says Garda Coleman gently. "It's all part of the procedure."

"Tell me about your mother's relationship with Maurice McQueen," says the sergeant.

"There was no relationship. He was only trying to . . ."

"Trying to what?"

I open my mouth and then pause. "Nothing. I dunno."

Detective Sergeant Grace unclasps his hands and stretches his fingers while I try to ignore the screaming in my head.

"You said you wanted to kill Maurice McQueen when you found out he was going out with your mother."

"I didn't mean . . ."

I can't remember who I said it to, or if I even said it at all.

"You were obsessed with him, weren't you?"

"No."

"We have statements from Melissa Courtney, Aisling McWilliams, Stephanie Burke and Karina Kenny," says the sergeant, "who all say very similar things. That you spoke about your feelings for Maurice McQueen, often in a lewd and inappropriate way."

"That's not true."

"And that you took every opportunity to spend time with him, going to his office, asking for lifts, staying behind after class."

"That was all him," I shout. "He was the one who came after me."

I'm dizzy with the onslaught, the gunfire of names and accusations. Stephanie and Karina, even Melissa, I could almost understand, but I thought Aisling was my friend.

"You also made some serious allegations about him at school . . ."

My breath catches somewhere between my leaden breastbone and my throat and all I can do is shake in reply.

". . . after he spurned your advances."

"No."

"And we have in our possession a copy of a magazine in which you published your defamatory comments."

"It's all true," I shout, "and none of it makes me guilty of anything."

My voice slaps off the bare walls, shifting in tone and timbre until I'm too scared to utter another word.

"It's OK, Lou," says Garda Coleman. "We're not here to talk about that. We're just trying to find out what happened last night."

I can hardly remember. I need to get out of here and see Shauna, piece it all back together.

"Right," says Sergeant Grace. "Last night. You say you were not at the school between seven and a quarter past, the times Melissa saw you."

"That's right."

"You're certain?"

"Yes," I say, although I can barely hear myself. I already recognize the pattern of these questions and I know there's another wave coming.

"Melissa is not the only person who saw you at the school."

In a rush of panic, I try to remember a shape or shadow, but there is nothing.

"Shauna Power," he says, "saw you in the swimming pool complex during that time."

I wonder if he's talking about Sandra Powell, a fourth-year. He can't mean my Shauna; she'd never have told him that.

"No, you're lying," I say. "That's not possible."

Sergeant Grace flicks back a few pages on his notepad, looks down the bridge of his long nose and starts to read.

"Shauna told us that at around 7 p.m. you entered the pool area shouting Maurice McQueen's name. Mr. McQueen was in the storeroom and when he asked you to calm down you ran at the door, pushing it into him and knocking him to the ground."

"Oh no, Jesus."

It's my voice, but it's too distant to be me.

"Mr. McQueen tried to reason with you, but you were hysterical, shouting that you wanted to kill him. You shoved him again and he fell and smacked his head on the tiles."

The room fills with the growl of a low moan, guttural and sustained.

Muffled voices float above it, catching the rising pitch of a muted scream. I shut my eyes and let it drown me.

TIME PASSES IN WAVES OF light, pale shadows that drift like dust past the chink in the cell door. Minutes or hours slip by, measured only in the pulse of dreams. Flashes of dead eyes and bleeding bodies inhabit cycles of thin sleep punctured by bursts of jagged chatter. I can't be sure what's inside or outside my head and I don't know which voices to believe anymore. There's only one that hasn't yet denied me, the sole anchor I have left.

As soon as I enter the visitors' room Joe is on his feet. The tube lighting flickers and spits above him as the Guard instructs him to sit, and puts me across the table from him, no contact allowed. Joe's crumpled smile can't hide the fear in his eyes. It's the same expression he wore at Tina's funeral, an event that feels like it belongs to another realm, one where grief and time are human luxuries.

"I've been charged," I say.

"I know," says Joe, eyeing the Guard standing at the door behind me, as if I might forget.

He smiles, a desperate attempt to mitigate against everything that has happened in the last few hours, and it only makes me feel even more helpless.

"I just want to get out of here," I say, and the tears come at last, rolling down my cheeks as angry waves of despair shudder through me.

"Ah Lou, don't worry, please," he says, and he's crying too now. "I'm gonna do everything I can to get you out."

I know that means Kenny O'Kane, and I don't care. I want to wake up and find out that Kenny is the worst thing I have to worry about.

"I'd do anything for you, Lou, you know that?"

His eyes flare wide and I wonder what he means, if he's talking about an alibi, but it's too late for that. I've already told the Guards that I saw McQueen rape Shauna, that he went for me too before he slipped and fell. But there is something else he can do.

"Joe, I need you to find something for me."

"What is it?"

"I took a photo. Of Shauna with him, last night. I left the camera at the pool but the Guards say they never found it. Will you look for it? It's the only piece of proof out there."

"Yeah, of course I will. I'll do everything I can."

"Thanks."

I rub the tears from my eyes, but the exhaustion remains.

"Do people know yet?" I ask. "About me?"

"Yeah, I'm sorry," says Joe. "It's been on the radio and in the evening papers. I dunno yet about the telly."

"Oh god. Like, my name and everything?"

"Yeah."

He reaches his hands across the table and then pulls them back when the Guard looms over my shoulder.

"Did you talk to Mam?" I ask.

"I tried, but . . ."

"What?"

"She was . . . eh . . ."

"Drunk?"

"Upset."

I thought I couldn't sink any deeper, but there goes my heart.

"About him, I bet."

"Of course not. She's devastated about you."

I stare at the spasms of light on the ceiling as tears prick the corners of my eyes.

"I've made him into a martyr, haven't I?"

"You haven't done anything," says Joe firmly.

"No, fuck, I didn't mean . . ."

"I know, Lou," he says, glancing at the Guard.

My head throbs with the pain of remembering. What I did and didn't do, what I've said and should never say.

"I just meant . . . the press, they're going to idolize him and crucify me, aren't they?"

"So what if they do? None of that matters."

"And you, they're going to go after you too. That stupid fucking article."

"Please don't worry about me," he says. "Seriously, just focus on keeping yourself together while you're in here. Look, I've spoken to your solicitor and he's sure you'll get bail. You'll be home for Christmas, I promise."

Joe speaks with such certainty, but I shake my head.

"No, my hearing's tomorrow. They told me. In Dún Laoghaire."

"But . . ." He sucks his lips as he chooses his words. "You know that's the District Court? They can't set bail for a murder charge. You have to apply to the High Court for that. Didn't anyone explain it to you?"

When I was charged, there were voices and there were words, all merging into one discordant hum as I retched and spat onto the floor in front of me. After that, I clung to the one thing I could decipher: tomorrow's court date.

"Your solicitor said you should get a High Court hearing within two weeks," says Joe. "And then you'll be out. That's what you've got to focus on."

I look at him in bewilderment, this boy who's become a legal expert in the course of one day, who can talk murder charges with lawyers as if it's simply another academic module.

"No," I say.

"I wish I could do more, but look, it's just another few days and then, once you're out, we'll be able to make sure you never have to come back."

"No." I'm louder this time, breath coming quicker as the rage builds, as Joe slips further away.

"Ah god, Lou. I'd swap places with you if I could, you know I would."

"No," I scream. "I can't stay here."

I push back my chair and stand up, and the Guard is on me, a hand on each of my arms.

"Lou," says Joe, his face cracked with despair. "They won't keep you here. You'll be in St. Patrick's while you're on remand."

I try to shrug off the Guard, but he wraps an arm around my chest and pulls me to the door.

"It'll be way better there," says Joe as we leave, but he is wrong. After one night in St. Patrick's, I'll be begging for the luxury of Dundrum Garda Station.

42

The stench of urine sticks in my throat, long after I've left my six-by-eight-foot hole in the basement of St. Patrick's institution. The fetid odor was interred in the floors, the walls, frozen into the bitter, callous air of the place and I cannot cleanse myself of it, even as I step out of the Four Courts into the fading city light.

It's only when we make it to the safety of the taxi that I realize how drunk Mam is. I could see the flush in her cheeks across the courtroom, smell her sour breath as she hugged me tight after my bail was granted. But it's the roll of her eyes, inches from mine now, that leaves me in no doubt. There will be no respite at home, no day of grace tomorrow to forget and wallow in Christmas cheer. Joe puts his hand in mine and I rest my head on his shoulder and tune out the rising pitch of Mam's voice.

We crawl along the quays, every window in the city lit and the last-minute shoppers scurrying toward them like moths to a flame. As if nothing in the world has changed. Later, they'll catch a pint and a bit of camaraderie, and the merriment of the last bus home to their loved ones. Like a film on a loop, they won't even have to think about what comes next.

At the front door, Mam fumbles for her keys, pulling her bag apart until Joe takes it from her and opens the door himself. The signs of her decline are apparent, even before I switch on the lights. Letters scattered in an arc on the hall floor, dirty cups lined up on the half-moon table. I follow the smell of rotting food into the kitchen, and I have to turn away when I see the carnage.

"I was going to tidy up," she says without conviction.

I feel my top lip curl, rage concealed only by exhaustion.

"I'll do it," says Joe. "Why don't you both go and sit down? I'll bring in some tea."

"Thanks, Joe," says Mam. "I don't know what we'd do without you."

I follow her to the living room, where the furniture is decorated with discarded clothing and crockery. Mam pulls back the duvet on the sofa and I peel a pair of tights from the arm of a chair. A box of decorations sprawls in the space between us, strands of mismatched tinsel daring me to think of the alternate universe I left two weeks ago. There is no tree in the house, no sign at all that Mam has made any effort other than a single trip to the attic. I suppose I should be grateful she made it down in one piece.

I grab the remote control and turn on the telly. Jimmy Savile's belly hangs over a shiny blue tracksuit as he chats to the two starstruck young girls next to him. I'm about to flick over when I see Mam bend down and reach under the sofa. She resurfaces with the guts of a naggin of vodka and a smile as limp as her resolve. I do not smile back.

"Ah love, would you give me a break? It's Christmas Eve."

"You wouldn't know it in here. Have you done anything except drink for the last two weeks?"

Mam puts her hand to her mouth and tears pool in the dark circles under her eyes.

"You know it's been absolute hell for me?" she says.

"Well, I've had a ball in prison. Can't wait to go back."

A strangled sob catches in Mam's throat.

"I knew you'd be like this."

"Like what?"

"You don't understand what it's been like for me. It's not just a daughter I've lost, it's . . . it's . . ."

She drops her face into her hands, tears spilling through her fingers as the vodka falls to the floor, and I try not to think about what she means.

"No," I say. "Don't you dare."

Her shoulders heave and I'm on my feet, holding a finger up to her.

"If you mention him in this house ever again, I will fucking kill you, do you understand?"

I snatch the vodka from the carpet and march to the door.

"Lou, please," cries Mam, and I stop before I realize it's probably the bottle she's really after.

"I'M SAVING HER FROM HERSELF," I say to Joe as I crack some ice into a glass. "Want some?"

"Nah. Thanks."

I don't protest. He's elbow-deep in the washing-up and that's probably more use to me than a drinking buddy.

"I don't know how long I can survive here," I say as I search the cup-
boards for a mixer. "She's acting like he was the great love of her life."

"It's probably all been too much of a shock for her," says Joe. "And she
hasn't been in the right state of mind to process any of it."

"Oh god, she hasn't been making a show of herself, has she?"

I'll face all the accusations thrown directly at me, but I can't handle the
pitying looks and unsolicited advice that Mam's relapse will generate.

"I don't think so," he says. "I haven't seen her outside the house anyway."

"Well, that's one less thing to worry about."

I throw some orange juice on top of the vodka and ice and knock it back
in one. It takes a grimace and a shake of the head to get it down safely and
I stick my tongue out in disgust as I sit down at the table. Joe turns back to
the sink and I unfold the *Evening Herald* that's half hidden under a tea towel.
It takes a moment to realize the grainy photo dominating the front page is
me. And then the headline: *He Deserved It.*

My heart races as I look at the inset photo, the yellow hair and stone-
washed denim of Sonia Curley, my Garda station cellmate, and I learn the
first rule of defense: admit nothing.

The small print tells of Sonia's brush with me in custody, her inside
knowledge of McQueen's abuse.

"I'm not saying she did it," says Curley, "but he deserved to die. He was
abusing loads of girls at that school."

My face flushes with the naive stupidity of what I've done.

"I had to say something because these bastards are everywhere." Curley
goes on to allege abuse of her own at the hands of a national school
teacher, now deceased. "I never said anything because I didn't think anyone would believe me. But he made my life hell. I still have nightmares
about him."

It takes me several paragraphs to realize this is not the hatchet job I
expected but the start of an exposé that could help my defense. Not that I
plan to say I killed him because he was a monster. But it certainly gives me
hope that this could help a jury answer the other allegations leveled at me.

Curley's claims are backed up by Manson herself in an interview with the *Rathmines College Chronicle* earlier this month.

I gasp and Joe spins around, suds dripping from his hands onto the lino as he sees the photo.

"Oh god, sorry Lou. I didn't know that was there."

"No, it's OK," I say. "I think it might even be good. Here, look."

He dries his hands as he skims through the piece.

"Jesus," he says as he takes it all in. "That's . . . something."

"It's a start," I say, "but I need to talk to Shauna."

Joe throws me a look of disbelief.

"No way."

"You don't understand. She's my only hope."

An exhausted sigh spills out of him and he leans his elbows on the back of a chair.

"She's the main prosecution witness. You absolutely cannot go anywhere near her."

"But she's lying. And I know she wouldn't do that to me, not unless . . ."

"Unless what?"

"Someone must have made her do it."

"Who would do that?"

"Highfield? Her parents?"

"And you think Shauna would just go along with it?"

"I dunno, Joe. But if you're not asking these questions, what does that mean? Do you believe her?"

Joe never found the camera, the one piece of evidence that could back up my story. Either it's been discarded unwittingly, or one of the nuns has destroyed it and my chance of absolution with it. There are too many with too much to lose, the full force of the establishment against me now.

"No," he says. "Of course not."

"So you see why I need to talk to her?"

"Look, we'll sort all this out after Christmas, OK? Just promise me you won't do anything stupid before then?"

"What? Like murder someone?"

I see the fight go out of him and his eyes flick to the clock on the cooker. It's five to six.

"I'm sorry Lou, I can't stay much longer. I've promised my ma."

"Yeah, go and leave me, I'll be fine here with the alco rape-apologist."

"It's just . . ." he says quietly, "it's her first Christmas without Tina."

It's as if Joe has managed to freeze time, stills of the last year laid out like photos in an album. Tina dancing at Faces on New Year's Eve, Tina's tears painting tracks down her cheeks on that last night, Tina's bloodless body like a waxwork in the open coffin. And all the scenes I've had to live without her, from Santa Maria to Highfield, from Dalkey to jail, and the two of us back here at the house, trying to make sense of it all.

"Ah god, Joe, I'm sorry," I say. "I wasn't thinking."

"It's OK. We all have a lot going on."

It's only a few weeks since I kept her with me everywhere I went. Now it's *his* face that fills my days and nights, stealing her from me once again.

"I haven't forgotten her," I say, "if that's what you think."

"Of course I don't."

The weight of his kindness is all it takes to crack the outer shell and I crumble, grief pouring out of me in tears and wails as the strength goes from my legs. I collapse onto a chair and Joe is on me, his arms folded around my shoulders. I lean into the warmth of his neck, the silky sheen of his paisley shirt and, for now, this makes more sense than anything.

The moment is shattered by the toll of the doorbell, and I pull away from Joe and wipe my hands across my face.

"I can get it," he says. "You've been through enough already today."

"No, I have to face up to people round here at some stage."

As I pass the living room door, I'm relieved to see Mam asleep on the sofa. I don't know who I'm expecting to see in the half-light of the doorstep, but the sunken face of Derek Brady from next door is not on my list.

"Oh," he says, and pulls at his knuckle until it cracks, a single splintered snap of bone against tendon.

I shiver, trying not to look at his hands with their ripped fingernails and protruding veins.

"Is yer ma there?" he asks.

"She's in bed."

Another crack. And another, ligaments twisted and stretched to their elastic limit.

"What d'ye want, Derek?"

"Yeah, eh . . ." He can't look me in the eye. "I need to tell her something."

"Well, spit it out then."

I fold my arms across my chest to ward off the bitter wind that whistles up the drive.

"Right, yeah . . . she's late."

"Late for what?"

"Her payment. She didn't have it yesterday and I've been knocking in all afternoon."

"Oh, I get it," I say. "You're doing Kenny O'Kane's dirty work now, yeah?"

Derek kicks a pebble against the doorstep, eyes to the ground.

"And you thought it'd be a good idea to call round to your neighbors of, what, ten years, on Christmas Eve to demand his blood money?"

"Look, she owes the money. I'm just doing my job."

"Your job, yeah, right."

He looks up now, a vacant stare that cares nothing for me or Mam, and I can't help myself.

"D'ye know what I've been charged with, Derek?"

"I do, yeah."

"Well, if you don't fuck off out of here right now, I'll make sure you're next."

Derek puts his hands in his pockets and he's considering his options when I hear footsteps behind me.

"Everything OK, Lou?" says Joe.

"Joe," says Derek, "you're here."

"I am."

"You've saved me a trip."

Joe pushes past me on to the doorstep and pulls the door behind him. Through the crack, I see him pleading with Derek.

"I told you I'd sort it out on Monday."

"Well, the boss says there's nothing he can do. First payment was due yesterday."

Joe folds his hands behind his head and paces the drive.

"I only borrowed the money on Friday, it hasn't even been a week."

"It's cos of Christmas," says Derek. "Nobody'll be working until Monday."

"So let me pay then. What's the difference?"

"It's due now. If I let you off till Monday, there'll be a penalty."

"How much?"

"Fifty quid."

"Fuck," shouts Joe as he walks to the gate.

Derek follows and more words are thrown before he leaves, his hunched and haggard shape shuffling out of the light.

"What are you gonna do?" I ask Joe when he returns.

"I'll sort something out."

"It's the bail money, isn't it?"

"Yeah, but don't worry about it, you've got your own shit going on here."

"Thank you, Joe," I say. "I really mean it."

He smiles. "Are you going to be OK?"

I doubt Mam has any money stashed away, but we have a small amount of pawnable jewelry between us, enough for now anyway.

"Yeah, I will be when I get some sleep."

"OK. Look, I'm really sorry, Lou, but I gotta go."

"Yeah, of course."

Joe puts his arms around me, and I hold on tight.

"Thanks, again," I say, "for everything."

"I'll call round tomorrow, to see how you are."

And then he is gone, and I'm alone with space to breathe and think. I feel the ravages of endless broken sleep and the weight of decisions to come, and I know the only thing I can handle right now is oblivion. I don't bother with the ice this time, I just drown the vodka in the orange juice, hold my nose and hope for the best.

43

The phone is a distant drone, closer with each pulse, until sleep is snatched from me and my brain jolts into action. For a moment of blind panic, I can't make out the shape of the room and my eyes flit through the darkness looking for an anchor. As I gasp the air into me, I see Mam draped across the sofa, one arm hanging over its side, and relief pounds my chest. It's OK. I'm home.

I remember the contours of the day now, Mam's dole money taken by that little prick next door, only enough left for a bottle of vodka, not even the Coke to wash it down. I let the phone ring out and check my watch. It's 5:45 p.m., the afternoon gone from us and only a dry mouth and a full bladder to show for it. The ringing starts again and Mam groans, but she doesn't move. She's used to letting life unfold around her hangovers. I sit up in the armchair and nausea forces me back down, and I give up on the phone.

Nobody rings here anymore so it's either very important or another abusive crank threatening rape and violence. Friends and neighbors have been frightened away by the verdicts delivered by vested interests in the media, at the pulpit and in schools across the country. There was the sermon by the archbishop that warned of the deadly power of lust and the obligation of every parent, teacher and clergyman in Ireland to stamp it out before more of our young women are possessed by it. And the Irish Swimming Association have wasted no opportunity to sanctify their hero and call for a swift and merciless sentence. When I leave the house, I half-expect to see my mugshot, Myra Hindley–style, plastered across billboards with a target on my head.

The phone starts again, and I hoist my queasy body off the chair and into the hall. It's Russell Geary.

"Lou, how are you?"

"Fine." I groan with the effort it takes to squeeze a pleasantry out of me.

"Good, good, good, good. Tell me, what do you know of a Sonia Curley?"

My former cellmate has been talking to any tabloids and pirate stations that will have her. I've kept as much distance as possible from the media and it's only from Joe that I hear the edited highlights. Apparently, Sonia's been speaking about her own sexual abuse and pointing out the hypocrisies in the discussion of mine.

"I met her in Dundrum Garda Station. I might have said something to her."

"Yes, I gathered that from a certain newspaper article."

"Oh yeah, sorry about that."

"No, no, no, don't be sorry. Sonia called me and she's found something. Or someone."

"What do you mean?"

It's bound to be nothing, but I can't help a flutter of hope.

"She was on Radio Freebird, one of the small pirates, based out in Santry or Swords or somewhere, and this woman called in to say she'd been abused at Highfield too."

"Oh my god," I say. "Who is she?"

"She wouldn't give her name, unfortunately. It was a good few years ago so you probably wouldn't know her anyway, but get this, it wasn't Mc-Queen she was talking about. It was Aidan Heffernan, do you know him?"

I feel nauseous at the thought of another rapist in my life.

"I've heard of him. He coached at the club a few years ago."

"Yeah. According to this source, he moved to another club after her parents made a complaint. But they weren't the only ones. It took several victims and their parents to come forward first."

"Jesus Christ. How many of them are there?"

"Enough to give us hope. If we can find people to talk, we can paint McQueen as an aggressive rapist operating in a culture of abuse. The sort of person who wouldn't think twice about trying to attack a young woman like yourself. You see where I'm going with this?"

"Yeah."

It's all we've got. Especially as the Guards claim they found none of my blood at the pool, the one piece of evidence we'd hoped would back up my story of a struggle.

"So I'm going to get this Sonia into the office to talk about how she can help us find other victims who might be willing to speak up and we'll see if we can turn this conversation around, OK?"

"OK," I say and, despite myself, I let Russell's newfound enthusiasm in. For the first time in a long time, I feel like I can breathe on my own.

RUSSELL'S OFFICE IS NINE SQUARE yards of scuffed floorboard at the top of a Georgian terrace in the north city center. Wind clatters against the sash window behind him and scuttles into the room through cracks in the panes, and the rest of us brace against it, arms folded and coats pulled tight. Only Russell doesn't seem to notice, sleeves rolled and the usual flush in his cheeks as he leans his elbows on his desk. Across from him is Julie Gillespie, a beautiful and poised woman in her early twenties with perfect skin and big ash-blonde hair. She contacted Sonia Curley after hearing her on one of the late-night pirate stations and she's here to tell an all-too-familiar story of Maurice McQueen.

When Julie speaks, we all listen, Sonia Curley beside her, and myself and Joe leaning against the wall behind.

"I met him at a gala at King's Hospital when I was fourteen. I only came third, but he still went and talked to my dad and, next thing, I was going to Highfield. I didn't need any convincing, I'd dreamed about joining a club like Highfield and Maurice made me feel so special. He told me I could make the Irish team, the Olympics even."

Julie speaks slowly and methodically, as if she has rehearsed every line.

"On trips to competitions around Ireland, he'd give me a lift and he'd put his hand on my leg as he drove. At the time, I didn't think he was doing anything wrong. I wanted him to like me more than anyone else and I thought that meant he did."

Her voice shakes for the first time and she stops.

"Can I get you a glass of water or anything?" I ask.

"Yeah, thanks." She turns around and smiles gratefully.

"I'll do it," says Joe.

"Sorry," says Julie. "It seems so stupid now, but I trusted him."

"Of course you did," I say. "Everyone trusted him, that's how he was able to get away with it."

"You know, when I heard you on the radio," says Julie to Sonia, "I couldn't stop crying. I just sat in my flat for hours with your phone number on a piece of paper in front of me."

Sonia leans across and takes Julie's hand.

"I thought I was the only one," Julie continues. "Hearing you talk about the others, I couldn't believe it. It made me feel I wasn't alone, but at the same time, I was so angry. Not just at him, but at myself for thinking I was special. If I'd said something back then, maybe none of this would have happened."

"This is not your fault," I say.

I remember how firmly Matron said those words to me, how empowering it was to have someone believe me. I wish I'd told her the truth now, that I'd named McQueen as my abuser, because Russell insists any testimony that suggests I made accusations against multiple men will do more harm than good.

"He's the only one to blame here," I say, "and it's not your duty to help me or anyone else. But I'm very grateful that you want to."

"Thank you," she says.

Joe returns with a glass of water and Russell picks up his pen.

"You were saying about the lifts he gave you," he says.

"Yes. He started with a hand on my knee, and then it was kissing, on the mouth, tongues and everything. I was so confused. I thought he wanted to be my boyfriend and, honestly, I would have let him back then, I was so eager to please him. But he started ignoring me in training and I couldn't work out what I'd done wrong. I was swimming better than I ever had in my life, winning medals at every gala, and that still wasn't good enough for him."

She stops to take a drink and a deep breath.

"It was only when he left me off the team that I confronted him. It didn't make any sense. Why would he choose swimmers who weren't as good as me? So that evening, I waited until everyone else had gone home and asked him outright. He told me his feelings for me were too strong, and he couldn't bear to be around me anymore. He even cried and said he'd tried so hard to fight it. And I remember calculating in my head that if I let him touch me, he'd have to put me back on the team."

"Bastard," says Sonia, still holding on to Julie's hand.

"That's how it started. I never meant to let it go very far, but when he got what he wanted, he was nice to me, and when he didn't . . . it got to the point where I'd just get it over with so I could swim."

"I'm very sorry," says Russell, "but I have to ask, did he have intercourse with you?"

"Yes, many times," she says quietly. "The first time, I kept saying no, but he wouldn't stop. After that, I just tried to block it all out until it was over."

I look at Joe, biting his lip as he takes in the cold reality of it for the first time. I slip my fingers through his and he squeezes his appreciation.

"What age were you then, the first time?" asks Russell.

"Fifteen."

"And where did it take place?"

"In his car."

Disinfectant coated in the bitter smell of aftershave.

"Was it always in his car?" asks Russell.

"No, most of the time it was in the storeroom at the end of the pool. Once in a hotel room after a competition."

"And how often did it take place?"

"About twice a week for two and a half years."

Joe sucks air through his teeth and I feel his arm stiffen.

"How did you stop it, in the end?"

"I gave up swimming. I just walked away from it. I'd made the Irish team, but he was coaching them by then so there was no escape. I was starting college and I wanted a clean break. So I left. Nobody understood it. My dad never forgave me. But I'm not sure I'd be still here if I'd stayed."

"Do your family know?" asks Sonia.

"No, and I was round at my parents' last week after your radio show, and there was something about it in one of the papers and my dad said, 'I don't believe a word of it.' He still thinks he was God."

AS JOE AND I LEAVE Russell's office, I feel relieved that of all the Highfield victims out there, Julie is the one to come forward. This is a woman people will listen to. It's not just her looks and her Dublin 4 accent, she has that delicate balance of dignity and vulnerability that will play well with a jury.

"She's good," I say to Joe when we get out into the bracing wind.

"Too good."

"I'm sorry, that must have been really tough for you to hear."

"Well, yeah," he says, "seeing as I'd been deluding myself about the extent of it."

"We don't know it was like that for Tina," I say, but he shakes his head.

"Fuck it, d'ye wanna go for drink?"

"Oh, I dunno," I say, looking at my watch. It's gone four, so I only have two hours before my court-imposed curfew kicks in.

"Go on," says Joe. "I'm buying."

"OK, maybe just a quick one then."

He hooks his arm through mine, and we walk down Marlborough Street to the Plough, a dive of a pub with cheap beer and colorful clientele. A few old lads prop up the bar and Joe chats to them while he waits for his pint to settle. I steer clear of the punks and find a booth in a secluded corner. Scrawled on the wall next to the ripped vinyl seat is an anarchist symbol and a quote.

WE ARE NOT IN THE LEAST AFRAID OF RUINS: DURUTTI

It sticks with me, the idea that destruction means a beginning as much as an end. I am used to ruins, to making something out of nothing. In some ways, it's who I am.

The first pint goes down smoothly and, by the second, the tension is seeping out my fingers and toes. When Joe comes back with a third round, he pushes in beside me. I rest my hand on his thigh and he links his fingers through mine.

"I think we've turned a corner," he says. "I really do."

"I dunno. We could have ten Julie Gillespies, but they only need one Shauna Power."

"But it's only her word against yours."

"Ah come on, Joe," I say, squeezing his knee. "Even you're not that naive."

"Hey," he says in protest, but he's smiling, his leg pressed up against mine and, for the first time in months, I feel normal. Three pints and some human warmth is enough to suspend the guilt and the dread for just a moment, and I could barely be more grateful.

WHEN WE HIT THE BRACING cold, it's already twenty to six and there's no time for a bus or a DART. Joe hails a taxi and I don't protest, even though I'm sure he can't afford it. Mam's behind on her payments and I don't know how Joe's keeping up with his, the interest galloping past the principal already.

In the back seat, I rest my head on his shoulder and he wraps his arm around me. Just an ordinary couple making our way home from town. It could be that easy.

"You up to anything for the night?" asks the taxi driver.

"Nah," I say, "we're just going home."

"Quiet night in?"

"Yeah," says Joe. "Something like that."

I look up at him, those trusting hazel eyes that only ever see the best in me.

"Could do with one of them myself," says the taxi driver.

I don't allow myself another thought and I lean into Joe until my lips brush against his. He hesitates and then pulls back, and I wonder if I've made a terrible mistake.

"Are you sure?" he whispers.

"Yeah," I say, "I think so."

I'm not sure of anything, but I can only work with the ruins I have. When we kiss, it's soft and intimate and safe. And I'm pretty sure it's not going to end in murder, and that's enough for now.

When the taxi pulls up outside my house, I don't let go.

"Will you come in?" I ask.

"If you want me to."

"Yeah. I mean no. I need to talk to you. There's something I need to say."

I don't know how shocked or hurt Joe will be, but I need to tell my-self. If he hears it for the first time in court, he might never trust me again.

44

I can see them all from up here on the bench. The nuns, teachers, parents, neighbors, classmates. They've all come to bear witness. An eerie calm hangs in the space between us, the air dazed and diffused with an illusive distance. I'm on display, isolated and confined, already an outcast. So much for the presumption of innocence.

The court registrar calls Melissa Courtney and heads turn to see the young woman approach the witness box. She's dressed in a single-breasted gray suit, modest and mature. An everywoman. I've been instructed to go softer, younger, to try and dispel the media narrative of a crazed and jealous stalker. I'm in a blue shift dress and a yellow cardigan with my hair combed flat and I'm surprised my own mam recognizes me. I glance over and her grimace softens to a smile, but I see how uncomfortable she is, squeezed into a bench with Sister Keating and Sister Mullen whispering behind her. It's a wonder she made it at all, the state of her this morning, but I'm grateful for it.

Melissa's voice trembles as she is sworn in. The prosecution barrister stands, and I sit up and brace myself. Mr. Sullivan is a short, round figure who'd be lost under his wig and gown if it wasn't for the resonant voice he projects across the courtroom. No syllable is left unenunciated as he delivers his proclamations.

"Miss Courtney," says Mr. Sullivan, peering through the wire-framed glasses that sit at the end of his nose. "I understand you were at Highfield on the night of the eighth of December, 1986."

"Yes."

"I understand there was a Mass to celebrate the Feast of the Immaculate Conception."

"Yes."

"Can you talk me through what happened after the Mass, when you left the chapel?"

Melissa turns toward the jury in a move that must be rehearsed. All but one of the twelve, two women and ten men, have their eyes on her. Only the young woman with the bleached fringe and the blue satin shirt looks to me for a reaction, and I give her my deepest despair in response. She will be my focus, the one person I need to believe in me.

"We had a procession through the school in the dark with everyone carrying torches," says Melissa. "We put this colored crepe paper over the torches so they glowed in different colors, and that's all you could see really. I saw Lou's light go off in front of me and then she turned off by the music room, so I followed her."

"Why did you follow her?" asks Mr. Sullivan.

"I was worried she was going to the pool."

"Why would she go there?"

"Shauna had training with Mr. McQueen. Lou had this idea there was something going on between them and she wanted to break them up."

My eyes flick over to Joe, sitting behind the bar table, shaking his head. We knew it wouldn't be easy, but they are going for it. Russell scribbles a note and hands it across the table to Mr. Fagan, my barrister. He's a restless man, fingers drumming on his thigh or running through the shock of white hair that protrudes from the back of his wig. I'm really not sure what to make of him and can only hope his agitated bluster is a tried and tested technique. He reads the note and holds a palm up to Russell, as if to say, let's wait and see where this goes.

"Why?" asks Mr. Sullivan.

"Because she was jealous," says Melissa.

"Of Miss Power?"

"Yes. She was obsessed with Mr. McQueen."

"Why do you think that?"

"She used to tell me how much she fancied him, and she was always hanging around after class and going to see him in his office."

"And was there anything going on between Miss Power and Mr. McQueen?"

"No, of course not."

Mr. Fagan pushes his chair back from the bar table, ready to pounce, and Mr. Sullivan takes his cue to move on. He flicks over a page of his notes and takes a deep breath.

"Miss Courtney," he says. "What happened when you went after Miss Manson?"

"I followed her out of the school to see where she was going. She said she was going home so I took her word for it and went back to the procession."

"And what time was that?"

"Ten past six."

"When did you next see her?"

"I left the school at seven and I saw her walking to the swimming pool. She went in the main entrance, and I waited at the back of the school till she came out again."

"What time was that?"

"A quarter past seven. She went to the bike shed, got her bike and cycled past me on her way out."

I want it to end there, for Melissa to grant me that mercy at least. But she sits still and poised, waiting for instruction as her barrister clears his throat.

"What did you do then?" he asks.

"I went over to the pool. The lights were off, but Mr. McQueen's car was outside so I went in to look for Shauna. I couldn't see her at the entrance so I called her name. When she didn't answer, I went into the changing rooms and she was just standing there in her swimsuit, crying and shaking. When I asked her what was wrong, she said, 'She killed him.'"

Those three words reverberate around the courtroom, and I have to grab on to the brass rail in front of me. It was Melissa. She's the one who turned Shauna against me, who talked her out of the plan we'd agreed together. The juror in the blue shirt stares right at me, but I can't muster the strength to react. I feel only numbing resignation.

"What did she mean by that?" asks Mr. Sullivan.

"She said that Lou had attacked Mr. McQueen and he was dead."

"Did she say exactly what had happened?"

"She was in shock. I helped her get dressed and it was only after we left the school that she said she saw Lou push Mr. McQueen and that he fell and hit his head."

Melissa falters, the final words sticking in her throat.

"Thank you, Miss Courtney, and please, take a moment if you need one."

He is only delighted to let Melissa's testimony linger as she has a drink of water and composes herself. I glance over at Joe, rubbing the back of his neck, and then Mam, head in hands. I don't mean to stare at Sister Mullen, but I catch her eye and she looks away, refusing me any suggestion of sympathy.

"So," says Mr. Sullivan, thumbs tucked into the pockets of his waistcoat, "where did you go after you left Highfield?"

"We got a taxi to Shauna's house."

"Why didn't you go straight to the Guards?"

"Shauna wanted to talk to her dad, Charles Power. He's a solicitor."

Mr. Sullivan nods. He knows him well, I'm sure.

"What time did you get there?"

"A bit before nine."

"And yet you didn't go to Dalkey Garda Station until eight forty-five the next morning. Why?"

"Mr. Power didn't get home until after seven in the morning. He was out, working late on a case."

She keeps a straight face, but she must know that's a lie. I bet Charlie Power had some explaining to do.

"So as soon as you spoke to him, you went to the Guards?"

"Yes."

"Thank you, Miss Courtney," says Mr. Sullivan.

Mr. Fagan gathers his papers, arranges them on the podium and then leans his elbows on it and folds his hands together in a move as measured as I've seen him make.

"Did you know Miss Manson was in a relationship with Miss Power?"

"What?"

It's out before Melissa has time to think and her shock is echoed across the room.

"Oh yes," he says. "They were very close. In fact, I think it's fair to say that neither of them would have had any interest in Maurice McQueen, or any man for that matter."

Mr. Sullivan is on his feet, hands and gown swinging.

"My Lord, this is ludicrous and utterly irrelevant. I apply to have it ruled inadmissible."

Judge Campion is a man of measured calm, and he takes his time to consider this.

"Please, My Lord," says Mr. Fagan. "I'm trying to establish that Miss Manson was not jealous of Miss Power, nor was she obsessed with Mr. McQueen. I'd like to show the jury two photographs that support this."

The judge beckons both barristers to the bench and examines the pictures, Shauna posing in her bra, the two of us kissing.

"I'll allow it," he says. "Please continue, Mr. Fagan."

Despite the exhaustion, the grinding sense of doom, I can't help feeling a flourish of victory as Mr. Fagan lays down the two Polaroids in front of Melissa. She shakes her head at the first and puts her hand to her mouth when she sees the second. She looks straight at me with a sadness I didn't expect, and I wonder if she's having second thoughts.

"Miss Courtney, do you recognize the two young women kissing in the photo?" asks Mr. Fagan.

"Yes."

"Can you tell me who they are?"

"Shauna and Lou," she says, and the whole room inhales at once.

I've never tried to label my feelings for Shauna, I never dared think beyond the heat of the moment. I didn't want to allow outside voices in because I knew what they'd say. I hear it now in the gasps and mutterings and I want to shout, no, it wasn't like that.

I look over at Joe, unfazed and stoic, though it can't be easy for him. He's taken it all quite reasonably, as if it comes with the territory, and I hope he's not saving his resentment for later. Mam, on the other hand, has not been forewarned and the news is like a shot of adrenaline to the heart. Wide-eyed and alert, she has shed her aura of self-pity and I almost dare to hope she finally gets it.

As the photos are passed around the jury, I pray that some of them can see beyond the inevitable scandal to the human side of it. It's a huge risk and I know the press will gorge themselves on it, but it may just provide enough reasonable doubt to my motivation and put a question mark over Shauna's too. I know it could go either way, amplify the monstrous caricature that's already out there, but it's all I've got and I have to hope at least one of the jury can understand.

"Miss Courtney, I want you to take us back to Highfield on the night of the eighth of December. You say that you were following the procession around the school when you saw one of the torch lights in front of you go off. You noticed it belonged to Miss Manson, who then slipped away down a corridor."

"Yes, that's right."

"If you were behind Miss Manson in the procession, how could you have known it was her torch?"

"I . . . I don't know. I just did."

"Was it because you were watching Miss Manson, following her?"

"I could see her ahead of me."

"Did she already tell you of her plan to go to the swimming pool to check on Shauna?"

"She might have said something."

I almost feel sorry for Melissa, the flush in her cheeks as she scrambles to save herself.

"By 'something,' do you mean the numerous times Miss Manson told you that Miss Power was being sexually abused by Mr. McQueen? Was that why you were both so interested in going to the pool that night? Because you wanted to stop your friend from being raped by her teacher?"

Mr. Sullivan is up, scuttling to his podium amid a flurry of cries and gasps across the room.

"My Lord," he says, "I apply to have this evidence ruled inadmissible. It's hearsay and it's also completely irrelevant."

Judge Campion holds up his hand and leans forward to talk to the court registrar before making an announcement.

"I'm going to ask the jury to leave the courtroom, and then I will hear submissions from both sides."

As the members of the jury file out, I look over at Russell, and he shrugs. Across the table, Mr. Fagan flicks through a ring binder as though his life depends on it.

"My Lord," begins Mr. Sullivan. "This is nothing more than an attempt to smear the deceased, an honorable man who is not here to defend his good name. But more pertinently, his sexual proclivity is simply not relevant to the matter before this court."

"Mr. Fagan?" says the judge.

"My Lord, I put it to you that it is indeed relevant, in fact it is the single most relevant consideration in determining what happened at Highfield that night. Miss Manson has given a statement to the fact that not only was she abused by Maurice McQueen, but that she witnessed Miss Power being raped by him in the storeroom at the pool that night."

"My Lord," says Mr. Sullivan, "Miss Power vehemently denies that any such incident ever took place."

"We have two witnesses," says Mr. Fagan, "Julie Gillespie and Paula Fletcher, who will testify to being sexually abused by Maurice McQueen in that very storeroom over a number of years."

Unease ripples through the spectators as excitement turns to discomfort. Murder they could handle, but rape allegations against such a powerful man is not something anyone wants to face.

The judge takes his time, makes some notes while Mr. Fagan crosses and uncrosses his arms, shifts his weight from one foot to the other. Each anxious movement hits like a punch to the gut until I can't look anymore. I close my eyes and pray.

"Mr. Sullivan, Mr. Fagan," says Judge Campion, and nobody moves a muscle. "I agree with Mr. Sullivan. I am ruling this inadmissible. Mr. Fagan, you may not present any further evidence that relates to this matter."

Mr. Fagan throws his head back and shuts his eyes, and I know I'm done for. All our work, all our hopes have relied on this inconvenient truth. Without it, it's just me against Highfield, and I already know how that one goes.

45

I wake from nothing into the trance that's been shadowing me like a cloud since that night. Today, it doesn't wait for me to leave the house, to engage with the world. It clings to me as I struggle to wash, dress and breathe through the thought that Shauna is about to deliver the blow that will send me back to prison for a decade.

The doorbell rings and I take my cue to pull myself together. It'll be Joe, both the harbinger of reality and the comfort from it. I've almost beckoned him in before I notice the mop of red hair and the wily smirk on that angular face. Kenny O'Kane is the last person I want to talk to this morning but here we are.

"Mornin', Lou."

He holds his fists in the pockets of his leather jacket as if he's got a gun in each hand.

"What do you want?"

"I'll be brief," he says. "I know you have to rush off and prove your innocence. And I believe you by the way, millions wouldn't."

I hold his gaze but say nothing.

"So yeah, you owe me money, you haven't paid me that money and I'm starting to think you're never going to pay me at all."

"We will," I say. "Just as soon as—"

"Just as soon as wha'? You walk outta that court a free woman? You're not Houdini and your ma's not Betty Ford."

I look away then, the undeniable truth laid bare in the words of Kenny O'Kane.

"So I've been thinking," he says, "what do you have that's worth something to me? You know, something that would wipe the slate clean for you, for your ma and for bleeding-heart Joe there across the way?"

I dread to think what Kenny has up his sleeve, but I'd agree to almost anything to get rid of him right now.

"You know what I want? I want you. All to myself. For one night, and then you can walk away from both of the debts."

For a few seconds, there is nothing but the ringing in my ears, as if time has stopped to wait for my answer. It's only now I feel the true terror of the choice that feels like no choice at all, a kind of death instead. Like Shauna, like Tina. And yet, in these seconds of stillness, I'm already considering it. Just one night to end the constant panic of it, for me and for Mam and Joe.

"It's a win-win situation for you, love," says Kenny, as if he gives a shit about any of us.

If today doesn't go well, it's over for me anyway, but maybe I can numb myself enough to scrape out a win for Mam and Joe before that happens.

THE WIND LASHES AN ICY rain at us as we push through the crowds of press and rubberneckers that line the footpath outside the Four Courts. Joe ushers me forward and I keep my head turned away from the voices that clamor for position, lobbing questions as we pass.

"Was it a crime of passion, Lou?"

"Did you plan the murder together?"

"Were you in love with Maurice McQueen?"

"Ignore them," whispers Joe as he leads me up the steps to the front gate.

Beyond the baying mob, I see a banner, *WAR: Women Against Rape*. Sonia Curley's there, and Julie Gillespie and Paula Fletcher and twenty or thirty other women chanting, "No means no," all doing their best despite the judge's ruling. I take comfort in the fact that no matter what happens, something bigger than me has begun.

COURT HAS BEEN DELAYED SO I pace the floors while Joe and Russell strategize and Mr. Fagan talks to the judge. Mam's not here; she didn't even make it out of bed this morning. When I get to the end of the corridor, I almost walk smack into Charles Power, bulling around the corner. I mumble an apology, but he is unmoved, his cold blue eyes filled with such hatred it scares me. He bats me away with a flick of his hand and the truth of it hits me. This is nothing but damage limitation for him. He doesn't care about justice, he's only here to protect his lot.

Mr. Fagan returns from the judge's chambers with even more fluster than usual, rubbing his temples and massaging his head as he explains that Shauna has been delayed and won't be here until after lunch. The prosecution will call another witness this morning instead.

Sister Shannon is grace personified as she sits upright in the witness box, one hand resting on the other as if she is as much at ease here as anywhere else. She delivers her testimony with great sadness, clearly devastated she was unable to contain my obsession with McQueen, despite her best efforts. The court is subjected to the whole unraveling, my spurned advances, my attempts to discredit him and the subsequent breakdown he witnessed in my home.

Mr. Sullivan leans into his deference, as if every word Sister Shannon says is blessed by God Himself. They've got the crowd with them, the mothers clutching their scarves, the girls on the edges of their seats.

"Highfield Manor has a long history of helping the underprivileged," says Sister Shannon as though she is giving a sermon. "Our ethos is one of compassion and charity for those less fortunate than ourselves. And it was with these Christian values that we took Louise on, despite the many flaws in her background."

I want to scream that I was paying as much as anyone else to attend her poxy school.

"Although Louise is an illegitimate child, we would never hold that against her. But I suppose growing up with a convicted criminal for a mother has left its mark."

She looks up and I follow her line of sight all the way to Charles Power in the front row. He looks away, breaking eye contact with her, but not before I know what he's done.

"My Lord," says Mr. Fagan with a flap of his gown, "this evidence, if it is indeed true, is irrelevant and being used purely to prejudice the jury against my client. I ask that it be ruled inadmissible."

"I agree, Mr. Fagan," says Judge Campion, and he turns to address the jury, but I already know it's too late. Sister Shannon and Charles Power have got exactly what they wanted; the jury won't just forget what a gurrier I am. I rest my head in my hands, relieved at least that Mam's too hung over to be here today. I wouldn't want her drinking herself into another arrest.

Sister Shannon concludes her testimony with a eulogy of Maurice Mc-Queen and we're left with an impression of the goodness in him that, even after everything, he wouldn't press charges against me. I don't know why it's deemed admissible to refer to his good character when we're not allowed to give testimony to the contrary, but nobody else seems concerned about this.

Mr. Fagan takes the floor from Mr. Sullivan with a sweeping flourish of his long, black gown.

"Sister Shannon," he says, "thank you for coming today. I know it can't be easy for you or any of the staff at Highfield to be here under these circumstances."

"No. Thank you," says Sister Shannon.

"I understand that you were rightly concerned about Miss Manson's well-being, especially in the light of her interactions with Mr. McQueen. What I want to know is why you thought Miss Manson was interested in a relationship with Mr. McQueen. Did you see any evidence of this yourself?"

"Well, no, not specifically," she says.

"So why did you make that assumption?"

"I didn't assume anything," she says with a hint of irritability. "Mr. McQueen told me himself."

"And did you have any evidence to the contrary?"

"I had no reason to disbelieve Mr. McQueen. He was a teacher of the utmost integrity."

Mr. Fagan pauses, hands on hips, as if he is confused.

"So you didn't know Miss Manson was in a relationship with Miss Power?"

Voices rise and fall again in anticipation, maybe hope, of another salacious revelation.

"No, I don't believe that for one minute," says Sister Shannon.

There's something about Mr. Fagan's nod, both sympathetic and skeptical, that signals the calm before the storm.

"Sister Shannon," he says, "I understand that on the morning of the first of December of last year, you gave a talk to all the sixth-years in the music room at Highfield."

"I . . . I don't know," she says, her eyes darting to Mr. Sullivan and back.

"Let me refresh your memory," says Mr. Fagan. "You were concerned about a, quote, 'gross breach of conduct and morality' that had been reported to the school. You spoke to the girls about the dangers of, again quote, 'shameful, unnatural acts' and the damage this could do to Highfield's reputation. Do you remember now?"

"Yes," she says quietly.

"Was this talk, that you gave to the whole year, brought on by the fact that Miss Power and Miss Manson were seen kissing in Highfield Park the previous Thursday lunchtime?"

"No, absolutely not," she says, her words submerged in the swell of surprise from the crowd.

"Are you telling me you have no memory of speaking on the phone to Margaret Behan, the woman who made the complaint about Miss Power and Miss Manson, on Friday the twenty-eighth of November?"

"I don't know," says Sister Shannon, eyes down, both hands balled into fists. "I don't remember."

"Because she remembers talking to you. She was so upset by what she witnessed that she had no choice but to let you know and you assured her that you would take the matter in hand. In fact, you went as far as to say the two young women, whom you seemed to recognize by their descriptions, would be suitably reprimanded."

Sister Shannon glares at the prosecution, as if she can summon the powers that be to rescue her as they always do. I look at Joe, the coy smile lingering in the corners of his mouth. This is his work, a few white lies and the persistence of a professional newshound. He'll go far.

"I'd have to consult my diary," says Sister Shannon. "I deal with so many people every day I couldn't possibly comment without checking."

"Are we to believe, Sister Shannon, that the incident that inspired your impassioned talk to the entire year was only one of many transgressions committed by Highfield students that same day?"

As Sister Shannon fumbles for words, Mr. Sullivan steps up to his podium.

"My Lord," he says, "Sister Shannon has already explained that she does not remember the details."

"I am simply trying to establish," says Mr. Fagan, "that Miss Power and Miss Manson were indeed having a relationship, and that this relationship had been brought to the attention of Sister Shannon as early as November, a time when she insists Miss Manson was chasing Mr. McQueen."

"I'll allow it," says Judge Campion.

"Sister Shannon," says Mr. Fagan, "did you know that Miss Manson had been spotted in a passionate embrace with Miss Power in Highfield Park?"

"I was aware that girls matching their descriptions were involved, yes."

"Thank you, Sister Shannon."

I'll take that small victory, but I know it could well be overturned by the battle yet to come. Shauna's no pushover on her own, but with the weight of her family and Highfield behind her, I'm not sure I stand a chance.

THE AFTERNOON SESSION IS ALSO delayed, and I wait outside the court-room with Joe, his hand resting on my knee to stop it bouncing like a jack-hammer. No amount of platitudes can calm me down and I'm up, pacing the corridor to try and break the tension. As I reach the corner, I see the outline of a gray veil and a familiar beaked nose protruding from it. I try to turn back, but it's too late, I'll have to face her.

"Louise," says Sister Mullen, not unkindly. "How are you?"

"I've been better, Sister."

"I'm sure it hasn't been easy for you."

"No, Sister."

She attempts a smile of sorts.

"God is understanding and compassionate. He knows your intentions and he sees the bigger picture. If you seek forgiveness, you will find it."

If I didn't know they were all against me, I might think this was some sort of vague acknowledgment of McQueen's actions. I'm about to leave when I realize I have nothing left to lose.

"Sister?"

She turns away, as if she already knows she's said too much.

"You knew, didn't you?" I say.

"I should go now," she says.

"No, please, Sister."

I step in front of her, blocking her path.

"You know what Mr. McQueen did to all those girls. And Mr. Heffernan too."

Her eyes flare, just enough to make me wonder if the Heffernan revelation is new to her.

"You have to help me," I say. "You have to speak up. Not just for me, but for all the other girls, too. Or this won't be the end—can't you see that?"

She sucks in a breath and for a moment I think I've got her.

"Only God can save you, Louise. He's the one you need to talk to."

She clasps her hands together, bows her head and walks away with a practiced piety that only fuels my rage.

"You have blood on your hands," I shout. "You all do."

I hear the gasps behind me and I don't want to turn around to the shocked and disapproving faces. I put my head down and march straight to the toilets. In the solace of a cubicle, I sob silently at the stupidity of the girl who thought she could take them all on. That justice for Tina was ever an option. I know now that the only person I can ever hope to save is myself.

I don't hear her come in, but when I leave the cubicle she is there, corkscrew curls hanging over the collar of her fitted gray jacket. She stares red-eyed into the mirror, watching me as I approach.

"Melissa," I say, and she nods.

I wash my hands and she takes her time, wiping a finger slowly under each eye.

"Are you OK?" I ask.

"No."

I want to ask her what she expected, if she really thought fucking me over would be easy, but I sense an opportunity.

"What's wrong?"

We speak to our reflections, the mediators of this uneasy exchange.

"It's Shauna," she says. "She's disappeared."

"What do you mean she's disappeared?"

My whole body is gripped with the fear that something irrevocable might have happened.

"Nobody's seen her since last night, and . . ."

"What?"

"She hasn't been well." She puts her hands to her face. "I don't know what she might do."

"Melissa," I say, "you need to explain to me exactly what you mean by that."

She turns and looks me in the eye, as if she knows I am the only person who can help.

"I think she might try and kill herself."

"Fuck, no," I shout, and bang my fists on the basin.

I've been through this before with Tina; I can't survive it again. I need to do whatever I can to find Shauna before it's too late.

46

As soon as court is adjourned I tell Joe I'm going to the toilet and I pick up pace until I'm outside, racing down the quays to Tara Street DART station. The sky is dark and mottled and the wind lashes the rain against my bare legs. I turn up the collar of my blazer, but it is poor protection against a day determined to drown me in its sorrows.

As the DART rumbles south along Dublin's coastline, I'm only half-focused on the swell of the gray-green sea, the broken rhythm of the waves as they hurl their weight onto the shore. In my mind's eye, I see Tina on that last night, cross-legged on the orange rug as she sucked joylessly on a cigarette and told me about McQueen. How he'd first put his hands on her at age fifteen, kissed her at sixteen and then raped her only a few weeks later. How she couldn't tell me because it would make it real and she'd lose everything, the promise of a career most kids on our estate couldn't even dream of. And all I could think about was the betrayal of his hands on her body, that she would let him touch her like that when it was all I'd ever wanted.

Tina will never know why I questioned her story, why I wouldn't go with her to England for an abortion. She will never understand why I walked out and left her crying and pleading on that orange shag-pile rug. I just didn't have the guts to tell her how I really felt about her. And no matter how many times I say he killed her, I know it's not true. She's not dead because of him. It's because of me.

In Dalkey, I run through the rain-drenched streets until I reach the sea-front. At the edge of Dillon Park, the waves bloom onto the rocks below and I wonder if I've made a mistake. The tide is almost in, the rock where we shared our first kiss half-obscured already and Dalkey Island barely visible in the distance.

As I climb down, the wind whipping the rain at my face, my thin pumps slip and slide on the loose stones, and I have to hold tight to the overhang of bristled shrubs. There is no shore below, the usual sliver of sand buried

under the rush of the waves, and I lurch sideways until I reach a large boul-
der and scramble to the top.

That's when I see her, wrapped in an anorak, bare feet and legs hanging
over a ledge in the nearby rockface. I slither down and claw my way across
the rocks, scraping a groove down my shin in the process. When I get to
her, clothes stuck to me and blood painting a line down my leg, she is silent
and unmoved.

I push in beside her and say nothing, our knees touching, our breathing in sync. The sea swells and crests, swells and crests, each silent threat
released and restated. A wave breaks below us, the tide creeping closer
with every outburst. In five, ten minutes, it will be upon us, forcing us out
of here. I shudder with the fear of it, the crippling force of its raw power.

"What's going on?" I say.

She stares straight ahead, as if she hasn't seen me at all.

"I can't do it."

"Do what?"

"Court."

My heart sinks and I know I'm going to have to fight for her.

"You'll have to do it eventually. If you don't, you could go to prison and,
trust me, you wouldn't like it."

"I'm sorry." She bows her head and silent tears fall onto her lap. "For
everything."

"It's not too late," I say cautiously. "You can change your testimony.
Even if you said what really happened, that would make things easier
for me."

"There's no point," she says. "You're better off if I just disappear completely. The case will fall through without me."

"What do you mean, disappear completely?"

Her hair falls forward across her face so I can't see it.

"Shauna, you're scaring me. Please tell me what you're talking about."

The sea sprays onto our bare legs, salt stinging my open wound.

"I have nothing, Lou. I've destroyed everything."

"What do you mean? You have so much—your family, your friends,
swimming."

She pushes her hair behind her ear and I see the hollows of her eyes for
the first time.

"Is that it?" she says.

"You'll be going to college next year," I say, scrambling for scraps. "That'll be a fresh start for you."

She shakes her head as if she doesn't want any of it.

"And me," I say, taking her hand, "I don't want you to . . . disappear."

Shauna pulls her hand away and covers her face.

"How can you say that after what I've done?"

The sea is at our feet now, the cold water filling my shoes, but I don't move.

"I know it's not you, Shauna. It's everyone else trying to turn you against me."

"Melissa was only trying to help me."

"I know," I say, although the confirmation is crushing. "But whatever you've done, we can get past it. It's not too late."

"You don't understand," she cries, her face obscured by her hands. "Mr. McQueen. It was all my fault."

The rage rushes out of me, the absolute fury that, after everything, he still has the power to make her believe that.

"Do you know what?" I shout. "He deserved to die. If he was alive, he'd still be raping you and all the others. It was never your fault, not one bit of it. People will understand that. You have to tell the truth, not just for me but for everyone else he's hurt too."

"I can't, I'm sorry," she says as a wave crashes against our legs. "I ruined everything. I hurt the one person who . . ."

"What?"

"It doesn't matter," she says. "Nothing matters."

I reach out my hand, but she jerks it away and then she's on her feet, teetering on the edge of the rockface before I have time to think about what she's doing.

"It's better for you this way," she says.

"Shauna, no," I scream, and I grab at her as she pushes off the ledge and plunges into the water.

She swims out into the waves and I'm left behind, paralyzed by the fear of going after her and the terror of doing nothing. Seconds feel like minutes and I stand frozen as my brain tries to calculate the probability of survival for any given action. I kick off my shoes, pull off my blazer, close my eyes and jump.

Under water, time flickers and flares as the shock of the cold tears through me. The silence roars in my ears and all I can do is let go and trust my body to catch the rhythm of the waves. I could swim before; I can do it again. I kick and grasp at the water, lift my mouth to the air, and all I can think is, I can't let this happen again.

"Shauna," I shout, but she doesn't hear and I carry on, thrashing at the tattered sea, pushing through the pain.

I call again and this time she turns, her head bobbing as I wave, and I think I've done enough to save her. She knows how terrified I am of the water; she has to see this as the grand gesture it's intended to be. But it's not enough. She pulls away, putting even more distance between us until I have no choice but to save myself. With the wind howling and the rain clattering around me I do the one thing that is still within my power.

"Shauna," I shout, her name ripping through my throat, "I love you."

The light is fading from the day, and I can no longer see the shape of her in the water.

"I love you," I roar again and again until the breath is gone from me, and I have to turn back.

I can only hope the sea hasn't drowned me out, the wind hasn't twisted my words. I've done everything I can and I have to let Shauna make her own decision now. She's a strong swimmer; she'll make it back to shore, if that's what she wants. If her heart hasn't been gouged to nothing by Maurice McQueen.

47

I choose my clothes for court carefully. Not the bland, juvenile costume of before: I want the jury to see me today. My life is in their hands and I am not an abstract prototype, a sample version of a teenage girl gone bad. I want them to think about what music I like, what books I read, where I like to hang out with friends on a Friday after school. When I look that young, satin-shirted juror in the eye, I want her to wonder if our paths have crossed, if she's ever seen me at Faces or a gig at the SFX.

It's not just the jury I'm thinking of, it's Shauna too. When she enters the courtroom, and I pray with all my heart she does, I want her to remember who I am, no matter what her parents or the nuns or the swimming authorities might have said to her since I left her last night.

I'm tucking a black shirt into the waistband of a long pencil skirt when the doorbell rings. It's too early for Joe, but it's not him I'm expecting anyway. I slide on my brogues and take my time on the stairs, my resolve building with each downward step.

"Howiye, Lou," says Kenny, an unlit cigarette hanging from the corner of his mouth.

"Kenny," I say with a nod.

He flicks open a lighter and pulls hard on his cigarette as it flares to life.

"I've just dropped round to wish you luck in court today," he says, "and to finalize our business agreement."

It's stopped raining, but the ground is still black with evidence.

"I need to get my hands on you while I still can."

He laughs and takes another drag of his cigarette.

"So tonight's your lucky night. I'll come round at eight."

He inhales and waits for my surrender. I let him blow his smoke into the ether before I show my hand.

"In your dreams, Kenny," I say, holding up a big wad of notes.

"What's that?"

"It's your money. Every penny of it."

I hand it over and he leafs through it.

"Where d'ye get this?"

"That's none of your business. And *we* are none of your business anymore."

I wait for Kenny to count the cash, my hand on the door.

"Hold on a minute," he says. "This is what you owed last week. I only put the interest on hold because I thought we had a deal."

There comes a time in every girl's life when she's had enough of playing by rules that are rigged against her. When she realizes the consequences of breaking them are no worse than following them.

"You do know, Kenny, that I have the whole country's press hanging on my every word? Wouldn't they love to know that my poor mam is being threatened by illegal money-lenders, even after she's paid everything she owes? D'ye reckon that'd be good for business, having the Guards sniffing around? Sure everyone knows they're just waiting for any excuse to lift you."

His upper lip curls and, for a moment, I'm afraid he's going to go for me.

"You think you're so fucking smart," he says, walking away. "Wait till you're sent back to St. Patrick's. I know people everywhere."

I think about what lies in wait for me there and I don't let Kenny see me shudder. But I need to forget about that for now, I've another day in court ahead.

IT FEELS LIKE EVERY PHOTOGRAPHER in Dublin is outside the Four Courts, and I make use of the opportunity to stand with Sonia Curley and Julie Gillespie and the rest of the *WAR* women and we raise our fists in solidarity with all victims of sexual abuse. It's the enduring image from the case, even if it is used to illustrate my defiance. Before I leave, I hug every one of the women and thank them for raising the money to save me from Kenny O'Kane. I promise to join them in protest as soon as I can.

EVERY HEAD IN THE ROOM turns to see Shauna as she walks to the witness box. My heart skips with relief that she is here, and then sinks when I take in the navy business suit, the hair pinned back into a tight bun. The styling is an intervention that has surely come from Charles and Olivia, and I fear her words will be scripted by them too. They're sitting tall at the front of the court with Ronan, who looks at me with such animosity I can't help but throw it back at him. Behind them, I see a row of classmates, and I have to look away before any of them can get into my head. I glance at Joe, in his usual spot behind the bar table, and Mam beside him, bleary-eyed but present.

Shauna is sworn in and takes her seat without once looking my way. The overhead light wraps her in a soft glow that feels both intimate and distant and I can't predict which way she will go. My teeth grind with the stress of it, the anticipation of the words that will release me or condemn me to rot in St. Patrick's.

Mr. Sullivan clears his throat and waits for the crowd to pipe down before addressing his star witness. This is his moment to shine, to nail this case shut once and for all.

"Miss Power, I understand you've attended Highfield Manor school since you were three years of age."

"Yes."

Her voice is small and tight, her body upright and rigid.

"And you're an honors student and a prefect there?"

"Yes."

"I understand you've been a member of Highfield swimming club for the last six years."

"Yes."

"And you're planning to swim in the Olympics in Seoul next year?"

"Well . . ." she says, and a slight grimace cracks the facade. "I hope so."

"I understand Maurice McQueen was your coach since you were thirteen," says Mr. Sullivan.

"Yes."

"How would you describe your relationship with him?"

"He was an excellent coach."

Mr. Sullivan waits for Shauna to continue, but she is not forthcoming.

"Did you ever have any . . . issues with him, personally or professionally?"

My pulse slows to a dull thud as I clench every muscle in my body.

"No."

My head falls into shaking hands, and I try to stop the breath from rushing in and out of me. When I look up, Joe has his arm around Mam, her head buried in his chest.

"Is it true to say that he went out of his way to help you?" asks Mr. Sullivan.

"Yes. He gave me private training and drove me to galas and other competitions."

"I understand he even brought you to Florida last year."

"Yes, for a training camp in a fifty-meter pool there."

"So would it be fair to say that his death has been a considerable blow to you?"

"Yes."

Until now, I'm not sure I ever truly believed she would go through with her planned testimony. I was convinced that our relationship would be enough to stop her. That once she saw me in court, she'd have no choice but to save me. But now I'm paralyzed by the certainty that she will only save herself.

"On the night of the eighth of December last year, you were training with Mr. McQueen at the Highfield pool."

Mr. Sullivan's chest is puffed like a pigeon as he lays the groundwork for his big reveal.

"Yes."

"I understand you finished at seven o'clock and then you helped Mr. McQueen tidy away the equipment into the storeroom at the back of the pool afterward."

"Yes."

"And I understand it was at this point that Miss Manson arrived."

"Yes."

"Can you tell us exactly what happened when she entered the pool area?"

Time unspools as Mr. Sullivan speaks, his words melting into a slow-motion drawl, and I'm underwater again, plunging into the hazy darkness. Only this time, there's nobody else to save. Nothing I can do except sink and hope that someone will catch me.

"She came in through the changing rooms while we were still in the storeroom."

There's not a shadow of remorse on her face, her expression resolute as she prepares to deliver the final blow.

"Mr. McQueen went out to see who was there."

I can't look anymore. I close my eyes and wait.

"He shouted at her that she shouldn't be there, and she told him she'd come to see me."

Even with my brain numb to proceedings, I know these are not the words I read in her statement. The ones I rolled around my head a thousand times. I open my eyes and the first thing I see is Mr. Sullivan, leafing frantically through his notes.

"When I heard Lou's voice," continues Shauna, "I looked out the storeroom door and Mr. McQueen was walking toward her."

"Miss Power," says Mr. Sullivan, his voice rising, "may I remind you that you are under oath. Can you tell me again what happened when Miss Manson arrived at the pool and, this time, please refer to the statement you gave to the Gardaí on the ninth of December."

Shauna clears her throat and turns from Mr. Sullivan to face the jury.

"Lou didn't push him," she says. "He slipped."

The strength goes from me, and I slump forward onto the brass rail in front of me, the shapes of the courtroom fading to a gray haze. It's not the lies that will kill me, it's the hope. And I'm not sure how much more of it I can take.

48

The air is cooler in the corridor, and I rest my drowsy head on Joe's shoulder as the wigs and cloaks scurry past. There's no sign of Russell or Mr. Fagan, nobody to tell us what's going on or what to expect. Court has been adjourned while Mr. Sullivan speaks to Shauna, and I can only imagine the pressure Charles Power is putting on her right now. Mam clings to my hand, sucking a shivering breath through her teeth while I try to ignore the Highfield girls, who feel entitled to stand and stare.

Russell rounds the corner, and Joe is up and on him.

"Even if Shauna goes back to her original story," says Russell, "we'll move for a mistrial. She's been proven unreliable and the prosecution's whole case depends on her."

"That's good news, right?" says Joe. "Lou will be acquitted?"

"It's not that simple," says Russell. "Even if the case was dismissed, it's likely it would be tried again."

"Oh my god," I say. "I can't do it, I can't."

I bury my head in Joe's coat to try and stifle the cries that shudder out of me. And then Mam's at it, wailing in harmony as Joe tries his best to calm the pair of us.

"Is that really the best we can hope for?" asks Joe, but I hear no reply.

When I look up, Russell is already gone and I am being ushered back into court. I'm going to have to face this alone, again, myself and Shauna head to head one final time.

A LEADEN SILENCE FALLS ON the courtroom as Shauna arrives back to the witness box and Mr. Sullivan takes position at the podium. Shauna's rigid posture gives nothing away, but it's Mr. Sullivan's relaxed movement that tells me it is surely over. I can't take the stress of another performance and I wish they'd just spit it out and put an end to this torture.

"Miss Power," he says, "please take us through what happened on the night of the eighth of December, after Miss Manson arrived at the swimming pool. You stated that she arrived around 7 p.m., shouting Maurice McQueen's name."

"Yes," she says.

"And what happened then?"

"She pushed him, and he fell."

Her voice is robotic, emotionless, as dead as I feel inside.

"Can you clarify, please, Miss Power? Who pushed whom?"

"Lou pushed Mr. McQueen."

"This is when you were in the storeroom?"

His arm tight around her neck as she struggled to breathe.

"No," she says. "I mean, yes."

"In your statement, you said Miss Manson ran at the door, pushing it into Maurice McQueen and knocking him to the ground. Is that what happened?"

Her shivering body crumpled against the wall.

"Yes."

"And how did Mr. McQueen react?"

"He . . . he tried to get Lou to calm down."

His hand sharp against my cheek, my blood splattered across the tiles.

"What did he do?"

His flexed body looming over me, that twisted grin on his face.

"He said . . ." She closes her eyes. "He said . . ."

Slut, skanger, cunt.

"Miss Power? Can you please tell the court what happened when Maurice McQueen confronted Miss Manson?"

She opens her eyes and looks straight at me as a solitary tear paints a trail down her cheek.

"He slipped and hit his head on the tiles and fell into the pool."

The gasps come first and then the murmurs, and I turn to see Mam, already crying, Joe hugging her tight. Mr. Fagan and Russell lean across the bar table in frenzied discussion while Mr. Sullivan waves his arms in the air.

"My Lord," he shouts, "I wish to consult with the witness."

"Yes," says Judge Campion, turning to face Shauna. "But first, I would like to talk to you myself."

I see a weary defeat in the slump of Shauna's shoulders, and I realize,

there is no judge or jury to declare her innocence, no one to absolve her of
what she's done, even if we both get to walk out of here today.

"Miss Power," says the judge, "your testimony today contradicts that
which you gave in your statement to the Gardaí. Which are we to believe
is the truth?"

"I'm sorry," says Shauna, a quiver in her voice. "I lied to the Guards. Lou
never touched him."

Mr. Sullivan slaps his hands on the bar table, his face flushed with frustration.

"I must ask you to consider very carefully what you've told us," Judge
Campion says to Shauna. "Your testimony will determine the outcome of
this case and I need you to tell us with absolute certainty what you saw
that night."

There isn't a whisper in the court as we wait for Shauna to speak, not a
breath taken from any of us.

"I was in the storeroom with Mr. McQueen when we heard Lou outside. He went out and told her to leave but she said she wanted to see me."

She stops and reaches for her glass of water, and I see the shake in her
hand.

"Mr. McQueen was walking over to her," she continues, "when he
slipped and hit his head on the side of the pool. He fell into the water and,
when he didn't surface, I told Lou to go. I knew she'd get blamed for it, even
though she did nothing wrong."

It's a version of the truth, one that releases me from culpability and
Shauna from the stigma of abuse. I can only hope it will be enough to rid
us both of the ghost of McQueen.

"Why did you lie to the Guards?" asks Judge Campion.

Her breath stutters and she takes a moment to steady it.

"I was afraid we'd be accused of killing him because . . ."

Terror surges through me and I'm underwater once more, paralyzed
with the fear that she is going to steal it all away from me again.

". . . because . . ."

And then I'm swaying, struggling to my feet, and it's out before I can
stop myself.

"No," I shout, and time slows to nothing as every eye in the courtroom
turns to me.

"Miss Manson," says the judge, "please remain quiet or I will have to hold you in contempt of court."

Silence rings in my ears as I take in the scene around me, Joe and Mam clinging to each other, the girls and nuns on the edge of their seats. Russell's hand moves up and down, a gesture for me to sit, and I fall back onto the bench. I can't look at Shauna; I can only pray I've done enough.

"Miss Power, please continue."

"I was scared we'd be blamed for Mr. McQueen's death," she says quietly, "because we didn't try to save him."

Below me, Mr. Fagan pumps his fist discreetly and my heart jolts with it.

"Thank you, Miss Power," says the judge.

There's a new momentum in the courtroom now, the whispers and gestures and half-hidden grins that spread across the public benches. And in front of them all, Charles and Olivia and Ronan Power, upright and unmoved, as if none of this had anything to do with them at all.

As Mr. Fagan takes to the podium, Russell gives me the thumbs-up, but I still don't know what this means.

"My Lord, the defense believes there is no case to answer and we wish to apply to have it dismissed."

Judge Campion nods and begins to write. I close my eyes and count to ten repeatedly while the unbearable tension screams from every corner of the room.

"I have no choice," says the judge as the numbers pound a rhythm in my head, "but to dismiss this case."

It's not until I hear Mam's cries that I dare open my eyes, and she is pushing past Joe, clambering to get to me, when Mr. Fagan holds up his hand and the blood drains out of me. It's not over yet.

"Mrs. Manson, one moment, please." He turns back to the judge. "My Lord, we wish to seek a dismissal of all charges on the basis of Miss Power's evidence."

Judge Campion nods slowly in acknowledgment.

"Mr. Fagan, Mr. Sullivan," he says, "there is no case to answer. Miss Manson, you are acquitted and you are free to go."

I may have screamed or shouted, and I must have fallen forward because Mam has me in a headlock, her muffled wails ringing in my ear. And Joe is crying and kissing my face, and all around is muted chatter and fractured movement as I try to stand and make my way along the bench and out into the slow-motion swarm. I feel Mr. Fagan take my hand in his and Russell's arms around my back, and the lights are blinding, forcing me inside my head as Joe kisses me full on the lips and leads me past Shauna and her family with their cold eyes and sleeping secrets, and we walk out of the courtroom, me, Mam and Joe, through the Round Hall to the entrance, the waiting press and the life beyond.

PART FIVE

Now

49

The sun slips into the bay, casting its red-gold shimmer on the water as I make my way along the seafront. There's a fire in the fading light, a burning memory that calms and steels me at the same time. I've spent my first day of exile at home, making plans, preparing speeches and trying to silence the voice in my head that tells me to leave Highfield and Melissa well alone. That I'm no match for the power and wealth of any of them. I've grown so accustomed to that cynical voice I've forgotten it's not part of me. At least, it never used to be.

My mind races with the challenges ahead—a trip to see Melissa in London tomorrow and a showdown at Highfield on Monday. I'm going to explain all of it to Alex tonight, but first I want to make sure I've got my head straight. I need advice from the only person who will get it. I need to talk to Joe.

Katie answers the door with five-year-old Danny by her side.

"What are you doing here?" she asks.

"Well, I'm not here to see you, if that's what you're afraid of."

"Daaaaad," she shouts, and the two of them scoot back into the TV room while I wait at the door for Joe.

"Hey, Lou," he says, coming out of the kitchen with a tea towel in his hand. "What's up?"

"Have you got a minute to chat?"

"Yeah, yeah. I'm just making dinner, but come on in."

I sit at the kitchen table while Joe seasons a pot of Bolognese and I tell him about my forced eviction from work and the deal I've made with Mick Craddock at the *Evening Express*. I say nothing of my planned trip to London; I'm not sure how I'd explain the Melissa situation to him.

"Oh Jesus," he says, and I hold my breath until a smile breaks across his face.

"What?" I say.

"It's just . . . this is exactly the sort of thing teenage Lou would have done."

I appreciate the sentiment, but Joe never knew teenage Lou as well as he thought. Despite everything we've been through together, he still doesn't know the full horror of what I've done.

"And look where that got me," I say.

"It never got you what you deserved. But now?" He laughs. "This is some top-level doxxing combined with nerves of steel. You're crazy but you're also kind of a genius, you know that?"

"Well, that's a relief," I say with a smile. "I was afraid you were just going to tell me I was crazy."

Joe turns off the hob and sits across from me.

"Look," he says, "I certainly think you've got enough to force a settlement out of Highfield. But you can't rely on the likes of the *Evening Express* to carry the weight of this story. You need a more established outlet behind you if you want to blow the whole thing open. Let me talk to some people and see what I can do."

"God Joe, that'd be brilliant."

"It won't be the *Irish Times*, of course, but I have someone in mind. It will have to wait till next week though. We're off down to Rosslare tomorrow for the night."

"Nice."

"I asked Katie if she wanted to come with us, but she tells me she has plans."

"Yeah, thank god," I say. "She's going to the cinema with some of the girls from school. I hope it'll pull her out of this slump and maybe even help her get back to swimming."

Joe raises his eyebrows and I hold my hands up.

"I know, I know. But she loves it, she's good at it and I owe her."

His earnest hazel eyes hold my gaze and the whole thirty years passes between us.

"I feel like I owe it to Tina too," I say quietly.

Joe takes my hand between both of his. "Let's hope this is all the start of something better, for both of you."

I have to believe he's right. That we just have to get through this and then we can finally leave predatory men far behind us.

THE CAR IS IN THE drive, so I know Alex is home, even though the house is in darkness. When I get in, I shout her name, but there is no reply. I try again, and nothing. I tread nervously up the stairs, trying to remember her plans for the day, when I notice a crack of light under our bedroom door. I throw it open to find her folding clothes into a backpack.

"What are you doing?" I ask.

"I'm going to my mum's," she says without turning around.

"But why?"

"Because she doesn't lie to me all the time."

"What do you mean?" The quiver in my voice betrays the rush of panic to my head. The terror that she has finally discovered who I really am. She turns and looks at me with a contempt I've never seen before and I grab the door handle for support.

"You didn't answer earlier so I called your office. Judy reminded me that you're off until further notice."

I exhale long and hard, that this is the worst of it. For now.

"Please, let me explain," I say as Alex grabs underwear from a drawer and shoves it into the backpack. "I was forced to take leave and I was going to tell you, of course, but there was already so much bad news yesterday . . ."

"No, no, no, no, no," she shouts. "Don't you dare put this back on me."

In the stunned silence that follows I find the only words I have left.

"I'm sorry."

Alex puts her hands on the bed to steady herself.

"I know you're going through a stressful time," she says, "but it feels like ever since the Powers have come back into your life you've been hiding something from me."

"It's not that . . ."

"Wait," she says, and I stop. "I don't ever expect to understand what you went through but I've always tried to be here for you and I can't do that if you won't be honest with me."

My mind is racing and I can't separate the things I should tell her now from those I never will. All I can think is, I haven't said I'm going to London in the morning and she needs to be here for Katie.

"I don't want you to leave," I say.

"Please don't make this any harder," she says as she hangs her head. "I've already decided I'm going for the weekend. It'll give you some time to think about what you *do* want because I'm not sure you know anymore."

WITH ALEX GONE AND JOE away, I have only one option left. I'm going to have to ask Mam to mind Katie. I've been avoiding her as she wants to interrogate me about the lawsuit, even though I've told her it's got little to do with me. It's not that I don't trust her, I just don't want to drag her back there with me. She's been sober for over twenty years and she's kept busy with the vegan café she runs in Bray with her husband, Steve, but I can't reason with the part of my brain that's been taught to say nothing, deny everything.

She answers on the second ring, as mams do, even though I can hear the hum of the café in the background.

"Please tell me you've been able to get out of this court case."

"It's fine, Mam, it's no big deal. I just had to give a statement."

"I swear to god," she says, "have those people no shame? After everything they did to you."

I wonder how much Mam really remembers about that time, about what she did to me, or if it's just a trait of the Manson women that we learn to forget.

"Well, that was then," I say. "We're all different people now. Listen, I was wondering if you could take Katie for a couple of nights."

"You know we're always delighted to see her. When were you thinking?"

"Tonight and tomorrow?"

"Ah Lou, could you not have given me some notice? We're open late Fridays and Saturdays now."

"She'll be doing her own thing. You don't need to babysit her anymore."

Mam lets out the weary sigh of a mother's lot.

"What's the occasion? Are you off anywhere nice?"

"Yeah, London. And Joe's away too."

"Well, I can't exactly say no then, can I?"

"Thanks, Mam, you're a star. I've to pick her up from Joe's and then I'll drop her over in the next couple of hours."

KATIE'S HAVING NONE OF IT. She swings her schoolbag off her shoulder and it slaps onto the hall floor.

"No way. Alice has already booked the cinema."

"Look, I'm really sorry, Katie. I know you were looking forward to it, but you can do it another time."

"I can't. They're not gonna ask me again if I back out now."

I recognize the desperation in her eyes, that yearning for autonomy and acceptance, and the guilt eats away at my resolve.

"Gran and Steve will be working in the café, love. They won't be able to pick you up."

"Nobody has to pick me up. I'll get the bus home and I'll be fine here on my own."

I think about the photos, the dangers that are inside her phone, and I don't know if leaving her alone with it all weekend is any less of a risk than letting her meet her friends in town.

"OK, here's the deal. You stay with Gran, and you can go to the cinema, but you're on a DART back to hers by nine o'clock."

"What's the point? The movie won't even be over by then."

"Ten o'clock, final offer."

A smile curls at the ends of her lips and I'm happy for her, the adventure ahead. I relax and congratulate myself on the fine balancing act of keeping her safe while building her resilience, all done with my eyes wide open. Now I can focus all my energy on tomorrow's showdown with Melissa.

50

The soft October light threads through the branches of the rowans that line Melissa's street in Islington, north London. Sunbeams glaze the ruby-red berries in an autumn vignette as illusory as a dream, while adrenaline keeps me moving through it. It's eleven already and I just hope I'm early enough to catch her before she leaves to start preparations for tonight's show.

She never replied to my email, but it wasn't hard to find her address online. In contrast to Shauna, every aspect of Melissa's life is available on one platform or another. A large brass knocker hangs on the yellow door of the Victorian terrace I recognize from a home tour in *Hello!* magazine, the intricate fanlight and the stained-glass panel surround even prettier in real life.

She opens the door on the third knock. In the moment before she realizes, I catch a glimpse of celebrity Melissa, slim and smiling in a Breton top and skinny jeans. It's still her, even if the shape of her face has changed, her cheeks high and plump, the skin taut across them. Her smile freezes and then falls, and the longer she says nothing, the more afraid I am she'll close the door and leave me out here in the cold.

"Can we talk?" I ask. "Please?"

"Lou, what a surprise," she says, one hand still on the door. "I . . . I'm busy right now, I have to get ready for the show. Maybe tomorrow? Or Monday. Let's set something up for then, OK?"

"Melissa," I say loudly, "we can either do this out here right now or you can invite me in and we can speak in private. But I'm not leaving until you talk to me."

Melissa glances right and left, and then opens the door and ushers me in. She leads me along a bright and airy hallway with ornate coving and varnished timber floorboards.

"Nice house," I say as we continue down a staircase to a kitchen–dining room that opens onto a lush, sheltered garden.

"Thanks. Would you like coffee?" she says in a voice tainted with resignation.

"Sure."

I look out at the garden while Melissa packs coffee into the filter of an elaborate espresso machine.

"So," she says as I take a seat opposite her at the marble-topped island, "what did you want to talk about?"

"Liam Kelly."

"Who's that?"

Her delivery is so genuine I could almost believe her.

"I know you're Liam Kelly."

She holds on to her innocent indignation for several seconds until I stare her out of it. The mask falls slowly before she speaks.

"How?"

"Does it matter?"

She shrugs and a rush of rage catches me unawares. And I realize I'd wanted her to feel some remorse, some duty of care toward me.

"I need to know why you don't want me to testify."

"I thought I made that clear," she says. "Shauna's not able for this."

"What do you mean by that? Ronan said she's fully behind the action."

"Ronan's too close or maybe too busy to see it."

"To see what?"

She eyes me up, deciding just how much to reveal.

"Shauna was my best friend," she says, "and I had to watch her lose everything. You didn't hang around for the worst of it. She lost her career, her health, all her hopes and dreams. She never got over what McQueen did to her. She was never able to trust anyone again."

"What about Nigel?"

"That fucker?" Melissa shakes her head. "He was the last person she should have married. He wanted the beautiful, thin, wealthy Shauna. He had no time for anything below the surface."

"Oh god," I say. "I wanted to hear she'd been happy."

"She never had any luck with men." She looks at me. "Or women."

The flush in my cheeks surprises me and I look down into my coffee cup.

"How do you know about Nigel anyway?" asks Melissa.

"Carol told me."

"You talked to Carol?"

"Yeah, she's all right now."

"So I hear. I remain a skeptic."

I laugh. I don't blame her.

"But I still don't understand why you're so against the lawsuit. I mean, I was reluctant too, but surely it's the right thing to do? And after everything Shauna's been through, don't you think she deserves some sort of closure?"

Melissa takes a deep breath and exhales through pursed lips.

"Because it will kill her."

The grim intensity of her stare leaves me in no doubt she believes this.

"What? How?"

"You'll just have to trust me on this."

It's that Highfield circle of silence again and I refuse to yield to it anymore.

"Jesus Christ, Melissa, you expect me to take your word after all the lies you've told?"

"It was never personal," she says with a defensive pout. "I did it for Shauna."

"Can you hear yourself? I honestly don't know how you sleep at night. I went to *prison*."

"It was Shauna or you. I made a choice, that's all."

I feel her slipping from my grasp, but I can't stop.

"You're delusional," I say, voice rising out of control. "It's not just what you did back then. Have you forgotten your email threatened my family too?"

Melissa folds her arms and I'm sure my time is up.

"You weren't the only one who suffered," she says. "You've no idea how hard it was for Shauna. And for me too. I had to clean up his blood, for fuck's sake."

In the screaming silence that follows, everything I've ever questioned about that night starts to make sense.

"You were at the pool?"

"I thought . . ." she says, confused. "Shauna said she told you."

"She never told me that."

Panic spreads slowly across Melissa's seamless face as she realizes what she's done, how the balance of power has shifted.

"I thought you found her in the changing rooms," I say. "That's what you said in court."

"I . . . eh . . ." she says, struggling for words.

"It was you," I say. "You're the reason I went to prison. The reason I lost Shauna."

I slap my hands onto the marble worktop and Melissa's afraid to say another word. As if her silence could save her now.

"You forced Shauna to testify against me. You cleaned up the murder scene to frame me."

I'd always wondered why there was no blood found, mine or his, evidence of the struggle I'd described to the Guards. I pace up and down behind the kitchen island as each new implication lands.

"You lied in court."

She is so still I'm not even sure she's breathing.

"And now, the email. You were scared I'd tell."

The skin strains across her cheeks as tears swell in her eyes.

"I only ever did any of it to protect Shauna," she says.

"From me?"

"No," she says. "You don't understand. She was delirious when I got to the pool. She didn't know what she was saying, she would have confessed to anything. You left her there to deal with him alone and I had to step in and take over."

The tears run down her cheeks and we are both back there, eighteen and exposed.

"We'd already worked it all out," I say. "Shauna was going to say that he slipped and fell. She was supposed to go and get help."

"But that was before," she says.

I struggle to remember, to put together the pieces that never quite fit.

"Before what?"

It's just a flicker, a split second of panic on Melissa's face.

"Before, eh . . . I arrived," she says as her breath picks up pace. She looks away and wipes her fingers across her cheeks, but I can't let it go.

"Did something happen? When you arrived?"

She covers her face with her hands and shakes her head.

"Tell me," I shout. "Tell me what happened."

"No," she says. "I can't. I just can't."

"What's going on, Melissa?" I say as my mind races with the possibilities. "If something happened after I left, don't you think I deserve to know?"

Her shoulders heave with the force of her sobs but she says nothing.

"Well, if you won't tell me," I say, "you'd better give me some way of contacting Shauna. Or I swear to god I will go to the press with all of this. I have nothing left to lose, and you have everything."

When Melissa finally slides her hands from her face it's not fear or anger I see. It's pure sadness. Neither of us speaks as she opens a drawer, takes out a pen and notepad and starts to write. She can barely look at me as she tears out the page and hands me a Dublin address. It's what I've been looking for all this time. A chance to confront Shauna and her version of the truth. And now I'm more afraid of it than ever.

51

The plan was to fly back in the morning, but I'd only spend the night riding this wave of anger and confusion in the solitary confinement of my hotel, so I've rebooked on to a late flight. I'll get some sleep at home before my showdown with Shauna tomorrow. As I stroll through the airport, I try not to speculate about Melissa's secret, but still my mind slips into its darkest corners. I have a whole life constructed around the fallout from that night and I'm not sure I have the strength to rebuild the narrative, whatever it is. I wanted so much to believe Carol, that Shauna was ready to make amends, and now I have to face the prospect that she was lying to me all along.

I'm at the departure gate when my phone rings. It's Mam.

"Lou? You're not to freak out now, but Katie hasn't come home yet and I need you to—"

"What do you mean?" I say as I check the time on my phone in a panic. "Has she called?"

It's five to eleven. She was due back by ten.

"I've called her and I've texted her, but she's not answering. Can you call her friends' parents and check with them?"

I've never spoken to them. I'm not even sure I know their names, never mind their numbers.

"Shit."

"What's wrong?" asks Mam.

"I don't know the parents."

"What do you mean you don't know them? You let your daughter go out without checking who she'd be with?"

"Jesus, Mam, I don't remember you being parent of the year. Do you want me to tell you what I was up to at fourteen?"

"OK, OK, Lou," she says, "but what are we going to do?"

"I'll see if Alex has the numbers. You wait at home for Katie. I'm sure she's just pushing boundaries, you know what teenagers are like."

"I certainly do," says Mam. "And I hope you're right."

I call Katie and it rings out three times. I send a WhatsApp message in the hope she'll read it, even if she doesn't want to talk to me. But the two gray ticks don't turn blue, no matter how long I stare at them. I check my parental control app for her last known location and I'm relieved and alarmed to see she was at a pub on Middle Abbey Street only twenty minutes ago. I have no choice, I'll have to call Alex.

"I'm sorry," I say over and over in the silence after I've explained.

"Jesus Christ," says Alex quietly. "Let me think."

The last of the passengers board the plane and I am forced out of my seat and through the gate.

"OK," she says, "I'll go over to Middle Abbey Street straight away, and you keep trying to get in touch with her."

"I'm sorry, I can't for much longer. I'm boarding now," I say, my voice cracking with the strain. "Can you call Joe?"

"Jesus," she says. "Yeah, sure. Call me as soon as you land."

"OK," I say. And then, "I love you," but she has already hung up.

AS I WAIT FOR THE plane to take off I call Katie over and over, my heart pinned to the vacant pulse of the ringtone. Until it stops. The call connects to an out-of-area message and I lash open the parental controls. My chest tightens when I see her battery is dead, and her location has not been updated. I flick through her recent online activity for any clues, but there are only a few Google searches from a couple of hours ago. I usually wouldn't look twice at any of that stuff, but I need to be sure I'm not missing anything.

At 8:35 p.m. Katie searched for "Will Pearson age," "William Pearson age" and then "willpears age." A popstar or an actor, I presume, but I find no evidence of any Will or William Pearson of note. As the cabin crew run through the safety routine, I find an Instagram account with the handle "willpears" and alarm bells start to chime in my head.

Will looks like the sort of boy who could charm any teenage girl, with his dark eyes and tousled hair and a sultry smile that sets me on edge. I click on a photo of Will holding a puppy and skim through the comments until I come to the one thing I didn't want to see: my daughter's profile pic and, next to it, the words "So cute!" Underneath, Will has said, "Not as cute as you," and my stomach lurches, but it's not enough, I need to be sure. I race through one photo after another, a whole series of flirty interactions between them, until I see a comment that leaves me in no doubt: "You're not like other girls, that's what makes you so special."

It's a line McQueen used on me, and probably every one of his victims. But I was seventeen and I already knew too much. Katie is so young, so innocent, I don't know if she'd spot any of the warning signs. And that's when it hits me, the search terms: she is with him and he is older than she expected.

"Excuse me," says the flight attendant, pointing at my phone, "you need to turn that off now."

"Yes, sorry," I say as I lean down to the bag under the seat in front of me. As the plane taxis down the runway, I send a final message to Alex: "Katie is with willpears on Instagram. He is a predator. Call the Guards."

And then I turn off my phone and beg, plead and pray that they get to her in time.

52

As the landing wheels hit the tarmac, I turn on my phone, shaking and waving it to try and catch a signal, but there is nothing. Through the window, Dublin is a dark and silent place and I want it to scream into action, to understand what's at stake. It takes ten suffocating minutes before we start to disembark, several more before I reach solid ground, and it's only then, under the pale drizzle of night, that my phone bursts to life. I call Alex with shaking hands and I'm almost faint with fear when she answers.

"We found her," she says, and her words strike me with such force, I double over.

"Thank god, thank god," I cry as I try to catch my breath. "Is she OK?"

The pause that follows is devastating.

"Alex? Please."

"We're in an ambulance," she says, her words cut with jagged sobs. "On our way to the Mater hospital."

"What's wrong with her?" I shriek. "She's not . . . she's not . . . ?"

"No, she's just out of it. Drugged. One of the Guards said it looks like ketamine."

"Ketamine?" My voice is warped with relief and confusion as I wave my apologies to the staff who steer me toward the terminal. "What the fuck was she doing taking ketamine?"

"I don't think she did take it," says Alex. "It looks like her drink was spiked."

"What do you mean?"

"You were right. He is a predator. The Guards found him dragging her along Liffey Street. Lou, she could barely stand up."

I reach the airport building and it's all too much, too crushing. My legs buckle with the strain and I fall against a railing. As I suck the air into me, I try to find the words to form the question I never wanted to ask.

"Did he touch her?"

"I don't know," whispers Alex.

ALL SENSE OF TIME IS abandoned in the stark fluorescence of A&E, the windowless waiting room full of Saturday-night casualties. There's a collective resignation among the myriad faces, a shared acceptance that they are all here for the long haul. I can't see Katie or Alex among them and I can only hope the time-sensitive nature of Katie's visit has bumped her up the list. I make myself known at reception and I'm ushered into a corridor lined with trolleys. In the distance, Alex sits on the edge of one, Katie's long, bare legs stretched out beside her. I run toward them, trying to hide my shock at my daughter's pale and crumpled face.

"Oh baby," I say as I wrap my arms around Katie. She hugs me back and I hold on, breathing in the coconut scent of her tangled hair.

"Are you OK?" I whisper in her ear.

"Yes," she says, but when I pull back, there's a glassy distance in her eyes. "I'm sorry."

"No, I'm sorry, Katie. None of this is your fault. I'm the one who hasn't been there for you and I don't want you to think I'm angry or that I blame you for any of this."

I feel Alex's hand on my shoulder and I turn to see a sympathetic smile. I grasp her fingers and she nods toward the exit.

"We'll be back in a minute," I say as I let go of Katie.

I try to gauge Alex's expression as we walk the corridor, my pulse pounding in my ears.

"They found ketamine in a urine sample," she says as she pushes open the door to the waiting room. "She swears she knows nothing about it so it looks like she was spiked."

The confirmation winds me but I need to know more.

"Is that . . . all they found?"

"Yes. She hasn't been hurt, if that's what you mean."

The relief hits me even harder and I lean back against the wall.

"And she's going to be OK?"

"Yes, she's going to be fine. We're just waiting to give a statement to the Guards and then she can go home and sleep it off."

"Oh thank god," I say, tears racing down my cheeks.

"And he's in custody, he's been arrested, all thanks to you. You saved her."

"Tell me what happened," I whisper.

She takes a deep breath and I brace myself.

"She's been chatting to him for a few weeks, but this is the first time they've met. She says nothing happened but he was pressuring her to have sex and she didn't want to. Lou, it must have been him, the ketamine. He must have been trying to loosen her up."

"The utter bastard," I say. "Oh Jesus, you don't think he did it and she doesn't remember?"

"She's been examined and there are no physical signs and, anyway, it doesn't sound like there was time. She remembers being in the pub around half ten and then, sometime later, she felt really heavy and sick, like she wasn't really there, she said. The Guards found them at twenty to twelve, not far from the pub. Wherever he was bringing her, it looks like they intercepted him."

Sobs start to shake my body and Alex puts her arms around me.

"My god, Alex. What did he think he was doing?"

"I'd say he spiked her drink and just didn't think she'd have such a strong reaction."

"She's fourteen, what did he expect?"

"I think he expected it to go exactly as it usually does for him."

She lets that sink in and do its job.

"We're going to destroy him," I say.

"Yes we are."

53

I've driven past Highfield's stone pillars on occasion, seen the cedars rise above the granite walls, but it's the first time I've stepped inside these wrought-iron gates in over thirty years. I've prepared myself to try and forget, to focus only on the now, but nothing here has changed. The grand oak entrance doors still open on to the vast foyer, walls covered in gilt-framed photos of past glories. And there, taking pride of place in the center of them all, is Maurice McQueen at the 1984 Olympics, arms folded across his chest and that mustache curled into a pompous grin.

I don't walk away. I stand and confront him, the respect he still commands in this place, the power he has to silence his victims. And I realize that forgetting has been a mistake, a symptom of the control he still has over me. I've spent thirty years not talking about him, trying to hide from the horror of what I did while his legend grew unchallenged. That photo was on the wall the day I entered Highfield and it's still there because I haven't had the courage to speak. I need to do it now, not just for Josh Blair. I need to speak for myself.

I take the stone staircase to the first floor and walk past the toilets where Shauna first asked me out. The door to the 6A form class is closed and I picture Sister Mullen behind it, lashing her tongue at some poor grammar victim. I turn right on to the corridor with the black-and-white tiles, my shoes clicking against them as I make my way to the principal's office. I have an appointment this time, Ms. Flynn is expecting me.

"Come in," she says with a pleasant lilt and I open the door to a very different room. Sister Shannon's dark, mahogany enclosure has been transformed into a bright and colorful office, with two armchairs that look out through the large sash window on to the hockey pitches. Ms. Flynn gestures to one and I sit opposite her, instantly disarmed by her relaxed, informal approach. I expected to be challenged, not charmed, and I can't let it blunt the edges of my resolve.

"I appreciate it must be difficult for you," she says, "coming back here after all this time. What exactly did you want to talk about?"

"Damien Corrigan," I say, and she flinches.

"I'm sorry, that matter is with the courts now and I am not permitted to discuss it with anyone."

"Well, let me do all the talking, then." I take a folder out of my bag, open it and hand her a series of printouts. "These are the posts of a user by the name of funboy23 on the website Irish-Punters.com. If you look at the last two pages, you'll see that funboy23 has the same mobile number as Damien Corrigan. You probably have it yourself on file somewhere."

Ms. Flynn's expression changes from confusion to alarm as she reads, although she says nothing. I take my phone from my bag, unlock it and hold it up to her.

"This is the live site. You can look it up yourself."

I click on funboy23's username and his posts line up, one under the other.

"And this," I say as I offer another pile of papers, "is a selection of the private messages Damien Corrigan sent on that website."

She holds my gaze as she takes the pages from me and I sense a shift in her stance, the stark reality of it too much to ignore. As she reads, I watch her face, the intake of breath and the flare of her eyes more telling than any words could be.

"The *Evening Express* is going to print the allegation in this afternoon's paper that Corrigan has solicited and paid for sex with underage boys. You have until midday tomorrow to offer a full settlement and an admission of guilt to Josh Blair or every last detail of Corrigan's behavior will be splashed across tomorrow's *Express*."

I stand up to leave but Ms. Flynn doesn't move from her chair. Her eyes are wide with the questions she wants to ask but she is bound to silence by the same machine that kept so many quiet for so long.

"I really do hope you'll do the right thing by Josh," I say. "For all our sakes."

As I walk back down the staircase, past the stained-glass window and the wood-paneled walls, I don't stop to look back at any of it. Not the veneer of privilege, the debt of obligation. And certainly not the gilt-edged reverence of Maurice McQueen. I've had enough of that.

WILL PEARSON'S INSTAGRAM IS PRIVATE now but his profile pic is still smiling, those dark eyes still exuding the perfect balance of burgeoning strength and boyish warmth. Except Will Pearson is not a boy, he's a twenty-three-year-old man, and his real name is Cian Murray. Joe mutters expletives as he reports the account and does his best to console me.

"You *are* a good mother," he says as my tears run tracks down my face. "I didn't keep enough of an eye on any of this stuff either."

"She could have died," I say, spluttering out the stress of the day.

We're just back from court, where bail was set for Cian Murray after he was charged with poisoning and sexual exploitation. The media were there to greet us, and I wanted to turn around and leave, but it was Katie who held my hand and kept me going. When she told me it was good they were reporting it, I couldn't have been any prouder. The last thing any of us needs is another court case, but this is one we plan to nail.

"But she didn't die," says Joe.

"Why do you have to be so bloody forgiving?" I say, and he laughs.

"Just as well for you that I am. Here, I'll put the kettle on."

He makes his way around the kitchen island and I call up to Katie to offer her a cup of tea.

"No, thanks," she shouts back.

"She seems a bit better," says Joe.

"Yeah, she's starting to open up about it. She's confided in me more in the last couple of days than she has all year, so that's something at least. And I think she's learned her lesson, but Jesus fucking Christ, I don't know if I'll ever learn mine."

"What do you mean?"

"Oh god, Joe, where do I start? I've never been able to protect the people I love. I could've saved Tina and I didn't."

"Ah Lou, Tina made that choice herself."

He exhales heavily. We've been through this so many times, never with any clear resolution.

"And Shauna," I say. "I fucked that up as well. But I might have a chance to resolve things now."

"What are you talking about?" he asks.

I take a deep breath and hope that Joe will support me, as he always does.

"I have Shauna's address. I'm going to go and see her."

"I dunno," he says, frowning. "That doesn't sound like a good idea."

"There are things . . . I need to know. And I feel like I owe her the same too."

Joe stops, a teabag in each hand and a look of pure anger on his face.

"You did everything for her, Lou, and look what she did to you. You owe her nothing."

"You don't know what it was like for her," I say, recoiling at his righteous fury.

He shakes his head and drops each teabag into a cup.

"She had everything to lose," I say.

"Why?" says Joe. "Because she was an elite athlete and you were just some skanger from Ballybrack?"

I wince at the violence of that word, one I haven't had thrown at me in decades.

"I'm sorry," he says, "but they hung you out to dry, Highfield, the Powers, the lot of them."

Shauna and I have so much unfinished business, more than Joe could possibly imagine. I could never tell him how much she meant to me; it would have hurt him too much. And I never confessed to the killing of Maurice McQueen. Joe might have stood by me, but I couldn't take the risk that it would change how he saw me once he knew what I was capable of. That's the guilt I've always kept hidden deep inside, the one thing that's secured my silence. I can't be tried for it again, but it's my own demons that haunt me, more than anything else ever could.

"Look, I know you, Lou," says Joe. "You're gonna do what you're gonna do, and I can't stop you. But don't be blinded by nostalgia, Shauna was never the one for you. You have everything you need right here in this house."

Maybe he's right, maybe it'll all end in tears, but one thing is certain: if I don't face Shauna, I'll never be free of her.

WHEN THE END COMES, IT doesn't feel like it. Ronan arrives at my front door just after Joe has left, and I know before he's said a word.

"I can't stay, but I wanted to let you know," he says. "It's over. Josh has accepted a settlement from Highfield."

"Oh?" I say, trying to act surprised. "What sort of settlement?"

"A suitable sum of money. And Corrigan has resigned from the club."

"But what about . . . ?"

Justice, revenge, retribution? Or was that just what I wanted?

"This is the best outcome for Josh," says Ronan. "He's been vindicated and he gets to return to the sport he loves without the threat of Corrigan hanging over him. All Josh ever wanted was to protect himself and his friends, and he's done that."

"So we just let him . . . get away with it?"

As I blink away the tears, I realize for the first time that I would have taken that stand and confessed it all if I had to. And maybe that's because young Josh Blair has given me that courage, but I know for sure now that this is not the end. It can't be.

"Look," says Ronan, "I didn't take on this case to get back at Highfield or avenge Shauna. I did it for one reason, to try and give Josh whatever he needed to move on with his life. In the end, he didn't want the stress or stigma that comes with a trial. He just wanted to swim."

It's a turning point. I could feel it in the principal's office at Highfield, and I feel it now. But it won't help those of us who came before.

"And Damien Corrigan will never coach again," he continues. "His name is all over the internet thanks to the *Evening Express*. He may not have been convicted of anything, but he hasn't got away with it either."

I try to smile, but my mouth is rigid with regret.

"It's not enough," I say quietly. "It's not enough for me."

Ronan reaches out and rests his hand on my arm. "That's exactly what Shauna said."

54

As soon as I've finished my last lecture I make my excuses and pack up. The afternoon sun cuts through my office blinds, the light glowering from the lacquered surface of my desk. I'm relieved to be back, but I've had enough of the side-eye and mutterings, the subtle changes in my colleagues' behavior. I've been here for seventeen happy and successful years, and still Maurice McQueen has managed to cast a cloud of suspicion on me, just as he always did.

For the day that's in it, I have The Smiths on Spotify, *Hatful of Hollow* in my earbuds as I pass from the sheltered calm of Trinity's front square into the buzz of the city beyond. I'm still reeling from the revelations of the past few days and now I have to steel myself for one final confrontation. It's killing me, what Melissa said and didn't say, how tethered I still am to her, to Shauna. I might be the one who's had to live with the trauma of taking a life but we're all still dealing with the fallout. So no matter what happens in Shauna's house today, I need to walk out of there with some sort of closure or I'll be looking over my shoulder for the rest of my life.

I slip into the newsagent's by the bus stop and pick up a copy of the *Evening Express*. The Highfield case has made the front page yet again, a brief rundown of the settlement but no further allegations about Damien Corrigan. Those will come, I'm sure of it. Mick Craddock was like a dog with a bone when I spoke to him yesterday so I've every faith he'll find what he needs for a full-blown exposé. And once that information is in the public domain, the Guards will have no choice but to act on it.

I step off the bus in Rathgar village to the fading glare of the sun. It's only a short walk to Shauna's house, a three-story Victorian red-brick that has lost its luster. I'd expected something more glamorous, more secluded, but I don't know Shauna now; maybe she enjoys a simpler life.

I lift the latch on the front gate and walk down the weed-strewn path to the front door. In the pause before I knock, my heart pounds the blood through my veins and I taste the fear I've held close for over thirty years.

The door is opened by an attractive young woman with dark hair pulled back tight into a ponytail.

"Hello. Can I help you?"

Her accent is Spanish, maybe Latin American.

"I've come to see Shauna Power," I say, as casually as I can.

"I'm very sorry," she says, "but I think you have come to the wrong house."

I feel the sting of betrayal once again, although I'm not sure who to blame this time. I'm about to turn away when I realize I have nothing to lose.

"Can you tell Shauna it's Lou Manson?" I enunciate my name with care.

"I'm sorry," she says sweetly, "but there is no Shauna here."

I stand rigid on the porch, afraid to break eye contact and lose all connection to this place. As the pent-up rage and frustration takes over, I know that the balance of my future is in this moment. I take a step forward and put my palm flat against the door.

"If I turn around and walk out of here without seeing Shauna, I'm going to regret it for the rest of my life. So please go and tell her I'm here because I am not moving until I talk to her."

Her smile fades and she looks behind her at the staircase that runs up along the wall.

"Is that where she is?" I ask. "Upstairs?"

She shakes her head without conviction.

"Shauna," I shout. "Shauna, it's Lou."

The young woman steps back and I slide past her, into a hall devoid of decoration. Adrenaline carries me up the stairs, into one room after another until I come to the bedroom at the front of the house. I take a deep breath, put a smile on my face and open the door.

At first, I think it must be an elaborate joke, a cruel trick designed to derail my endless curiosity. And then I'm sure it's a mistake, a completely different Shauna, because this is not anyone I know, this sickly woman with white hair and yellow teeth, propped up on one side of a double bed, her arm hooked up to a hospital machine.

She stares at me for several seconds before she speaks.

"I didn't want you to see me like this."

It's not the voice, hoarse and wavering, that convinces me. It's the eyes, still bright and blue under hooded lids, that couldn't belong to anyone else.

"Shauna?"

"You never did know when to give up," she says.

It takes me a moment to react, for my eyes to adjust to the contours of her face. The last of the day's sun streams through the two large sash windows behind me, lighting her pallid skin with a ghostly glow. This is not who I expected to see here and I'm paralyzed with the shock.

"How did you find me?" asks Shauna.

"Melissa."

"You spoke to Melissa?"

"Yes. And I need you to tell me exactly . . ."

The young woman steps into the room and looks from me to Shauna.

"It's fine, Carla," says Shauna. "Lou's a good friend."

Carla hesitates and gives me a cold, hard stare before she leaves and closes the door behind her.

"What happened that night, Shauna? After I left."

I try to ignore the jut of her shoulder, the deep crevices of her face.

"I wanted to talk to you for so long," she says, "but I never had the courage."

Her breath is fast and shallow and I realize she is more terrified than I am.

"I've had . . . problems. Ever since the trial. Probably way before that if I'm completely honest with myself. It was bulimia at first, then anorexia."

I remember the scar on her inner thigh, the vomiting at school.

"In my third year of college, I was so ill I spent eight months in St. John of God's psychiatric hospital."

"Jesus, I had no idea."

"I did have some good periods," she says, "and I'd think it was all over, but it never left me."

"By it," I say gently, "do you mean him?"

"Yeah."

I've been so determined to wrench the truth out of Shauna I almost forgot who the real culprit was.

"He never left me either," I say.

She winces. "I'm sorry."

"I don't need you to be sorry, I just need to know you're not going to talk about . . . what I did. Even if I can't be tried for it again, it would ruin me."

"Oh Jesus," she says, and for a moment there is nothing but the fractured sound of her breath. "It's all my fault. Everything is my fault."

"He wasn't your fault."

"Yes," she whispers, "he was."

It's the tone of her voice that scares me, the weight of the words unspoken.

"You said that before, by the sea. But I still don't understand."

"Oh god," she says, her head in her hands.

Everything else fades to a distant echo as Shauna turns and hooks me with a dead-eyed gaze.

"You didn't kill him," she says.

The fist of my heart stops pounding as I watch the words take shape on her lips.

"I did."

55

Shauna turns away, unable to look at me as I try to remember, as I start to understand.

"But I saw him," I say.

"He was still alive."

I couldn't look at his face. I didn't question it when she told me he was dead.

"What did you do?" I ask, dizzy with hope and terror.

She exhales and closes her eyes.

"After you left," she says, her voice barely a whisper, "he spluttered. Not just once. He did it three or four times, and I was so scared I didn't even think. I pushed and pulled and kicked him into the pool."

I put my hands to my face, almost afraid to believe her.

"I stood at the edge of the pool and I watched him sink," she says, "and I stayed there until I was sure he was dead."

None of this seems real, not the scale of Shauna's deception nor the haggard shape of her in the bed.

"I was going to work out a story when Melissa arrived and I let her take over."

The syllables of her name spasm to life inside me, as if they might bear the weight of this betrayal instead.

"Melissa?" I say. "She made you do it?"

"No, of course not."

"Well, what happened then? We agreed we were going to say he slipped and fell."

"I don't know. I don't remember anything after we left. I just went along with whatever my dad said, and then it was too late."

"Even though you knew I could be convicted for it?"

"I couldn't do it," she cries, "I couldn't testify."

"But you let me believe I killed him."

Shauna closes her eyes and wraps her arms around her shaking body, the breath shivering in and out of her.

"All this time," I say, "I've been haunted by what I thought I did, and you didn't think I deserved to know the truth? Did you ever think of me at all?"

"Yes," she cries. "I never stopped thinking about you."

There's a rap at the door and Carla swoops in and stands between us like a shield.

"I think you should leave," she says.

I don't wait to be asked twice. I gather myself and march across the landing and down the stairs. I make it out the front door and I'm almost at the gate when the legs go from under me and I fall to my knees, shaking and sobbing onto the weed-punctured paving. There's nothing I can do to stop the onslaught, wave after wave of attack and release. A lifetime of sorrow for the eighteen-year-old girl who never stood a chance.

I can't quite grasp what's been stolen from me, my link to the past, my faith in the future. I never had the easy composure of an ordinary life, but I could have got there, if I'd had absolution. The grit and gravel pierce my hands and graze my knees and I don't care who sees my bruised and bloodied grief, not even when I hear the footsteps and see the shadow of the figure standing over me.

"Please come back," says Carla. "Shauna's sorry. I'm sorry."

I sit up on my haunches, dust the dirt from my hands and look back at the frayed facade of a once-proud place, the weather-bowed sash windows, veiled and forlorn. And behind them, the one person who can help me, the only one who can close the door on the events of that night.

SHAUNA'S TEAR-STAINED FACE IMPLORES ME as I stand over her bed, arms folded against the rapid beat of my heart.

"I tried so hard to find a way to tell you," she says. "You have to believe me."

It would be so easy, but I don't know what to believe anymore.

"Please," she continues, "I'll do anything to make it up to you. I've had to live with what I did and now I'm going to have to die with it."

I search the hollows of her eyes and find nothing but a planet of regret.

"What's that supposed to mean?"

She says nothing, just shakes her head slowly.

"Is that what all this is?" I gesture to the equipment.

"Yes," she says. "Dialysis."

I stare at the equipment, the numbers and colors on the monitor, the blood rushing through the tubes, the swellings on her arm at the access points.

"But you'll get better? You're still young."

"Oh, Lou," she says. "I'm not going to lie to you anymore. All those years of starving myself, I have some serious heart issues too."

I stare at the ceiling, hands on hips, trying to make sense of what's been given and taken away from me.

"There must be something you can do," I say as tears blur my eyes. Shauna's crying too and I don't know which of us to pity most. All I ever wanted was her mercy and now I see that's what she wants from me too. And as much as I wish I could walk out of here and take my forgiveness with me, I know I can't carry the weight of it for the rest of my life.

"There is something I want to do," says Shauna, wiping away her tears. "Since Ronan's lawsuit, I know for sure that I'm ready to tell the full story. Everything he did and exactly how Highfield enabled him."

And that's when I know what my choice is: to hold a broken teenage girl responsible for a desperate decision or to seek justice for all of us.

56

Shauna hands me a tissue and I sit on the edge of the bed and bury my face in it.

"I feel the same way," I say. "I want to tell the world everything."

She smiles and I force one back at her.

"Can I get you anything?" she asks. "Tea or coffee?"

I hesitate, looking at the tubes in her arm.

"I mean, Carla will get it. She's my carer."

"Oh, right. Yeah, tea would be great."

Shauna speaks into an intercom at the side of the bed. In the reprieve, I look around the room, the lack of adornment or any markers of a life.

"Where is all your . . . stuff?" I ask.

"It's all in there," says Shauna, pointing to an antique mahogany wardrobe in an alcove. "Go on, I want to show you something."

I open the wardrobe door to the meticulous arrangement of Shauna's life. Dresses, skirts and trousers hang neatly on top while the shelves below are filled with perfectly folded T-shirts and jumpers. Between the two is a single drawer with a crystal handle I can't help but touch.

"In there," she says, "in the box."

I pull the drawer and open a Prada shoebox. Inside is a collection of photos of young Shauna, and my heart skitters at the memories.

"Bring the whole lot over," she says.

I put the box on the bed between us and Shauna pulls out one photo after another, smiling tentatively as she shows them to me. Tiny Shauna at the beach with her mother, in Highfield purple already at only three years old, teenage Shauna in that gold lamé skirt, her whole life ahead of her.

"There it is," she says, lifting up a square Polaroid picture.

She hands it to me and my heart clenches with an unexpected pain that feels like grief. It's me at eighteen, hair spiked and eyes lined in black, posing in my bra and underpants with my hands behind my head. Despite all the reminders, I can hardly remember who she was. This girl, this young woman, is so full of hope and confidence I can't bear it.

"Oh god, not again," I say as a tear slides down my cheek.

"You were so gorgeous," says Shauna.

"Yeah, I was."

Carla arrives with the tea and I put the photo back in the box with the rest of the faded memories. She nods as she hands me a cup and I smile graciously.

"You know," I say after she's left, "for a moment, I thought you were going to show me a different photo. The one from that night."

She stares at me and then flicks her eyes, as if blinking away the memory of it.

"I . . . I don't know what happened to that."

The revelation hits harder than I expected, as if I'd been holding on to the possibility of proof all this time.

"It could have changed everything," I say.

She shakes her head.

"I think people still wouldn't have believed it. They were so invested in him they weren't prepared to accept he was capable of it."

I think about Sonia Curley and the WAR women who supported me at my trial, how I'd vowed to join their campaign as soon as I was acquitted. I'd meant it at the time, but afterward, it was the last thing I wanted, to relive the futility of it.

"Do you really think people would believe us now? When the DPP won't take a case and Highfield still stands by him?"

"I do. I think if we're honest and open then people will listen. And anyway, what choice do we have, now that we know it's still happening? Think of all those kids at risk, their whole lives ahead of them. It's not good enough for Highfield or the swimming authorities to say they have safeguards in place. Men like him, they don't respect those boundaries. People need to know how they operate, or they'll just keep getting away with it."

She speaks with such conviction it's contagious.

"But how?" I say. "Now that we're not going to have our day in court, what can we do?"

"Write a book," she says with a smile. "There's still such massive interest in our story, publishers would be fighting over it."

My pulse quickens as I sit upright.

"You want us to write a book?"

"No, not me, I have no experience. But you're a fabulous writer."

"How would you know?"

"I've read every paper you've ever written."

I can hardly catch my breath with the excitement.

"I'll back up everything you say," says Shauna. "I'd been planning to leave a sworn statement with Ronan anyway. And there are several others who will do the same."

I'm dizzy with this turn of events. I've spent the last few weeks so afraid Shauna would tell the truth, and now she's offering it to me like a prize.

"But what about the consequences?" I ask.

"Don't worry," she says. "I don't plan on throwing anyone under the bus. You and Melissa are safe. And what are they going to do to me in this state?"

She holds up her intubated arm, the blood pulsing in and out of it.

"Do it, Lou, please," she says, mistaking my silence for reluctance. "For all of us."

"OK, I will. But . . ."

I turn away from those piercing blue eyes as I try to work out what I want to say.

". . . I can't be the only one to take control of our shared history."

"What do you mean?"

"I mean, you're handing me all the power. But what about your own story? Shouldn't you be the one to tell that?"

I don't know if it's a lifetime of shielding behind others or the fear of a backlash, but Shauna flinches at the thought.

"I can be there for you too," I say, taking her knotted fingers in mine. "I'll stand beside you and support whatever you say."

She shrugs, but the half-smile gives her away.

"I don't even know how I'd go about it," she says.

"Well, neither do I, but we can work it out."

Her eyes spark with something like hope, and I feel it too. For the first time in years, I can see a path, not just away from the trauma of the past, but toward something new, and all I want to do is tell Alex.

"Thank you," I say, "for this gift."

She exhales and the strength goes out of her as her head falls back onto the pillow.

"I owed you," she says.

THE SOFT GLOW OF THE antique streetlamps blur the light with the dark as I make my way back to Rathgar village. The air is sharp and smoky, and I think of a roaring fire, the three of us curled up on the sofa in front of it. My mind is a whirl of possibility as it dances through the opportunities that Shauna's offer poses. Inviting McQueen back into my life won't be easy, but this time, it will be on my terms. And I know if I want to beat him, I'll have to fight him first.

57

It arrives in a handwritten registered envelope marked "Private." I take it into the kitchen and open it as the kettle boils. Inside is a photo, dark and grainy, with a yellow Post-it attached and a message scrawled across it: *I'm sorry. I made the wrong choice.*

The words hit deep before I've even deciphered them, and I snatch the paper from the surface of the photo. Underneath, it's exactly as I see it in my mind's eye every time I think of that night. Shauna's tear-stained cheek flat against the wall, eyes shut tight as his body presses into her. I look at his face, eyes flared red with the flash of the camera, and it doesn't seem like a distant memory. It feels like part of me.

I grab the envelope, just to be sure, and there it is, stamped across the queen's head: Islington Mail Centre. The girl who was the guardian of Shauna's confidence for all these years has handed over the privilege to me. And I realize it's not too late for her, for us. There's still a way for her to make the right choice.

As the kettle roars to a climax, I hold tight to the photo—my lifeline, my proof. It might not have made a difference back then, but it changes everything now.

THE DAY HAS RETREATED ALREADY, but a warm glow spills from every window of Shauna's house. Ronan opens the front door with a phone to his ear and I give him a wave as Alex and I pass by. The living room has been transformed, with mid-century furniture and colorful artwork filling in the blank spaces and Melissa in the middle of it all, directing a camera crew and lighting technicians. Even in a muted blue shift dress, her star power is clear as she guides her team with confidence and control. As soon as she sees us, she comes over and kisses Alex on the cheek before taking my hands in hers.

"She's upstairs," she says. "She wants to see you before we start."

"Thank you," I say as I take in the sights and sounds of the operation unfolding around us.

Joe has kept his promise and used his contacts to set Melissa up with a segment on RTÉ's *Prime Time*. I don't remember the last time there's been this much buzz around a TV broadcast.

"No, thank *you*," she says, and squeezes my hands.

"You go on up," says Alex. "I'll wait here."

I push open the bedroom door and Shauna smiles and beckons me in. She's sitting on the edge of her bed while a young woman with bronzed skin and perfect eyebrows sweeps powder across her face.

"This is Jenny," says Shauna.

Jenny nods to me, a sort of deference that suggests I need no introduction.

"I'm finishing up here," she says. "I'll leave you to it."

Shauna's white hair is slicked back in a ponytail that adds poise and professionalism to the clean lines of her blouse and blazer. The dark shadows of her illness are tempered by Jenny's handiwork, but I can still see the trepidation behind it, the fear of the words yet unspoken.

"You're going to smash this," I say as I sit down beside her.

Her face cracks and I'm worried a tear will escape and dissolve her painted veneer.

"No, no, no," I say. "No tears allowed."

"Oh, don't worry, I'm not going to cry," she says. "I'm too happy. I mean, we're finally doing this."

"Yes, we are."

I offer my arm and she grabs it with both hands and stands up slowly, unsteadily.

"Do you want me to get Ronan?" I ask.

"No. I want to walk in there with you."

There's a surreal glare to the studio lights as we enter the living room and I guide Shauna into an elegant teak chair. Melissa takes a seat opposite her and runs through the beats of the interview while the crew make their final preparations and I retreat behind the light. I wave when I see that Joe has made it, the circle now complete, and we embrace before joining Alex and Ronan on the sofa.

As the cameras roll and Melissa starts to speak, I finally understand what makes her such a great presenter. It's not just her eloquence when she introduces Shauna, the gravity with which she conveys her story, there's a compassion in her tone and delivery that makes it impossible not to believe in her. By the time she hands over to Shauna, I have no doubt that this will change the conversation. As Shauna finds her voice, I hold tight to Joe's hand to my left and Alex's to my right.

"Maurice McQueen raped me for the first time when I was only fifteen years old. But his grooming of me started long before that . . ."

IN THE END, WE'RE THE ones who have to live with the stories we tell ourselves. This is mine.

ACKNOWLEDGMENTS

Every book is a collaboration, and I could not be more grateful to all the talented people who worked on *When We Were Silent*.

Thank you to my brilliant agent, Rachel Neely, and to Juliet, Kiya, Liza, Alba, Catriona, and Emma at Mushens Entertainment.

To my wonderful coagent, Jenny Bent, and everyone at the Bent Agency.

To my two incredible editors, Christine Kopprasch and Imogen Nelson, for your vision and expertise that helped make this book the very best it could be.

To the whole amazing team at Flatiron: Nancy Trypuc and Maris Tasaka for marketing, Cat Kenney for publicity, Maxine Charles for assistant editorial, Emily Walters for managing editorial, Jeremy Pink and Eva Diaz for production, and Sue Walsh for design.

To Keith Hayes and Gregg Kulick for such a beautiful and striking cover.

To Hannah Cawse for producing such a compelling audiobook and to India Mullen for your exceptionally moving performance as Lou.

To my first reader, John Braine, for support and encouragement as well as sound advice.

To Laurie Murphy, Alan Mulconry, Anthony O'Donovan, Enda Treacy, Conor Gunn, and everyone in the Dublin City University writing workshop. Thank you for so much close reading and suggestions that helped shape the book from the start.

To Sarah Starr Murphy for your invaluable insight and feedback, and to everyone at the *Forge Literary Magazine*.

To Hannah Redding for your encouragement when I was almost but not quite there.

To Alan Mulconry (again!) and Caoimhe O'Reilly for a final read before I sent the manuscript out into the world.

To Andrew Sheridan for always being on call for legal advice and guidance.

To Ken Early, Sarah Early, and Brian Sweeney for swimming help and information.

To Marina Carr, Darran McCann, Kit Fryatt, Ferdia Macanna, and everyone at DCU for getting me started.

To the Arts Council for the literature bursary that allowed me to focus on writing.

To the Crime Writers' Association for seeing something in an early draft.

For help with the small details, thank you to Kate Butler, Emma Kennedy, Edel Kirley, Alan Coholan, Ben Walsh, Sinéad Casey, Dorothy Kelly, and Geraldine Clements.

To Colette Woods for deadline dinners.

To all the writers I have met along the way, thank you for the insider information, the stories, and the laughs.

To Joan, Paddy, John, and Liz McPhillips for endlessly mining your memories of 1980s Dublin. And for a lifetime of love and support.

And to my children: James, Anna, and Harry. Thank you for making everything worthwhile.

ABOUT THE AUTHOR

FIONA McPHILLIPS is an Irish journalist, author, and screenwriter. She is an editor at the *Forge Literary Magazine,* and her own work has appeared in the *Manchester Review, Hobart,* and *Barren Magazine,* among others. *When We Were Silent,* the runner-up for the 2021 Crime Writers' Association Debut Dagger, is her first novel. Fiona lives in Dublin with her three kids, two cats, and a dog.